# WHO SPEAKS FOR THE DAMNED

*A Sebastian St. Cyr Mystery*

## C. S. HARRIS

BERKLEY
New York

BERKLEY
An imprint of Penguin Random House LLC
penguinrandomhouse.com

Copyright © 2020 by The Two Talers, LLC
Excerpt from *What the Devil Knows* copyright © 2021 by The Two Talers, LLC
Penguin Random House supports copyright. Copyright fuels creativity, encourages
diverse voices, promotes free speech, and creates a vibrant culture. Thank you for
buying an authorized edition of this book and for complying with copyright laws
by not reproducing, scanning, or distributing any part of it in any form without
permission. You are supporting writers and allowing Penguin Random House
to continue to publish books for every reader.

BERKLEY and the BERKLEY & B colophon are registered trademarks of
Penguin Random House LLC.

ISBN: 9780399585708

The Library of Congress has catalogued the
Berkley hardcover edition of this book as follows:

Names: Harris, C. S., author.
Title: Who speaks for the damned / C. S. Harris.
Description: First edition. | New York: Berkley, 2020. |
Series: A Sebastian St. Cyr mystery
Identifiers: LCCN 2019033100 (print) | LCCN 2019033101 (ebook) |
ISBN 9780399585685 (hardcover) | ISBN 9780399585692 (ebook)
Subjects: GSAFD: Mystery fiction.
Classification: LCC PS3566.R5877 W47856 2020 (print) |
LCC PS3566.R5877 (ebook) | DDC 813/.54--dc23
LC record available at https://lccn.loc.gov/2019033100
LC ebook record available at https://lccn.loc.gov/2019033101

Berkley hardcover edition / April 2020
Berkley trade paperback edition / March 2021

Printed in the United States of America

Cover images: cloaked running man © Roy Bishop /
Arcangel; brick tunnel by Hayden Verry / Arcangel
Cover design by Adam Auerbach

*For Steve*

*Who speaks for the restless and the damned?*

—CHARLES GRAMLICH

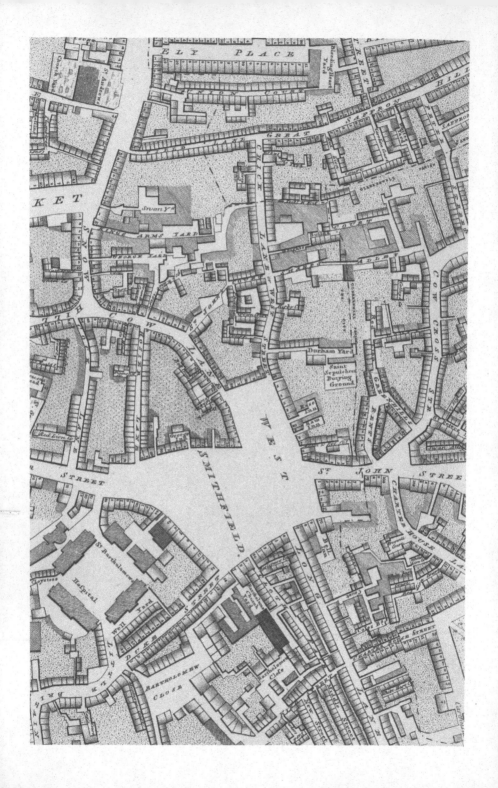

# WHO SPEAKS FOR THE DAMNED

# Chapter 1

*A*lone and trying desperately not to be afraid, the child wandered the narrow, winding paths of the tea gardens.

Ji could hear laughter and the voices of other garden visitors in the distance. The day had been hot—unusually so for June, the child heard people say. But the sun was beginning to sink in the clear lavender blue sky, lengthening the shadows beneath the arbors and hinting at the chill of coming evening. The scent of roses and peonies drifted sweetly on the moist air, stirring unbidden memories of the shady walkways and placid canals of the Hong merchant's private gardens. A wave of home-sickness washed over the child, bringing a painful lump to Ji's throat, and the sting of threatening tears.

Ji swallowed and pushed the dangerous thoughts away.

Ji had grown up hearing tales of the faraway misty islands of Britain, and somehow in the child's mind the British Isles had blurred with the Garden Islands of the Eight Immortals. Ancient Chinese legends told of island palaces made of gold and silver, where there was no pain or winter, where the rice bowls were always full, and those who ate the fruit of the enchanted trees would live forever.

"Britain's not like that, child," the man called Hayes, his face taking on a pinched look, had warned Ji. "It's not like that at all."

"Then what is it like?" Ji had asked. "Is it like Canton?"

"No. It's not like Canton either."

A gust of wind rustled the leafy branches of the lime trees overhead, jerking the child back to the present. Ji fumbled in the pocket of the strange clothes Hayes had insisted the child wear ever since that wretched day when they'd rowed out to the ship in Canton's harbor and sailed away from everything Ji loved. Everything familiar and beloved except for Hayes.

"Give me until seven," he'd said after they'd eaten a dinner of thinly sliced roast beef and hot bread and butter in one of the tea gardens' boxes.

"How will I find you? Or know what time it is?"

"Stay close to the pond," he said, handing the child his watch with a smile. "I'll find you."

The child hadn't been worried. Not then. But now Ji flipped open Hayes's watch and saw it was nearly half past seven.

Where was he?

Something dangerously close to panic bubbled up within the child. Ji began to walk in ever-widening circles around the tea gardens' ornamental pond. Past the bowling green, past the river, where late patrons lingered at the tables and chairs set out beneath the row of willows. Then a high brick wall loomed ahead, forcing Ji to curve back around.

It was there, in a small clearing not far from the wall, that the child found him. He lay facedown in the grass, one arm curled up at his side, his blue eyes open but staring blankly.

And from the torn, blood-soaked cloth of his coat protruded the workworn handle of a sickle, its sharp, curving blade buried deep in his back.

*Chapter 2*

*H*alf an hour later, in the exclusive part of London known as Mayfair, Sebastian St. Cyr, Viscount Devlin, sat cross-legged in the middle of his elegant drawing room floor. The heir to the powerful Earl of Hendon, he wore formal knee breeches, a white silk waistcoat, and a cutaway dress coat, for he and his wife, Hero, were planning to attend the Prince Regent's reception for the visiting Allied Sovereigns later that evening. But they always tried to devote the hour before dinner to their sixteen-month-old son, Simon.

"Where's the watch?" Sebastian asked the boy, bringing two closed fists from behind his back.

Golden eyes sparkling with anticipation, Simon pointed to Sebastian's left fist, then squealed in delight when Sebastian uncurled his fingers to display an empty hand.

Simon tapped Sebastian's right fist. "D'ere!"

Sebastian opened another empty hand, and the baby laughed so hard he fell over backward.

"Isn't that cheating?" asked Hero with a smile.

"Not a bit of it. It's teaching him that things aren't always where you expect them to be."

"I think it's teaching him that his father sometimes cheats."

"Another valuable lesson," said Sebastian as the child scrambled behind his back to pounce on the missing watch.

"He's going to chew on it," she warned.

"It won't be the first time."

A warm breeze shifted the curtains at the open windows, drawing Hero's attention to something in the street below. As Sebastian watched, a faint frown creased her forehead.

"What is it?" he asked.

"There's a child out there, by the lamppost. He's been staring at the house for the past five minutes or more."

Sebastian pushed up from the floor and went to stand beside her. The streets of London were filled with children, many of them ragged, barefoot paupers eking out a precarious existence. This boy looked to be perhaps eight or nine, but he was no beggar or street sweeper. His clothes were those of a tradesman's son or shopkeeper's apprentice, sturdy and respectable. As they watched, he took a step forward, only to stop, then lean his back against the lamppost and throw an apprehensive glance around.

Hero said, "Have you ever seen him before?"

"No."

As if sensing their attention, the child looked up, the brim of a round hat lifting to reveal delicate features and wide eyes. It was a haunting, vaguely exotic face, and there was something about the child's troubled expression that caught at Sebastian in a way he couldn't have explained.

"Whoever he is," said Sebastian, "I think something's wrong. Perhaps we should—"

He broke off at the sound of the kitchen door opening below. As they watched, Sebastian's valet, Jules Calhoun, climbed the area steps toward the child. A slim, lithe man in his thirties with even features and straight fair hair, Calhoun had been with Sebastian for almost three years now. At the sight of the valet, the unknown lad's chest jerked with what looked like a sob and he threw himself forward.

Sebastian heard Calhoun say, "Ji, what is it?" But the child's answer was lost in the rattling thunder of a passing brewer's dray drawn by a team of six stout shires.

Uncomfortably aware of inadvertently witnessing something personal, Sebastian went to retrieve his watch from his teething son. But a few moments later a quick step sounded on the stairs, and Calhoun appeared in the drawing room doorway with an apologetic bow.

"I beg your pardon, my lady." The valet's normally cheerful face was uncharacteristically serious, his voice tight with strain. "If I might have a word with you, my lord?"

Hero came to scoop the baby into her arms. "I'll take Simon upstairs to Claire. It's nearly dinnertime." Her gaze met Sebastian's, but all she said was "Tell Papa good night."

"We saw the lad outside," said Sebastian as Hero turned toward the door. "I take it he's brought a message?"

"He says there's been a murder up at Somer's Town, in Pennington's Tea Gardens. The victim is Nicholas Hayes, the youngest son of the late Earl of Seaforth."

"Nicholas Hayes?" said Sebastian in disbelief. Nicholas Hayes had been a legend in England for nearly twenty years, his life a cautionary tale used by alarmed parents as a dire warning to curtail the wayward behavior of their rebellious offspring. It wasn't often an earl's son was convicted of murder and transported to Botany Bay. "I thought he'd died ten or fifteen years ago."

"Reports of his death were . . . premature."

"Evidently. The message came from Bow Street?"

"No, my lord. The lad found the body himself. Unless someone else has reported it, the authorities have yet to be informed."

Sebastian remembered the child's relief at the sight of the valet, and Calhoun's quick *Ji, what is it?* "Why did the boy come to you with this?"

"I . . . It so happens I was somewhat acquainted with Hayes."

Sebastian studied his valet's guarded face. "And the boy knew this?"

Calhoun blew out a shaky breath and nodded.

"Did he see the murder?"

"No, my lord. He says Hayes had arranged to meet someone in the gardens, but Ji—that's the boy—doesn't know whom. By the time Ji found him, Hayes was dead. Someone stabbed him in the back with a sickle."

"Good God. And what is this child to Hayes?"

"They came together from China."

"China?"

"Yes, my lord."

"The boy is downstairs in the kitchens?"

"He is, my lord."

"Best bring him up right away."

"Yes, my lord."

But when Calhoun went back downstairs, the child was gone.

Hero watched Devlin toss a black silk cape over his shoulders. "You're going to investigate a murder dressed in evening clothes and a chapeau bras?"

"I am. I know your father is expecting you at tonight's reception, so please go ahead without me, and I'll catch up with you there later if I can."

"You've sent a message to Sir Henry?" Sir Henry Lovejoy was one of the Bow Street Public Office's three stipendiary magistrates. Not so long ago, when Sebastian had been on the run for a murder he didn't commit, Lovejoy had been responsible for bringing him to justice. But in the years since, the two men had grown to both respect and like each other.

"He's meeting me up in Somer's Town."

"You haven't had dinner."

Devlin adjusted the tilt of his black bicorn hat. "I'll live."

She crinkled her nose at him. "Can it really be Nicholas Hayes?"

"Calhoun doesn't seem to have any doubts."

"How does Calhoun know him?"

"He didn't say."

She went to stare out the window at the gathering darkness. "You think the little boy went back to the tea gardens?"

"I hope so. Because if not, then where the hell is he?"

# Chapter 3

The area known as Somer's Town lay just to the north of Bloomsbury. Home to artists and writers and the middling sort of refugees from
the revolution in France, it was the site of market gardens, brickfields,
and several different tea gardens. The gardens were close enough to the
densely crowded streets of London to make them an easy walk for young
apprentices and seamstresses as well as the families of tradesmen, artisans, and shopkeepers. For sixpence, one could spend the day enjoying
the fresh air of the country and listening to music while drinking tea or
ale and eating roast beef and cakes.

*And maybe getting stabbed in the back with a sickle,* thought Sebastian as
the carriage rolled through the hot, darkening streets of the city.

He shifted his gaze to the valet on the opposite bench. "So, are you
going to tell me how you came to be acquainted with an earl's son transported to Botany Bay eighteen years ago?"

Calhoun brought up tented hands to cover his nose and mouth, then
let them fall. "I knew him before that—before he was accused of murder
but after he was disowned by his father, the Earl. He had a room at one
of my mother's inns."

"Ah." Calhoun's background was unusual for a gentleman's gentleman. The son of an infamous underworld figure named Grace Calhoun, he'd grown up hanging around the most notorious flash houses in London. "The Blue Anchor?"

The valet gave a faint shake of his head. "The Red Lion."

"Good God." Situated in a back alley near Smithfield, the Red Lion was a known resort of thieves, cracksmen, blacklegs, and beau-traps. "What the devil was he doing there?"

"To be honest, I think he came there planning to kill himself." A faint smile that hinted at old, fond memories lifted one corner of Calhoun's mouth. "He changed his mind."

"How long was he there?"

"Nearly six months. Shortly before he arrived, my mother had hired an ancient, broken-down valet to teach me how to 'act and talk flash,' as she put it. But my sixteen-year-old self was less than impressed with the dotard, and I didn't want any part of her scheme. Then I met Hayes."

"How old was he at the time?"

"Twenty, or thereabouts. My mother let him stay for free, hoping he'd succeed where the dotard had failed—teach me to dress, walk, and talk like a gentleman. She had ambitions of me becoming a confidence man, you see. Near broke her heart when I decided to take everything I'd learned and become a valet instead."

"No doubt," said Sebastian, who had met the formidable Grace Calhoun. She was the kind of woman a wise man didn't turn his back on— or cross in any way.

Calhoun's smile faded as he shifted to stare out at the shadowy streets flashing past, his body swaying with the motion of the carriage. "If it hadn't been for Hayes, I'd probably have been hanged long ago."

"I was under the impression he'd been transported for life, without eligibility for parole."

"He was."

"Yet he came back to England?" For a man transported for life to return to Britain without a pardon was to court a death sentence. "Why?"

"I don't know."

"But you've seen him since he came back?"

Calhoun nodded.

"Why did everyone believe he'd died in Botany Bay?"

"He told me they had a flash flood on some big river out there that swept him away from the chain gang he was on. When he came to, he was lying next to a dead man of about the same height, build, and hair color. The fellow was a freeman who'd once been a soldier, and he'd obviously spent some time in irons and been flogged, because his body was scarred. Hayes changed clothes with him, took his papers, and bashed in the dead man's face with a rock until he was unrecognizable. And then he seized the first chance that offered to get away from the colony."

*Jesus*, thought Sebastian. "And went to China?"

"Eventually."

"Why did he contact you?"

"He said he might need my help, and he wanted to know if I'd be willing to give it."

"Your help with what?"

"He didn't say."

"And what did you tell him?"

The valet met Sebastian's gaze, and held it. "I told him yes."

"Dead bodies in my gardens?" muttered Irvine Pennington, sweating heavily as he led the way along a central allée of pleached hornbeam underplanted with low-clipped hedges of boxwood and waves of purple allium. "It's an insult, it is, even to suggest such a thing. An insult!"

The owner-manager of Pennington's Tea Gardens was a short, stout man in his middle years, with heavy jowls, a long upper lip, and bushy side-whiskers. They'd arrived in Somer's Town to find that the tea gardens closed early on Thursdays. Pennington had resisted Sebastian's request that he reopen the gardens for them and scoffed loudly at the idea that one of his patrons might be lying dead somewhere within. But at the magical words "Bow Street," the garden owner's opposition evaporated. Leaving one of his lads at the gate to await the magistrate and constables, he insisted on personally accompanying Sebastian.

"So, where is this mythical corpse?" Pennington grumbled, holding his horn lantern high. "Hmmm? You tell me that."

Sebastian glanced at Calhoun, who said, "According to Ji, he's lying somewhere to the west of the pond, near a brick wall." They'd hoped to find Ji waiting for them at the tea gardens, but they'd yet to see any sign of the child.

"Where's your pond?" asked Sebastian.

"Just up ahead. But it's nonsense to suggest—"

"Then let's go left."

Without waiting for Mr. Pennington, Sebastian veered onto a narrow path that wound through a shrubbery toward the high wall that separated the gardens from the hayfields to the west.

Mr. Pennington hesitated a moment, then charged after them, his lantern held high. "Wait, wait!" Pennington shouted. "How can you even see where you're going?"

"I have good eyesight."

"But it's too dark! What a fool's errand this all is. Your lad probably saw someone who'd simply lain down and dozed off after drinking too much ale. Havey-cavey it is, accusing me of leaving corpses littered about my gardens. Why, I've a mind to—"

"There," said Sebastian.

The man lay facedown in a small clearing just off the path, his head turned to one side, his widely staring eyes already beginning to flatten and film. His clothes and boots were of a similar quality to those of the missing boy, respectable but neither fashionable nor expensive. The back of his coat was dark and shiny with the blood that had spilled out around the sickle buried deep between his shoulder blades.

Pennington gave a gasp and stumbled to a halt, his lantern swinging wildly. "The Lord preserve us."

"Grab that lantern before he drops it and starts a fire," Sebastian told Calhoun.

Calhoun lifted the lantern from the garden owner's unresisting grasp and brought the light closer. "Is he dead?"

"Very," said Sebastian, hunkering down beside the body.

Nicholas Hayes—if this was indeed Hayes—couldn't have been more than thirty-eight or thirty-nine, not too many years older than Sebastian himself. But life had been hard on this earl's son. His once-dark hair was thickly laced with gray, his complexion weathered by years of hard labor beneath the blazing hot sun of New South Wales. Born with all the advantages of wealth and lineage, he should have lived a comfortable, dignified, even productive life. Instead he'd endured nearly two decades of unimaginable horrors that ended in . . . this. Sebastian felt the tragedy of the man's wasted life and senseless death press down on him like a heavy weight of sadness mingled, he knew, with an unsettling realization of just how easily this man's miserable life could have been his.

"Is it Hayes?" he asked his valet.

Calhoun crouched down beside him, the lantern dancing a macabre pattern of shadow and light across the still, alabaster flesh of the dead man's face. "Dear God. It is."

Sebastian glanced over at him. "Not simply the man you saw recently, but the man you knew eighteen years ago?"

"Oh, yes. I'm certain of it. He's older, but I knew him the instant I saw him."

Sebastian brought his gaze back to the body before them. He'd been a handsome man, Nicholas Hayes, tall and leanly built, with a long, straight nose, straight dark brows, and high cheekbones. Why would a man so easily recognizable return to England? Why come back and risk near-certain death?

Sebastian looked at the tea gardens' owner. "Is this sickle one of yours?"

Pennington began to back away. "Mine? Oh, surely not. What a thing to ask."

"It strikes me as a reasonable question."

Pennington backed into the trunk of a linden tree and stopped, his head shaking slowly back and forth, back and forth. "This won't be good for business. It won't be good for business at all. Perhaps we could—" He licked his lips. "Perhaps we could shift the body? Just a tad? There's an access gate in the wall near here. If we were to—"

"No."

"Who would care? Look at him. He's—what? A shopkeeper, perhaps? A cobbler or maybe a—"

"As it happens, he's the youngest son of the late Earl of Seaforth."

"The Earl of—" A succession of emotions flickered across the garden owner's face as shock gave way to wonderment, followed almost immediately by a gleam of hopeful avarice. "Really? Well, well, well. Perhaps this won't ruin me after all. I could make the site into a special attraction. Yes, that might work. I could even fence off the area and charge a separate admission. I wonder if they'll let me have the dead man's clothes. I could have them stuffed and restage the murder scene. I could even—"

"Why, you sick, greedy bastard," swore Calhoun, surging to his feet. "The man is dead, and all you can think about is—"

Sebastian just managed to snag his normally mild-mannered valet's arm and haul him back. "Calhoun," he said softly.

Mr. Irvine Pennington threw up both hands and scuttled around behind the linden tree as if using the trunk as a shield. "Merciful heavens."

"May I suggest you await the arrival of Bow Street at the entrance gate? That way you can direct them where to go when they arrive."

"Yes, yes, I'll do that. I'll do that right away." He hesitated, then added timidly, "May I have the lantern back, please?"

Sebastian waited until the garden owner trotted off, the lantern light swinging wildly over the darkened shrubbery. Then he let the valet go.

"I beg your pardon, my lord," said Calhoun, smoothing the tumbled hair from his forehead and repositioning his hat with unsteady hands. "That was unforgivable of me."

"Yet understandable." Sebastian brought his attention back to the dead man at their feet. "I suspect Bow Street won't take kindly to the realization that you knew Hayes was an escaped convict and yet failed to report him to the authorities. We need to come up with a convincing story to tell Sir Henry. Quickly."

*Chapter 4*

*U*nbelievable," said Sir Henry Lovejoy, holding his lantern high as he peered at the dead man's face over the rims of his spectacles. "It really is Nicholas Hayes."

The Bow Street magistrate was a small, balding man with a rigid moral code and a serious demeanor. Earlier in life he'd been a moderately successful merchant, but the tragic death of his wife and daughter some years before had led him to change course and decide to devote the rest of his days to public service. Far too many of London's magistrates were either venal, lazy, or both. But Lovejoy was neither. Dedicated, scrupulously honest, and clever, he had a tendency to see each murder, each violation of the public's trust, as a source of deep personal sadness.

"You knew him?" said Sebastian in surprise.

"Not personally, no. But I remember the trial quite clearly. Such a tragic, sordid affair it was. The woman he killed—the wife of the Count de Compans—was so young, and quite lovely." Lovejoy shifted his lantern to let the light play over the bloody sickle still embedded in Nicholas Hayes's back. "Ghastly. You say a lad brought you word of this?"

"Yes."

"How very odd. Why didn't he go to the local authorities?"

Sebastian glanced over at Calhoun, who was busy staring fixedly into the surrounding darkness. They'd decided to simply fudge some of the particulars. "Certain segments of society do tend to have a virtually inbred fear of the constabulary."

Lovejoy frowned. "Any possibility this lad could be involved in the murder himself?"

"I doubt it. He was a mere child. Unfortunately, he took off without giving us his direction."

"Most unfortunate, indeed." Lovejoy drew a handkerchief from his pocket and pressed the neatly folded square against his damp forehead. "Goodness, it's warm tonight." Handkerchief still in hand, he straightened to glance around the small clearing. He'd set a couple of his constables to going over the area as best they could by lantern, but they'd need daylight for a more thorough search. "The use of the sickle suggests a crime of both opportunity and passion, although I suppose simple robbery could also have been the motive. I'm tempted to leave the weapon in place and send the body as it is to Paul Gibson."

"Probably a good idea," said Sebastian. No one in London could read a corpse better than the former Army surgeon.

Lovejoy was silent a moment. "It makes no sense—Hayes coming back here, I mean. Somehow the man must have managed to escape from Botany Bay with everyone thinking he was dead. Why risk everything by returning to England again?"

"I suspect the answer to that might tell us who killed him."

"I hope you're right. Because the palace isn't going to like this. They aren't going to like this at all."

Sebastian knew only too well what that meant. The palace had a tendency to see sensational crimes involving the nobility or the royal family—whether as victims or perpetrators—as threats to the established order of society. Their first instinct was to shut down any and all investigations, usually by finding a convenient scapegoat to blame.

Lovejoy pressed his handkerchief to his sweat-dampened face again. The magistrate had always been abnormally sensitive to cold, but lately he'd begun to have trouble tolerating heat as well. "We'll need to move quickly to inform the current Earl of Seaforth before he hears of this from elsewhere. He's—what? Nicholas Hayes's brother?"

"First cousin. I believe Hayes did have brothers, but all died before the previous Earl."

Lovejoy tucked his handkerchief away. "Only a cousin? How very awkward. So the man has been calling himself the Earl of Seaforth for years when the rightful heir was alive all along."

"Well, no one could dispute that he's the rightful Earl now," said Sebastian, his gaze on the still, pallid face of the dead man at their feet.

*Chapter 5*

**H**is Royal Highness George Augustus Frederick, Prince of Wales and Regent of the United Kingdom of Great Britain and Ireland, looked out at the bejeweled, highborn crowd overflowing his palace's stifling-hot reception rooms and smiled. His color was high and his eyes sparkled with pleasure, for the Regent was in fine spirits on this, the third day of the Allied Sovereigns' visit to London.

At the Regent's invitation, a glittering assortment of Europe's hereditary ruling families had descended on London to celebrate the recent defeat of Napoléon: the Tsar of Russia and his sister the Grand Duchess of Oldenburg; King William of Prussia and his sons; Princes Metternich and Leopold and dozens of other, lesser princes and war heroes. The city was lit in a glorious three-day Illuminations of Joy, and the streets were constantly filled with jubilant, cheering crowds. The fact that they were cheering not the Prince of Wales but his royal guests had yet to penetrate the Regent's overweening sense of amour propre.

"It's quite the defining event of the Season. Wouldn't you agree, Jarvis?" said the beaming royal.

"Undoubtedly, sir," said Charles, Lord Jarvis, the Prince's most trusted advisor and distant cousin as well as the real power behind Wales's fragile Regency.

"Everyone is saying it was a stroke of genius, my inviting all the Allied Sovereigns here for a grand visit to commemorate our victory."

Those who knew their self-absorbed Prince were actually predicting he would quickly tire of sharing the attention he so desperately coveted. But Jarvis wasn't about to tell him that. "They are indeed, sir."

The Prince's smile faded as he watched the Tsar's beautiful, proud, ostentatious sister Catherine, the Grand Duchess of Oldenburg, go down the line of a country dance. "Does it look to you as if she dislikes music? You remember when she told me she doesn't like music and made me stop the orchestra I had playing at my banquet in her honor?"

"Perhaps she only dislikes music when she's dining," suggested Jarvis. Privately he suspected the Grand Duchess's announcement had been made to spite the Regent, who'd been bragging about personally selecting the pieces to be played with each course of the banquet.

"Possible, I suppose. Still, it's odd, wouldn't you say?"

"Well, she is Russian."

"There is that."

Jarvis let his gaze drift over the gathering of the Kingdom's wealthiest and most powerful and found his attention settling on his own daughter, Hero. She was exceptionally lovely tonight in a silver silk gown of half-mourning worn in memory of her dead mother. Her looks were not of a type he admired. Jarvis preferred blond, petite women with winning ways, whereas Hero was brown haired, alarmingly tall, and far too masculine in both her features and her interests. But he had to admit that marriage and motherhood had improved her.

Her choice of husband still rankled him to no end.

"Excuse me, sir," he said with a bow to the Prince.

The crowd parted before him easily, for Jarvis was a large man as well as being so powerful—well over six feet tall and fleshy, with a pene-trating gray stare and a well-earned reputation for being utterly ruthless. "I don't see that scapegrace husband of yours," he said, coming up to his daughter. "Is it too much to hope you've finally decided to dispense with him?"

The gray eyes she had inherited from him lit up with amusement. "Good evening, Papa. As it happens, something came up. He hopes to be able to join me here later."

Jarvis frowned. "It's never a good sign when you use that airy tone."

She laughed out loud, but he noticed her attention had strayed to the small cluster of people around Gilbert-Christophe de LaRivière, the Count de Compans. A close confidant of both the newly restored French King Louis XVIII and his brother Charles, the Count was acting as a kind of surrogate for the absent Bourbons, who had already returned to Paris to claim their throne.

"It was LaRivière's wife that Nicholas Hayes was convicted of killing all those years ago, was it not?" said Hero.

"It was. Her name was Chantal, and she's been dead for over eigh-teen years now. Why the sudden interest?"

"A man believed to be Nicholas Hayes has just been found murdered up in Somer's Town."

"Impossible," said Jarvis, his gaze going to where Ethan Hayes, the Third Earl of Seaforth, was deep in conversation with a man who had his back to them. "Nicholas Hayes died a convict in New South Wales in 1799."

"Evidently not."

As Jarvis watched, a familiar lean, dark-haired man in his early thir-ties walked up to Seaforth and said something in the Earl's ear.

Jarvis said, "I take it Devlin has involved himself in this murder. In Somer's Town, did you say? What a dreadfully plebeian locale."

The Earl of Seaforth hesitated a moment, then turned to walk away with Devlin.

Hero said, "It does look as if the dead man really is Nicholas Hayes, doesn't it?"

Jarvis shifted his gaze to where the Prince Regent now stood in conversation with the Count de Compans. Without even looking at Hero again, he said, "Excuse me," and walked away.

## Chapter 6

Sebastian had arrived at Carlton House to find the Prince Regent's
Pall Mall palace stuffed to overflowing with the most select members of
the Upper Ten Thousand, all flushed and sweating from the heat but
eager for a close-up look at the Allied Sovereigns.

Working his way with difficulty through the crowd packing the Regent's gilded, silk-hung reception rooms, he finally came upon Ethan
Hayes, the current Earl of Seaforth, deep in quiet conversation with a
middle-aged man Sebastian vaguely recognized as one of the Directors
of the East India Company.

Slightly built, rusty-haired, and of medium height, the current Earl
of Seaforth was perhaps a year or two younger than his ill-fated cousin.
His gray eyes were small and closely set, his freckled cheeks ruddy, his
jaw line decidedly on the weak side. His estates were in Ireland, but he
visited them seldom, preferring to spend most of his time in the North
Audley Street town house he inherited from his uncle, the Second Earl.
He had a vague tendency toward dandyism, but otherwise was considered solidly respectable, carefully avoiding the popular pitfalls of gam-
bling and highfliers that were bankrupting so many of his peers. Married

for ten years, he was said to be exceptionally devoted to his plump, rather plain wife and growing brood of children.

"Good evening, my lord," said Sebastian, walking up to him just as Seaforth's companion was turning away. "I wonder if I might have a word with you in private. It's rather important."

Seaforth opened his eyes wide, for Sebastian barely knew the man. "I suppose," said the Earl.

He followed Sebastian to a small withdrawing room hung with figured red silk and stuffed with black lacquered Chinese furniture and a few dozen pieces of the Regent's vast collection of Ming dynasty porcelains. "Bit irregular, this," said the Earl, drawing up just inside the door.

"I have some disturbing news, I'm afraid. Your cousin Nicholas Hayes has just been found dead at Pennington's Tea Gardens up in Somer's Town. He's been murdered."

Seaforth stared at him for a moment, his nostrils flaring on a quickly indrawn breath, his features slack and expressionless. Then his face hardened. "Is this some sort of jest? If so, I take leave to tell you it's damnably rude. Nicholas died fifteen years ago in the most sordid circumstances imaginable, and everyone in London knows it."

"No jest."

The Earl turned away to go stand beside the room's empty hearth with one hand resting on the marble mantelpiece. He was silent for a moment, his gaze fixed on nothing in particular as if he were struggling to compose himself—or perhaps simply choosing how best to respond. He finally said, "You're certain?"

"Reasonably so, yes. Bow Street is sending the body for a post mortem."

"A post mortem? How barbaric. Is that really necessary?"

"I'm afraid so, under the circumstances."

Seaforth swung to face him again, his forehead beaded with sweat. "Why are you the one telling me this?"

"It seemed preferable to having someone from Bow Street cause a stir by barging into the Regent's reception with the news."

Seaforth's eyes narrowed. "Yes, but why you? What has any of this to do with you?"

Rather than answer, Sebastian said, "You didn't know your cousin had returned to London?"

"No, of course not."

"Any idea why he might have decided to come back?"

"I told you, I thought he was dead."

"That doesn't mean you can't think of a reason why he might decide to return, if he were alive."

"How's this for an answer? I have no idea what he was doing in London." The Earl's lips flattened into a pinched expression. "Although I probably should have guessed he'd find one more way to embarrass and disgrace the family. I don't suppose there's any possibility of keeping this from becoming widely known?"

"No," said Sebastian. "When was the last time you heard from him?"

"Nicholas? I never heard from him again after he left England. Actually, I never spoke to him at all after his arrest—or in the months before that. The man was a disgrace. Why would I?"

"You weren't close?"

"Hardly. I don't know how familiar you are with his history, but my uncle had already disowned him for abducting an heiress a good six months before he was arrested for murder. No one in the family had anything to do with him."

Sebastian hadn't heard this part of the tale. "An heiress?"

"That's right."

"What was her name?"

"I don't know." The tone was testy. Annoyed. "What difference does it make?"

"Do you recall the names of your cousin's friends?"

"No, I don't. I told you, I try not to think of the man." Seaforth glanced beyond Sebastian to the noisy, crowded reception rooms. "And now you really must excuse me. I didn't come to Carlton House tonight to discuss Nicholas." And with that, he brushed past Sebastian and began to push his way through the throng.

Sebastian went to stand in the doorway, his gaze following the Earl's progress. He was still standing there when Hero came up beside him.

She said, "Do I take it the dead man up in Somer's Town actually is Nicholas Hayes?"

"Apparently so."

"Was Ji there?"

"No."

"That's worrisome." She was silent, her gaze, like Sebastian's, following Seaforth as he worked his way across Carlton House's vast, opulent hall. "How did he take the news of his cousin's return and death?"

"With anger and bluster but not a great deal of surprise—and not even a hint of feigned grief."

"You think he knew Nicholas Hayes was in London?"

"I can't say for certain, but I think he might have."

"Discovering that the rightful owner of the titles and estates you've been calling your own for years is actually very much alive strikes me as a powerful incentive for murder. If one were the murdering sort, of course."

Sebastian watched Seaforth turn to glance back at them, as if aware of both their scrutiny and their speculation. "It does, doesn't it?"

## Chapter 7

*J*i couldn't stop shivering.

The night was warm, the dark sky above clear with a scattering of stars. And still the child shivered. Drawing back into the shadows of a crumbling, deeply recessed doorway, Ji stared across the narrow lane at the ancient inn. The warm golden glow of light from the familiar mullioned windows beckoned like a comforting old friend, but Ji's heart was thumping with fear and uncertainty.

Trying desperately not to cry, the child listened to the outbursts of laughter from the inn's taproom, the clink of glasses, the murmur of strangely accented male voices. Then the tavern's door crashed open and a couple of drunken drovers staggered out to stand legs astraddle and relieve themselves against a post. The air filled with the acrid stench of their urine.

Everything in this place, England, was so strange. The crush of carriages filling the streets with the thunder of horses' hooves and the clatter of iron-rimmed wheels over cobbles. The women—so many women, not only servants and concubines but also ladies from good families, or so said Hayes—walking in the streets, their dresses thin and filmy, their huge hats decorated with bows and flowers and towering feathers. And the smells! Canton smelled of open sewers, incense, roasting ducks, and steaming dumplings. But one of the most pervasive odors in London was a pungent burning aroma that Hayes identified as roasting coffee, mingled always, everywhere, with the dung of horses and the tang of ale.

"Well, Englishmen do like their horses. And their ale," Hayes would say whenever Ji commented on it.

"Why? It's nasty stuff," Ji had said just that afternoon as they walked the shady paths of the gardens. "And they don't know how to drink tea. They put *milk* in it!"

Hayes had laughed at the expression on the child's face. "You should try it."

"Never!" said Ji, and Hayes had laughed again.

Ji was trembling now, the child's mind skittering away from the dangerous places it kept wanting to wander, to images of a shadowy clearing . . . memories of the sharp, raw smell of blood . . . a pale, dearly beloved face . . .

Choking back a sob, the child pushed away from the dank, rough bricks of the old archway and was about to cross the lane toward the inn when the shadow of a man shifted near the corner. Shrinking back, Ji watched as the man sucked on a pipe and the warm glow of burning tobacco illuminated his face. It was only for a fleeting instant, but it was enough for Ji to recognize him.

*Poole,* Hayes's friend had called the man they'd noticed following them earlier in the week. Titus Poole.

"That's a funny name," Ji had said. But then, most English names sounded funny to the child.

"It is a bit," Hayes agreed. "But there's nothing the least bit funny about Mr. Titus Poole, from what I'm hearing."

It was when he didn't think the child was listening that Hayes had told his friend Mott, *I'm afraid someone has hired him to kill me. Me, and perhaps Ji too.*

Heart pounding now so hard that it hurt, the child stared helplessly at the beckoning light streaming from the old inn's windows. If this man Poole knew where they were staying, then the inn was no longer the safe refuge it once had been.

With a spiraling surge of panic, Ji thought about going back to Hayes's friend Jules Calhoun. But Hayes hadn't trusted the nobleman and -woman Calhoun worked for and had carefully avoided going anywhere near their house himself. Hayes's death might have driven the child there, briefly, but Ji wasn't about to trust anyone Hayes hadn't trusted.

Again the shadowy man sucked on his pipe, the tobacco glowing in the dark. Ji watched him exhale, smelled the fragrant smoke drifting on the warm night air. *Was it you?* the child wondered, shaking now with fury as much as with fear and raw, unimaginable grief. *Did you kill him? Did you? Did you?*

As if aware of the child's gaze upon him, the man glanced around. Ji froze, not daring even to breathe.

It was going to be a long night.

## Chapter 8

*Friday, 10 June*

*T*he morning papers were filled with sensational tales of the sordid sins, unexpected return, and gruesome murder of Nicholas Hayes. After reading through one dubious account of the man's scandalous history after another, Sebastian sat down in his library with Jules Calhoun and said, "I need you to tell me everything you know about Nicholas Hayes."

The valet met his gaze squarely. "Where do you want me to start, my lord?"

"You can begin with where he's been staying since he arrived in London."

"That I don't know, my lord. He wouldn't tell me—said it was better I not know."

"He didn't trust you?"

"I don't think it was that. He was afraid of what might happen to me if he was caught."

"Do you know when he arrived in London?"

"Sometime near the end of last week, I believe. But I don't know precisely."

"On a ship from China?"

"Yes, Canton. That's where he's been since not long after he left Botany Bay."

"When exactly did you see him?" asked Sebastian.

A faint trace of color rose in the valet's cheeks. "This past Sunday."

"He—what? Sent you a note?"

Calhoun nodded. "We met at Oxford Market."

"How did he know where to find you?"

"I don't know. He didn't say."

"So what did he say?"

Calhoun squeezed his eyes shut for a moment and pinched the bridge of his nose. "He told me how he'd escaped from Botany Bay. How he'd been living in Canton."

"Interesting place to take refuge."

"He said he left Botany Bay on an American whaler and spent a season working with them. But then they ran into a storm and had to put into Canton for repairs. Right before they were to leave, he came down with a fever. The monsoons were about to hit, so they left him. Everyone thought he was going to die, but he didn't."

"And he's been in Canton ever since?"

Calhoun nodded. "He was working with one of the Hong merchants. Seems the fellow was happy to have someone who not only spoke perfect English and French—along with a smattering of other languages—but could understand European ways of thinking as well."

Merchants from Britain, Europe, and the United States were all eager to trade with China, the ancient source of silks and porcelains and the increasingly popular tea. After having been rigidly closed off for centuries, the country was finally beginning to open up. But the Qing emperors insisted on tightly controlling their subjects' contact with the barbaric West. By Imperial decree, all trade was funneled through the city of Canton and the nearby island of Macau, with foreigners forced to do business through specially licensed middlemen known as Hong merchants.

"Did you ask him why the hell he threw it all over to risk his life by coming back here?"

"I did. But all he'd say was he had his reasons. And then he said he might need my help, and asked if he could count on me."

*And you said yes*, Sebastian thought, *no questions asked*. It revealed much about the strength of the bond between the two men.

Aloud, Sebastian said, "Tell me about the child. What is he to Hayes?"

"I honestly don't know."

"Is he a servant, do you think?"

"I don't believe so, no."

"Any chance the boy could be Hayes's son?"

"I wondered that myself. He does look half-European. But he didn't say and I didn't ask."

Sebastian studied his valet's fine-boned, tensely held face. He'd known Calhoun for years now. In general, he was an affable man, calm and easygoing. But Sebastian had always suspected that there was another side to the valet, a hidden side that was the legacy of all those growing-up years spent in the dangerous back alleys of places like Seven Dials and Hockley-in-the-Hole. "Tell me about when you knew Hayes before—those months when he was staying at your mother's flash house. Did any of his friends or relatives come to see him while he was there?"

Calhoun looked thoughtful. "There was an Irish fellow who'd been up at Cambridge with him and came a few times, but I'm afraid I don't recall his name. It's been nearly twenty years, and I didn't pay that much attention anyway."

"No one else?"

"Everyone else pretty much cut him off after his father disowned him—all except for his brother, of course."

"I thought he had several brothers."

"He had two. But it was only Crispin, the middle son, who came to see him. They were quite close, so his death hit Nicholas hard."

"Crispin Hayes died while Nicholas was in prison? Or when he was staying at the Red Lion?"

"It was right before the Frenchwoman's murder."

"How did he die?"

"He drowned."

*Jesus. What a tragic family*, thought Sebastian. "Tell me about Nicholas Hayes himself—what manner of man he was."

Calhoun drew a deep, pained breath. "I know what they said about him in the papers this morning, how they made him out to be some ne'er-do-well, depraved reprobate. But he wasn't like that. I mean, yes, he was wild and maybe a bit reckless and hotheaded. But he was a good man—honorable and trustworthy and true."

"Most people would consider abducting an heiress fairly depraved."

Calhoun set his jaw and said nothing.

"So, why did he kill Chantal de LaRivière?" asked Sebastian.

"He said he didn't."

"Did you believe him?"

Calhoun met Sebastian's gaze. "Yes—then and now."

"Did you attend the trial?"

"No. Nicholas said he didn't want me to."

*Interesting*, thought Sebastian. Because Hayes wanted to spare the lad pain? Or because he didn't want Calhoun to realize he really was guilty of murder?

Aloud, Sebastian said, "Who do you think killed him?"

Calhoun drew his lower lip between his teeth and shook his head. "I don't know. But whoever it was, Nicholas must not have seen him as a threat. I mean, he turned his back on the fellow, didn't he? You wouldn't do that with someone you thought might kill you. Would you?"

"The killer could have crept up behind him."

"I suppose so."

"Ji didn't know the name of the man Hayes was planning to meet in the tea gardens last night?"

"No. Or, at least, he said he didn't."

"Do you have any idea where Ji might have gone or how to set about finding him?"

"No, my lord. Believe me, I wish I did." The valet took a deep breath. "With your lordship's permission, I'd like to spend the day looking for the lad."

Sebastian nodded. "We need to find him, and quickly. Was Ji with Hayes when you met him at Oxford Market?"

"He was, yes."

"Would he run if he saw you, do you think?"

"I don't know. He ran away from me last night, didn't he?"

"True. But he was scared."

Calhoun thrust up from his seat by the cold hearth and went to stare out the front windows. The sun was already high and hot; it was staging up to be another brutal day.

After a moment, he said, "Is Ji in danger, do you think?"

Sebastian was aware of a sense of disquiet settling low in his gut. "That child might not know whom Hayes was meeting last night. But if the killer thinks there's a chance he does, then I'd say yes, he's in danger. Grave danger."

## Chapter 9

*H*ero was dressed in a plain walking gown of soft gray sarcenet and positioning a simple high-crowned bonnet on her head when Sebastian came to stand at the entrance to her dressing room.

"You're going to look for that child, aren't you?" he said, watching her.

She kept her gaze on her reflection in the mirror as she tilted the hat just so. "How can I not? It's ghastly to think about such a young child all alone in a strange city. In a strange *country*."

"I thought you were planning to start the interviews for your next article today." Much to the disgust of her father, Hero was writing a series of articles for the *Morning Chronicle* on the poor of the city. She'd profiled everyone from London's street children to its pure finders and night-soil men, and each article enraged Jarvis more than the last.

"I am. But I don't see any reason why I can't do both. This article is about the city's street musicians, and it occurs to me that one of them might have seen the boy. There can't be that many half-Chinese children roaming around London, and street performers do tend to pay attention to their audiences."

"I've given Calhoun leave to search for the boy as well. I think he plans to begin in Oxford Square, which is where he and Hayes met."

Hero glanced over at him, her arms falling to her sides, her gray eyes clouded with worry. "If you were a child alone in a strange land, where would you go?"

"I don't know. It's possible he's gone back to where Hayes was staying. But at the moment I haven't the slightest idea where that was."

"How will you even begin going about finding who killed him?"

"All I can do is start with the evidence I have—which at the moment consists mainly of Nicholas Hayes's body."

Paul Gibson's surgery lay in a narrow medieval lane on Tower Hill, virtually within the shadow of the great Norman castle that had guarded London and the Thames for over seven hundred years. He'd been an Army surgeon at one time, until a French cannonball tore off his lower left leg, leaving him racked by phantom pains. When the pains—and his increasing consumption of the opium he used to control them—grew to be too much, he'd come here, to London, to open his surgery and teach anatomy at the hospitals of St. Bartholomew's and St. Thomas's. But he continued to work at expanding his knowledge of death and the human body, largely by way of surreptitious dissections performed on cadavers filched from London's overflowing graveyards by gangs of body snatchers euphemistically referred to as "resurrection men."

Irish by birth, Gibson was in his thirties now and thinner than he should be, thanks to his opium consumption. His friendship with Sebastian dated back nearly ten years to the days when both men had worn the King's colors and fought the King's wars across the Old World and the New. It was Sebastian who'd held his friend down when they sawed off the mangled remnant of Gibson's shattered calf, and Gibson who'd helped save Sebastian when some painful truths about his parentage came close to destroying him. Theirs was a bond that transcended class, nationality, and other such trivialities.

The surgeon performed both his official post mortems and other, less legal activities in a stone outbuilding at the base of the yard behind his ancient house. It was there Sebastian found him that morning, with Nicholas Hayes's naked body lying faceup on the raised stone slab in the center of the room. Gibson had a scalpel in one hand and was about to make his first cut on the dead man's chest, but paused when Sebastian's shadow fell across him.

"Ah, there you are," said the Irishman, looking up. "Thought I'd be seeing you soon enough. Is it true, what they're saying? That this is Nicholas Hayes?"

"It seems to be."

"I thought he died out in Botany Bay."

"So did everyone," said Sebastian. "Christ, look at those scars."

Thick, ugly bands of scar tissue encircled the dead man's wrists and ankles. Shackles left scars like that on a man, especially when he was forced to do hard labor in them—deep, humiliating marks of base servitude that never, ever went away.

"He must have worn those chains for years, night and day. They obviously festered badly." Gibson gave a faint, disbelieving shake of his head. "Why the hell would someone like that come back to England?"

"Love? Revenge? Homesickness? I honestly can't begin to fathom it. What can you tell me about his death?"

"Not a lot so far that you don't already know, although I'm only just getting started." Gibson set aside his scalpel. "Here, help me turn him over."

They rolled the stiff body onto its stomach. The fatal gashes left by the sickle gaped red and raw, but Sebastian found his attention riveted not by the new wounds but by the thick mat of crisscrossing old flogging scars that completely covered Nicholas Hayes's back.

*When he came to,* Calhoun had said, *he was lying next to a dead man of about the same height, build, and hair color. The fellow was a freeman who'd once been a soldier, and he'd obviously spent some time in irons and been flogged, because his body was scarred. Hayes changed clothes with him, took his papers, and bashed in the dead man's face with a rock until he was unrecognizable.* At the time, Sebastian had wondered how desperate a man would need to be to do such a thing. Now he understood.

"He's lucky to have survived that flogging," said Gibson. "Looks like two hundred lashes or more, laid on hard."

"I'd be surprised if he was only flogged once."

They called them "special prisoners" out at Botany Bay: men who could read and write, and who were unlucky enough to talk like gentlemen. The soldiers tended to single such men out for particularly harsh treatment. They didn't usually survive long.

Sebastian shifted his focus from Hayes's old flogging scars to the wounds that had killed him. "Looks like he was hit with that sickle— what? Two or three times?"

"Depends on how you count them." Gibson turned to pick up the bloodstained sickle from a shelf that ran across the back of the room. "The blade on this thing is razor-sharp, so it wouldn't have taken much force for the killer to drive it in deep. It looks to me as if he sank the sickle into Hayes's back, dragging the blade down through the tissue in a kind of swiping slash the first time. Then he yanked it out and sank it in again deeper. The first blow would have stopped Hayes if he were walking away, but it's probably the second one that dropped him to his knees."

"Was he still alive then?"

"I'd say so. I'll know more when I get a good look at the heart, but I suspect that once Hayes fell, your killer grabbed hold of the sickle's handle again and twisted the blade in the wound, driving it deeper and hitting either the heart or a major artery."

"Lovely." Sebastian went to stand in the doorway and look out at the sun-drenched garden that had recently replaced what was once a weedstrewn wasteland.

"You've no idea who did it?" said Gibson, watching him.

"At the moment, my only suspect is the man who's been calling himself the 'Earl of Seaforth' all these years—and that's simply because he has an obvious motive." Sebastian turned to glance around the room. "Where are his things?"

"There," said Gibson, nodding to a shelf behind the door where the dead man's clothes lay neatly folded beside his boots and an old wooden platter containing a fat purse and the other contents of his pockets.

"Doesn't look like the motive was robbery," said Sebastian, reaching for the purse.

"Don't see how it could be," agreed Gibson. "Footpads wouldn't have bothered to stab him more than once; they'd simply grab that purse and run. Why waste time sticking around to make certain the fellow's dead?"

Sebastian studied the scattering of disparate personal objects on the platter: a few loose coins; a silk handkerchief; a small metal disk of some kind; an ivory toothpick in an enameled brass case. "No watch?"

"No."

Sebastian picked up the bronze disk, which was about the size of a large coin and decorated with a relief of an ancient-looking stone building with a row of arched windows and an exotic dome; the other side was the same. "Must be a token of some kind. It looks vaguely familiar, but I can't place it."

"Does it? Don't think I've seen it before."

Sebastian bounced the token up and down in his palm. "If you were an escaped convict fresh off a ship from Canton, where would you stay?"

"Canton? Is that where he's been?"

"For most of the time, yes."

Gibson looked thoughtful. "I think I'd be tempted to go back to someplace that was familiar, but not so familiar that I'd need to worry about people I didn't trust recognizing me." He paused. "Although if Hayes was worried about being recognized, why come back at all?"

"Whatever his reason, it was obviously important to him—important enough to risk being caught and dying for."

"What's important enough to lure a man into risking both his freedom and his life?"

Sebastian closed his fist around the token and brought his gaze back
to the dead man's silent, yet oddly peaceful-looking face. "Maybe the
question isn't, What? Maybe the question is, Who?"

*Chapter 10*

$O$xford Market lay just to the north of Oxford Street. A large, sunlit square of stalls and shops bordering an old wooden arcade, it was a popular spot for a variety of street performers, from hurdy-gurdy players and barrel organ grinders to fire-eaters, conjurers, street singers, jugglers, and a little old man with three trained dogs.

Strolling through the market early that morning with a broad parasol to protect her from the sun, Hero found her attention caught by a tall, dark-haired, copper-skinned man dressed in a loose knee-length tunic over trousers of the same cloth. He had with him a slim boy of perhaps six or seven—also dark haired but much lighter skinned—who wiggled through the crowd with a cup to collect offerings while the father sang a haunting, undulating melody and beat out the rhythm on a barrel-shaped drum.

Joining the crowd gathered around him to watch and listen, Hero caught the little boy's attention and bent down to his eye level while holding up a shilling. "Tell your papa he can have three more of these if he'll talk to me for a few minutes."

The boy's eyes widened and he nodded as his fist closed around the coin.

She watched him dart back to his father. The man glanced over at Hero, then finished his song with a flourish.

His name, she learned, was Dinesh Chakravarty, and his English surprised her. "You want to know how I came to do what I do?" he said when Hero explained she wanted to interview him for an article.

"I do, yes."

"That is very strange."

Hero laughed out loud. "The article is on London's street musicians." It was hard not to ask the man right away if he knew anything about Ji, but Hero suspected she'd have a better chance of getting an honest answer if she approached the subject in a more roundabout way. "Where were you born?"

The man's teeth flashed in a wide smile. "Calcutta."

"How long have you been in England?"

"Eight years. I came here as a servant to a British Army officer." The smile faded. "He died."

"That's when you became a street musician?"

"Not at first, no, my lady. I tried to get another position as a manservant. But with my last master dead, I had no letter to recommend me. You can't get a position without a character reference, so I bought the drum." He cocked his head and beat a little flourish on the drumhead.

"Do you make a good living?"

"Good?" Again, the smile. "No. I did better at first. That's the way it always is, you know? When something is new and different, everyone stops to watch and listen. But now I'm lucky if I make six or eight shillings a week. Winters are always worse."

Hero found herself looking at the little boy. "It must be hard to keep a family on that."

"It is, my lady. My wife, she sometimes takes in washing, but it is hard when she's so heavy with child."

"Your wife is English?"

He smiled. "Scottish. I also pose for artists at the Academy. They say I have 'the look' they want, whatever that means."

He would be interesting to paint, Hero thought, with his hawklike nose and deep-set eyes and arresting bone structure. "Have you thought about going back to India?"

A wistful expression crept into the man's sad, dark eyes. "I'm afraid my Marie wouldn't like it there. But I think of it all the time, especially in the winter. I doubt there's a Bengali in London who doesn't think of it."

"Are there many?"

"Oh, yes, my lady. They come here as Lascars." Lascars were Asian sailors who served as seamen on British ships to replace the sailors who tended to die at such alarming rates in the East. Particularly during the war when the British Navy was impressing so many sailors, the East India Company was often seriously short of crews for their return voyages.

Dinesh drew a deep breath that flared his nostrils. "So many of the young men, they think it'll be a lark, or at least a way out of misery. But they don't know what they're getting themselves into—the floggings, the wretched holes they're expected to live in. The East India Company, they pay Lascars only one shilling for every five they pay an Englishman—and give them less food too. A lot of the men, they reach port and they won't go back on a ship. So they starve here instead of in Calcutta."

Hero had heard horror stories about Lascars starving to death in the streets of eastern London. She said, "How do people tend to treat you?"

He stared across the square, to where Hero could see Jules Calhoun talking to a woman selling apples. "Sometimes people insult me, call me ugly names," Dinesh said slowly, the flesh seeming to pull tight across the bones of his face in a way that left him looking gaunt and troubled. "Some even hit me and spit on me. They have much hate in their hearts for anyone who looks different from them. They think the color of our skin makes us less than them—as if we were more animal than man. I am glad my son's skin is so light. It will be easier for him."

"What about the Chinese?" asked Hero, aware of a strange burning in her chest that was half shame and half rage. "Are there many Chinese people in London?"

"Not so many, no. Some also come as Lascars to replace the English sailors who die on the way to China. But they tend to stay close to the port."

"I'm told there's a little half-Chinese boy who hangs around this part of London—a child of perhaps eight or nine." Hero was careful to keep her voice light. "I'm thinking it would be interesting to interview him. Do you know him?"

Dinesh shook his head. "No, my lady. Sorry."

"You haven't seen him?"

"No, my lady."

"Where would a child like that go, do you think?"

"Is he a street performer? Because most street performers move around. We need to. People get tired of seeing or hearing us. So he could be anywhere from Billingsgate to Covent Market to Portman Square."

Hero was aware of Calhoun working his way back around the arcade, his alert, watchful gaze raking the crush of shoppers and sellers. "He might be a beggar," she said. *Or he could be reduced to stealing,* Hero thought with a sudden upsurge of alarm.

"Beggars usually stay farther east," said Dinesh. "Workingmen and -women tend to be more generous with beggars than folks around here."

"That's a sorry comment on the people of Mayfair," said Hero, handing the musician his shillings.

Dinesh gave a very Eastern shrug. "It is what it is."

"Anything?" Hero asked Calhoun when he walked up to her a few minutes later.

He blew out a harsh breath and shook his head, his gaze still hopefully scanning the crowd. "No, my lady. No one's seen him."

"Yet he was here just last week."

"He was. But he was with Hayes then. People might not have noticed him as much."

Hero watched a couple of ragged, appallingly dirty boys dart past, one tossing a loaf of bread—doubtless purloined—to the other. "Perhaps Devlin is having more luck."

"Perhaps," said Calhoun. But she knew from the pinched look on his face that he didn't believe it any more than she did.

*Chapter 11*

*W*here would a man such as Nicholas Hayes go to hide?

Sebastian pondered the question as he guided his curricle and pair through the narrow lanes leading away from Tower Hill. A sailor could lose himself in the crowded alleys and miserable boardinghouses near the docks, but how well would a man such as Hayes blend into that environment? Not well, Sebastian suspected.

*Someplace familiar,* Gibson had suggested, but not so familiar that he'd run the risk of being recognized. Obviously not St. James's or Piccadilly. But what about a place where he'd taken refuge once before? A place where constables were unwelcome and the locals knew not to ask too many questions.

A place like the Red Lion off Chick Lane.

Situated not far from the vast, death-haunted meat market of Smithfield, Chick Lane—or West Street, as it was increasingly called—lay in an insalubrious section of London infested with thieves and highwaymen and the kind of prostitutes who were as likely to rob a man as smile at him.

Dominated by two foul parish workhouses and a collection of aging breweries, the area had already been in decline twenty years ago. It was even worse today.

The Red Lion was a ramshackle three-hundred-year old inn that backed onto one of the last free-flowing stretches of the Fleet left within the city. What had once been a clear, navigable waterway was now mostly built over and reduced to an underground sewer. These days, the few sections still above ground were usually referred to as Fleet Ditch rather than the River Fleet.

Sebastian had visited the Red Lion only once before. When he drew up outside the ancient inn, he decided it looked even worse than he remembered. The original plaster of the second and third stories had mostly fallen away, exposing the *brickette-entre-poteaux*, or brick-between-posts, construction beneath. Left to the mercy of the elements, the old, poor-quality Tudor bricks were slowly crumbling away. Someone at some point had covered the ground-floor facade with wood, but even that was now weathered and worm-eaten.

"I remember hearing tales about this place when I was on the street," said Tom, Sebastian's young groom, or tiger. Craning back his head, he squinted up at the inn's leaning chimneys and crooked casement windows. "Heard they throw the bodies of those they murder out the rear windows into the Fleet."

"I'll keep my wits about me," said Sebastian, handing the boy the reins. "But if I'm not back in half an hour, send the constables in after me."

Tom laughed.

Inside, the heavily beamed ceiling was low, the wainscoting dark with the smoke of ages, the worn flagstone paving underfoot covered with sawdust. It was early enough that the taproom was nearly deserted, with only a couple of rough-looking characters in an old-fashioned booth near the front windows and a dark-haired, middle-aged man with the broken nose and brawny build of a retired Gentleman of the Fancy behind the bar.

"I'm looking for Grace Calhoun," said Sebastian, walking up to him. "Is she around?"

The man—who was at least six-two and so muscle-bound as to make his movements slow and ponderous—screwed up his lips and shot a stream of tobacco juice in the general direction of a battered spittoon. "Who's askin'?"

"Devlin."

"Huh." The barman turned and disappeared through a doorway behind the bar.

Sebastian could hear whispers—the barman's hushed voice, then a woman's. Their words were pitched low enough that they surely had no expectation of being overheard. But Sebastian's hearing, like his eyesight, was abnormally acute.

"'E don't say wot 'e wants," whispered the barman.

"You know what he wants."

"I kin tell 'im ye ain't 'ere."

"No. I'll see him. Why not?"

She appeared a moment later, a tall, upright woman with unusual, striking features and thick black hair beginning to shade to gray. Sebastian thought she must have been quite young at the time of Calhoun's birth, because she didn't look much above fifty now. Her black eyes were shrewd and cunning and utterly merciless.

"How did you know?" said Grace Calhoun, coming straight to the point. There was no need for her to spell out the obvious by saying, *How did you know Nicholas Hayes was staying here?*

"Deduction. Someone had to tell him where to find Jules."

She sniffed.

Sebastian said, "When did Hayes come here?"

"Couple weeks ago. Why?"

"Calhoun seems to have the impression he'd only just arrived in London."

"He figured the less my Jules knew, the better."

"Yet he contacted him," said Sebastian. *And you obviously told him how to do so.*

"He didn't want to. But he was afraid he might need help."

"With what?"

"He didn't say, and I ain't one for askin'."

Sebastian studied the woman's hard, carefully shuttered face. The particulars of her life were unknown to him, but no one reached her position in London's dangerous, cutthroat underworld without being tough and brutal and very, very clever. "Why let him stay? He was a danger to you."

"If he'd been caught, you mean?" She gave a dismissive twitch of one shoulder. "Who's t' say I knew who he was? The last twenty years been hard on him, that's for sure."

"Did anyone come to see him while he was here?"

Grace Calhoun cast a questioning look at the barman, who spat again and said, "Didn't see nobody 'cept that boy 'e brung wit him."

"You mean Ji?"

"Aye."

"Is the boy here now?"

Grace Calhoun shook her head. "We ain't seen him since yesterday."

The faint hope Sebastian had nourished that he'd find the boy here, safe, died. "Do you know the name of the man Hayes was planning to meet in Somer's Town yesterday?"

"No. Why would I?"

"Because you're far more knowledgeable than you like to appear."

She remained silent, but a faint gleam of what might have been amusement lit up her dark eyes.

He said, "May I see Hayes's room?"

"What for?"

"It might help me figure out who killed him."

Her head tilted to one side. "Why you care who killed him?"

"I care," said Sebastian.

She was silent for a moment, considering his request and its various ramifications. Then she glanced at the ex-boxer standing nearby with his arms folded at his chest. "Show him."

*Chapter 12*

$S$ebastian followed the silent barman up two narrow flights of stairs to a room overlooking the Fleet. Furnished with a heavy old bed and a smaller trundle for the boy, the room was both neat and noticeably cleaner than the rest of the inn. A Chinese porcelain shaving cup, a razor, and other personal items were lined up on the washstand; two sets of silk slippers—one pair large, the other small—were visible beneath the edge of the mattress, their toes embroidered with colorful butterflies and birds. On a table beside the bed rested a *chinois* enameled frame containing a miniature portrait of a young Chinese woman.

"Do you know anything about the woman?" asked Sebastian, going to pick up the miniature. She'd been painted with her face turned partly away and a faint smile curling her lips. She was lovely.

The barman shook his head. "'E didn't talk much, that cove."

Curled up beside the portrait lay what Sebastian recognized as a set of Buddhist prayer beads. Made from the wood of the bodhi tree, they were worn and obviously well used. Two talismans or amulets flanked the beads' decorative tassel: one a silver spiral, the other a symbol Sebastian didn't recognize. He stared at it a long moment, then turned away to begin searching the room.

The shelves of the wardrobe contained spare clothing for both the dead man and the missing child. Hayes's clothes were all European in style, but there were a small *changshan* and a *magua*, presumably for Ji. Sebastian fingered the fine, colorful silk, wondering again about the relationship between man and child. A stack of well-read books rested on the top shelf, and he scanned the titles: Milton's *Paradise Lost*; Shakespeare's *Tragedies*; Plato's *Republic*. Interesting reading for a man infamous for kidnapping an heiress and killing a French countess.

"Ye 'bout done there?" demanded the barman, shifting restlessly.

"Almost."

The bed was easy enough to search, its lumpy mattress resting directly on leather slings. A sea chest stood at the footboard, but it was nearly empty, containing only a winter greatcoat small enough to fit the child and a few other miscellaneous pieces of clothing. At the very bottom, tucked beneath a scarf, was an unloaded flintlock pistol and a powder horn, along with a leather kit containing a brass funnel, lead shot, extra flints, cloth patches, and cleaning materials. The pistol was not new, and Sebastian found himself wondering why the hell Hayes hadn't taken the weapon with him to Somer's Town. The man had obviously misjudged whomever he went to meet.

Leaving the gun where he'd found it, Sebastian was replacing the clothing when a folded sheet of newspaper fluttered to the floor. Picking it up, he realized he was holding the third and fourth pages from the *Morning Post* for the last Tuesday in May. Densely printed, the pages contained everything from notices of property sales and upcoming horse auctions to a section headed "Fashionable Arrangements for the Week." He quickly skimmed the list.

THIS EVENING: *the Countess of Balcarra's rout, Cumberland Place*
TOMORROW: *the Duchess of Warton's ball, Berkeley Square*

THURSDAY, JUNE 2: *Lady Forbes's rout, St. James's Square*
*Mrs. Drummond's ball, Half Moon Street*
FRIDAY, JUNE 3: *the Marchioness of Hertford's ball, Manchester Square*
SATURDAY, JUNE 4: *Mrs. Campbell's rout, Grosvenor Street*
SUNDAY, JUNE 5: *Mr. and Mrs. James Mortimer's public breakfast,*
*Oaklawn, Blackheath*

It was the final item that caught Sebastian's eye:

MONDAY, JUNE 6: *the Comte de Compans's soirée, Dover Street*

"Ain't got all day, ye know," grumbled the barman.

Sebastian tucked the folded news sheet into his pocket and closed the chest's lid. "I've finished."

Alistair James St. Cyr, the Fifth Earl of Hendon, was striding purposefully across Palace Yard toward Whitehall when Sebastian came upon him.

One of the most powerful men in Britain after Lord Jarvis, Hendon had served as Chancellor of the Exchequer under a succession of three prime ministers. There'd been a time when he'd been taller than Sebastian, although these days the Earl had begun to stoop. He had a blunt, heavy-featured face, thinning white hair, and the piercing blue eyes that had been the hallmark of the St. Cyr family for generations but were so noticeably lacking in Sebastian. Sebastian had grown up calling this man "Father," although he'd recently learned that their relationship was considerably more complicated. The rift that discovery had caused was beginning to heal, but slowly.

"I'm surprised you're not at Ascot with the Regent and the Allied Sovereigns," said Sebastian, falling into step beside him.

Hendon made a gruff noise deep in his throat and kept walking.

"We're looking at two solid weeks of endless balls, routs, dinners, receptions, banquets, and reviews. They don't need me at Ascot."

"Understandable."

Hendon threw him a quick glance, his jaw tightening. "I saw this morning's papers. Is it true, what they're saying? That Nicholas Hayes was found murdered up in Somer's Town?"

"It is, yes."

"What a sordid affair. Please tell me you haven't involved yourself in it."

"I have, actually."

Hendon's jaw tightened. "You were—what? Eight? Ten?—when he killed that Frenchwoman?"

"Thirteen. Fourteen by the time he was transported."

"Huh. Well, I doubt you paid much attention to it at the time, but if you had, you'd know not to have anything to do with this. You'd simply be glad the wretched man is finally dead and let it go."

"Oh? So tell me about him."

Hendon drew up abruptly. "You can't be serious."

"But I am."

Hendon cast a quick glance around the crowded Yard. "We can't discuss it here."

"Then let's go for a walk."

They walked across Westminster Bridge, toward the sun-dazzled south bank of the river.

"How much do you know?" asked Hendon.

"Nothing beyond the fact that Hayes was transported for murdering the Countess de Compans, and that she was very young and very beautiful."

Hendon stared off across the river, his eyes narrowed against the glint bouncing off the water. "She was beautiful, with the palest blond hair and eyes the color of violets. To be honest, she was the most exquisitely beautiful woman I've ever seen. Chantal was her name. Chantal de LaRivière. She was younger than the Count—no more than twenty or twenty-one when she died. She left a child barely a year old."

"Tragic."

"It was, yes."

"So exactly what happened?"

"LaRivière found Hayes trying to force himself on her. When he pulled the bastard away from her, Hayes drew a double-barreled pistol and shot first the Count, then Chantal. The bullet only grazed LaRivière's head, but Chantal was killed."

"Sordid, indeed," said Sebastian.

"Hayes insisted he was innocent, of course."

"Oh? What was his story?"

"He denied that LaRivière found him trying to force himself on the Countess. Claimed she was simply present at an argument between the two men and that the pistol was LaRivière's. According to Hayes, the Count threatened him with the gun, and it went off when he tried to defend himself. He said the same bullet that wounded the Count killed Chantal outright."

"Surely the servants would have been able to count the number of gunshots."

"He didn't dispute that the gun went off twice. He claimed the first bullet—fired by the Count—had gone wild, although it was never found."

"And the jury didn't believe his story?"

"Given the man's disreputable history? Of course not. Hayes had no good excuse for being where he was. And while he claimed they were arguing, he refused to say about what. If he'd only admitted it, he might have been found guilty of manslaughter. Instead, he was convicted of murder. I'm surprised he didn't hang."

"Did you know him?"

"Hayes? No, not really. Knew the father, of course. He was up at Oxford with me."

"The Second Earl? What did you think of him?"

Hendon was silent a moment, his lips pressing into a tight line. "He was a pompous, vain, arrogant man, yet extraordinarily touchy about the fact his title was only an Irish one and relatively recent at that. It's a bad combination, in my experience—arrogance and wounded pride. It sours a man."

"Nicholas was his third son?"

"He was, yes. The middle son, Crispin, drowned just a few days before Chantal de LaRivière's murder. And the heir—Lucas, I believe was his name—died childless a year or two before the Earl."

"And when was that?"

"That Seaforth died? Must have been ten years ago, at least."

"That's when the title passed to the Earl's nephew, Ethan?"

"That's right. He was the heir presumptive, given that Nicholas was dead—or so everyone thought." Hendon frowned. "You're certain this fellow killed up in Somer's Town really was Nicholas Hayes?"

"There doesn't seem to be much doubt about it."

Hendon paused for a moment, his gaze on a wherryman rowing his fare across the river. But Sebastian had the impression his thoughts were far, far away. After a moment, the Earl said, "Why the devil would someone like that return to England?"

"I can think of one rather obvious explanation."

Hendon turned his head to stare at him. "You can? What?"

"What if Nicholas Hayes told the truth eighteen years ago? What if he really didn't kill Chantal de LaRivière?"

"What are you suggesting? That the Count accidently shot his own wife and then blamed Hayes for it? That's absurd."

"It would explain why Hayes came back."

"For revenge, you mean? Against the Count de Compans? Please tell me you aren't suggesting that Gilbert-Christophe de LaRivière of all people killed Hayes. Good God, Devlin! Eighteen years ago, LaRivière was just another impoverished French nobleman struggling to survive in exile. But he's now a close confidant of both the newly restored French King and his brother—who will no doubt be King himself soon enough. The only reason LaRivière isn't in Paris with the rest of them is because he agreed to stay and represent the Bourbons during the Allied Sovereigns' visit."

Sebastian studied Hendon's hot, angry face. "Just because I see it as a possibility to be explored doesn't mean I intend to accuse the good Count out of hand, if that's what concerns you."

Hendon's lips flattened into a thin line. "I'd hoped when you married and became a father you'd give up this nonsense. It's not at all a proper thing for you to be doing, chasing after murderers. Especially when the victim is a man of such despicable character. It's . . . unseemly."

Sebastian gave a faint shake of his head. "Murder is unseemly. Making certain a killer doesn't get away with what he has done is an obligation we the living owe to the dead—no matter how unsavory we consider them to be."

"I suppose so—but that's why we have magistrates and constables."

"Am I not my brother's keeper?" said Sebastian softly.

Hendon pointed a shaky finger at him. "Don't start."

"Are you saying it's not relevant?"

Hendon didn't try to deny it, although his face grew even redder. "But *this* murder, Devlin? The dead man was himself a murderer."

"And what if he wasn't?"

"Of course he was."

Sebastian held his peace. Yet he found himself thinking of two sets of embroidered Chinese slippers, one large, the other small, tucked neatly away beneath a lumpy mattress.

And a set of Buddhist prayer beads curled up beside the miniature portrait of a faintly smiling young woman.

*Chapter 13*

*J*i had awakened that morning just before dawn, still slumped in the recess of the old doorway. Jerking up, mouth dry with a rush of terror, the child scanned the narrow lane, listening, watching. The man Poole was gone.

But the child was still too afraid to return to the Red Lion. Instead, Ji took off running, darting down noisome alleys, past stinking breweries, through streets crowded with shabby secondhand dealers and bawling hawkers who wouldn't have been too out of place in Canton. On and on the child ran. Only when the familiar inn and the danger it had come to represent were left far, far behind did Ji draw up, chest heaving, lungs gasping, head spinning with fear and confusion mixed with mind-numbing grief and a paralyzing sense of failure.

*I should have been there when he died,* Ji kept thinking over and over again. *I should be with him now.* Worse than the heart-stopping fear, almost worse than the tide of overwhelming grief, was this shameful sense of having failed Hayes at the time of his greatest need. As death approached, Ji should have been at his side chanting the holy protective verses and helping Hayes feel calm and at peace. Instead, Hayes had died alone. Alone and in pain.

Ji knew Hayes had lived a good life filled with good deeds. He had accumulated good karma that could enable him to transition to an auspicious new life rather than be reborn as a hungry ghost or a hell creature. But Ji knew too that Hayes had done things in his past—dark things. In the transition from one life to the next, the final moment of consciousness was the most important of all, and Hayes's last moments must have been hideous. He would need assistance on his path, yet in this vast, unfriendly alien city, who was there to help? Ji didn't even know where Hayes was now. Was his body being treated gently and with respect? Was someone setting up an altar with offerings of incense, flowers, and fruit? Where?

As his breathing slowed, Ji washed at a public pump, then bought bread and gave half of it to the birds while chanting sutras to generate merit that could be transferred to Hayes. But it wasn't enough. Hayes was now in the intermediate state—what Ji's Tibetan nurse, Pema, called the Bardo. Some taught that in the First Bardo—the four days right after death—the dead often didn't even know they were no longer alive.

*Do you know?* thought the child, choking back tears. *Do you know you're dead?*

There were special chants that could reach the dead in such a state, to help them. But Ji had never learned them. If they were in Canton, the Hong merchant would hire monks—one hundred and eight of them— to burn incense and open the road to the next world. Hayes would be carefully bathed and dressed in proper burial clothes, and a priest would divine the most propitious minute to place the body in its coffin. The temple would be hung with odes and eulogy scrolls, and everything would be done as it should be. Except here, in this strange city, Ji didn't even know where to sleep.

"Oh, Hayes," whispered the child, "I don't know what to do. What do I do?"

*What do I do?*

*Chapter 14*

Sebastian arrived at the Dover Street residence of Gilbert-Christophe de LaRivière to find a team of sweaty, foam-flecked grays and a dusty chaise drawn up before the French nobleman's house. The Count himself was just descending from the carriage.

"Walk 'em," Sebastian told Tom, handing his chestnuts' reins to the tiger. "I doubt I'll be long."

Hopping down to the pavement, Sebastian caught up with the Frenchman as he was about to mount his front steps. "Good afternoon, my lord. If I might have a word with you?"

The Count turned, one hand fumbling for the quizzing glass that hung around his neck from a black riband. Eighteen years before, at the time of his lovely wife's death, LaRivière would have been a man of thirty or perhaps thirty-five. Now he was a widower in his late forties or early fifties, his black hair still only lightly streaked with gray, his eyes dark and deeply set, his nose long and narrow. Unlike many nobleman of his age who'd grown soft and fleshy, LaRivière was still trim, his movements quick and sure. He was known as a fine dresser and a connoisseur of the arts who personally designed his own fobs and collected ancient artifacts. He also had a reputation as something of an artist himself and could frequently be found sketching London's old churches and picturesque Renaissance houses.

Now he stared at Sebastian through his glass long enough to convey both annoyance and the faintest hint of derision. Then he let it drop and said in English only faintly accented by his native French, "You're Devlin, I believe?"

"I am." Sebastian paused at the base of the steps and said again, "If I might have a word with you, my lord?"

"I've just come from Ascot and am due to dine with the Queen this evening."

"It shouldn't take up too much of your time."

The Count's eyes narrowed in a way that told Sebastian the Frenchman knew exactly why Sebastian was here. "Very well. Do come in."

Sebastian followed LaRivière to a richly appointed library filled with hundreds of leather-bound volumes artistically interspersed with fragments of Greek and Roman statues. For a man who had fled France a penniless refugee twenty years before, Compans somehow contrived to live quite comfortably. And Sebastian found himself wondering how.

"Brandy?" offered his host.

"Please."

The Count went to a small inlaid table bearing a crystal carafe and glasses. "You're here because of Hayes, I take it?"

"How did you know?"

"Seaforth was also at Ascot."

"Of course."

He eased the stopper from the carafe. "So it's true, what they're saying in the papers? That the dead man found up in Somer's Town really is Hayes?"

"I believe so."

"How very odd."

"When was the last time you saw Nicholas Hayes?"

"Me?" LaRivière poured brandy into two glasses. "Eighteen years ago I watched him sentenced to death for murdering my wife. And then, much to my disgust, I saw that sentence commuted to transportation for life."

"Did you know he had returned to England?"

The Frenchman handed Sebastian one of the glasses. "I thought he was dead."

"Any idea why he might have come back?"

LaRivière sipped his drink, then ran his tongue across his upper lip. "Some men are simply irrational. There is no coherent, linear thought behind their actions. Their behavior is as unpredictable as a dog deciding which of a thousand flea bites to scratch, or the direction of a playbill fluttering in a whirlwind."

"You're suggesting Hayes risked his life by returning to England for no reason?"

"Presumably the flea-bitten dog has a reason for his selection. But I doubt the ability of anyone to divine it."

Sebastian took a slow swallow of his own brandy. "How well did you know Hayes?"

"Not well. I was better acquainted with his brother Crispin." LaRivière brought up one hand to rub his forehead, and it was a moment before he could go on. "I beg your pardon. I find thinking about those days trying. It may have been eighteen years ago, yet in so many ways it seems like only yesterday."

"I'm sorry," said Sebastian. "I understand this is painful. You say you didn't know Nicholas Hayes. But I take it he knew your late wife?"

LaRivière let his hand drop, his lips tightening. "She knew who he was, of course. But they were hardly friends, if that's what you're suggesting. Chantal was a very beautiful woman. Men sometimes became obsessively infatuated with her. It could be awkward."

"You're saying Nicholas Hayes became infatuated with her?"

"Embarrassingly so, to the point he made her uncomfortable."

"Why? What did he do?"

"The usual—staring at her, following her around. That sort of thing. She avoided him when she could, but he was alarmingly persistent."

"Where was she killed?"

"Here in this house. Upstairs in the drawing room." LaRivière went to stand at the window overlooking the street, his gaze on a passing donkey and cart, one hand playing with the gold fob on his watch chain. It was a moment before he continued, his voice cracking with the strain of emotion. "I blame myself. I sought to save her, but in the end she was killed."

The words, like the pose, were tragic: the aging widower still struggling to come to terms with a crushing burden of guilt for what he considered his own failing. And yet . . . And yet somehow it all didn't quite ring true, even if Sebastian couldn't put his finger on precisely why.

He said, "I'm told Hayes claimed there was an argument between him and you. He said that argument led to a struggle, during which the gun went off."

LaRivière's face hardened. "That's what he claimed, yes. Although he couldn't even manage to come up with a believable explanation for this mythical argument." He drained his glass in one long pull. "The man was a rogue. Months before he killed my wife, he abducted some heiress."

"Do you know her name?"

"No. The point is, he didn't belong in polite company. I don't understand how he managed to escape from Botany Bay, but it's where he belonged, and I'm glad he's now dead. He should have been hanged eighteen years ago."

"Do you know of anyone who might have wanted to see him dead?"

"Besides me, you mean?" A faint hint of a smile touched one corner of the Frenchman's thin lips. "I take it that is why you are here?"

"Do you know of anyone?"

LaRivière shook his head. "As I told you, my acquaintance with the man was limited."

Sebastian set his brandy aside. "Thank you for agreeing to speak with me. I understand those days must be difficult to revisit."

The Count met his gaze and held it. "Do you?"

"Yes."

Sebastian turned to go, then paused to draw Hayes's strange bronze disk from his pocket and say, "Do you know what this is?"

"No. Why?"

"It was found in Hayes's pocket."

"Sorry. And now you really must excuse me."

"Of course. Thank you for your assistance."

"Have I been of assistance?" said LaRivière, walking with him toward the entrance hall. "I've heard you frequently interest yourself in such matters, although I fail to understand why—particularly in the case of this murder. What could Hayes possibly mean to you? You didn't know him, did you?"

Sebastian found himself hesitating. What could he say? That no, he hadn't known Hayes, but somehow that didn't stop him from feeling personally invested in the man's death in a way that had nothing to do with ties of friendship or kinship? That he'd looked at the dead man lying on Gibson's slab and felt a jolt of powerful emotion that went beyond empathy, far beyond it, to something he couldn't identify but suspected was at least partially colored by a cold breath of fear? For Sebastian was an Earl's son who'd once been accused of murder. He understood all too well how easily a man's life could be shattered. He himself had once come uncomfortably close to being forced to endure the horror, pain, and humiliation that Hayes had suffered. Those shackle and flogging scars could easily have been his.

Except of course he could say none of those things.

"No," said Sebastian as a footman reached to open the Count's door. "I didn't know him."

It was the truth. And yet the denial had the flavor of a lie and left a bad taste in his mouth.

*Chapter 15*

$\mathcal{T}$he palace is unhappy," said Lovejoy as he and Sebastian walked down Bow Street toward the magistrate's favorite coffeehouse on the Strand. The chaos that tended to characterize the district around Covent Garden Market in the morning was beginning to subside, the crush of carts and barrows in the streets easing. "They don't like the newspaper headlines reminding people that a peer's son once committed such a shocking murder. I'm afraid they may move to shut down our investigation."

"And blame—whom?" said Sebastian. "Footpads?"

Lovejoy rarely smiled. But a brief, faint suggestion of amusement lightened his normally somber gray eyes. "What would we do without footpads to blame?" The amusement faded. "The Earl of Seaforth came to see me first thing this morning."

"He did? Why?"

"Ostensibly to inquire as to the location of Nicholas Hayes's body. But I suspect in reality to attempt to convince me to quietly end Bow Street's investigation into his cousin's murder."

"Interesting."

"He also informed me—quite without my asking—that he dined at his club yesterday evening before going directly from there to Carlton House."

"An enviable alibi, if true." Sebastian watched a costermonger turn his empty barrow into Vinegar Yard. "LaRivière was also at Carlton House last night—although that might not mean anything, given that we don't know how long before the discovery of his body Nicholas Hayes was murdered."

"We have a better idea than we did. A couple of my lads spent the morning up in Somer's Town interviewing the tea gardens' staff as well as searching the area. One of Pennington's daughters was working the entrance yesterday, and she says she remembers Hayes arriving fairly late in the afternoon."

"She's certain?"

Lovejoy nodded. "She saw the body as the men from the deadhouse were removing it. Pennington's house is next to the front gate, and the man made no effort to keep his family from turning out to watch the spectacle. She says Hayes had a young boy with him, and she particularly noticed the child because he was so striking—perhaps wholly or at least partly Chinese. Does that sound like the lad who came to Brook Street?"

"It does, yes." Sebastian chose his words carefully. "It appears likely that Hayes came here from China and brought the boy with him, although I'm not certain as to the exact nature of their relationship."

"China? Good heavens, is that where he's been? Well, if the boy is Chinese, it will certainly make him easier to find." There were probably no more than two or three hundred Chinese in all of London, most of them men. And they tended to stick close to the docks of the East End. "I'll set one of the lads to see if he can find the ship Hayes came in on. The officers and crew might be able to tell us much that we do not know."

"That would help," said Sebastian. "Did Pennington's daughter work the entrance all day?"

"Most of it. If we can come up with the culprit, she might be able to identify the fellow." They were passing St. Mary's burial ground, and Lovejoy had his frowning gaze on the cemetery's crumbling entrance. It was a moment before he spoke. "I've been reading the transcripts of Hayes's trial at the Old Bailey, hoping to understand why he came back to London."

"And?"

Lovejoy shook his head. "Nothing leaps out at me. From what was said at the trial, Hayes sounds like a thoroughly disreputable fellow. It's beyond shocking in one of his rank and lineage."

"Did no one defend him?"

"There was a young Army ensign named Noland—James Noland— who spoke on Hayes's behalf. No one else."

"I wonder where this Ensign Noland is now."

"I looked into him. He enjoyed a distinguished career and rose to the rank of colonel before being killed at Vitoria."

"Unfortunate. Was he Irish, by chance?"

"As it happens, he was. His father's a vicar in County Carlow. How did you know?"

"Someone said Hayes's friends and family abandoned him after his father disowned him, all except for an Irish fellow and one of his brothers."

Lovejoy shook his head. "There was no mention of a brother in the transcripts."

"As I understand it, Crispin Hayes died shortly before Chantal de LaRivière was killed."

"Ah. That explains it, then. Hayes expressed no remorse for what he'd done, by the way—continued to insist to the end that he was innocent."

"Perhaps he was."

"Oh, surely not."

"Think about this," said Sebastian. "If Hayes was innocent—if La-Rivière did accidently kill his own wife and managed to get Hayes transported for it—then I can see a man who'd suffered the hideous brutality that Hayes endured in Botany Bay vowing to come back to England and kill the man he held responsible for it all."

Lovejoy drew his chin in against his chest. "There's no denying it would explain Hayes's puzzling return. But . . . what a shocking miscarriage of justice, if he was innocent and yet was convicted anyway."

"It happens," said Sebastian. *It could have happened to me.*

Lovejoy looked unconvinced. "LaRivière has a reputation as an accomplished swordsman, does he not?"

"I believe he does, yes."

"If Hayes had been killed by a sword thrust, one could with reason cast suspicion on the Count. But a common sickle? In the back? It seems unlikely, wouldn't you say?" Lovejoy looked thoughtful. "It might be worth having the lads look into Pennington's groundskeepers. One of the gardeners may have an unknown past association with Hayes."

*I hope not,* thought Sebastian as they reached the Strand. *Otherwise the poor fellow is liable to end up quickly charged with murder.*

*Whether guilty or not.*

"Why we going back up t' Somer's Town?" asked Tom as Sebastian guided the chestnuts north along St. Martin's Lane.

Sebastian cast an amused glance at his tiger. "You still planning to become a Bow Street Runner someday?"

"I am," said the boy solemnly.

"Then think about this: If you were going to murder someone, would

you do it in a place where you knew your arrival and departure were
certain to be observed by the person taking admission at the gate?"

"Don't seem real smart."

"That's why I want to take another look at Pennington's Tea Gardens."

He found Irvine Pennington's daughter once again manning the tea gardens' entrance. A winsome, freckle-faced girl named Sarah, she had a
sunburned nose and a wide, toothy smile. But her smile faltered when
Sebastian walked up, introduced himself, and asked for her father.

"Begging your lordship's pardon," she said, dropping a quick curtsy,
"but he ain't around. We don't know where he's taken himself off to."

"Perhaps you can help me," said Sebastian. "You were working the
entrance yesterday, weren't you?"

She dropped another curtsy. "I was, your lordship. M'father spelled
me a few times, but I was here most of the day."

"Did many people visit the gardens in the afternoon?"

"Oh, we was right busy, that's for sure. Not as busy as on Sundays, of
course. But it's been so hot lately, lots of folks've been coming out."

"Did you get many gentlemen yesterday?"

"You mean, proper gentlemen? Like yourself?"

Sebastian smiled. "Yes, like that."

"We don't get too many fine ladies and gentlemen anymore. Time
was, we did. But it's mostly common folk these days."

"But you did get some yesterday?"

"Well, probably one or two."

"Do you remember them? If they were old or young? Tall or short?
Thin or fat?"

She screwed up her face with the effort of memory. "I'm right sorry,
your honor, but I don't reckon I could say, for sure. One day just kinda
blends into the next."

"But you remember the man who was killed?"

"Oh, yes, your honor. On account of the boy he had with him. Prettiest little boy I ever did see. Like a porcelain doll, he was."

Sebastian squinted against the sinking sun as he studied the garden's eight-foot-high brick wall. "Is there another entrance to the tea gardens?"

"No, your honor. This is the only one."

"I thought your father said something about a gate in the western boundary wall."

"Well, there is a gate goes out to Cow Lane. The gardeners use it to haul in manure and such. But it's kept locked otherwise."

Sebastian fished in his pocket for a coin and paid his entry fee. "What time do you close?"

The girl handed him a ticket with another smile. "Not till midnight, your honor. We only close early on Thursdays."

"Thank you."

Walking up the tea garden's main promenade, Sebastian was conscious of following in the footsteps of Nicholas Hayes and the missing child. He kept trying to imagine the dead man and Ji relaxing and enjoying these flowery walks and shady arbors, but he could not. A string quartet was playing chamber music in the great room, and the strains of Haydn drifted through the open windows to the horseshoe-shaped arrangement of booths, where a chattering, laughing crowd was eating syllabubs and cakes washed down with tea and ale. And all Sebastian could think was *What an incongruous spot for murder.*

Circling around a bowling green and skittles yard, he came upon an ornamental pond where he paused to watch the half dozen or so children gathered there sail toy boats. A splashing fountain played merrily; the children laughed and called to one another. And Sebastian found himself wondering, *Why would Nicholas Hayes arrange to meet someone here of all places?* Why Pennington's Tea Gardens, a fading pleasure spot that had once attracted the "better sort" but now catered more to shopkeepers

and apprentices? Was that the reason? Because it was so out of the way
and unfashionable? It was, after all, why Hayes had chosen to stay at the
Red Lion.

It made sense, Sebastian decided. But it did nothing to explain whom
Hayes had come here to meet, or for what purpose.

"Bloody hell," said Sebastian under his breath, and turned away.

He followed a narrow path through the shrubbery until he hit the
brick wall that bounded the garden on its western side. Winding back
around, he soon ran across the small clearing where Nicholas Hayes had
died. His corpse might be gone, but his death was still an almost palpa-
ble presence here, the grass flattened by both his body and the boots
of Lovejoy's constables. A bare patch of earth showed dark from his
blood.

Going to stand in the center of the clearing, Sebastian could hear the
distant play of the fountain, the laughing voices of the children, the liquid
crystal song of a robin lost somewhere in a nearby clump of holly. The
evening sun filtering down through the leafy branches overhead felt hot
on his shoulders, and he stood silently for some minutes, trying to understand what had happened here. Searching for answers that eluded him.

Frustrated, he was turning to leave when a flash of white caught his
eye. Someone had spread a small square of white cloth in the shade of a
peony. On the cloth rested a clutch of blossoms—foxglove and white li-
lacs and lady's lace—along with two oranges and a pile of ash surrounding the remnants of what he realized was a joss stick. If he breathed
deeply, Sebastian could just catch the faint scent of sandalwood hanging
in the air.

He quickly crossed the clearing and crouched down beside the
makeshift altar to touch the ash. It was still warm.

"Ji?" he said, rising to his feet. His gaze raked the surrounding shrubbery as he listened intently for the faintest footfall or hushed sound. "Are
you there, Ji? I'm a friend—Calhoun's friend. I won't hurt you. I want to
help you."

He paused. For a moment he imagined he could feel the weight of the child's grief still lingering in this death-haunted clearing as unmistakably as the scent of the wafting incense.

"Ji?" he called again.

But he was alone.

*Chapter 16*

That night, Sebastian watched his wife stand at their bedroom window, one hand on the heavy curtain at her side. She was staring at the darkened street below, but he knew her thoughts were far, far away.

"We're trying," he said, coming up behind her to slip his arms around her waist and hold her close. "That's all we can do."

She tipped her head back against his, her gaze on an elegant chaise dashing up the street below, a crest emblazed on its panel, the lamplight gleaming on the backs of its high-stepping team of matched bays. "And yet it's not enough. That little boy must be so afraid—alone and afraid. I keep imagining Simon in a similar situation, and it's unbearable." She paused. "At least we know Ji's still alive, thanks to the makeshift altar you found."

"It's possible the killer doesn't know the boy exists."

"Perhaps. Yet even then, he's still alone and in danger."

"I know." He turned her in his arms to thread his fingers through the thick fall of her hair and lift her chin with his thumbs. Her eyes were dark and glittering with unshed tears, and he touched his lips to hers. He heard her breathy exhalation as her hands slid up his back to grasp his shoulders. He kissed her half-closed eyelids, her cheeks, the arch of her nose, then came back to capture her mouth again.

She clung to him, her fingers splaying over his bare flesh, her breath raspy as she pressed herself against him. Then she drew back, her hand finding his to tug him toward the curtained recesses of their bed.

They fell together, legs tangling, lips coming together again. He touched her breasts, kissed the tender flesh of her stomach. She gasped, arching against him, her palms cradling his face. "Now. Please," she said, and he rose above her. There was an urgency to their lovemaking, a desperation he couldn't quite define even as he understood its source. Then he felt her body convulse with her release, and he cried out as she pulled him over the edge with her.

Afterward they lay together, his hand caressing her bare arm. They shared a companionable silence for a time. Then he felt the tension begin to coil within her again, and he knew that while she had found some solace in their lovemaking, her thoughts had again returned to the missing child.

He said, "Ji is unusual enough that I think we have a good chance of finding him."

She shifted her head against his shoulder. "I wish I knew where to look next."

"If I had to guess, I'd say somewhere around either the tea gardens or the Red Lion."

"Dear God. I hope he's not sticking close to the Red Lion. That's an appalling neighborhood. Although you're right. It's probably the part of London he's most familiar with."

She was silent a moment, then said, "I've been thinking about what Nicholas Hayes might have been doing in the days before he contacted Jules Calhoun. Grace told you he and the boy arrived in England at least two weeks ago, yet he didn't see Calhoun to ask for his help until last Sunday. What if he spent those days trying to do something but failed?

That could be why he finally reached out to Calhoun, even though he doesn't seem to have wanted to, at first."

"Hmm. It's an interesting theory. Although if you're right, the question then becomes, what was he trying to do?" He pressed his cheek against the top of her head, breathed in the sweet fragrance of her hair. "Calhoun describes Nicholas Hayes as a headstrong and passionate but nonetheless honorable man, while everyone else talks about him as a scandalous son disowned by his father for abducting some heiress. And yet no one seems to know her name."

"Well, it is the kind of thing her family would try to keep quiet, isn't it?"

"It is. But I'd like to know who she was."

She turned in his arms with a smile. "I can think of someone who might be able to tell you."

*Saturday, 11 June*

The next morning, Sebastian paid a call on his aunt Henrietta, the Dowager Duchess of Claiborne. Born Lady Henrietta St. Cyr, she was Hendon's elder sister and thus not actually Sebastian's aunt, although they hadn't allowed that truth to interfere in their relationship. Now in her seventies, she was one of the grandes dames of London society, famous for her ability to ferret out—and remember—every scandal and on-dit to have convulsed the *ton* over the past sixty or more years.

A blunt-faced, fleshy woman with the famous blue St. Cyr eyes, the Dowager was known to never leave her room before twelve or one o'clock. But when Sebastian arrived at her Park Lane town house early the next morning, he was surprised to find her not only up and dressed in a lilac gown trimmed with pink silk, but already breakfasting on toast and tea in her morning room.

"Good heavens, you're up," said Sebastian cheerfully when her butler, Humphrey, showed him in. "Why? It's barely past nine."

The Duchess groaned and brought up one hand to shade her eyes. "Don't remind me, you unnatural child."

He laughed and came to take the seat opposite her. "Never tell me you're planning to join in the day's festivities for the Allied Sovereigns? What's on the schedule for today? A visit to the Tower? A balloon ascension? Or just another grand reception or two or three?"

She gave a faint shudder. "I've no idea. But whatever it is, I haven't the slightest interest in attending. The way Prinny boasts and struts around in his ridiculous uniforms, you'd think all the credit for defeating Bonaparte is personally his and his alone, when everyone knows he's never been anywhere near a battle in his life. It's beyond mortifying. And nauseating."

"So why are you up?"

"Emily. Her latest is being christened. You'd think at her age she'd be done with breeding, but she keeps popping them out. Claiborne says I'm being indelicate to speak of such things, but I've no patience with these modern missish ways. Calling breeches 'unmentionables' and blushing at the mere mention of a chicken thigh. What next?"

Claiborne was Aunt Henrietta's middle-aged, straitlaced son and the current Duke, while Emily was her youngest child, forever in disgrace for having, as her mother always put it, "married badly." Last time Sebastian counted, his cousin was the proud mother of thirteen offspring—and happily adored them all.

"Then I suppose I should be grateful to Emily's fertility for saving me a scold."

The Dowager gave a faint *harrumph*. "Hendon tells me you've involved yourself in another murder. He's most put out, you know."

"Yes, I do know."

"Is that why you're here? To ask me about Nicholas Hayes? I'm afraid I scarcely knew the young man—they packed him off to Botany Bay barely a year after he came down from Oxford. And all I know about that French countess's murder is what was in the papers."

"So tell me about the heiress Hayes was said to have abducted."

Henrietta leaned back in her chair. "Oh, that."

"It actually happened?"

"Well, yes and no. The bit about the 'abduction' was just a ridiculous tale put about to save the girl's reputation."

"I don't understand."

"They eloped, of course."

"Ah. Who was she?"

The Duchess gave him a fierce look. "I trust you to use whatever information I give you discreetly."

"Of course."

"Very well. It was Theo Brownbeck's daughter, Katherine."

"Good Lord." Few in London were unfamiliar with Theodore Brownbeck, a banker who'd made a vast fortune through adroit investments. He was still a powerful figure in the financial affairs of the City, but lately he'd taken to devoting more and more of his time to producing an endless outpouring of works on religion, morality, crime, and the poor. The theme that ran through them all was the conviction that any attempt to educate or improve the living standards of the lower classes was a crime against God and nature. According to Brownbeck, what he sneeringly called "the good intentions of the feebleminded" would only result in inculcating a "sense of entitlement and lethargy" amongst a class ordained by their Creator to be worthy of nothing more than a life of hard work and an early death. Unsurprisingly, he had a passionate and long-running feud with Hero, who had challenged the validity of both his statistics and his harsh prescriptions to cure society's ills.

Sebastian stood up to fetch a teacup from the sideboard. "Why did they need to elope? Why couldn't they simply have married?"

"Because they were under twenty-one, and their fathers refused to countenance the match."

"Seaforth and Brownbeck both opposed the marriage?"

"That's right. The old Earl was a pompous, arrogant ass who thought a Cit's daughter—even a wealthy Cit's daughter—wasn't good enough for an earl's son, even an earl's *youngest* son. And Theodore Brownbeck had no intention of allowing his only child and sole heir to throw herself away on the untitled offspring of an upstart Irish peer and spend her life following the drum."

Sebastian looked up from pouring himself a cup of tea. "Nicholas Hayes was in the Army?"

"No, but he was planning to buy a pair of colors. Of course, that became impossible when his father cut him off without a penny."

"So what happened?"

"Once they realized there was no changing their parents' minds, the young couple ran off. A foolish, woefully improper thing to do, of course, but it was no abduction. Didn't make it halfway to Scotland before the old Earl caught up with them."

"Who started the tale of the abduction?"

"That was Brownbeck. He thought it would reflect better on his daughter when the rumors leaked out. But word of the elopement never really got around. It was the 'abduction' story that people talked about, and it discredited Nicholas Hayes in a way he didn't deserve."

"That's when Seaforth disowned him?"

Aunt Henrietta nodded. "Cut him off without a farthing."

Sebastian came to sit again, the teacup in his hands. "What happened to the girl—Kate Brownbeck?"

"Her father married her off to Sir Lindsey Forbes."

"Of the East India Company?"

"The same. Nasty man, but rich enough—there's no doubt about that. And of course he's even richer now, thanks to his marriage and subsequent years in India."

Sebastian took a slow sip of his tea. "How do you know all this?"

"I knew the girl's mother. She was an Osborne—much better born than Brownbeck, obviously. I understand he paid through the nose for the privilege of aligning himself with the family. She died about a year after her daughter married. Brownbeck is a pompous, self-righteous bore, but Kate was fortunate enough to take after her mother. I remember her as a lovely young woman, full of spirit and laughter. Quite charming."

"She's dead now?"

"Kate? Oh, no. She's just not like that anymore. It's as if marriage to Forbes sucked all the life and joy out of her. It's quite sad." Henrietta sighed. "I suspect Hero knows her; she's part of the Annabelle Hershey set these days."

Sebastian was familiar with Annabelle Hershey, thanks to Hero. A general's daughter, Miss Hershey kept a salon for those with keen wits and sharp intellects and interests in everything from philosophy and literature to science and technology.

He took another sip of tea. "Do you think Nicholas Hayes did it? Killed the Countess de Compans, I mean."

He expected his aunt to say, *Of course he did.* Instead she was silent for a moment, her lips pressing into a frown. "I honestly don't know. The entire affair never rang true to me."

"Why not?"

"Partially because he was so desperately in love with Kate just a few months before. But mainly because I remember Chantal de LaRivière."

"I understand she was very beautiful."

"She was indeed—utterly exquisite. But I always suspected she was a bit of a coquette."

"Oh? And what do you think of Gilbert-Christophe de LaRivière?"

"I know everyone keeps referring to him as a close confidant of both the French King and his brother. But the truth is he's far closer to the Count d'Artois than to Louis—which tells you all you need to know about him."

"It does, indeed," said Sebastian. Charles, the Count d'Artois, was the saturnine younger brother of the newly restored French King Louis XVIII and a man known as an ultraroyalist, ultrareligious reactionary. "So what do you think happened to Chantal de LaRivière?"

"I never could figure it out." She was silent for a moment, her fingers reducing her toast to crumbs. Then she said, "What a tragedy Nicholas's life was. An unnecessary tragedy. How differently it all would have turned out if the young couple had simply waited. In another few years, Kate would have been twenty-one, and Nicholas would have been his father's heir."

"But they couldn't know that."

"No."

"How soon after the elopement did she marry Forbes?"

"Three weeks, I believe."

"Hasty."

"It was, yes. But it wasn't because she was with child, if that's what you're thinking. She never had children."

It was what he'd been thinking, of course. Sebastian took a sip of his tea, found it had gone cold, and set it aside. "If she wasn't with child, then the pressure Brownbeck put on her to bend to his wishes like that must have been brutal."

"I suspect it was. She was never the same afterward. And then she and Forbes went off to India."

"Where her husband helped starve to death something like a million people," said Sebastian. "I should think that would change almost anyone."

"Not Forbes. He's still every bit as arrogant, smug, self-righteous, and insufferable as he's always been."

"But rich." Sebastian pushed to his feet. "Very, very rich."

Aunt Henrietta eyed him thoughtfully "You will remember you promised to treat what I've told you with the utmost discretion?"

"I'll remember."

He bent to kiss her cheek and was surprised when she put her hand on his arm and said, "And you will be careful, Sebastian? There's something particularly ghastly about anyone who could sink a sickle into another man's back."

"I'm always careful."

She lowered her eyebrows and pursed her lips. "No, you're not."

But at that, he only laughed.

Sebastian was walking up the front steps of his Brook Street house, his thoughts lost in the troubled past, when a breathless messenger boy came running up with a note.

"It's from Sir 'Enry Lovejoy, 'im o' Bow Street," said the boy with a gasp.

Sebastian handed the boy a coin and broke the missive's seal to read Sir Henry's neat penmanship.

*Irvine Pennington found stabbed to death in Cat Alley, Somer's Town.*

## Chapter 17

The tea gardens' owner lay sprawled on his stomach, arms flung stiffly out at his sides, head turned and eyes open wide as if in shocked disbelief. Flies buzzed furiously around the dried blood on the back of his ripped coat and crawled in and out of his gaping mouth. The heat in the close, rubbish-strewn alley was intense, the stench of death overwhelming. After six years at war, Sebastian was painfully familiar with the sights and smells of death. But sudden, brutal murder still troubled him.

"Looks like he's been dead for a while, doesn't it?" he said, hunkering down beside the dead man. "Perhaps as much as a day."

Lovejoy nodded gravely, a folded handkerchief held over his nose and mouth. "According to his wife, he's been missing since yesterday morning."

Sebastian remembered the swift expression of consternation that flitted across Sarah Pennington's face when he'd asked for her father. *We don't know where he's taken himself off to. . . .*

"Damn," said Sebastian.

Lovejoy cast a thoughtful look around the noisome alley. "Perhaps we've been wrong in our thinking about Nicholas Hayes's death. Perhaps his murder had nothing to do with *who* he was and everything to do with *where* he was. Perhaps we should be looking for a killer with a link to the tea gardens or Somer's Town rather than to Hayes."

"Perhaps. Although it's also possible Pennington is dead because he was working the gardens' entrance when Hayes's killer arrived and thus could have identified him. His daughter did say her father spelled her a few times."

"True."

Sebastian studied the four or five blood-encrusted slits in the back of the dead man's coat. "I don't think our killer used a sickle this time."

"No." Lovejoy squinted up at the blazing sun overhead. "I sincerely hope the men from the deadhouse arrive with their shell soon. The stench is appalling."

The men from the deadhouse took their time.

While waiting, Lovejoy set his constables to interviewing the villagers in the area. Several people thought they remembered seeing Irvine Pennington the previous day . . . although they weren't quite sure.

"Passed by here all the time on his way to the Grecian Coffeehouse, he did," said a stout, middle-aged woman with an oyster stall near the corner. "Always thought it queer. I mean, what's a fellow with his own tea gardens doin' goin' t' a coffeehouse? Hmm?" But she couldn't recall for certain if she'd seen him that Friday. "Could've been the day before," she admitted. "One day's pretty much like the other, ye know?"

The owner of the coffeehouse, a Mr. Ned Dashiell, had the same problem. "I think he was here yesterday, but I couldn't say for sure. He didn't come this morning, though. That I do know."

All the villagers agreed on one point: They hadn't seen anything or anyone suspicious lately.

Sebastian said, "If Nicholas Hayes's killer is methodical enough to eliminate the person who took his money at the entrance to the tea gardens, then I suspect he was careful to make certain he wasn't seen again."

"I almost hope you're right," said Lovejoy, his face pink with the heat, "because whoever this killer is, he's ruthless. Ruthless and deadly."

Clarendon Square lay to the west of Pennington's Tea Gardens, just on the edge of where the shops and houses of Somer's Town gave way to the rolling hills and open fields of the countryside. Built in the last decades of the eighteenth century on the site of what had once been a Life Guards' barracks, the square formed a vast rectangle around an unusual inner ring of newish houses with curving facades known as the Polygon.

When Hero arrived at the square midway through the morning, she found only two performers—a harpist who had set up near the French Catholic chapel and a hurdy-gurdy player on a far corner. But like so many street musicians, both were blind, and the hurdy-gurdy player was so awful that Hero suspected the residents paid him to go away. In the end, she decided to interview a penny-profile cutter—a sad-eyed, middle-aged German woman who cut silhouettes out of black paper for a penny each.

"You only vant to talk to me?" said the woman, her accent thick as she stared at Hero with obvious suspicion. A stocky woman dressed in ragged but clean clothes, she had fading fair hair and a scar from what looked like a saber slash running the length of one side of her face. She said her name was Anja Becker, and that she was originally from Hanover. "I don't like to just talk."

"Well, you can cut my profile while we talk, if you'd like."

"I zink I'd rather do zat." She picked up her scissors and reached for a piece of paper. "Look at zee Polygon."

"How long have you been doing this?" asked Hero, watching her. Once, she must have been a pretty woman. "Cutting silhouettes, I mean."

The old scar across the side of Anja's face seemed to darken as she squinted assessingly at Hero. "Since I vas fourteen, maybe fifteen. But you need to turn zee head sidevays and look at zee Polygon."

Hero obediently shifted her gaze to the curving facades of the ring of houses at the center of the square. "You've been in England that long?"

"No. Started in Hanover, I did."

"How did you end up in London?"

"I don't vant to talk about zat," said the woman.

Given all that had happened in Hanover in the last twenty-plus war-torn years, Hero suspected it wasn't too hard to guess at the vague outlines of this woman's life. She said, "Do you always work here in Somer's Town?"

"*Ach*, no. I like to vork here because I can see zee fields and zee hills, but I move all over, I do. If I stayed in one place, I vould soon cut zee profiles of most all zee folks who vant zem, now, vouldn't I?"

"True."

"Keep zee head turned," snapped the woman when Hero's gaze drifted sideways.

"Sorry."

"I do my best business at zee fairs. Used to be, there vas a fair some-where around London most every week, at least when zee veather's fine. But they're shutting them all down now, more and more. Too rowdy, they say." Anja made a scoffing noise deep in her throat.

"How did you learn to cut profiles?"

"Learned it from an old voman in Hanover, I did. I vas born in zee countryside, but ended up in zee city after zee French soldiers burned our farm and killed my *mutter* and *vater*. At first, I used to just bronze and frame zee profiles zee old voman cut—I can bronze zis one for another fourpence, if you want, and frame it for another ten. But after a while, zee old voman, her hands started shaking so bad, she had to have me do zee cutting too."

"I should think it would be a difficult thing to learn."

"You need to have a good eye and a steady hand, *ja*. I'm not as good as zat old voman was. But I'm good enough."

"What happened to her?" asked Hero.

"She vas killed by soldiers."

Hero watched a young man in yellow pantaloons and a coat with a nipped-in waist come down the steps of one of the houses in the Polygon and let himself out the iron gate. "Is it hard to make a living cutting profiles, now that they're restricting the fairs?"

Anja blinked and glanced away for a moment, her throat working when she swallowed. A gust of naked fear passed over her features before being quickly, ruthlessly suppressed. But that rare moment of raw vulnerability told Hero everything she needed to know. "Hard enough," said Anja, "especially in zee vinter."

The woman was so determinedly strong and independent, thought Hero, so formidably controlled. She'd survived so much, her life constantly torn apart by wars begun by kings and princes and a certain upstart Corsican to whom women like Anja meant nothing. Nothing at all. Hero found herself aching for her and all the countless others like her, and had to clear her throat before she could say, "I'm looking for a little boy I'd like to interview—a little half-Chinese boy of eight or nine. Have you seen him?"

"A Chinese boy?" Anja pursed her lips as she thought about it. "I don't zink so, no."

"He may be half-English."

"Don't zink I've seen him. Lots of French around here, but I've never seen any Chinese." Anja set aside her scissors and held up Hero's profile. Despite the woman's earlier self-deprecating remarks, it was startlingly good. "So. Do you vant zis framed?"

Hero was standing on the far side of the Polygon, the framed silhouette in one hand and her parasol in the other, her thoughtful gaze on the feathery tops of a distant line of trees lifting in the hot wind, when she saw Devlin walking toward her.

"Any luck?" he asked, coming up to her.

"Nothing." They turned to walk together along the lane that ran toward the open countryside, and Hero shifted the parasol to keep the hot sun off her face. "What are you doing here?"

"Irvine Pennington was found stabbed to death in an alley near his tea gardens this morning."

"Good heavens. Why would anyone kill him?"

"Lovejoy is inclined to think both killings may be related to the tea gardens themselves—that it's possible Nicholas Hayes's history had nothing to do with his death at all."

"But you don't agree?"

"I don't. Although I have nothing to base that on besides a gut feeling." They'd reached the rolling fields and market gardens of the open countryside, and he paused to watch the warm wind ruffle the ripening grain. He said, "You're familiar with the set that frequents Annabelle Hershey's salon, aren't you?"

"I am. Although somehow I doubt that's an innocent question."

"Have you ever met Lady Forbes, the wife of Sir Lindsey Forbes?"

"Kate Forbes? Yes, of course. She's published several fascinating books of the drawings she made of the native plants of the Malabar Coast when she was in India with her husband. Why do you ask? What has she to do with anything?"

"According to Aunt Henrietta, she eloped with Nicholas Hayes six months before he was arrested for killing Chantal de LaRivière."

Hero turned to stare at him. "You can't be serious."

"I'm afraid I am. It was her father, Theo Brownbeck, who set about the false tale that Hayes had kidnapped some heiress."

Hero gave an inelegant snort. "Now, that I can believe. No doubt he even has a pet Bible verse to trot out to justify it all. I've never understood how such a sanctimonious, pompous hypocrite managed to produce someone like Kate."

"You like her?"

"I do."

"Then I suspect he left her upbringing to her mother."

"No doubt." Hero was silent for a moment. "However did he manage to set about such a story while still keeping Kate's name out of it?"

"Perhaps by announcing that she was betrothed to Forbes. The marriage took place just three weeks later."

Hero's lips tightened, her nostrils flaring on a quickly indrawn breath. "What a beastly man."

Sebastian said, "I could try talking to Lady Forbes about Nicholas Hayes, but it would be rather indelicate."

"Huh. If Aunt Henrietta is right, it's going to be indelicate no matter who does it." When he remained silent, she said, "Let me guess: You want me to approach her?"

His eyes crinkled in a smile, and she cuffed him playfully on the chin. "Coward."

*Chapter 18*

Sir Lindsey Forbes's impressive town house in St. James's Square was famous as a showcase for his extensive collection of artifacts, mainly Indian brasses, religious sculptures, and silk paintings but also an impressive number of priceless Chinese porcelains, for the East India Company had long enjoyed a monopoly over British trade with China as well as with India.

Although Hero knew Lady Forbes from Annabelle Hershey's salon, she had never visited the former Kate Brownbeck at home. When Hero arrived at the square shortly after nuncheon, she half expected Lady Forbes to decline to see her. But a few minutes after Hero sent up her card, the butler returned with a bow to say, "This way, my lady, if you please."

She followed him up a gleaming broad staircase to a cabinet lined with mahogany shelves filled with row after row of colorful Chinese porcelain jars. Lady Forbes herself stood at the red lacquered table in the center of the room. She had a crisp white apron pinned over her fine muslin gown and was carefully measuring out a portion of what Hero realized must be tea leaves. The rich aroma of fine teas filled the air.

The former Miss Kate Brownbeck was an attractive woman somewhere in her mid- to late thirties, her fair hair as yet untouched by gray, her features strong and even. She had a reputation for grace, poise, composure, and calm self-mastery. But today her eyes were red and puffy, her expression that of a grief-stricken woman struggling to maintain a facade of equanimity. "I hope you'll pardon me for receiving you like this," she said, "but I didn't want to interrupt the process."

Hero perched on a nearby stool indicated by her hostess. "You're mixing tea?"

"I am, yes. I've made my own blends for years."

"Thank you for agreeing to see me," said Hero, watching her.

Lady Forbes carefully poured the measure of tea into a larger container, then glanced over at her. "You say that as if you thought I might not."

"I take it you know why I'm here?"

"I can guess. I've heard Lord Devlin is looking into the murder of Nicholas Hayes, and your presence here suggests he's discovered that Nicholas and I once . . . knew each other."

"Did you know Hayes had returned to London?"

"No." The denial came quick and decisive.

"Do you have any idea why he came back?"

"No. How could I?" She turned to select another jar from one of the shelves, her voice airy and calm and everything Hero knew she was not. "Does Lord Devlin have any idea as to who might have killed him?"

"Not yet." Hero hesitated a moment, but she could think of no delicate way to phrase it and so simply said bluntly, "Do you think his return could have been motivated by revenge?"

Lady Forbes froze with her arms extended over her head, then slowly lifted the jar she'd been reaching for from the shelf and turned. "What do you mean?"

"Could he have come back here to kill someone?"

She was silent for a moment, obviously giving the idea—or at least her response to it—some thought. "No. Nicholas wasn't like that."

"Twenty years ago, perhaps not. But a brutal life can change people.

I notice you don't say you can't think of anyone he might have had reason to kill."

Lady Forbes's face hardened unexpectedly. "Who wouldn't be tempted to kill the man who destroyed his life?"

"You mean the Count de Compans?"

"Yes."

"You're suggesting Hayes didn't actually kill the Count's wife?"

"Of course he didn't."

"How can you be so certain?"

"Because I know him." She paused, then said more softly, "Knew him."

The sound of the entry door opening floated up from below, followed by a man's crisp voice asking something Hero didn't catch and the butler's murmured reply.

Hero said, "Can you think of any other reason he would risk coming back to England?"

Kate Forbes shook her head as approaching footsteps sounded on the stairs. The anxious fear in her eyes was unmistakable. "No. It makes no sense. But please—"

She broke off as Sir Lindsey Forbes appeared in the open doorway. "Ah, there you are, my dear. I was—" He gave a faint start, as if only becoming aware of Hero's presence even though she knew he must surely have learned of it from his butler. "I do beg your pardon, Lady Devlin. Am I interrupting?"

He was a good-looking man, probably in his late forties or early fifties, with thick, prematurely silver hair, dark eyebrows, and a strong chin. The fourth son of a Devonshire reverend, he had joined the East India Company as a simple cadet at the tender age of sixteen and distinguished himself in the campaign against Hyder Ali on the Malabar Coast. After that, he'd risen quickly to become quartermaster general of the Bombay Army. It was the kind of position that enabled a man to accumulate an extraordinary fortune in a short time, if he was ruthless enough—and from everything Hero had heard, Forbes was more than ruthless. Under his stewardship, the company had forced the area's farmers to shift from growing grain to the production of opium. When a famine hit, close to a million people starved to death. But whenever the topic came up, Forbes would simply shrug and say India was overpopulated anyway. As far as Hero was concerned, that sentiment told her all she needed to know about the man.

"I saw your father at this morning's reception for the Allied Sovereigns at the Bank of England," he told Hero with a smile.

"Was the Bank on today's schedule of events?" said Hero pleasantly. He had the soft blue eyes and ageless, angelic face of a choirboy, and it was all so disconcertingly misleading that she found it chilling.

"It was—along with a banquet this afternoon and a visit to the Opera this evening. Do you and Devlin attend?"

"Probably not."

"It should be entertaining. There's a rumor the Princess of Wales plans to put in an appearance. Needless to say, the Regent is in a pother over the possibility. If he could have his way, I suspect he'd have her locked up for the rest of the Allied Sovereigns' visit."

"Well, he's managed to bar his wife from Court and from all official receptions and banquets. But I doubt he'll succeed in keeping her from the Opera."

Forbes caught his wife's eye and something passed between them, a silent exchange that Hero couldn't begin to decipher. Then he said, "Has Kate been showing you our selection of teas? We have samples from nearly all the tea-growing regions of China. One of these days the company is going to get its hands on the secret process the Chinese use to make the stuff, along with some seedlings of their precious *Camellia sinensis*, and then we'll be able to grow and produce tea ourselves in India. No more having to deal with these ridiculous Qing emperors and their grasping Cantonese Hong merchants. It's either that, or send in the British Navy and force them to be more reasonable in their trade with us."

Hero looked at him with interest. "Have you been to Canton?"

"A few times, when I was in Bombay. They're impossible people to deal with, you know—the Chinese, I mean. They insist we pay for their silks, porcelains, and tea with silver because they have no interest in anything Europe produces. And the one thing we could use to trade with them, opium, they refuse to allow into the country."

"Rather understandable, is it not?"

"It's outrageous—that's what it is. They can't deny the market is there. The Chinese people can't get enough of it, and we could produce tons of the stuff in India. But we have to smuggle it in, which the emperors have made shockingly risky."

"Shocking, indeed," said Hero with a tight smile. To Lady Forbes, she said, "It was good seeing you again. No need to ring for a footman; I can show myself out."

She thought Sir Lindsey might offer to walk with her to the door, but he did not. Instead he stood at the entrance to the tea-blending room and watched her walk away with such intensity, she fancied that she could feel his gaze boring into her back.

# *Chapter 19*

*A*fter Hero left to pay a visit to St. James's Square, Sebastian drove east to Tower Hill, where he found Paul Gibson easing the sturdy shoes off the still-dressed cadaver of a small older woman laid out on his stone slab. Four other corpses rested on the shelves behind him: Nicholas Hayes's, Irvine Pennington's, and two blood-drenched corpses in workingmen's clothes unknown to Sebastian.

"What is all this?" asked Sebastian, pausing in the open doorway. Despite the thick stone walls, the heat in the room was intense, the smell of death even more acute than usual.

Gibson swiped at a bead of sweat rolling down his cheek. "The woman's a former milliner, found near Soho Square, while the two navvies appear to have killed each other in a knife fight in an alley over by Ratcliffe Highway. I presume you know about the tea gardens' owner. If you ask me, this heat is making everyone cranky and short-tempered."

Sebastian studied the distorted features of the woman on Gibson's table. Her gray-streaked dark hair was wildly untidy, her face swollen and discolored, her eyes projecting grotesquely. A wide purple bruise such as might have been left by a strap showed just above the high neck of her modest black stuff gown. "Who'd want to strangle an aging milliner?"

"Footpads, I'm afraid. Her earrings are missing." Gibson nodded to her bloody left hand. "And her knuckles are so swollen from arthritis, they had to cut off her finger to get her wedding ring."

"Good God." Footpads were still a dangerous menace on the streets of London; it was the reason they so often served as a ready excuse whenever the palace wanted to deflect public attention from a delicate death. Sebastian shifted his gaze to the shelves running along the back wall. "I take it you haven't finished Hayes yet?"

Gibson shook his head and blew up a hard breath that ruffled the tousled graying dark hair on his damp forehead. "I wanted to take a preliminary look at the rest of this lot before going back to him. His inquest isn't till Monday morning, so there's time."

"Did the Earl of Seaforth come to view his cousin's body yet?"

Gibson set aside the woman's first shoe and went to work on the other. "No. No one's come. Why? Were you expecting him to?"

"I thought he might. He asked Sir Henry where the body was." Sebastian crossed his arms at his chest and rocked back on his heels. "If someone were to suddenly show up claiming to be my long-dead cousin and the rightful heir to the titles and estates I'd been calling my own for years, I think I'd want to take a look at the fellow and see if he really was my cousin."

Gibson set the second shoe beside its mate. "So would almost anyone, I suspect. So why do you think he hasn't?"

"The most obvious answer is that he already knew Nicholas Hayes was alive because he'd seen him."

"And then killed him?" said Gibson, going to work on the woman's sensible stockings.

"Seems reasonable, doesn't it?"

"So why bother to ask Sir Henry about the body?"

"Perhaps he thought it was expected of him." Sebastian circled the room to stare down at the two dead navvies. Both were heartbreakingly young, surely no more than sixteen or seventeen, their faces smooth and beardless, their features relaxed now into a semblance of calm serenity he found oddly disturbing, given the way they'd died. They had managed to slash each other to ribbons before blood loss and shock completely overcame them; their clothes were ripped and soaked a gory red.

"So then, why didn't he come?" said Gibson, watching him.

"I've no idea." Sebastian wiped the back of one wrist across his damp forehead as he turned away from the dead boys. "Damn this heat."

As he drove away from Tower Hill, Sebastian found himself going over and over everything they knew about Irvine Pennington, trying to see if it cast any kind of light on the death of Nicholas Hayes. But the heat made it hard to think. The streets of the City were miserable, the aging, close-packed buildings trapping both the brutal heat and all the noisome smells of too many people and too many horses jammed into too small an area. Even the air wafting up from the river smelled pungent and dead.

"I'm thinkin' maybe somebody's followin' us, gov'nor," said Tom as Sebastian passed through Temple Bar.

"Bloody hell." Sebastian resisted the urge to glance back over his shoulder. "Describe him."

"'E's just an ordinary-lookin' cove on a bay. 'E ain't stayin' real close, but I seen 'im before, when we was up in Somer's Town."

"You're certain it's the same man you saw before?"

"Oh, aye. I noticed 'im when ye was talkin' to Sir 'Enry. The cove was jist standin' there, 'oldin' 'is 'orse, when this dog comes nosin' along, and that cove, 'e went outta 'is way to try to kick that poor old dog."

"What color coat?"

"The man or the dog?"

Sebastian found himself smiling. "The man."

"Brown."

He pulled up outside a chandler's shop and handed the boy the reins. "Wait here."

Hopping down, Sebastian got his first look at the cove on the bay. Of medium height and build, he looked to be perhaps thirty or thirty-five, with brown hair and a nondescript face. His brown corduroy coat and round hat were respectable without being fashionable, his horse serviceable but not showy. He was utterly forgettable, and Sebastian suspected Tom would never have noticed him if not for that act of cruelty toward a stray dog.

The man checked for only an instant before riding past the stopped curricle. But as Sebastian turned to go into the chandler's, Brown Coat reined in farther up the street, his gaze drifting over the surrounding shops as if he were looking for something.

"May I help you, sir?" said the boy behind the chandler's counter.

"Sorry," said Sebastian. "Wrong shop."

Walking back out into the sunshine, Sebastian turned up the street to where the man still sat on his horse, studiously looking at anything and everything except Sebastian.

"Have something you care to say to me?" said Sebastian, walking right up to him.

The man gave a start of surprise that Sebastian suspected was utterly genuine. "Yer honor?"

"I assume you've been following me for a reason. If you didn't have something you wished to say, then I can only conclude that your interest in me is less than benign."

The man's eyes widened. "I don't know nobody named Ben Nigh."

"Oh? So who set you to following me?"

"I ain't been followin' ye!"

"You'd have me believe we've simply been coincidentally visiting the same parts of a metropolis of one million people?"

The man's eyes narrowed. "I ain't been followin' ye."

"Well, there's obviously no point in you continuing to do so, because if I see you again, I'll set the constables on you—"

"But I ain't done nothin'! Ain't no crime in a free Englishman ridin' his horse down the street."

"—so you may as well tell your employer—whoever he is—that he needs to find a new hireling."

"I ain't been followin' you," said the man again.

Sebastian took a step back. "What did you say your name was?"

"Jack. Jack Smith."

"Right then, Mr. Jones—"

"It's Smith!"

"Mr. Smith. I'm going home now. If I see you anywhere near me or mine again, I might not bother calling the constables. I might just shoot you."

"You can't do that!"

Sebastian took another step back. "I suggest you not try testing that theory. Now, get out of here."

## Chapter 20

Sebastian was in his library, pouring a tankard of ale from a fresh pitcher, his thoughts far, far away, when an angry, insistent knock sounded at his front door.

"A Mr. Brownbeck to see you, my lord," said his majordomo, Morey, appearing at the library door a moment later.

Sebastian took a deep swallow of ale. "Show him in."

Theo Brownbeck came in with a quick, decisive step. A stout, self-important little man in his late fifties or early sixties, he had thinning iron gray hair, heavy jowls, and thick, bushy eyebrows. His dress was typical of the older merchants and bankers of the City, his silver-buttoned coat cut square and with a stand-up collar, his waistcoat long with flap pockets, his short breeches buckled at the knee. He drew up just inside the door, his breathing agitated, his color high, his face damp with perspiration. "You know why I'm here," he said without preamble.

"Actually, I don't," said Sebastian. "But please, do have a seat."

"Thank you. I prefer to stand."

"May I offer you some ale?"

The banker looked as if he'd prefer to refuse, but he was hot enough that temptation overwhelmed him. "Please," he said grudgingly. "I'm told Lady Devlin visited my daughter a short time ago."

Sebastian went to fill another tankard with ale. "Who told you that?"

"Good God, man, that's not the issue here."

"Oh? So what is the 'issue'?"

"I'll not have my daughter's name dragged through the mud by that villain's reappearance."

Sebastian held out the ale. "By which I gather you're referring to the murder of Nicholas Hayes?"

Brownbeck wrapped a meaty fist around the tankard, then pointed a shaky finger at Sebastian. "You stay away from my daughter, you hear? You and Lady Devlin both."

Sebastian took another sip of his own ale. "Did you know Nicholas Hayes was in London?"

Brownbeck's eyes widened. "Merciful heavens, of course not. If I'd the slightest suspicion he was anywhere in England, I'd have gone straight to the authorities."

Sebastian studied the older man's red, angry face. "Would you?"

"Of course I would—as would any right-thinking man."

"It's curious that he returned, don't you think?"

"To be honest, I hadn't given it any thought."

"Can you think of a reason why he would come back?"

"In my experience, it's useless to try to ascribe rationality to the dangerous incorrigibles of this world. And while Hayes may have been an earl's son, he'd long ago betrayed his birth and breeding and cast himself down into the gutter."

"You must get on well with the Count de Compans."

Brownbeck looked vaguely baffled. "What's that supposed to mean?"

"He sounds just like you."

Brownbeck's lip curled. "I know Lady Devlin believes that the poor are somehow the innocent victims of society's inequities, but those familiar with the frailties of the flesh and the ways of our world know better. The unfortunate, painful truth is that what the kindhearted mistake for misfortune is actually the predictable result of a fatal lack of discipline, sobriety, decency, and prudence—as Hayes's descent into opprobrium so glaringly illustrates."

"I've been wondering if revenge might have had something to do with Hayes's return," said Sebastian, carefully keeping his voice even.

Brownbeck sniffed. "I wouldn't know. As I said, it's a waste of time attempting to discern the motives of such a degenerate. If you ask me, the authorities would do well to look for his killer amongst the denizens of the underworld."

"A footpad, you mean?"

Brownbeck snorted. "Footpads, prostitutes, sharpers—he consorted with them all. After his father disowned him, the scoundrel actually hired a thief to break into Seaforth's house and steal from him."

"Oh? Where did you hear that?"

"The old Earl told me about it himself."

"Someone burgled the late Earl of Seaforth's house, and he blamed his own son? Bit of a stretch, wasn't it?"

"It was obvious."

"Oh? How's that?"

"Because of what was taken, of course."

"What was taken?"

"A stash of banknotes whose location was known only to the rogue, and a watch that once belonged to the First Earl and that the lad had long coveted."

"Nothing else?"

"No."

"So what led the Earl to leap to the conclusion that Nicholas had hired a thief? Couldn't he simply have entered the house and taken the stuff himself?"

Brownbeck shook his head. "Not unless the cad had recently acquired some specialized skills. It was a professional job, no doubt about that. The wastrel sank fast, you know, after Seaforth disowned him. Took to consorting with the lowest sort of company. I can't imagine why you've decided to concern yourself with his death. The man ought by rights to have been hanged eighteen years ago."

"That seems to be a common consensus."

"I should think so." Brownbeck drained his tankard. "To be frank, I was hoping none of us would ever have reason to think of the scoundrel again."

"Yes, I can see how that would have been more convenient for you."

Brownbeck's jaw sagged. Then his features tightened. "Amuse yourself by dabbling in the detection of murder if you must. But you keep my daughter's name out of this, do you hear?"

Sebastian gave the man a hard smile. "Shall I ring for a footman to show you out?"

Brownbeck set aside his empty tankard with a thump. "I'll see myself out. Thank you."

"One question," said Sebastian as the man turned to leave. "Have you ever seen something like this before?"

Brownbeck glanced at the small bronze token Sebastian held out. "No. What is it?"

Sebastian closed his palm around the mysterious disk. "I've no idea."

Morey was closing the door behind their visitor when Hero came down the stairs.

"How much of that did you hear?" Sebastian asked her.

"Enough to be impressed by the extent to which you kept your temper."

Sebastian went to pour himself more ale and drank deeply. "Pompous ass. How do you think he learned of your visit to St. James's Square so quickly?"

"I could be wrong, but I doubt he heard it from Kate. Which means Forbes himself must have sent word to his father-in-law."

Sebastian nodded. "That's what I was thinking."

Hero went to stand at the front window, her gaze on the sunbaked street. "What do you make of his tale of Hayes hiring someone to burgle his father's house?"

Sebastian came up beside her as Brownbeck's carriage pulled away from the kerb. "I think I need to pay another visit to Chick Lane."

Sebastian found the Red Lion's ancient taproom filled with a hot, sweaty, boisterous crowd and Grace Calhoun focused on filling six tankards of ale.

"Was wondering when you'd be back," she said, throwing him a quick glance as he walked up.

"Oh? Why's that?"

Rather than answer, she scooped up all six tankards at once and carried them to a table of what looked like highwaymen huddled in the murky depths of the room.

When she came back, he said, "Have you seen Ji?"

She scooted behind the bar without even looking at him. "No."

*Damn*, thought Sebastian. Aloud, he said, "Can you think where he might be hiding?"

"No."

Sebastian studied the woman's handsome, hard face. "I'm told Hayes befriended a cracksman when he was staying here eighteen years ago."

"He was a right personable fellow, Nicholas. Made friends easy, he did."

"Did he?"

"When he wanted to."

"I'm told he used this cracksman to break into his father's house. Do you know anything about that?"

"Me? Why would I?"

"Because I suspect you know your customers better than a vicar knows his parishioners."

A gleam of amusement shone in her dark eyes, but she remained silent.

Sebastian said, "Is he still around, that cracksman?"

"Been a long time. Maybe he's dead."

"I'd like to talk to him if he isn't."

"What makes you think he knows anything?"

"I don't know that he does."

Grace Calhoun swiped at a pool of some spilled liquid on the sur-face of the bar with a rag. "Heard tell the owner of them tea gardens got found dead over in Somer's Town."

Sebastian nodded. "This morning."

"Why you think that happened?"

"I don't know."

She looked up at him. "Don't you? Seems to me you ain't lookin' for no common cracksman."

"I never said I suspected the cracksman of killing Nicholas Hayes. I'm hoping he can tell me more about what happened eighteen years ago."

Grace Calhoun tossed the rag aside. "There's lots o' folks could tell you about what happened eighteen years ago."

Sebastian watched her turn away to start stacking dirty glasses in a tub. "Were you here that night? The night Hayes killed Chantal de La-Rivière?"

"He didn't kill her."

"So certain?"

"I reckon I'm a pretty good judge of a man's character."

Sebastian couldn't argue with that. She had to be to have not only survived but flourished in her business. He said, "Did he come back here that night? After the shooting, I mean."

"He did."

"And?"

"I wanted him to hide."

"Where?"

Again, that faint gleam of amusement that was there and then gone. "We've places."

Sebastian had heard about the Red Lion's "places." Secret doors and false walls and hidden passages that enabled those wanted by the authorities to simply disappear. "But he wouldn't do it?"

"No. Said he hadn't done nothing wrong. Said he wasn't gonna hide like he had."

"How was he caught?"

"His cousin—him that's now the Earl of Seaforth. He told on him. Constables picked Nick up near Smithfield Market."

*Nick*, noted Sebastian. Aloud, he said, "Seaforth betrayed him?"

"That's right. Only, he weren't the Earl of Seaforth then. He was just Mr. Ethan Hayes, son of a younger son and lookin' at a humdrum life spent as a simple barrister. But he's sure enough an earl now, ain't he?"

*Chapter 21*

*E*than Hayes, the Third Earl of Seaforth, sat sipping a glass of fine brandy in the Reading Room of White's, his eyes narrowed in a squint as he leafed through the latest copy of an arch-Tory publication called *The Anti-Jacobin Review.*

Sebastian settled in the red bucket chair beside him and said, "Good evening."

Seaforth scowled and cast a quick glance around, as if to ascertain who might be near enough to overhear them. "What the devil are you doing here?"

"As it happens, I am a member."

"That's not what I meant and you know it."

"Ah. Well, you see, I wanted to talk to you."

"Here?"

"That's a problem? Have something you don't want to get around, do you?"

A faint flush darkened the other man's cheeks. "Of course not."

Sebastian signaled for a brandy. "I've been trying to get a better picture of what happened eighteen years ago, when Nicholas Hayes was accused of killing Chantal de LaRivière."

"He wasn't simply 'accused' of killing her. He did kill her."

"So certain?"

"He was convicted."

"Innocent men have been found guilty before."

"Not this time. You didn't know Nicholas. I did."

Sebastian settled more comfortably in his seat. "So tell me about him."

Seaforth continued to hold his journal open in both hands in a not-too-subtle expression of his attitude toward this interruption. "What is there to tell? He was wild and reckless to a fault, quick-tempered and heedless of all conventions and norms, and utterly lacking in either the virtues of his class or any semblance of Christian morality."

"Is that why you informed on him?"

Seaforth was silent, his nostrils flaring on a quick intake of air. Then he said, "Who told you that?"

"So you did, didn't you? How did you even know where he was?"

"Crispin had told me some months before. Not the exact inn, but that it was near Smithfield Market. That was enough."

"Your cousin Crispin must not have known you well."

"What is that supposed to mean?"

Rather than answer, Sebastian said, "I understand Crispin and Nicholas were close."

"They were."

"How long before Chantal de LaRivière's murder did Crispin die?"

"A day or two. Something like that. Why?"

"He drowned?"

"That's right."

"In the Thames?"

"Yes."

"What was he like?"

"Crispin? Nothing like Nicholas, if that's what you're thinking."

"Yet they were close?"

"They were. I could never understand it. Crispin was everything Nicholas wasn't—sober and responsible and upright in every way."

"I'm told Nicholas was planning a military career."

"He was, yes. He was always army mad, from the time we were boys."

"From the sound of things, I suspect he'd have made a fine officer."

Seaforth stared at him. "You can't be serious."

"But I am."

Seaforth shook his head and reached to take a sip of his brandy.

Sebastian said, "Tell me about the older brother, Lucas. I take it he and Nicholas were not close?"

"No. But then, there were eight or nine years between them. And Lucas was always sickly. If I remember correctly, by that time he was virtually bedridden."

"He died—when?"

"Ten or twelve years ago, at least. Before his father."

"He never married?"

"No. To be honest, no one expected him to live as long as he did. Consumption, you know."

"So at the time you informed on your cousin Nicholas, his eldest brother was known to be dying and the second brother was already dead."

Seaforth stiffened. "I take leave to tell you I resent the implication of that statement."

"You mean the implication that you informed on Nicholas because you had ambitions of inheriting his father's titles and estates in his stead? You have my leave to resent the implication as much as you like. It's rather glaringly obvious, you know."

"You would have had me do what instead? Shelter a murderer?"

"You weren't exactly hiding him in your basement."

Seaforth sat up straighter in his chair and adjusted his cravat. "I behaved as any honorable man would have done."

"Somehow I doubt Nicholas saw it that way."

"What difference does it make how Nicholas saw it? As if I care what the scoundrel thought of me."

"Not then, while he was in custody, or now that he's dead. But if you heard he was alive and on the loose and had returned to England? I can see you being afraid that he might decide to pay you back for what you did to him all those years ago."

Seaforth sucked in a quick breath, then hissed, "What are you suggesting?"

"You know what I'm suggesting."

A naked succession of emotions flickered across the Earl's face, consternation mingled with outrage and fury and something that looked like fear. "Don't be ridiculous. If I'd known Nicholas was in town, all I'd have needed to do would be to inform the authorities and let them kill him."

"If you knew where he was. But if you didn't?"

Seaforth pushed up from his chair with such force that he sent it thumping back across the carpet. "You go too far, Devlin. You hear me? You go too far."

Sebastian rose slowly to his feet, his hands curled loosely at his sides. "Believe me, I've only just begun."

He thought for a moment that Seaforth might try to throw a punch. But the man simply tossed his journal aside and strode rapidly away.

Having sent Tom home with the curricle, Sebastian walked the hot, dusty streets of Westminster, his thoughts on the past. The sun was sinking low in the sky, casting long shadows. But even close to the river, the heat was still oppressive.

He couldn't stop thinking about the man Nicholas Hayes had once been—an earl's youngest son, army mad, reckless, headstrong, and passionate. A man much like Sebastian himself. But Hayes's life had gone disastrously awry, beginning with an ill-fated elopement that led to banishment and a dangerous refuge. And then . . . what? Theft? Attempted rape? Murder?

Sebastian found himself doubting it all. Yet he knew too that his tendency to see his own life reflected in the life of Nicholas Hayes could be blinding him to an ugly reality.

*So what do we actually know?* thought Sebastian as he reached the Thames. He paused to look out over the sun-sparkled expanse of the river and felt a welcome evening breeze lift off the water to cool his face. *What do we know for certain?*

The truth was they knew almost nothing about the man found dead up in Somer's Town except that he'd spent three miserable years as a convict before using a rock to obliterate the features of a corpse and stealing its identity to escape the living hell to which he'd been condemned. Then after fifteen years of freedom he'd risked it all by returning to England. Why?

The only explanation that made sense was a burning desire for revenge unquenched by the passage of time. So then the question became, revenge on whom?

His cousin, the new Earl of Seaforth, for betraying him to the authorities and appropriating the inheritance that should by rights have been his? The Count de Compans—particularly if the Frenchman had lied about the circumstances surrounding his wife's death?

Who else?

Theo Brownbeck, for refusing to allow Hayes to marry his daughter? Also possible, Sebastian decided, although that seemed more of a stretch.

So, LaRivière and Seaforth, and possibly Brownbeck. But as he stared off across the darkening waters of the river, Sebastian found his thoughts returning to the flintlock pistol he'd found lying at the bottom of the sea trunk in the Red Lion. If Nicholas Hayes had been planning to meet either LaRivière or Seaforth that night in Pennington's Tea Gardens, surely he would have taken the pistol with him. So why hadn't he?

The obvious explanation was that he'd gone to the gardens that night planning to meet someone else. So who?

*Who?*

## Chapter 22

Someone was following him again.

Sebastian became aware of the man's persistent presence as he walked up Cockspur Street toward home. The light was fading slowly from the sky, casting the street into deep purple shadow. The breeze from the river was growing stronger, flickering the flames of the recently lit streetlamps and scuttling a loose playbill along the gutter.

When Sebastian paused to gaze into a pastry shop's window, the following footsteps stopped. When he walked on, the footsteps started up again, carefully matching Sebastian's speed.

He caught a glimpse of the man as he crossed Piccadilly: a middle-aged tradesman, by the looks of him, in a shabby corduroy coat and greasy waistcoat. They continued up Berkeley Street to the square, then Davies. Whistling softly, Sebastian abruptly turned into the narrow entrance to John Street and flattened himself against the brick wall of the corner shop. The unknown shadow was perhaps fifteen steps behind him. Sebastian could hear the man pick up his pace lest he lose his quarry.

He came around the corner quickly, a man with several days' worth of grizzled beard on his face and the pasty flesh and bloodshot eyes of someone who spends too much time in gin shops. Stepping away from the wall, Sebastian grabbed the man by the arm and shoulder to swing him around and slam him face-first against the bricks.

"'Oly 'ell!" yelped the man, his head craning around sideways, eyes wide as he attempted to see who'd grabbed him. "Wot'd ye want to go and do that fer?"

Sebastian tightened his hold on the man's arm and bent it back at an awkward angle. "You're following me."

"Oy! That 'urts, it does."

"Why are you following me?"

"She said ye wanted t' talk t' me. Never said nothin' about ye meybe manhandlin' me."

"Who? Who said I wanted to talk to you?"

"Miss Grace."

"Grace Calhoun sent you?"

"Aye. Said ye wanted t' know 'bout the nob what got shipped off t' Botany Bay back in 'ninety-six."

Sebastian took a step back and let the man go. "You're the cracksman?"

The man turned cautiously to face him, then set about straightening his clothes with a calm dignity. "Not anymore. Cain't hold it against a feller wot 'e did in 'is salad days, now, can ye?"

"And what do you do now?"

"Got me a dolly shop in Cheapside, I do. Down by St. Mary-le-Bow."

A dolly shop was—ostensibly—a pawnshop. But most dolly-shop owners were also to some extent fences. "So you've graduated from theft to receiving, have you?"

The man looked affronted. "Me? No. Never."

"Right. What's your name?"

The former housebreaker snatched off his hat and clutched it to his chest with a bobbing little bow. "Tintwhistle. Mott Tintwhistle, at yer service."

Sebastian eyed the man's haggard, lined face. "How good is your memory, Mr. Tintwhistle?"

The retired cracksman wet his lips with his tongue. "Works better wit a few quid and meybe a bit o' Blue Ruin t' lubricate things."

"That can be arranged."

They retreated to the George and Dragon at the corner of Bond and Brook streets, where Sebastian bought a bottle of brandy and two glasses from the stunned barman and retreated to a dark corner lit by a guttering candle.

"Now, tell me how you came to know Nicholas Hayes," said Sebastian, splashing alcohol into the glasses.

Mott Tintwhistle threw back his shot and smacked his lips. "Right good stuff, this. Better'n Blue Ruin any day."

Sebastian poured the man another generous measure. "Nicholas Hayes."

"Aye." Tintwhistle pursed his mouth and took a more judicious sip. "'E was staying at the Red Lion in them days, ye see."

"Yes."

A strange, faraway light shone in the cracksman's eyes. "Miss Grace, she's a fine-lookin' woman yet today. But twenty years ago, she was somethin' else, I'm tellin' ye. Reckon we wuz all more'n a bit in love wit 'er."

Sebastian took a slow sip of his own brandy. "Yes?" he prompted when the man paused as if momentarily lost in thoughts of the past.

Tintwhistle swiped a hand across his mouth and took another drink. "Well, when she asked me t' 'elp that young nob, I done it."

"Grace Calhoun asked you to help Nicholas Hayes?"

"Aye."

A vague suspicion was beginning to form in Sebastian's mind. But all he said was "So you broke into the Earl of Seaforth's house?"

"Me? No. I jist 'elped that young gentleman get into 'is da's 'ouse and take wot was 'is t' take. That's all."

"Hayes was with you?"

Tintwhistle nodded. "Normally I liked to work alone, ye see. But that young nob, 'e insisted on comin' in wit me."

"I suspect he wanted to maintain control over what you lifted."

Mott Tintwhistle gave a heavy sigh of longing undiminished by the passage of years. "Wouldn't let me take nothin'. Coulda been set fer life, I coulda, if I'd 'ad me way."

"So what did you take?"

"Next t' nothin'! 'E wanted me t' break into a strongbox in the old man's library. Like somethin' out o' the Dark Ages, it was, covered wit strips o' iron and bolted t' the floor in a cupboard. When I first seen it, I says, 'Jig's up, me lad; I ain't clever enough t' git us into that. I've heard o' these things, and they take one o' them fancy keys ye gotta insert jist right.' But 'e says no, it's all a hum, that what looks like a keyhole is jist fer show. And then 'e slides away this bit o' brass and I see there's this *other* hidden keyhole, and sure enough, me lockpick opens it real easy."

Sebastian poured the cracksman another drink. "What was inside?"

"Next t' nothin'. Jist some papers and an old watch."

"Some papers and a watch? No banknotes?"

"Nope. Jist the watch."

"What was he expecting to find?"

"That's what 'e said 'e wanted—the watch. Said it was 'is by rights, given t' 'im by 'is granddaddy when 'e was a wee tyke. Said they was always real fond o' each other, and 'e weren't gonna let 'is da keep the watch jist t' be mean."

"You didn't help yourself to anything else on the way out?"

A sly smile slid across the old man's face. "Well, maybe I tried t' lift a purdy little statue that was jist sittin' there by the door. But Hayes seen me and made me put it back."

"And that was it?"

"That was it."

"You didn't take any banknotes?"

Tintwhistle's eyes bulged. "No. Not sayin' I wouldna taken 'em if I'd seen 'em, but there weren't none."

"When was the last time you saw Hayes?"

"Me? Come into the shop jist this last week, 'e did."

"He did?"

"Aye. Meybe Tuesday or Wednesday."

"Alone?"

"Well, 'e 'ad a little nipper wit 'im. Can't remember the lad's name. Real quiet and polite, 'e was."

"Do you know where the boy is now?"

Tintwhistle gave him a blank look. "No. Why would I?"

"The child is missing."

"Huh. Don't know nothin' about that."

"Why did Hayes come to see you?"

Tintwhistle looked vaguely affronted. "Wot ye think? That a feller cain't stop by t' see an old friend?"

"I was under the impression yours was more of a business relation-ship than a friendship."

"Well that jist goes to show wot ye know, don't it? Tried to 'elp 'im, I did, when the constables jumped 'im in Smithfield that day. Weren't no use, of course. But 'e come by t' thank me fer it anyway."

"I've heard that Hayes's cousin, Ethan, told the authorities to look for him in Smithfield."

"That's right."

"Did Hayes know that?"

"Sure enough did. Swore 'e'd kill the man too if'n 'e ever got the chance."

"He did?"

"Course 'e did. Who wouldn't?"

"He told you when he came to your shop that he was planning to kill Seaforth?"

"What? No, I'm talkin' about what he said all them years ago, when they was gonna hang him."

"So the only reason Hayes came to see you at your dolly shop was to thank you for trying to help him eighteen years ago?"

"That's right."

"Did you see him again?"

"Why would I?"

Which wasn't, Sebastian noted, precisely the same as saying no. He reached for the bottle and topped up the man's glass. "You heard that Hayes was murdered two days ago?"

"Aye."

"Who do you think killed him?"

Sebastian expected the man to say, *How the blazes would I know?* Instead, Tintwhistle laid a finger along the side of his nose and said, "Who ye think?"

"I honestly have no idea."

"Huh." The retired cracksman leaned forward and dropped his voice. "Seen somebody, I did, when 'is nibs was in the shop. Somebody I recognized. Looked t' me like 'e was followin' 'im."

"Someone was following Nicholas Hayes?"

"That's right."

"Do you know this person's name?"

Tintwhistle turned his head and spat on the floor. "Lots o' folks know that cove. Used t' be a Bow Street Runner, 'e did. If'n there was any justice in this world, they'd 'ave 'anged 'im fer murder. But there ain't no such thing as justice in England. Not fer poor folk like us."

Sebastian shook his head. "Who did you see?"

"Poole. Titus Poole."

"Never heard of him."

Tintwhistle stared at Sebastian. "Ye ain't? Well, I wish I ain't neither—that's fer certain."

"This Titus Poole was following Hayes?"

"That's what I'm sayin'."

"You're certain?"

"Sure enough looked that way t' me."

"Why would Poole be following Nicholas Hayes?"

"Reckon somebody was payin' 'im. Why else? That's wot Poole does these days, ye know. Hear tell 'e makes more money now than 'e ever did as a Runner."

Sebastian studied the ex-cracksman's alcohol-ravaged face. "Who do you think was paying him?"

"Somebody wanted Hayes out o' the way, I reckon."

"You're suggesting someone paid Poole to kill Hayes?"

Tintwhistle sniffed. "Seems likely t' me. Don't it t' you? Otherwise, why didn't 'e just nab 'im and 'and 'im over t' Bow Street?"

"Did you tell Hayes someone was following him?"

"I did."

"And?"

"'E said he knowed it. Didn't know the feller's name till I told 'im, though."

"Did he say who he thought might be paying the man to follow him?"

Tintwhistle laughed. "Said he reckoned it could be any one of four people. But he didn't name 'em."

Sebastian watched the man purse his lips and squint as he drained his glass again. "So why did Hayes really come to see you?"

"I told ye: 'E wanted t' thank me."

"You weren't tempted to turn him in?"

Tintwhistle's eyes bulged. "Hell, no. Grace'd gut me fer even thinkin' o' such a thing."

Sebastian refilled the man's glass. "Do you know why Hayes came back to England?"

"Said 'e 'ad somethin' 'e 'ad t' do. I didn't ask 'im what. Ain't too hard t' figure out, though, if'n ye gets me drift?"

"You mean, you think he came back here to kill someone."

"Ain't no other reason I can think of, now, is there? Well, is there?"

"Who do you think he came to kill?"

"That cousin o' 'is, of course."

"Can you think of anyone else?"

"Well, if I were 'im, I reckon meybe I'd wanna kill me da too. That old Earl was one nasty son of a bitch. But he's already dead, ain't 'e?"

"How about someone Hayes quarreled with while at the Red Lion? Anyone?"

"Nah. Weren't a real quarrelsome fellow, 'is nibs."

"He was convicted of murder."

"Yeah. Well, sometimes things happen different from what we expect 'em to." Tintwhistle emptied his glass again and squinted at the brandy bottle. "Anythin' left in there?"

"Four men?" said Hero after Sebastian relayed the conversation to her when they were alone after dinner. "Hayes told Tintwhistle any one of *four men* could have hired the ex-Runner to follow him?"

"Four," said Sebastian. They were sitting in the drawing room, Hero drinking a cup of tea with the cat on her lap, Sebastian with a glass of port. "Seaforth and LaRivière, obviously, and possibly Brownbeck. He seems a bit of a stretch, although he could have feared Hayes was nursing a grudge over his refusal to allow him to marry Kate. But that still leaves one."

"The fourth could be Forbes."

Sebastian took a slow sip of his port. "Perhaps. Hayes did once run off with the man's wife, but it also seems something of a stretch." He swirled the dark fortified wine in his glass. "The problem is, why didn't whoever hired Titus Poole simply turn Hayes over to the authorities rather than setting an ex-Runner to follow him?"

"Perhaps that was the intent. But then Hayes confronted Poole and was killed in the resultant struggle."

"It's a scenario that would make more sense if Hayes hadn't been hit in the back with a sickle."

"There is that." Hero sipped her tea in silence for a moment. "It's interesting that, unlike Lady Forbes, Mott Tintwhistle had no trouble at all believing that Nicholas Hayes came back to London to kill someone."

"I suspect that, in some ways, Tintwhistle knew Hayes's capacity for violence far better than the former Miss Kate Brownbeck."

"Do you believe Tintwhistle's claim that they broke into the old Earl of Seaforth's house simply to take a watch?"

"It seems a reckless thing to do, I'll admit. But then, Nicholas was only twenty—and very, very angry with his father. So I can see it, yes."

The cat jumped down, and Hero rose from her chair to go stand at the bowed front window overlooking the street. The window was open to the evening air in the hopes of catching a breeze, but the room was still hot.

She was silent for a moment, her gaze on the street below. Then she said, "I keep looking, hoping he'll come back—Ji, I mean. I don't understand why he is staying away from Grace and Jules Calhoun."

"It doesn't make sense unless he's afraid."

"Of what?"

"Someone who knew about his ties to both Chick Lane and this house. Someone like Titus Poole and whoever hired him."

She glanced over at him. "If Ji is Hayes's son—and if Hayes somehow managed to marry the boy's mother and Ji can prove it—he would be the rightful heir to his grandfather's earldom, would he not?"

"I think he'd have a very good case to make. And it might explain one thing that's been bothering me."

"What's that?"

"Why Hayes brought the child back to England with him."

She drew a deep breath. "Would Seaforth do such a thing, do you think? Kill both Nicholas and that little boy, I mean."

"To keep his titles and estates?" Sebastian drained his port and set aside the glass. "I don't think he's a particularly evil man, but he is weak. And weak men can do some surprisingly evil things when they convince themselves that they're the victims in a situation—which they are very good at doing."

"Dear God," whispered Hero, her gaze on the dark, hot street below. "Where is that poor child?"

## Chapter 23

"Titus Poole?" said Sir Henry Lovejoy when Sebastian stopped by the Bow Street magistrate's Russell Square house that Sunday morning. "Don't tell me he's mixed up in this."

"That's what I'm hearing," said Sebastian, taking the seat Lovejoy indicated. The morning breeze blowing in through the parlor's open windows was already hot. "What can you tell me about him?"

Lovejoy rubbed his eyes with a splayed thumb and forefinger. "I'm surprised you haven't heard of the man. He was considered a genius when it came to tracking down and catching thieves. Up until five years ago, he was Bow Street's most famous Runner."

"Five years ago I was in Portugal."

"Ah. That explains it."

"So what happened?"

"Unfortunately, it became apparent that he owed much of his vaunted success to a habit of framing vagrants and lying at their trials. He was never prosecuted, I'm afraid—the last thing Bow Street wanted was to have one of their Runners linked to the kinds of perversions of justice associated with eighteenth-century thieftakers like Jonathan Wild and Quilt Arnold." Lovejoy gave a faint shake of his head. "I understand the desire to protect the Public Office, but at the same time I can't help but believe it was a mistake—in addition to being a serious failure of justice. The man left with his reputation intact and now enjoys a lucrative career as a private thieftaker."

Despite the establishment of the Bow Street Runners as a quasi police force, private thieftakers were still active in London and the surrounding counties. Typically they received fees for returning stolen goods to their original owners. But they also had a reputation for running protection rackets and lending their expertise to rich men with little respect for the law.

Sebastian said, "It's been suggested that someone was paying Poole to follow Nicholas Hayes."

"How odd. If someone knew Hayes had returned to England, why not simply inform the authorities and have the man taken up?"

"That I can't explain, but I suspect Poole could. Do you have any idea where I might find him?"

"Last I heard he'd married a woman who owns an inn in Warwick Lane, just south of Newgate Street. The Bell, I believe it's called."

Sebastian studied the magistrate's strained features. The graft and corruption of London's public officials had long been a source of severe aggravation to Lovejoy. "Could Poole kill, do you think? In cold blood?"

"The man's lies sent a dozen or more innocent men, women, and children to the gallows. I can't see someone like that balking at murder, can you?"

"No," said Sebastian.

Lovejoy reached for a small notebook lying on the table beside him and flipped it open to a marked page. "So far we've discovered no reasonable explanation for Pennington's death other than the possibility that he saw Hayes's killer that night. We've also found that Lord Seaforth did indeed spend Thursday afternoon and evening at his club before leaving directly for Carlton House, while the Count de Compans dined with the Regent himself that evening. So both men have solid alibis."

"It sounds like it. Although that's less significant when you consider that either man could have hired Poole to do his killing for him."

Lovejoy sighed. "True. I've also heard back from the lads who were trying to find Hayes's ship. Turns out only two ships from Canton have docked in London in the last several months: the *Dover Castle* and the *Morning*. Both arrived in a convoy with three whalers this past Monday."

"That's too late. Hayes was here before then."

"I thought so. There was another convoy of three ships in May—the *Clyde*, the *Earl of Abergavanney*, and the *Broxbornebury*. All three struck the Shambles off the Isle of Portland in a dense fog. The *Broxbornebury* and *Clyde* sank in the bay with great loss of life, but the *Earl of Abergavanney* managed to limp into Weymouth."

"That sounds like it's probably our ship."

Lovejoy nodded. "I've sent inquiries to the authorities in Weymouth, to see what they can discover. Presumably Hayes and this child traveled up to London by stage." He paused. "No luck yet finding the boy?"

"None. Which is worrisome, given that even if the lad doesn't know whom Hayes was meeting that night, he presumably knows where Hayes went and whom he saw after coming up to London. And that means he could be a threat to this killer."

"Perhaps that's why he's hiding—because he knows he's in danger."

Sebastian hesitated a moment, then said, "I've discovered nothing definitive one way or the other, but it seems reasonable to suppose that the child could very well be Hayes's son. And if he's legitimate . . ."

Lovejoy stared at him. "Merciful heavens." He was silent for a moment, absorbing the various implications of this possibility. Then he said it again. "Merciful heavens."

The ancient, winding street known as Warwick Lane ran south from Newgate Street toward St. Paul's Cathedral. Dominated by the fine octagonal dome of Wren's famous Royal College of Physicians, this was an area frequented by booksellers from Paternoster Row and busy with traffic going to and from the Warrick Arms, a famous coaching inn. But the looming nearby presence of Newgate Prison and the law courts of the Old Bailey cast something of a pall over the district—that, and the pervasive stench of raw meat from Newgate Market.

The Bell Inn was built around a narrow yard reached through an archway opposite Warwick Square. Dating to the time of Charles II, it was a small but reasonably respectable hostelry, with stables that stretched along the yard's eastern side. Titus Poole himself was in the yard talking to a coal monger when Sebastian walked up to him.

A balding man in his late thirties, the former Bow Street Runner was a good four inches taller than Sebastian and big boned, with a slablike face and small dark eyes that narrowed at Sebastian's approach. "I know who ye are," said Poole, turning away from the coal man. "Yer that viscount. Devlin, ain't it?"

"That's right. You're Titus Poole?"

Poole used his tongue to poke at the wad of chewing tobacco distending one cheek. "And if I am?"

"I'd like to know how you came to be following Nicholas Hayes."

"What makes ye think I was?"

"You were seen."

"Ah." Poole shifted the tobacco from one cheek to the other. "Just so happens I spotted him in Smithfield Market. Thought I recognized him, so I followed him."

"Why not simply notify the authorities?"

"I wasn't sure it was him."

"No?"

"No."

"For whom are you working at the moment?"

"No one."

"I don't believe you."

Poole gave a scoffing exhalation of air. "I don't rightly care what ye believe."

Sebastian watched a towheaded little girl bounce a ball against a nearby brick wall. "So what was Hayes doing when you *just happened* to see him?"

"Nothin' of interest. Just walkin'."

"When was this?"

"A week or more ago. Don't recollect precisely."

"And you were still following him this past Tuesday or Wednesday?"

Poole's eyes narrowed. "Who says I was?"

"The person who saw you."

Poole gave a dismissive twitch of one shoulder. "Told ye I didn't recollect exactly."

"Have you ever worked for the Count de Compans?"

"Don't think so. Don't hold with workin' for foreigners—especially Frogs. M'brother died in Holland, he did."

"What about the Earl of Seaforth? Ever work for him?"

"Not so's I recall."

Sebastian watched the little girl chase after her ball as it rolled away toward the arch. "You seem to have a shockingly poor memory for a former Bow Street Runner."

Poole set his jaw. "I pay attention when I need to."

"For whom are you working now?" Sebastian asked again.

"Ain't none o' yer business, is it?" said the man.

Which was a slightly different answer, Sebastian noticed, from "No one." He let his gaze scan the galleries fronting the second-story chambers that ran along two sides of the yard. "I'll find out, you know."

Poole took a menacing step toward him, his big head thrusting forward as his lips pulled back from his teeth in a sneer. "Ye reckon ye scare me? Because if that's what yer thinkin', yer thinkin' wrong, *yer lordship.*" He accentuated the title in a way that turned it into an insult. "People who know what's what, they're afraid of Titus Poole. Not the other way around."

Sebastian met the man's gritty gaze. "Is that a threat?"

"Just some friendly advice."

"Ah." Sebastian gave the man a hard smile of his own. "Then in the spirit of friendship, I have some advice for you: If you're smart, you'll come clean sooner rather than later. Because I'll be back."

# Chapter 24

*A*rriving at Tower Hill a short time later, Sebastian found Paul Gibson on the stoop behind his surgery emptying a basin of bloody water into the yard. He looked haggard, his face unshaven, his eyes sunken and almost bruised.

"You look like the devil," said Sebastian.

"Thank you. I've finished your dead tea gardens owner, if that's why you're here," growled Gibson, slapping his hand against the bottom of the upturned basin. "Did it late yesterday evening. And it's a good thing too, given that I spent all of last night and most of the morning stitching up stab wounds and binding broken bones. This heat has got to let up soon, or we're all going to die—or wish we could."

"Find anything interesting with Pennington?"

"Nope. He was stabbed four times in the back, probably with just your ordinary, everyday knife. That's all."

Sebastian narrowed his eyes against the fiercely blazing sun. "What about Hayes?"

"Finished him too. Didn't see anything to change my opinion about what happened the night he died. The second slash of the sickle is probably the one that brought him down, and then the killer twisted the blade, severing the artery and killing him."

"Would he have had much blood on him? The killer, I mean."

"On his cuffs, maybe. But probably not much beyond that. The initial cuts didn't hit anything vital. It's the internal damage that did the work, so the blood would have seeped out slowly rather than spurting all over your killer." Gibson gave his basin a final shake and turned. "How about a wee something to slake the thirst of this god-awful heat?"

Sebastian blew out a long, harsh breath. "Sounds good to me."

It was later, when they were sitting at the table in Gibson's kitchen, a pitcher of ale from the corner tavern on the boards between them, that Gibson said, "Did find one thing you might consider relevant—about your Earl's disreputable son, I mean."

"Hayes? What's that?"

"He was dying of consumption."

Sebastian felt a sudden chill sluice through him. "Do you think he knew it?"

"Don't see how he could help but."

"How much longer did he have to live?"

"Four to six months, at best. Probably less. Certainly no more."

Sebastian stared out the window at the sun-drenched ancient stone outbuilding at the base of the yard where Nicholas Hayes still lay. "That casts everything in a slightly different light."

Gibson nodded. "I thought it might."

*Chapter 25*

$\mathscr{H}$ero and Calhoun spent the morning searching the streets near Smithfield without any luck.

It was later, when she was in the library studying a map of London she had spread across the table, that she heard a visitor ply the knocker on the front door.

"Major Hamish McHenry to see Lord Devlin," said an unfamiliar Scottish voice when Morey answered the door. "Is he receiving?"

Turning her head, she heard Morey say, "I beg your pardon, Major, but his lordship is not at present at home."

There was a pause. Then the unknown major said, "I'll try again later."

Something about the depth of the disappointment in the man's voice brought Hero to the library door. "May I help you, Major? I'm Lady Devlin."

The major had been turning away, but at her words, he paused. He was a lean, sandy-haired man of medium height, probably in his early forties, with the chiseled features and weathered complexion of a man who'd spent many years serving his country in harsh, unforgiving climes. His eyes were framed by the kind of deep fan lines left by smiling or squinting into a bright sun, but Hero didn't think they were smile lines. His face was somber and a little sad, and she had the feeling that expression was habitual.

"You're very kind, my lady," he said with a bow. "But I wouldn't want to trouble you."

She smiled. "No trouble. It's so dreadfully hot out; may I offer you something refreshing to drink? Lemonade, perhaps? Or if you prefer, we've a barrel of ale delivered fresh from the brewery this morning."

A slow, answering smile spread across the Scotsman's face, transforming it. "Ale sounds grand."

"Then ale it is."

Later, when they were seated in the drawing room, the major with a tankard of ale and Hero sipping a cup of tea, she said, "Have you recently returned from France?"

"Not so recently. My mother fell ill not long after Christmas, and the doctors weren't holding out much hope for her recovery. My only brother's in India, so I came home in March and missed the end of all the fighting, I'm sorry to say."

"That must have been frustrating for you."

He gave a wry smile. "I won't try to deny it."

"And how is your mother?"

His grin spread. "Fit as a fiddle at an Irish jig."

"Thank goodness for that. Will you stay in the Army, now that Napoléon is finished?"

He nodded. "My regiment is being ordered to America. There's talk we may try to take Washington, D.C., or perhaps New Orleans."

"Ah, yes, of course. With all these endless celebrations for peace in Europe, it's easy to forget we're still at war with the United States." She took a sip of her tea. "Did you know Devlin when he was in the Army?"

McHenry cleared his throat and glanced away. "No, my lady. I'm here because I understand he's looking into the death of Nicholas Hayes."

"You knew Hayes?"

"Not well. But his brother Crispin and I were good friends."

"Crispin is the brother who drowned right before Chantal de LaRivière was killed?"

"Yes." He cleared his throat again, and Hero had the impression there was something he'd come here to say to Devlin but didn't feel comfortable telling her. "Has . . . has Lord Devlin identified who was responsible for Nicholas's death?"

"Not yet, no. Why? Do you know something that might help?"

"Not exactly. But no one will ever convince me that Nicholas killed that Frenchwoman—at least, not the way they say he did."

"How can you be so certain?"

"Because he was never in love with her. He blamed her for Crispin killing himself."

Hero's teacup rattled in its saucer. "Crispin Hayes committed suicide?"

"Yes. You didn't know?"

"No."

The major nodded. "Threw himself off London Bridge. His father the Earl managed to get the coroner to rule it an accident, but it wasn't."

"But . . . why? Why did he kill himself?"

To Hero's surprise, a faint flush rose to the major's cheeks. "I don't think anyone ever knew, precisely." He cast a quick glance at the clock on the mantel and set aside his tankard. "I've imposed on your generous hospitality far too long." He rose to his feet. "Thank you for the much-needed refreshment."

She rose with him. "I'll tell Devlin you called."

"Thank you. I'll be staying with my mother in Lower Sloan Street until my regiment is ready to set sail."

Hero walked with him to the top of the stairs. "Do you have any idea why Nicholas Hayes would risk his life by coming back to England?"

"I'm thinking there must have been something he felt he'd left unfinished—a wrong that needed righting."

"Or a man who needed killing?" suggested Hero.

The bluntness of her words obviously shocked him. But after a moment he gave a curt nod and said, "Or a man who needed killing."

Devlin came in some five minutes later, hot, dusty, and calling for ale.

"*Suicide?*" he said when Hero told him of Major McHenry's strange visit. "Crispin Hayes killed himself? Why the bloody hell didn't Calhoun tell me that? Or Seaforth? All he said was that Crispin drowned."

"Perhaps Seaforth was too ashamed to admit that his cousin killed himself."

"I doubt it. He wasn't too ashamed to talk freely about all of his cousin Nicholas's sins." Devlin took a long, deep drink of his ale. "Why do you think McHenry came today?"

"I could be wrong, but I had the impression there was something he wanted to tell you—something he didn't feel comfortable saying to me."

Devlin refilled his tankard and went to stand at the front window, his gaze on the heat-blasted street. "What he told you was explosive enough."

Hero was quiet for a moment, watching him. "Gibson is quite certain Hayes was dying of consumption?"

"Yes."

"I suppose that helps explain why he risked his life by coming back to London now, after all those years of freedom. He knew he was dying, so he didn't care if he was caught or not."

"Seems likely, doesn't it?"

"Do you think he came back to kill Gilbert-Christophe de LaRivière?"

"Either LaRivière or Seaforth. Or maybe both."

"Nicholas told Mott Tintwhistle that any one of four men could have hired Titus Poole to follow him. Seaforth and LaRivière are obviously two, and either Brownbeck or Forbes could be the third. But what about Hamish McHenry as the fourth?"

Devlin glanced over at her. "Why would Hayes want to kill his brother's good friend?"

"I don't know. But it might explain why McHenry came here today, wanting to talk to you."

Sebastian drained his tankard and set it aside. "I think I need to have a long talk with your major."

## Chapter 26

*J*i was hungry, tired, and afraid.

The few coins Hayes had left with the child on that dreadful evening had disappeared unbelievably quickly. After a night spent huddled in the doorway of an old church with no dinner and no breakfast, Ji knew something had to be done. And though it hurt even to think about it, the child eventually came to the conclusion there was only one thing to do: pawn Hayes's watch.

Hayes had told Ji, once, about the old watch given to him by his grandfather, and about the jeering soldier who'd taken it from him on the ship to Botany Bay. The first thing Hayes had bought after arriving in Canton was the watch Ji now had, and it was the only thing the child still possessed that had belonged to him. But if there was an alternative to selling it to a pawnshop, Ji couldn't see it.

Ji knew about pawnshops because Hayes had explained them to the child before they went to visit his friend Mott Tintwhistle. Ji thought about taking the watch to Tintwhistle himself, but then the child remembered that Titus Poole knew about Tintwhistle. And Ji was trying to stay away from any place Poole knew about—or might know about.

In the end, the child selected a pawnshop near the enormous white temple Hayes had called St. Paul's. The shop was a narrow, musty place jammed with everything from carpenters' tools and battered saucepans to fraying corsets and old carpet squares. In a corner near the counter, half buried beneath a dusty pile of fans, Ji even spotted what looked like an old Chinese bamboo flute.

"Help ye there, lad?" said the wizened man behind the counter when Ji hesitated to approach him. "If yer here jist t' drool or if yer thinkin' about maybe tryin' to lift somethin', ye can jist turn around and git."

The old man reminded Ji of the ancient, withered peasant who used to sell chicken feet in the market in Canton. He was short and skeletally thin, his skin gray and wrinkled like old parchment, the whites of his lashless eyes yellow. He had that old-man smell, and his shop reeked of dust and decay and damp.

Taking a step forward, Ji laid the watch on the counter and said, "What will you give me for this, sir?"

The old man looked at the watch, then at Ji. "Where the hell did ye get that, yer lordship?"

"Canton," said Ji. The "lordship" reference made no sense at all.

"Oh, ye did, did ye? And where might that be?"

"In the east." Too late, Ji suspected that burst of honesty about Canton was a mistake.

"Ho. Sure it ain't in the *west*?"

"No, sir. It's in the east," said Ji, not understanding the implications of the man's question.

"Who'd ye steal the watch from, then?"

"I did not steal it."

"Sure ye didn't." The man picked up the watch and held it to his ear to listen to the tick.

"It runs perfectly fine," said Ji, watching him.

The old man's lips pulled back into a nearly toothless grin. "Oh, it does, does it? *Perfectly fine*. Not *real good*, mind ye, but *perfectly fine*, ye say?"

Ji had the sense that they were holding two entirely different conversations, and the old man was the only one who understood both.

He said, "I'll give ye a shilling for it."

Ji stared at him. "But it's worth at least ten pounds! I know because I priced comparable items in the shops before I came here."

"So ye priced *comparable items*, did ye? Well, it may be worth ten pounds in a shop, new. But it ain't new, now, is it? For all I know, it could stop runnin' in an hour, or whoever ye lifted it off could walk in here this afternoon and claim it. And then I'd be out me shilling, now, wouldn't I?"

"I did not steal this watch."

"Sure ye didn't, lad." The man set the watch on the counter. "A shilling is me offer. Take it or leave it."

"Five shillings," said Ji, who had spent many a morning in the market watching Pema barter with everyone from fishmongers and butchers to greengrocers.

The old man snorted. "Two."

"Two and a half—*and* the bamboo flute there by the fans. If it plays."

The old man turned to stare at the instrument with an expression that told Ji he'd forgotten it was even there. "That?"

"Does it play?"

He extricated the flute from the jumble of other items and handed it to Ji. "You tell me."

The dizi was old and worn, the scarlet silk thread wrapping the bamboo dark with age, the tassel bedraggled. But it had once been a fine instrument; the protective ferrules were of jade, and Ji couldn't help but wonder what it was doing here, in this wretched dolly shop so far from China.

The child was afraid the dimo might be cracked or even missing. But when Ji sounded a tentative note, it hummed pure and true. At first Ji played with a soft-breath attack, and the tone was peaceful, floating. Then the child quickened, and the flute responded, the sound becoming sprightly and ethereal. For a moment, Ji was lost in the music, lost in a sound that spoke of plum blossoms and nightingales and trickling water—the sounds of home. Then an awareness of time and place returned, and Ji lowered the flute.

"I . . ." Ji drew a breath. "It still plays."

The old man was staring at Ji with a stillness that the child could not read, for the people in this land were too strange, their ways too different.

Then he cleared his throat and reached to close his hand around the watch. "Right then. Two and a half shillings and the flute. It's a deal."

*Chapter 27*

Major Hamish McHenry was not an easy man to find.

Sebastian went first to Lower Sloan Street, an area of modest but respectable brick row houses with white-painted double-hung windows and small front gardens filled with colorful splashes of roses and foxgloves and lilies.

He found Mrs. McHenry puttering about her rosebushes with a basket hooked over one arm and a pair of secateurs in hand. She was a small, white-haired woman probably in her late sixties or early seventies, dressed in a black stuff mourning gown and a wide-brimmed straw hat that threw a hatched pattern of light and shade across her plump face. When Sebastian introduced himself and asked after her son, her soft brown eyes crinkled with her smile.

"I'm afraid you've just missed him, my lord," she said with a lilting Scottish burr. "He was here for a bit and then went off again. Said something about meeting his mates for a pint, although he didn't say where. You might try the Scarlet Man in Cockspur Street. I hear all the officers go there these days, although when my George was alive they were always at the Bedford Arms."

"Your husband was in the Army as well, Mrs. McHenry?"

"Royal Marines," she said proudly. "Lieutenant Colonel George Mc-Henry. Served from India to Gibraltar to America, he did. Can't believe my Hamish will be going back there now to fight another war—to America, I mean. After all these years."

"When does his regiment set sail?"

"Soon, they say."

Sebastian watched her snip a spent bloom and place it in her basket. "Did you know Crispin Hayes?"

Her gaze flew to his, then slid away as her smile faltered. "I didn't, no. My George and I were living in Plymouth in those days. And now they're saying his brother is dead too." She turned to snip at another bush. "Shall I tell Hamish you're looking for him?"

"Yes, please," said Sebastian with a bow. "Thank you for your time."

She nodded, her smile once more firmly in place. But he was aware of her watching him as he walked away, the sun hard on her face and her secateurs slack in her hand.

Sebastian checked the Scarlet Man, the Bedford Arms, and several other pubs and coffeehouses popular with military men, all without any luck. Giving up on the major, he went in search of the Third Earl of Seaforth.

With its classical facade, gleaming black-painted door, and neat rows of silk-swagged windows, Ethan Hayes's elegant town house in North Audley Street was virtually indistinguishable from the other impressive residences in the street, a monument to its owner's wealth and status. But Sebastian found himself pausing at the top of the steps as he reached for the knocker.

Once, this house—like the Irish estates and titles that went with it—had belonged to a man whose three sons were now dead. Nicholas Hayes had grown up in this house, played in its nursery as a child, broken into its library as an anguished young man in search of something he considered his. Had his ghost haunted the current Earl all these years, troubling his conscience and dimming his pleasure in the enjoyment of what should never have been his? Somehow, Sebastian doubted it. Men like Seaforth always managed to find excuses for their own worst behavior, even as they loudly condemned the slightest transgressions committed by others.

Pushing the thought away, Sebastian let the knocker fall.

It was close enough to the fashionable dinner hour that Sebastian wouldn't have been surprised to be told that the Earl was already dressing. But Seaforth simply directed his butler to show Sebastian up to his dressing room.

Attended by a fussy, middle-aged valet, Seaforth stood in the center of the room, clad only in a long, open-necked shirt and drawers. His bare calves were pasty white and skinny despite the small potbelly that showed against the loose folds of his shirt. He dismissed his valet with a nod and said, "This is getting tiresome, you know. I only agreed to see you because I wouldn't put it past you to follow me to my dinner engagement and harangue me there."

Sebastian closed the door behind the valet and leaned back against it. "Acute of you."

The Earl reached for a pair of formal black breeches and pulled them on. "What do you want now?"

"I was wondering why you didn't tell me Crispin Hayes killed himself."

"I thought I did."

"No. You told me he drowned."

Seaforth buttoned the breeches, then smoothed on white silk stockings and pushed his feet into diamond-buckled shoes. "I suppose some people do fall into the Thames and drown by accident, but there can't be many."

"So why did he kill himself?"

Seaforth selected one of the neatly pressed cravats laid ready by his valet and turned toward the mirror. "I really don't know, although I always assumed it was a matter of unrequited love."

"Crispin Hayes was in love? With whom?"

Seaforth carefully wound the length of extraordinarily wide linen around his neck. "Chantal de LaRivière, of course." His gaze met Sebastian's in the mirror, and he laughed. "You really don't know much about those days, do you?"

"Obviously not. Care to enlighten me?"

"It's not a complicated story. The Countess was an extraordinarily beautiful woman, and Crispin fell madly, hopelessly in love with her."

"You're saying Crispin and Nicholas were in love with the same woman?"

"That's right." Seaforth kept his gaze on his reflection in the mirror as he tied the cravat. "To tell the truth, I've sometimes wondered if perhaps Crispin's death wasn't actually a suicide."

"Meaning . . . what?"

"Well, given what we now know about Nicholas, I wouldn't be surprised if he simply pushed his brother off the bridge in a fit of jealousy. Would you?"

Watching this smirking, condescending man calmly tie his cravat in the dressing room of the house that had come to him only through his betrayal of his cousin, Sebastian felt a wave of revulsion so intense that it was a struggle to keep his voice even. "You're suggesting Nicholas had a reason to be jealous of his brother? Why? Did the Countess favor Crispin?"

"That I wouldn't know."

Sebastian studied the other man's self-satisfied, smug face. "Are you familiar with a man named Titus Poole?"

Seaforth kept his gaze on his reflection in the mirror as he smoothed the folds of his cravat. "Poole? No, sorry; never heard of him. Why do you ask?"

"I understand he was once a rather famous Bow Street Runner, although he now works privately as a thieftaker."

"Oh?" Seaforth swung away from the mirror to reach for his white silk waistcoat. "I'm afraid I don't keep up with such people. What has he to do with anything?"

"He was seen following Nicholas shortly before he was murdered, and it's been suggested that someone had hired the man. You don't know anything about that?"

Seaforth tried to tuck his chin against his chest so he could see to work the waistcoat's buttons, but given the exorbitant width of his cravat, it wasn't easy. "No, of course not. How could I?"

"You didn't hire him?"

"Don't be ridiculous." He reached for his coat. "Are we about finished here? I promised my wife I'd look in on the nursery for a few minutes before we leave."

"Of course," said Sebastian. He turned toward the door, but paused with his hand on the knob. "Just one more thing. I've been wondering, was Crispin planning to buy a pair of colors like his brother and his friend Hamish McHenry?"

"Crispin? Hardly. He was never army mad like Nicholas."

"Oh? So what did he do?"

"I really don't recall. Why?"

"Just curious," said Sebastian, and let himself out.

## Chapter 28

*T*he evening breeze billowing in through the Brook Street house's open windows was warm and dry and smelled strongly of horse droppings.

Jules Calhoun sat in one of the chairs beside the library's cold hearth, his hands clasped between his spread knees and his head bowed. He'd been out most of the afternoon searching for Ji in the back alleys and crowded courts around the Red Lion, and he looked hot, tired, and uncharacteristically disheveled. "I don't know why I didn't say Crispin Hayes had killed himself," said the valet in answer to Sebastian's question. "I guess it didn't seem relevant."

"Is it possible that Nicholas Hayes killed his own brother?"

Calhoun's head came up. "Good Lord, no. Crispin defied the old Earl by continuing to visit Nicholas after their father disowned him. Anyone who saw the brothers together could tell how close they were. Nicholas was devastated when Crispin died."

"I've seen people devastated by the death of someone they loved but killed. Sometimes men act in anger, with little thought or conscious intent, and then regret it."

"No. I was with Nicholas when he heard about his brother's death. He wasn't simply grieved. He was shocked and horrified. He couldn't understand why his brother would kill himself."

"What did Nicholas do?"

Calhoun dug his palms into his eyes, rubbing back and forth. "He went off somewhere—I don't know where. When he came back to the Red Lion, he was in a tearing mood. I'd never seen him like that before."

"In what sense?"

"He was drinking heavily, but with a dark purposefulness rather than his usual reckless good cheer."

"How close was this to when Chantal de LaRivière died?"

"She died that night. Nicholas spent the better part of the day drinking, then went over there."

"To Dover Street, you mean? This was the same day his brother died?"

Calhoun shook his head. "No. He didn't hear about his brother until a good twelve hours after the body was found. So it was the next night."

"There was no suggestion of foul play in the brother's death?"

Calhoun looked at him blankly. "Not that I ever heard about."

"What do you know about a man named Mott Tintwhistle?"

A faint gleam of amusement lightened the valet's tense features. "The old cracksman? What about him?"

"Did you know he helped Nicholas break into his father's house?"

"I remember hearing about it. Why?"

"Do you know what they were after?"

Calhoun was thoughtful for a moment. "I did know, once. But I don't remember now. It was something Nicholas wanted—something he said was rightfully his."

"His grandfather's watch?"

"That was it. I remember thinking it was daft—breaking into the old Earl's house for something like that. Although to be honest, I suspect the watch was only part of it. I think he did it mainly to get back at the old man—show him he could."

"Did they also take some banknotes?"

"No. That was just a tale the old Earl spread around to make people see him as the victim of a 'bad son.' What kind of a father does that?"

"A horrible one."

Calhoun was silent for a moment. "It's funny, because I remember Nicholas as mature, sophisticated, and cultured—everything I wasn't but knew as soon as I met him that I wanted to be. I think of him as older and more mature than me because he was then. But looking back on it now, I realize he'd only just come down from Oxford. He was still a young man—very young. And he made a young man's mistakes."

"You don't have any idea where he went after he found out about his brother's death and before he started drinking?"

"No. He never said. When he came back, he just called for a bottle of brandy and started working his way through it. My mother tried to talk to him, but he asked her politely to leave him alone, so she did. And then he left for Dover Street."

"He said he was going to see the Countess?"

"No. The Count."

"Did he say what he was planning to do?"

"He said somebody had to stop those bastards, and it might as well be him."

"*Those* bastards? Not *that* bastard?"

"That's the way I remember it. But I could be wrong. It was so many years ago."

"How long was he gone?"

"A couple of hours. He came back covered in blood, but he wasn't hurt. He never tried to hide what had happened. Told my mother he and the Count had struggled over the gun and it went off, grazing LaRivière's forehead but killing his wife."

"Whose gun was it?"

"He said it was the Frenchman's."

"Hayes didn't take a pistol with him?"

"I honestly don't know." Calhoun thrust up abruptly and went to stand at the open window, his gaze on the darkening street now thick with the carriages of Mayfair's wealthy residents on their way to their evening's entertainments.

"If Hayes was drunk," said Sebastian, watching him, "he might not have remembered exactly what happened."

"He wasn't that drunk. He could hold his liquor like nobody I'd ever seen—until I met you."

Sebastian studied the taut, tired profile of the man at the window. "Did you know Hayes was dying of consumption when he came back to England?"

Calhoun swung to face him. "No. You're certain?"

Sebastian nodded. "He didn't give any indication?"

"No. I mean, I remember him coughing badly, but he said it was nothing. I asked why the hell he'd come back, and all he'd say was that there was something he needed to do. I told him he was daft, that nothing was worth dying for. And he said, 'This is.'"

"But you've no idea what he was talking about?"

"No."

"Did the boy say anything?"

"Nothing about why they were in London."

"How good is the lad's English?"

A smile lighted the valet's eyes. "As good as yours, my lord. Plop him down in Eton or Winchester—or the Court of St. James, for that matter—and he'd sound right at home. Even if he didn't stand out for anything else, you'd think a ragged lad living on the streets who sounds like a lordling would be remembered." A clock tower in the distance began to toll the hour, the dull chimes ringing out over the rattle of harness and the clatter of hoofbeats and iron-rimmed wheels on cobblestones. Calhoun glanced again toward the yawning darkness of the open window. "I can't believe we still haven't found him. Where could he be?"

"Any chance your mother could be hiding him?"

A faint suggestion of color rode high on the valet's prominent cheek-bones. "No. I asked her—when she told me you'd figured out Hayes had been staying with her." He paused, then added, "I honestly hadn't known about that, my lord."

"I never thought that you did."

Calhoun nodded. "She said the boy went off with Hayes the afternoon of the murder and never came back."

"Hayes didn't tell you anything at all about the child?"

"Only that he'd come from Canton with him."

"Did he tell you much about his life in China?"

"He told me about the Hong merchant he worked with, and how strange he found everything at first. He said their culture was so different, it took him a long time to adjust. He said that in many ways it was more cruel than ours, but there were some ways in which he thought it was better. And the longer he lived there, the more respect he came to have for their religion."

Sebastian thought about the Buddhist prayer beads left curled up beside the portrait of a smiling Chinese woman. "How much do you think he'd changed from the man you knew before?"

Calhoun was silent for a moment. "It's hard for me to say for certain. I mean, *I'm* different, aren't I? He was older than the man I'd known, obviously. But it wasn't only that. When I knew him before, there was a kind of coiled restlessness about him, a—a passionate, wild recklessness. That was gone. The man I met in Oxford Market was calm. At peace. There was nothing peaceful about the Nicholas Hayes I knew before. Nothing peaceful at all."

"Sometimes people who know they're going to die manage to find within themselves an unusual measure of serenity."

"Maybe that was it," said Calhoun.

Although he didn't sound as if he believed it.

*Chapter 29*

 he inquest into the death of Nicholas Hayes was held at eight
o'clock the next morning at the Swan, a tidy brown brick inn on the edge
of Somer's Town that dated to late in the reign of George II. Because
there was no officially designated site for inquests, they were generally
held in the nearest inn or public house large enough to accommodate the
crowds such affairs typically attracted. But the Swan was relatively modest in size, and the murder of an earl's notorious son had drawn massive
attention. By half past seven, the inn's public room was filled to overflowing with spectators and prospective jurors and a swarm of ragged, lithe
children doubtless taking advantage of the occasion to pick the pockets
of the unwary.

"This shouldn't take long," said Lovejoy, holding a handkerchief to
his nose. The atmosphere in the close room was stifling hot and smelled
strongly of spilled beer, sweat, and death, thanks to the presence of
Nicholas Hayes's four-day-old corpse.

Sebastian tried not to breathe any more than he had to. "Hopefully."

He let his gaze drift over the pushing, shoving crowd of gawkers eager for a glimpse of the bloody remains of the infamous murderer-turned–murder victim. "I don't see the Earl of Seaforth."

"He may not come. My office contacted him about making arrangements to release the body to him after the inquest, and he said he doesn't want it."

"He what?"

Lovejoy nodded. "He says we can dump the remains in the parish's poor hole for all he cares—which is what it looks like we'll be doing."

Sebastian felt a wave of revulsion pass over him. "No. If Seaforth won't give his cousin a decent burial, then release the body to me. I'll take care of it."

Lovejoy's eyes widened over the white folds of his handkerchief. "You're serious?"

"Yes."

"Very well." Lovejoy's gaze shifted to the door, where a debonair, exquisitely dressed older Frenchman was quietly slipping in through the crowd. "Ah. The Count de Compans has arrived."

"And Brownbeck," said Sebastian as the short, self-important merchant pushed his way in behind the Count.

Lovejoy shifted his handkerchief to pat at the perspiration on his brow. "Theo Brownbeck? What has he to do with this?"

"He and Hayes quarreled long ago," said Sebastian, mindful of his promise to his aunt Henrietta. "Before Hayes was transported."

"Interesting. There's talk of the man becoming the next Lord Mayor, you know. People like his no-nonsense attitude toward crime and the lower orders, although I must admit I question the validity of some of his statistics."

"With good reason," said Sebastian as the crowds near the door made way for another aristocratic latecomer: a slight, rusty-haired nobleman with vague inclinations toward dandyism and an exaggerated sense of his own importance.

The Earl of Seaforth might not be willing to take possession of his cousin's body, but he was obviously curious enough about the findings of the inquest to want to see it for himself. Drawing up just inside the door, he threw one long, contemptuous glance at Nicholas Hayes's bloody corpse, then walked over to a silver-haired gentleman who stood near the bar and leaned in to say something close to the man's ear.

"Who's that he's talking to?" asked Lovejoy, watching him.

"Forbes," said Sebastian as the man turned to glance their way. "Sir Lindsey Forbes, of the East India Company."

The coroner was a stout, middle-aged man named Norquist Gaffney, with full lips, a loud, gravelly voice, and a pugnacious, brusque manner. Dressed in a long powdered wig and a dirty black robe dusted liberally with snuff, he arrived ten minutes late, threw himself into the padded chair reserved specifically for him, and complained loudly about the heat and the crowd. Then he scratched beneath his wig and bellowed, "Right, then. Let's get this over with."

Called to testify first, Sebastian described his discovery of Nicholas Hayes's body in the blandest terms possible. He'd been careful from the beginning to characterize Calhoun's role as that of a simple servant, with the result that the valet hadn't even received a summons. Lovejoy likewise delivered his responses in a dry, forthright manner. The only vaguely sensational testimony in the entire inquest came from a rawboned, nervous gardener named Bernie Aikens, who haltingly admitted to having forgotten his sickle in the clearing on the day of the murder.

"What time did you leave the clearing?" snapped Gaffney.

"Around midday, yer honor," said the gardener in a small voice.

"What's that? Speak up, man."

"Midday, yer honor."

"And when did you realize you'd left your sickle there?"

"N-not till the next morning, yer honor," stammered Aikens, a bead of sweat rolling down his sun-darkened cheek. "It wasn't until I discovered me sickle wasn't with me other tools and heard that the fellow'd been killed in the clearing where I'd been working that I realized I musta left it there."

The coroner glowered at the gardener as if he were the most careless, forgetful, loathsome creature imaginable. "And yet you failed to inform the authorities of this fact?"

Aikens was sweating so badly now that his entire face glistened. "I told Mr. Pennington."

"When?"

"That morning, yer honor. Almost as soon as I knowed fer sure."

A constable standing beside the coroner leaned down to whisper in Mr. Gaffney's ear. The coroner's lips thinned, his frown deepening as his eyebrows drew together. But he nodded, then said to Aikens, "I'm told Mr. Pennington's daughter has confirmed your story. You're fortunate your carelessness hasn't earned you a murder charge."

Beneath his sunburn, Aikens's face had gone sickly white, and he was visibly trembling.

The coroner waved a dismissive hand at the gardener. "Just go away. Right, then," he bellowed. "Who's next?"

"Paul Gibson, yer honor," said the constable. "The surgeon what did the post mortem."

Slipping quietly from the room, Sebastian went in search of an undertaker.

They called it the "death trade," the lucrative business of taking care of London's copious supply of the dead. At the high end of the trade were the "funeral furnishers," a pretentious and rapacious set of professionals who had been known to bankrupt bereaved families by flattering and shaming them into signing up for elaborate funerals that included hiring a small army of mutes and professional mourners and draping their homes and churches in endless yards of black crepe. At the lower end of the business were simple carpenters and cabinetmakers who did a lucrative side business building coffins and organizing funerals for the poor. In the middle were the undertakers, which is what Sebastian decided he needed.

The discreet establishment of Joseph Summers, undertaker, lay on a narrow street not far from the Swan. A short, well-fed man with full cheeks and a balding head, Mr. Summers looked like the kind of fellow whose countenance was meant to be wreathed in cheerful smiles. It was not. Instead, he affected a sorrowful demeanor that somehow managed to be both ingratiating and faintly condescending at the same time—that is, condescending toward anyone who might show the least tendency toward anything other than mindless extravagance. When Sebastian introduced himself and explained what he wanted, Mr. Summers bowed so low, his nose almost hit his knees.

"We would be delighted to make all the necessary arrangements, my lord." The undertaker's plump white hands fluttered through the air. "Absolutely delighted. And where will interment take place, my lord?"

There was a pause. Mr. Summers blinked at him inquiringly, and it occurred to Sebastian that he should have given more forethought to the necessary particulars. "Probably St. Pancras, but I don't know for certain yet."

"I see." Mr. Summers's unctuous expression slipped only slightly. "Well, at any rate, the first step will be to convey the deceased from the Swan to your lordship's residence. We have two wonderfully capable women who will then come to wash—"

Sebastian thought about Joseph Summers delivering a bloody, decaying corpse to Brook Street and said hastily, "You can't bathe and prepare the body here?"

The undertaker's blobby nose twitched. "These things are generally done in the home of the deceased."

"This deceased doesn't have a home here. He's a visitor."

"Well. I suppose it is possible, although highly irregular." The undertaker paused significantly, a faint gleam showing in his eyes before he could hide it. "And far more costly."

"I understand."

Mr. Summers reached for his notebook and pencil. "Now, for the funeral procession itself, you'll be wanting two mutes, obviously. And at least six pages in addition to the bearers and—"

"There won't be a funeral procession or church service," said Sebastian. "I simply need you to pick up the body, have it washed and wrapped, and then deliver it directly to the churchyard."

Mr. Summers stared at him. "No funeral procession or church service?"

"No."

The undertaker swallowed. "You will be wanting a coffin, yes? I mean, I know St. Pancras has a coffin they rent out, but surely—"

"Oh, I want a coffin."

"Excellent. And let me hasten to assure your lordship that our coffins are made of the finest wide-planked, knot-free elm before being covered in black velvet and lined with padded silk—"

"Black superfine will do," said Sebastian. "And given that the man is dead, I don't think he needs padding."

"No padding? Black superfine?" repeated the undertaker in scandalized accents.

"Black superfine." Sebastian rose to his feet. "I'll let you know when I've spoken to the vicar of St. Pancras."

Mr. Summers rose with him and made a last-ditch effort to increase his revenue. "If you prefer, we would be more than happy to convey the deceased to his home parish for burial—wherever that may be."

"I don't think that would be practical in this case," said Sebastian, and beat a hasty retreat.

The ancient church of St. Pancras lay on the banks of the River Fleet, not far from the leafy gardens of the late Irvine Pennington. Most of the

crumbling stone building dated from the thirteenth and fifteenth centuries, but the church itself was older—far older, stretching back through
the ages to the seventh century if not beyond. As the only place in London that generally accepted Catholic burials, St. Pancras was popular
with French refugees. Sebastian decided it was probably a good place to
bury a man who kept a set of Buddhist prayer beads.

He had a frank conversation with the church's white-haired, sad-eyed
vicar. And then Sebastian went for a walk amongst the vast, sprawling
churchyard's moss-covered tombstones and centuries-old yews.

He was not wandering aimlessly.

He visited, briefly, the recent grave of an aged friend named William
Franklin. Then, turning toward the section of the churchyard that served
as the final resting place for the hundreds and hundreds of refugees from
the French Revolution who hadn't lived long enough to return home, he
found the grave of Chantal de LaRivière.

The Countess's headstone was a simple one of white marble, inscribed with nothing more than her name and the dates 1774–1796. With
the passage of years, the grave had sunken and was now overgrown with
long grass that lay wilted in the heat of the brutally sunny day. Hat in
hand, Sebastian stood beneath the spreading limbs of a nearby ancient
elm and tried to understand both this woman's death and the part it might
have played all these years later in the murders of Nicholas Hayes and
Irvine Pennington.

*What were you like?* Sebastian found himself wondering as he stared at
that starkly plain tombstone. All he really knew about Chantal de La
Rivière was that she was young and beautiful and that she had died violently. What else? He remembered someone saying something about a
year-old child. Was the child still alive? A boy or girl? He didn't know.
And it occurred to him that, despite having been relatively young at the
time of his wife's death, the Count de Compans had never remarried.
Why? Had he loved her that much?

Lifting his head, Sebastian gazed off across the sea of weathered, thickly clustered tombstones. From here he could see quite clearly the feathery treetops of Pennington's Tea Gardens. Nicholas Hayes's life had taken him halfway around the world, from the brutal shores of Botany Bay to the exotic, lotus-scented waterways of Canton. And yet in the end he had come back here to die just a few hundred feet from the grave of the woman he'd been transported for killing. What were the odds?

Sebastian brought his gaze back to the headstone before him. If Hayes had, in truth, been responsible for Chantal de LaRivière's death, then Sebastian supposed there was a kind of poetic justice to it all. But he couldn't shake the conviction that the true story of that fatal night eighteen years before had never been told.

"What happened?" he said aloud, as if the long-dead, long-buried woman could somehow hear him. "What really happened that night?"

A hot wind kicked up, rustling the leaves of the elm overhead and dancing patterns of light and shade across the eighteen-year-old tombstone. He could smell the ripening hay from a nearby field, hear the high, clear trill of a wren, feel the warmth of the sun on his face. And he realized that until now, he'd been thinking of this dead woman only in terms of the men in her life: her husband, the Count de Compans; Crispin Hayes, who had admired and desired her; and Nicholas Hayes, who'd been convicted of killing her. But once, he knew, she had been a living, breathing woman with her own hopes, fears, desires, and dreams.

Perhaps the answers he sought lay there, in her past.

## Chapter 30

℀ero spent the morning in Snow Hill, interviewing street musicians.

She spoke first to a cheerful blind man who imitated farm-animal sounds on a fiddle—everything from bulls and donkeys to dogs, peacocks, and roosters, all reproduced with an accuracy Hero found uncanny. He told her he used to play the violin at parties until he'd gone blind.

"The gentlefolk didn't like the look of my white, vacant eyes," he said, and then smiled. "I tried playing Mozart and Haydn on street corners, but that didn't answer too well. So I taught myself to do this." His grin widened. "Took me a while to perfect it, but folks do like it."

Farther up the street she found another blind man who simultaneously played the violin and the bells, a feat he managed by fixing the bells to a board with hammers and rigging up a system of wires and pedals he controlled with his toes. Each man had with him a young orphan he'd taken under his wing to serve as his guide and keep people from stealing the coins dropped in his cup. Hero asked the children if they had seen or heard of a boy who looked as if he might be part Chinese.

But first one lad, then the next looked at her blankly and said, "What's 'Chinese'?"

Frustrated, she moved to Cock Lane, where she talked to an old Italian barrel-organ grinder with a capuchin monkey. Dressed in a broad-brimmed felt hat with a jaunty red kerchief, the man played his organ while his monkey—clad in a red soldier's jacket and a Bonaparte hat—beat a drum and danced.

"I teach him with kindness, I do," said the old man, smiling as the monkey scrambled up onto his shoulder and gave a loud screech. "Only way to do it. I had a dog who dance too, and the monkey, he dance with the dog. Had that dog fifteen years." His voice broke. "But he die last winter, so now it's only Alessandro and me."

The old man had at least heard of China, but he hadn't seen any "Chinamen" since he'd been down near Portsmouth a decade or two ago when an East India Company ship wrecked along the coast. "Musta been a dozen or more of 'em washed ashore," he said. "But they was all dead."

Hero thanked him and started to hand the man his shillings for the interview, but he said, "No, give it to Alessandro." So she held the money out to the monkey, who screeched, then whipped off his hat and bowed.

It was when she was laughing at his response that Hero felt it—the powerful and unmistakable sense of being watched. She glanced quickly around, her breath catching, her gaze raking first the flagway's steady stream of passing tradesmen, apprentices, and shoppers, then the wagons, carriages, costermongers, and carts clogging the street. She couldn't see anyone who appeared to be paying her any heed. But as she continued up the street, talking first to a conjurer, then to a clown, the feeling of being stared at persisted.

Someone was watching her. And their interest in her was not friendly.

## Chapter 31

The Dowager Duchess of Claiborne was standing beside the counter of a fashionable Bond Street milliner when Sebastian pushed open the shop door with a jangle of bells.

Grandly dressed in an elegant gown of hyacinth-spotted silk with an intricately worked flounce, the Duchess had her eyes narrowed as she tried to decide between the rival merits of two caps: one with a fetching azure blue ribbon, the other ornamented with tasteful little tucks. At the sight of Sebastian, she drew her chin back against her chest and scowled. "Devlin. Good heavens. Whatever it is you want to know, I can't talk to you about it *here*."

He gave a soft laugh. "Am I so transparent?"

"In a word? Yes. Now, go away."

He leaned one hip against a nearby display cabinet and crossed his arms. "I can wait until you're finished."

"I can't decide which of these caps I want with you standing there."

"So buy them both. They're both lovely."

"They are, aren't they?" she agreed. She set them down and said to the clerk, "Both it is."

Leaving her abigail to supervise the wrapping of her purchases, Aunt Henrietta tucked her hand through the crook of Sebastian's arm as they left the shop and headed up Bond Street. "Right, then, what is it now?"

"I need you to tell me everything you know about Chantal de La-Rivière."

The Dowager gave him a speculative sideways glance. "What about her?"

"All I know is that she was young and beautiful, and she died. What was her background? Do you have any idea?"

"I believe she came from the lesser nobility or perhaps even the bourgeoisie. Her marriage to the Count de Compans was considered something of a coup. But then, she was very beautiful."

"That's all anyone ever says about her. 'She was beautiful.'"

"Well, she was. Enchantingly so."

"There must have been more to her than her looks."

Aunt Henrietta was silent for a moment, her eyes focused on something in the distance in a way that made him wonder what she was thinking. "Our society doesn't simply reward beauty in women," she said after a moment. "People act as if a woman's beauty is an outward manifestation of her inner goodness. As a result, there's a tendency to credit a beautiful woman with any number of positive characteristics that she may not, in fact, actually possess. Have you noticed? A beautiful woman—particularly if she's fair-haired—is automatically assumed to be sweet and gentle, loving and giving, innocent and good. At the same time, people tend to discount both her intelligence and her strength." Henrietta paused, then added, "And her potential for cunning."

"Somehow, I doubt you fall into the trap of that kind of thinking."

"Not often, perhaps. But I suspect I do sometimes. It's human nature, isn't it?"

"I suppose it is." He watched a pigeon flutter down to peck at some crumbs on the pavement. "So, what was Chantal like—*really* like—beneath her famous beauty?"

"It's difficult to say. She cultivated an aura of helplessness mixed with good-natured sweetness and one of those breathy little-girl voices that somehow make a woman seem simultaneously childlike and yet highly attractive to men in that way Claiborne is shocked to hear his mother talk about."

"But?" prompted Sebastian when she hesitated.

"I could be wrong, but I always suspected that beneath all the filmy white muslin and the wide, perfect smiles, she was shrewd, hard as granite, and utterly amoral."

"She was?"

"There, you see?" said his aunt. "You're shocked, aren't you? You've been picturing her as this gentle, innocent, tragic little thing, haven't you?"

"I suppose I have. What makes you think she wasn't?"

"A woman's intuition, mainly. But I also watched her work her wiles on several different men. She knew exactly what she was doing."

"Which men? Can you remember?"

"Crispin Hayes, for one. But there were others."

"Do you remember their names?"

Aunt Henrietta stared off down the street. "Hmmm. There was one young Scotsman in particular. I can't recall his name, but I remember wondering why she bothered with him. He was attractive, but not excessively so. And his father was nothing more than a Marine officer."

Sebastian drew up short. "You mean Hamish McHenry?"

"Ah, yes, that was his name. I don't know what became of him."

"He bought a pair of colors."

"Then that explains why he disappeared."

"Did you ever see the Countess 'work her wiles' on Nicholas Hayes?"

"No. Not that it would have done her any good. I told you, he had eyes only for Kate."

"Even after she married?"

"By the time she was married, Nicholas had been banished by his father."

Sebastian watched the pigeon take flight at the approach of a rumbling old landau. "I'm told Chantal de LaRivière left a child."

"Yes, Compans's heir."

"So he's still alive?"

"Last I heard. I believe he left for France with the Bourbons."

"And the Count de Compans never remarried?"

"No."

"Because he's still desperately in love with his dead wife?"

Aunt Henrietta sniffed. "To be honest, I don't know that he was ever in love with her. He was obviously proud of her beauty—saw her as reflecting well on him. And I believe he liked knowing that other men desired and coveted his wife. There's no doubt he now plays the part of the bereaved husband, although from what I understand it hasn't kept him from maintaining a string of mistresses over the years."

"In other words, Gilbert-Christophe de LaRivière is as much of a playactor as Chantal was. She played at being sweet and innocent, while he has now assumed the role of a bereaved widower forever in love with his murdered wife. So where lies the truth? I wonder."

The Dowager drew up at the corner and turned. "In my experience, the truth is generally the exact opposite of what such people would have you believe."

After leaving Bond Street, Sebastian paid another visit to Lower Sloan Street.

He found Mrs. McHenry alone in her parlor, tatting. "Oh dear," she said when a nervous young housemaid showed him in. "Hamish isn't here again. But you did find him yesterday, didn't you, my lord?"

"I'm afraid not." Sebastian was beginning to suspect Hamish McHenry had regretted stepping forward and was now trying to avoid him.

"Oh dear," she said again. "I think he's gone off to watch the barges on the river. The Regent is taking the Allied Sovereigns to Woolwich today, you know, for the launching of the *Enterprise*. Now that should be a grand sight. Hamish has always loved the tall ships."

"I'm surprised he bought a pair of colors rather than joining the Navy or the Marines like his father."

She leaned forward and lowered her voice as if imparting an embarrassing secret. "Well, to be honest, he gets frightfully seasick, you see. He's dreading this coming voyage to America." She settled back against the cushions. "Still enjoys seeing the ships, though. He was talking about going down to Woolwich for the launch, but I believe he decided simply to watch the barges from London Bridge." She glanced down at the watch she wore pinned to her shelflike bosom. "I suspect you could catch him there, if you hurried."

"Thank you," said Sebastian, pushing to his feet. "I believe I shall."

*Chapter 32*

The masses of spectators converging on the waterfront to gawk at the Allied Sovereigns' grand barge expedition were formidable. Finally forced to abandon his curricle and horses in Tom's care at the Strand, Sebastian worked his way through the jovial, laughing crowd toward the river. By the time he reached London Bridge, this stretch of the sun-spangled Thames was already filled with dozens of elegant barges rowed by uniformed watermen.

The barges carrying the Regent and his royal guests were the most opulently carved and gilded. But even those of the Admiralty and the Navy and the various city companies were impressive, draped with colorful bunting and silk flags that flew gaily in the warm breeze. All along both shores and crowding every bridge were masses of onlookers, cheering, waving their hats, and throwing flower petals.

It took Sebastian some time to push his way through the crowd to the center of the bridge, where a lean, trim man in Hessians and a military-cut coat was standing beside the stone balustrade, his gaze on the spectacle below.

"You're Hamish McHenry?" said Sebastian, walking up to him.

The man turned, his eyes widening in surprise. "I am. Who are you?"

"Devlin. My wife tells me you came to see me yesterday."

"I did, yes. But . . . how did you know to find me here?"

"Your mother."

"Ah." McHenry's eyes creased with what might have been a smile as he turned to look out over the flotilla of barges. "It's a grand sight, you must admit."

"That it is."

He kept his gaze on the river. "Did your wife tell you I was a friend of Crispin Hayes?"

"She did. She also said you never believed Nicholas killed Chantal de LaRivière."

A roar went up along the bridge and adjoining banks as the barge of the Czar of Russia and his sister came into view below, for the Duchess was a great favorite with the crowds. McHenry watched for a moment as the Duchess waved and smiled for her admirers. Sebastian had the impression he was choosing his words carefully. "Let me put it this way: I never believed it happened the way LaRivière claimed."

"Why not?"

The Scotsman brought up one closed fist to tap against his lips in the manner of a man considering his response . . . or perhaps regretting what he has already said. "It's difficult to explain, actually."

"Is it because you knew Nicholas?" suggested Sebastian. "Or because you knew Chantal de LaRivière?"

McHenry threw him a quick glance, then returned his gaze to the pageantry on the river. "Both, I suppose."

"What do you think happened?"

"Honestly? I think Nicholas went storming over there in a rage and got into a fight with LaRivière. Only, somehow or another, Chantal was the one who ended up dead."

"You don't believe Nicholas went there to rape her?"

"Good God, no. He was furious with her."

Sebastian watched the barge of the Ordinance Board shoot out from beneath the bridge, the oars of its liveried watermen throwing up cascades of water that glimmered like sheets of diamonds in the bright sunlight. "Anger and rape aren't necessarily mutually exclusive. Most people think men rape because they're overwhelmed by desire or uncontrolled lust. But from what I've seen, I'd say it's most often a tool of hate and punishment, or maybe a frustrated desire for control."

McHenry shook his head. "Nicholas wasn't like that. If the Count de Compans had accused him of walking in the door and simply shooting Chantal, I might have been able to believe it. But rape? No."

"Why was Nicholas so furious with her?"

McHenry was silent for a moment, the wind off the river ruffling his fair hair and flapping the tails of his coat. "Because he blamed her for Crispin's suicide."

"I've heard that Crispin Hayes was in love with Chantal. Is that true?"

"Oh yes. Desperately."

"So what makes you think Nicholas blamed her for his brother's death?"

"I know he did. Nicholas came to see me that day—the day after Crispin died."

"To tell you his brother's body had been found?"

"Not exactly. He was looking for answers. He said that right before he killed himself, Crispin had come to see him at that wretched inn where Nicholas was staying." McHenry paused, his face held tight. "The weather was horrible that night, with a howling wind and an endless hard rain like something you'd see in the tropics. Nicholas said Crispin was wild, saying all kinds of crazy things, most of which made no sense. But one of the things Crispin said was something to the effect that 'Hamish tried to warn me, but I didn't listen.'"

"Warn him about what?"

McHenry pressed his lips together and said nothing.

"Did you warn him that Chantal de Larivière was"—Sebastian

paused, searching for the right word, and finally settled on—"a coquette? That she'd been working her wiles on you too?"

A flare of surprise crossed the man's face. He turned to stare out over the river and after a moment gave a short, sharp nod.

"I take it Crispin didn't believe what you said about Chantal?"

"Not when I told him, no. He was furious with me for saying something like that about the woman he loved."

"So what happened to change his mind? It must have been rather drastic for the man to decide to kill himself over it."

McHenry let out a long, painful breath. "I honestly don't know."

Sebastian studied the major's sharp-boned profile, lit now by a pattern of dancing lights reflecting off the rough waters of the river below. "You didn't see Crispin that night—the night he died?"

"No. I hadn't seen him since I told him Chantal was playing with him—using him. Like I said, he was furious with me."

"How long between when you spoke to Nicholas and when he went to confront Chantal?"

"I don't know precisely, but it wasn't long."

"Did you tell the authorities about this?"

"Good God, no." The Scotsman looked genuinely shocked.

"Why not? Nicholas's life was at stake. He could easily have been hanged. As it was, they shipped him off to a living hell."

McHenry's hands curled around the balustrade before him. "Nicholas begged me not to. He didn't want it known that Crispin had killed himself, and the Earl was convinced that if Nicholas was convicted of anything, it would be manslaughter. Not murder."

"That's why Nicholas claimed he and the Count were arguing, but refused to say what the argument was about? Because he was protecting his dead brother?"

"Yes."

"Noble young fool," said Sebastian, half to himself. "And Compans refused to acknowledge the argument because he didn't want to admit his wife had a habit of playing the coquette."

"Yes."

Sebastian turned to look out over the sun-sparkled river. The barges had all come out from beneath the bridge now and were slowly making their regal way down the river. The music from the barge carrying a German band floated back to them on the gusting breeze. After a moment, he said, "Who do you think killed Nicholas Hayes?"

McHenry's nostrils had taken on an odd, pinched look. "When I went to see Nicholas in prison after he was arrested, he told me his cousin, Ethan—now the Earl of Seaforth—was the one who betrayed him."

"I know."

"So maybe Seaforth killed him."

"Is he capable of such a thing, do you think?"

"Seaforth? I don't know if he's capable of personally stabbing someone in the back, but I can easily imagine him hiring someone to do it for him. He's always been a sneaky son of a bitch."

"How well do you know him?"

"Not terribly well, but enough to know that. I mean, he used the authorities to try to kill Nicholas eighteen years ago, didn't he?"

"He did. So why would Seaforth hire someone to kill Nicholas now? If Seaforth knew Nicholas Hayes was back in London, why not simply inform on him and let the Crown hang him? Why go through all the bother and expense of hiring someone to murder him?"

"That I can't answer. Except that some people looked askance at Ethan eighteen years ago for informing on his cousin. If it came out that he'd done it again, and with both Lucas and the old Earl now dead? Everyone would be saying he did it the first time to get his hands on the title and the estates and then did it again to make certain he was able to keep what wasn't rightfully his. He'd be blackballed from society forever, wouldn't he? Well, wouldn't he?"

"Probably," said Sebastian. The barges were growing smaller and smaller in the distance, the men, women, and children on the bridge talking excitedly and laughing and calling to one another as the crowd began to disperse. Sebastian brought his gaze back to the man beside him. "Tell me this: Did you lie with the Countess de Compans?"

A betraying line of color rode high on the major's cheeks. "And if I did?"

"Did Crispin, do you think?"

McHenry hesitated a moment, then nodded.

"What if Crispin didn't actually throw himself into the Thames that stormy night? What if Compans pushed him?"

"He wouldn't," McHenry said quickly.

"Why not? Crispin was cuckolding him."

"Compans didn't care."

"That's a bit difficult to believe."

"They were . . . a strange couple. I could never understand them."

"If LaRivière didn't care, then why the fight with Nicholas Hayes?"

The major turned his face away to gaze down at the now-empty river, his throat working as he swallowed. "I don't know. I can't explain exactly what happened that night. All I know is that it didn't play out the way LaRivière claimed. And if you want to find out who killed Nicholas, I suspect you need to remember that."

## Chapter 33

*J*i watched the barges from a wharf near the grim, looming fortress Hayes had called the Tower of London.

The River Thames was a wonder to Ji. The waterways and canals of Canton were filled with vessels of every description—junks, chop boats, sampans, coffin boats, leper boats, and endless houseboats jammed one next to the other and occupied by people who lived their entire lives on water. Ji still found it amazing that there were no houseboats clogging this river.

But today's parade of carved, gilded barges with their flapping silk banners and rich carpets felt familiar to Ji—an ostentatious display of wealth and privilege that seemed expressly designed to emphasize the existence of a gulf much wider than the expanse of mere water that separated these special beings from the ragged, hungry crowds who cheered them from every bridge and wharf.

Ji had played the bamboo flute for the first time that morning. It was a form of begging, really, and that knowledge had brought feelings of great shame. But the battered old tin cup Ji had bought from a street stall filled quickly—too quickly, for the lilting, haunting music was so strange to English ears that it drew a great deal of attention. And too much attention could be deadly.

Ji would need to be careful, playing the flute just enough to buy a safe place to sleep at night and keep from going hungry, but not so much as to attract the man Poole.

Poole and whatever dangerous enemy had hired him.

## Chapter 34

*I* think he's hiding something," said Sebastian later that afternoon as he and Hero walked the shady gravel paths of Grosvenor Square with Simon.

Hero looked over at him in surprise. "Major McHenry? What could he possibly be hiding?"

"I don't know. But the story he tells doesn't quite hang together."

She was silent for a moment, obviously considering this. "You didn't even know the man existed until he came to Brook Street yesterday. Why would he seek you out, only to lie to you?"

Sebastian smiled as he watched Simon hunker down to study a pretty pebble in the gravel that caught his eye. "You have a point there."

"Perhaps what you sensed was his embarrassment over having lain with another man's wife."

"Perhaps. There's no denying it's an ugly tale. What do you think happened to cause Crispin Hayes to throw himself into the Thames that night?"

Hero reached out to catch Simon's hand before he could put the rock in his mouth. "Presumably he discovered the lovely Chantal de LaRivière was trifling with him."

"Would that be enough, you think?"

"For some men. Although I suppose it's also possible the Count de Compans gave Crispin a little push into the water."

Simon started to fuss at the sudden loss of his rock, and Sebastian swung the boy up onto his hip. "I feel like I'm missing something. Something that should be obvious."

"Only one thing?"

He huffed a laugh. "Multiple things." Shifting Simon's weight, he reached into his pocket to draw out the folded page from the *Morning Post* he'd found in Nicholas Hayes's room at the Red Lion. "When I first saw this, I immediately focused on the Count de Compans's name. My assumption at the time was that Hayes kept the page so he'd have Compans's address. But the Count told me he's still living in the same house where Chantal was killed, which means Nicholas already knew exactly where to find him."

Hero reached to take the page. "So why did Nicholas save it?"

"Look at the June second entry under 'Fashionable Arrangements for the Week.'"

"'Lady Forbes's rout, St. James's Square,'" Hero read, then glanced up. "Good heavens."

Sebastian nodded. "I skimmed right over it at first because I didn't know about Hayes's connection to Lady Forbes."

"Do you think he approached her?"

"Possibly. Although it's also possible he simply couldn't resist trying to catch a glimpse of her from afar."

A faint breeze had come up, and Hero was silent for a moment, watching the limbs of the trees shift against the hard blue sky. "What a tragedy it all was."

Sebastian nodded. "What I find particularly interesting is that when I arrived at Carlton House on the night of Nicholas's murder, I found Seaforth talking to Sir Lindsey Forbes. It meant nothing to me at the time. But then this morning, when Seaforth walked into the Swan for the inquest, the first person he paused to speak to was, once again, Forbes. That strikes me as an unlikely coincidence."

"It does, doesn't it? What could possibly be the connection between the two men?"

"I don't know. But I intend to find out." Simon began to squirm to get down, his tears forgotten. Sebastian set the boy back on his feet, then looked up at Hero. "Care to go to tonight's ball for the Allied Sovereigns?"

"I can't believe they're having a ball tonight on top of everything else."

"Yet they are. And I suspect both LaRivière and Forbes will be there."

That evening's event in honor of the visiting Allied Sovereigns was being hosted by the Earl of Cholmondeley. After sailing to Deptford and back that day, the visiting dignitaries had attended a formal dinner given by the Marquis of Stafford.

They were scheduled to leave for Oxford at six the next morning.

"Who do you think will collapse first?" asked Hero as they worked their way around the outer edges of Cholmondeley's hopelessly overstuffed ballroom. The Allied Sovereigns had been guests of honor at a week's worth of levees, dinners, balls, drawing rooms, banquets, and more, and yet fashionable London was still as anxious as ever for glimpses of the celebrated war heroes and assorted monarchs. "Prinny? King William? Or old Blücher?"

"Definitely not Blücher," said Sebastian as they watched the bewhiskered septuagenarian field marshal stomp down the line of a country dance with a pretty girl on his arm. "He's an old warhorse."

"I suspect you're right." She watched Blücher laugh and give his young partner's hand a squeeze. "Why on earth are they going to Oxford?"

"Honorary degrees."

"Seriously?"

"Seriously." He let his gaze drift over the perspiring, bejeweled crowd. "I don't see Forbes."

"There," said Hero, deliberately looking away. "By the orchestra, in conversation with Lady Jersey." She paused. "Do you even know him?"

"Vaguely."

"How precisely does one go about accosting a man in the middle of a ball in order to discuss the murder of someone who once ran off with his wife?"

"I don't know," said Sebastian. "But I'll think of something."

Sir Lindsey Forbes was turning away from Lady Jersey when Sebastian walked up to him and said cheerfully, "Ah, there you are."

Forbes stared at him. "Are you addressing me?"

"I am." Sebastian squinted up at the vast chandelier hanging over their heads. "Between the hundreds of hot candles and at least an equal number of hot guests, it's rather close in here, wouldn't you say? Shall we continue this conversation outside?"

"We're not having a conversation," said Forbes, and kept walking.

"Or," said Sebastian, raising his voice ever so slightly, "if you prefer, I could follow you across the ballroom, shouting my questions as we go. No doubt the Earl's guests would enjoy some of the revelations that might entail."

Forbes pivoted slowly to face him. The light from the endless blazing candles lent a soft shimmer to his carefully combed silver hair and surprisingly smooth, unlined face. But his eyes were narrowed and hard, his tight lips curled into something that was not a smile. "You bastard."

"The choice is yours."

Without another word, Forbes strode to the row of French doors overlooking the terraced gardens and thrust one open. Sebastian followed.

The night was hot and sultry, but after the stifling ballroom, the fresh air felt like a blessed relief. The wind that had come up that afternoon was even stronger now, thrashing the branches of the elms in the

Earl of Cholmondeley's gardens and banging a loose tile somewhere in the distance. His lordship had decked his garden with colorful little Chinese lanterns, but at least half of them had been blown out, while those that remained lit were dancing about chaotically, their feeble light seeming to accentuate rather than alleviate the dark, unwelcoming shadows of the wind-tossed trees.

"What the devil is this about?" demanded Forbes, walking to the end of the deserted terrace before turning to face him.

Sebastian went to stand some feet away from him, his gaze on the lanterns dancing in the wind. "Did you know Nicholas Hayes had returned to England? Before he was found dead, I mean."

"Of course not." It was said with just the exact touch of scorn and righteous indignation.

"You're certain?"

"Of course I'm certain. I'll have you know I'm a religious man, and I take our Lord's injunctions on honesty very seriously. Very seriously indeed."

"Oh? So what does your Lord say about carelessly starving to death a million or so wretchedly poor Indian peasants? Or can those injunctions be safely ignored?"

Forbes's nostrils flared. "I don't have to stay for this."

He started to turn toward the ballroom doors, but Sebastian stopped him by saying, "Just a few more questions."

Forbes swung about. "What?"

The air between them was palpably vibrating with the dangerous undercurrents of everything left unsaid—about Nicholas Hayes's elopement with the woman who was now Forbes's wife; about the hasty marriage that had surely been forced on young Kate Brownbeck by her father. But even Sebastian found himself shying away from addressing those issues directly.

He said instead, "How well do you know the Earl of Seaforth?"

"Seaforth? Well enough. Why do you ask?"

"Did you know his cousin Nicholas? Eighteen years ago, I mean."

"Goodness gracious, no. Why would I? By all reports the fellow was an incorrigible rogue. I really don't see why—"

"Are you familiar with a man named Titus Poole?"

Forbes's expression remained completely under his control, his face bland and pale in the wind-tossed moonlight. But Sebastian knew he was considering denying it. Knew too when Forbes realized such a denial could potentially be a mistake. "The company has used the fellow a time or two to retrieve stolen property. Why do you ask?"

"Because he was seen following Nicholas Hayes several days before he died, and it's been suggested someone might have hired him to kill Hayes."

"I don't see why you think that might have anything to do with me."

"Really? You don't?"

Forbes brought up one hand to stab the air between them with a pointed finger as he carefully enunciated each word. "You. Be. Careful."

"Just one more question," said Sebastian as the man started to leave again.

"What now?" The tone was one of annoyed exasperation, of a busy, important man humoring an irritating imposition.

Sebastian drew Nicholas Hayes's strange bronze disk from his pocket and held it out in the palm of his hand. "Do you have any idea what this is?"

Forbes gave the piece a quick, dismissive glance. "It looks like it's from those Turkish baths in Portman Square. Why do you ask? What has it to do with anything?"

"Perhaps nothing," said Sebastian, and closed his fist around the token.

Sebastian was working his way toward where he could see the Count de Compans near the ballroom entrance when the Prince Regent's powerful cousin stepped in front of him.

"What are you doing here?" demanded Jarvis.

Sebastian met his father-in-law's hard stare. "I was invited."

"You never come to these things."

Sebastian glanced over to where the French Count had paused to greet some acquaintance. "I do on occasion."

Jarvis followed Sebastian's gaze, his gray eyes narrowing. "I want you to leave Compans alone."

"Why?"

"What do you mean, *Why?* The man is currently acting as the representative of the King of France. These royal visits and all the pomp and celebration surrounding them are not intended simply to flatter the vanity of the Prince Regent, you know. They are serving a very real and critical purpose, and that is to solidify for the future a network of vitally important alliances. Our current alliances may have prevailed against Napoléon, but they are nevertheless fragile and vulnerable. Do you have any idea of the havoc you would wreak by casting an ominous cloud of suspicion over one of the pivotal men involved in reconstructing the old order?"

"You're suggesting the fate of the world rests on my not pursuing whoever is responsible for sinking a sickle into Nicholas Hayes's back?"

Jarvis's lower lip curled. "No one cares who killed Nicholas Hayes. If the authorities had managed to get their hands on the scoundrel, he'd have been hanged as fast as they could tie a rope around his neck."

"Undoubtedly. So did you never wonder why whoever killed him didn't use that option as the easiest means of dispatching the man?"

"No. Nor have I any intention of wasting my time ruminating on such sordid matters. The war may be over, but the peace is only beginning and it's delicate. If you want to go chasing after some sickle-wielding madman, then do so, by all means. But leave Gilbert-Christophe de LaRivière out of it."

"I'll be certain to give your preferences in the matter all the respect they deserve," said Sebastian, turning toward the door.

Jarvis put out a hand, stopping him. "I'm serious."

Sebastian studied his father-in-law's angry, set face. "So am I."

Jarvis let his hand fall. "As you wish. You've been warned." He turned and walked away.

Sebastian glanced again toward the ballroom entrance.

The Count de Compans was gone.

*Chapter 35*

$\mathcal{T}$'m beginning to suspect that Nicholas Hayes came back to England to kill all four of them," said Hero as their carriage rolled through the dimly lit streets of Mayfair toward home. "Seaforth, Compans, Brownbeck, and Forbes. And I can't say I'd blame him if he had."

Sebastian looked over at her and smiled. "To be honest, neither would I."

She fell silent, her gaze on the dark shops flashing past. Sebastian watched the light from the swaying carriage lamps limn her cheek with a soft golden glow, and knew what she was thinking. Reaching out, he took her hand.

She said, "It's been four days now. Where could that little boy be?"

"It's possible he—"

Sebastian broke off as the seat back between them exploded in flying fragments of cloth and stuffing, and the crack of a rifle shot cut through the night.

"Get down!" he shouted, pulling Hero to the floorboards. He caught her face between his hands. "Are you all right?"

"Yes. But what—"

"Stay down!"

The coachman was cursing, trying to rein in the plunging horses as Sebastian thrust open the carriage door and rolled out to hit the ground running. "Get the carriage out of here! Now!" he shouted as he darted toward the yawning black mouth of the alley from which he estimated the shot had come.

The night was wild, the hot wind sending bits of paper scuttling down the street and whipping at the tails of Sebastian's dress coat as he ran. A well-trained rifleman could typically fire three rounds a minute, maybe four. That kind of expertise was rare, but Sebastian was still counting the seconds as coachman John whipped up his horses and the carriage disappeared into the night with a rattle and clatter.

Sebastian had almost reached the alley when the night exploded again in fire and acrid smoke.

Eighteen seconds.

"Bloody hell," he swore, the knees of his elegant breeches sliding through rotten cabbage leaves as he dove behind a pile of overflowing, battered dust bins. He heard running footsteps that stopped abruptly, and knew that the shooter had relocated to a position farther up the alley.

*Eighteen seconds.* Either his assailant had brought two rifles, or Sebastian was dealing with an expert shooter.

Or he was facing more than one rifleman.

It was this latter possibility that kept Sebastian hunkered down behind the dust bins. One man could shoot and then reload while his partner took another shot. In which case confidently counting to eighteen could get Sebastian killed.

He was aware of the sweat rolling down his cheeks, his breath coming in quick pants, his throat so parched that the darkness of the night and the pungent stench of drifting gun smoke sent him hurtling back to another time, another place . . . a place of sun-blasted, dry mesas and sandstone villages that had already been old by the time of the Crusades. A distant rumble of thunder became the *boom* of cannons, the howl of a tomcat the cry of a frightened Spanish child, the enemy in the alley before him a foe he had battled a thousand nights in his dreams.

Drawing a steadying breath, he listened carefully, his gaze raking the shadows. The night might have been dark and alive with the wind, but Sebastian's senses were abnormally acute. One man, he decided— there, at the far end of the alley near some broken crates.

One man. Maybe two rifles, but Sebastian doubted it.

Wishing he had his boots and the knife he kept sheathed in one of them, Sebastian shifted his position and gave one of the dust bins a heave. It rolled out into the alley with a satisfying rattle and crash that flung rubbish in a wide arc and set a nearby dog to barking.

The rifleman obligingly, foolishly, fired again. Pushing up with a smile, Sebastian charged.

He saw the man rise from his position, the lower half of his face obscured by some kind of cloth, his eyes widening as he realized the hunter had suddenly become the hunted. Then the man turned and ran, his rifle hitting the paving stones with a clatter as he threw it away to lighten his load.

Sebastian knew an almost overwhelming urge to go after him. But the man had a good hundred-foot lead on him, and the possibility of a partner waiting somewhere out of sight remained.

Sebastian drew up just before the end of the alley, swallowed the strong, primitive need to give chase, and turned to pick up the abandoned rifle.

Then he went home to his wife and infant son.

That night Sebastian dreamt of a storm-tossed sky and of the pitiful wail of an infant lost somewhere in the howling darkness.

He ran through a desolate landscape shrouded by a wild, tempest-riven night, searching frantically, finding nothing. Then a tall, ancient wall built of crude sandstone blocks rose up before him, stopping him. He turned to say something to Hero, but she had vanished. She had been there, beside him. He was certain she'd been beside him. Now she was gone

"Hero?" he cried. But the wind snatched away his voice as if it had never been. Then the wailing of the child receded into the distance, and he heard his wife scream.

*"Hero!"*

He awoke with a jerk, his heart pounding in his chest and his mouth dry. Turning his head, he saw Hero lying awake beside him, her eyes wide and still in the darkness.

"Bad dream?" she said.

He reached for her, pulling her to him. She came hotly into his arms, her mouth opening to his as his head came up off the pillow seeking her hungrily. She slid on top of him, her thighs straddling his hips, her naked breasts heavy against his chest. He ran his hands up and down her back, finding solace in the solid warmth of her bare flesh beneath his touch.

"I lost you," he said. "You and Simon both. You were there, and then you were gone."

She took his face between her hands, her breath warm and soft against him as she gazed solemnly into his eyes. And he felt his love for this woman swell within him so powerful and frightening that it hurt.

"It was a dream," she said, and kissed him again.

Her lips were soft and tender, her hands seeking, her body opening itself to him. They moved as one, slowly at first, then quickening, lost in the heat of their passion and their need. He found himself swirled away, surrendering to the joy of the moment and the ultimate rapture of release. Then she smiled, murmuring, *"I love you. I love you, I love you,"* and he held her tight against him.

But the lingering whispers of that all-consuming fear remained.

*Tuesday,* 14 *June*

"You seem to have hit a nerve with someone," said Sir Henry Lovejoy the next morning as they walked through the crowded piazza of Covent Garden. "Any idea as to your assailant's identity?"

"None whatsoever." Sebastian gazed out over the colorful, bustling, brawling, shouting crowd of the marketplace. "The rifle was a common enough one, and I'm fairly confident the actual shooter was only a hireling. I've never known a man who could get off two shots in less than twenty seconds who wasn't a rifleman at some point. And even then it's rare."

"Ah. Goodness knows there are more and more ex-soldiers flooding into London every day, most of them desperate for work." Lovejoy paused, his face even more serious than usual.

"What?" said Sebastian, watching him.

"I heard the other day that Titus Poole has been going around bragging about hiring ex-soldiers. Seems he has ambitions of expanding his operation into something similar to the Bow Street Runners, only private. Those who are becoming increasingly frustrated by Britain's lack of a proper police force are actively encouraging him—despite his past history."

"Huh. Sounds like something Theo Brownbeck would support. I wonder if they know each other."

"Surely not."

Sebastian watched a ragged little girl steal an apple from a stall, and said, "I think I need to have another talk with Mr. Poole."

Titus Poole was behind the bar in the taproom of his wife's inn when Sebastian walked up and ordered a pint.

Poole pressed both hands flat on the polished surface of the bar and leaned into them, his small, nasty eyes narrowed in pugnacious hostility. "Ye ain't welcome here."

"No?" Sebastian gave the man a smile that showed his teeth. "Then let's drop all pretense of civility and simply have a frank, straightforward conversation, shall we? Word is, you've recently hired yourself an ex-soldier or two."

Poole's jaw tightened. "Ye got a problem with that?"

"On the contrary, I find it commendable. Any of those ex-soldiers happen to be a rifleman?"

"Why ye askin'?"

"Because someone took a shot at my carriage last night. Someone who's obviously very good at what he does."

Poole smiled, revealing tobacco-stained teeth and a half-masticated plug. "Scared ye, did he?"

"He nearly hit my wife."

"Ah. Now that woulda been a real shame."

Sebastian felt the skin of his face tighten, the blood pounding in his neck. "Let me make myself perfectly clear: If anyone harms, threatens, follows, watches, or even comes anywhere near my wife again, I'll hold you responsible. And you won't live long enough to hang—you or whoever is paying you."

Poole's color was high, his big head thrown back, his nostrils flaring. "Ye can't talk to me like that."

Sebastian adjusted the tilt of his hat. "You're lucky I didn't kill you." And then he turned and left before the urge to do this man damage became overwhelming.

*Chapter 36*

*T*he painted wooden sign outside Mahmoud Abbasi's Turkish Baths in Portman Square was small and discreet, but Sebastian knew he must have seen it several times, at least. Just below the proudly emblazoned name of the establishment, it depicted the same ancient stone building as Hayes's bronze token. And yet somehow Sebastian hadn't made the connection.

The baths had been open for business some six months. Prior to that, Mr. Abbasi had run the Hindu Kush Coffeehouse in George Street, serving a variety of curries and other authentic Indian dishes as well as providing hookahs and chilam tobacco. That establishment had not done well. Curries might have been popular with men who'd served in India with the British Army and the East India Company, but the taste was simply too exotic for most Londoners. And so Abbasi had closed his coffeehouse and opened the baths, which provided a hot room, a "shampooing" or massage room, a plunge bath, and a cooling and rest room.

Sebastian wondered if this venture was doing any better than the last.

He found the bathhouse's foyer decorated in an ostentatiously Eastern theme, with lots of red silk and shiny brass and colorful mosaics. At his entrance, a man who looked like he'd be more at home in the craggy, snow-covered mountains of the Hindu Kush came from behind the counter and bowed. "May I help you?" He was tall and wiry, with a dark complexion, thick black hair, and merry black eyes. In age he could have been anywhere between thirty-five and fifty-five, with even white teeth that flashed in a wide smile.

The smile slipped when Sebastian laid the small bronze token on the countertop beside them and said, "This was in Nicholas Hayes's pocket when he was found murdered up in Somer's Town last Thursday."

Abbasi held himself very still, in the manner of a man who senses danger but is as yet unsure of its nature. A silent, watchful boy of perhaps eight or nine came to stand in a nearby curtained doorway. His resemblance to Abbasi was unmistakable, but he was so much fairer than his father that Sebastian suspected the child must have an English mother.

When Abbasi remained silent, Sebastian said, "I'm not with Bow Street, if that's what's worrying you. The name is Devlin, and my only interest is in finding out who killed Hayes."

One corner of the man's mouth quirked up as if with an irrepressible bubble of amusement. "I must admit, you don't look like anyone from Bow Street I've ever seen. In fact, you remind me of a cavalry captain I once knew. He was with the Nineteenth Light Dragoons."

Sebastian found himself smiling in return. "I was with the Twenty-fifth. How could you tell?"

"I was a lieutenant with the East India Company. Long ago."

"Not so long ago, surely."

Abbasi laughed. "Long enough that I feel each old wound whenever a cold wind blows off the North Sea." The amusement faded. "What is your interest in Nicholas?"

*Nicholas*, Sebastian noticed, not *Hayes*. "They say we owe the living respect, but the dead deserve the truth."

Abbasi nodded, then quoted in perfect French, "'*On doit des égards aux vivants, on ne doit aux morts que la vérité.'"* He glanced over at the half-grown boy who still hovered in the curtained doorway. "Take over for me, Baba."

He led Sebastian to a small room covered from floor to ceiling with colorful Moroccan tiles and furnished with thick Persian carpets and piles of pillows. A shy, pretty little girl with black hair and huge brown eyes brought them thick Middle Eastern coffee as they sat cross-legged on the floor and talked of things common to military men all over the world, of brutal forced marches and the horses they'd known and fighting men they admired. Then Abbasi lit a hubble-bubble and said, "When I left the East India Company, I spent several years in Canton. It was there I came to know Nicholas."

Sebastian drew the cool, fragrant smoke deep into his lungs. "How long ago was this?"

"I left nine—no, almost ten years ago now."

"What was he like? I mean as a man."

Abbasi sucked on the hubble-bubble, his eyes narrowing against the smoke. "You've heard of his time in Botany Bay?"

"Some of it."

Abbasi nodded. "He was a man who had once been a certain way—a gentleman's son, heedless and gay and thinking little of tomorrow. Then he went through the worst kind of hell, and when he came out on the other side of it, he was inevitably . . . changed. Shattered. Hollowed out. But fate gave him a chance to remake himself into something else entirely, and so he did."

Sebastian found himself thinking about the worn prayer beads he'd seen in Hayes's room at the Red Lion. "He became a Buddhist?"

"He never called himself one. But he befriended a man who'd been a monk in Tibet and who taught him many things. I think you could say he eventually found a measure of peace."

"So why come back here, to England?"

"He said he had his reasons. I didn't ask what they were."

Abbasi's open acknowledgment of their recent meeting was unexpectedly frank. Sebastian said, "When exactly did you see him?"

"Last week sometime. Perhaps two or three days before he died."

"Here?"

Abbasi nodded. "We ate kofta and rice. Smoked the hubble-bubble. Talked of old times. I showed him that example of the tokens I'm planning to have made, and he said I should put the bath's name and address on the back rather than have both sides the same. I laughed, said he was right, and gave it to him as a souvenir."

"Was the boy with him?"

Abbasi looked puzzled. "What boy?"

"Hayes brought a boy of eight or nine with him from China. His name is Ji."

"No, he came here alone." Abbasi leaned back against his pile of pillows. "When I knew Nicholas in Canton, he had a little girl. But she would be older now—as much as twelve or thirteen. He made no mention of her, and I assumed she must have died."

Sebastian thought about the miniature painting of the young woman he'd seen at the Red Lion. "Did you know the little girl's mother?"

"No. She died before I ever met Nicholas."

"Who was she?"

"He told me she'd been a bondmaid, sold into slavery when her father fell out of favor with the Emperor and was executed. Her owner was getting ready to give her to some old man as a concubine, and Hayes offered double what the man was going to pay for her. He said once that his love for her was the only thing that got him through that first year after Botany Bay—that and her love for him. And then she died in childbirth."

"Was there another woman after her?"

"Not that I'm aware of. Although to be honest, I'm not certain the woman he told me about was his child's mother. I may simply have assumed it."

Sebastian was silent for a moment, overwhelmed by the relentless tragedy of Nicholas Hayes's life. He said, "I was under the impression foreigners aren't welcome in China."

"They're not. They're confined to their own quarter outside Canton and officially forbidden to set foot within the city walls. But exceptions are sometimes made."

"And exceptions were made for Hayes?"

"To a certain extent. I don't know how it came about, but he was quite close to one of the Hong merchants there, a fellow by the name of Chen Shouguan." He paused. "How much do you know about Canton?"

"Not much," Sebastian admitted.

Abbasi nodded. "The Hong merchants are the only ones permitted by the Emperor to trade with foreigners, and they are required to deal with the Westerners through one of five officially licensed linguists. All the linguists are Chinese, and despite being called 'linguists,' they don't actually speak English, just pidgin English. Most of the merchants don't really care. It's the linguists who negotiate terms with the foreigners and keep track of all the duties and fees required of their ships, so the emphasis is on their skills at negotiating and making deals rather than on their language abilities."

"But Chen was different?"

"Very. He wanted someone who could listen to the foreigners talk amongst themselves and know exactly what they were saying. That and understand how Europeans think."

"Wise man," said Sebastian. "Maybe that's why Hayes left China. Maybe something happened to Chen?"

Abbasi shook his head. "I asked Nicholas how the tough old bastard was doing, and he said Chen had just bought a new concubine. The man must be at least eighty."

"Charming."

Abbasi's teeth flashed in a grin. "It's a different world."

"So I'm told," said Sebastian. "Could Hayes speak Chinese?"

"He could, yes. It's forbidden by Imperial decree for foreigners to learn the Chinese languages, but . . ." He shrugged. "There are always exceptions. Nicholas learned both Mandarin and Cantonese."

"Impressive."

"He was a smart man. Very smart."

"I'm surprised he wasn't worried one of the Englishmen he interacted with in Canton might recognize him."

"But that's just it: He didn't interact with them directly. The official linguists were the ones who handled the actual negotiations. Nicholas's role was more to quietly watch and listen from the sidelines. Plus, he wore a thick, full beard." Abbasi's teeth flashed in a smile. "When he walked into my baths last week all cleanly shaven, I didn't recognize him until he spoke."

Abbasi paused, a frown creasing his forehead.

"What?" asked Sebastian, watching him.

"I take that back. There actually was one fellow who recognized him. It happened shortly before I left. Nicholas ran into him by chance in Macau."

"What was the man's name? Do you know?"

"Sorry. All I remember is that he was with the East India Company. Nicholas hated British East India Company men—myself excepted, of course." Abbasi flashed another smile. "He hated the British in general because of what His Majesty's own had done to him in Botany Bay, and he hated the company specifically because it is behind most of the opium being smuggled into China." Abbasi blew out a long stream of fragrant smoke. "I'm told that not long ago, the Chinese used opium the way we do, for pain. But now they've taken to smoking it the way we smoke tobacco, and it's become a big problem. The emperors forbade its importation, so the East India Company switched to smuggling it."

"Is the smuggling that hard to stop?"

"The thing is, the eradication of smuggling is the responsibility of the Hoppas—the customs superintendents. They're the same officials who collect the duties and fees in the port. And it's the opium smuggling that earns the East India Company the silver they then turn around and use to buy Chinese goods. So the Hoppas are afraid that if they crack down too hard on the opium smuggling, they'll see a corresponding fall in the revenues they send to the Imperial Court in Beijing. Obviously, that would impact their own income. And it also wouldn't be good for their necks." Abbasi illustrated the point by slashing a knifelike hand across his throat with a grimace.

"So one of the East India Company men recognized Hayes?"

"Not exactly. Nicholas recognized him. The first time he saw the man, we were on the streets of Macau." Abbasi paused. "Nicholas told me once that he was different when he was younger—impulsive and quick to anger. But the Nicholas I knew was one of the calmest, most controlled people I've met outside of a monastery. And yet the sight of that East India Company man drove him wild. I managed to hold him back then. But when we ran into the same man two days later on the waterfront . . ." Abbasi's voice trailed away, and he shook his head.

"What happened?"

"Nicholas got the fellow down on the dock and was slamming his head against the boards. And all the while he was doing it, he was screaming, 'You killed her. The two of you, you killed my baby.'"

*You killed my baby.* Sebastian felt the possibilities suggested by those words settle like an ache in his gut. "How did it end?"

"Some of the sailors from the East India Company ship ran up and pulled Nicholas off the man. But they didn't dare do anything to Nicholas because of Chen, so they let him go."

"You think the man recognized Nicholas?"

"He must have, because he kept shouting, 'I didn't kill the thing. It died.'" Abbasi paused, something that was not a smile curling his lips. "The 'thing.'"

"Did Hayes ever tell you what it was all about?"

Abbasi shook his head. "He simply apologized for losing control.

But over the years that I knew him, he said other things that led me to think that before he left England he'd been in love with a woman who had his child, only the child later died. I never knew how the East India Company man was connected to it all."

"Do you remember what the man looked like?" asked Sebastian, although he thought he already knew the answer.

Abbasi took a long pull on the hubble-bubble, then let the smoke stream out before answering, "I do, yes, because he was so unusual. He was still a fairly young man with a smooth, unlined face. But his hair was completely silver."

*Chapter 37*

The headquarters of the East India Company lay in Leadenhall Street, in the City of London. An early-eighteenth-century structure known as East India House, it had recently been remodeled and expanded. Boasting a classical facade with giant Doric pilasters and an elaborate frieze, the place was massive, with multiple meeting rooms, Directors' offices, an auction hall, and endless committee rooms as well as a courtyard and gardens. Over the years, the East India Company had also taken over most of the surrounding buildings, tearing them down and replacing them with endless rows of huge brick warehouses that virtually blocked out the sun.

Sir Lindsey Forbes was crossing the headquarters' ornate marble-clad vestibule when Sebastian fell into step beside him and said, "You didn't tell me you once had a nasty encounter with Nicholas Hayes on the waterfront of Macau."

Forbes's step faltered for only an instant before he resumed his previous pace. "I don't know what you're talking about."

"Yes, you do. He beat your head against the dock and accused you of killing his baby."

"The man was mad."

"So you admit the incident occurred."

Forbes drew up abruptly and swung to face Sebastian, his voice a low hiss. "What bloody difference does it make to anything?"

"It means you knew Hayes was alive. That he hadn't died in Botany Bay the way everyone thought."

"That doesn't mean I knew he'd returned to England."

Sebastian studied the older man's handsome, surprisingly ageless face. "Did you tell your wife? That Hayes was alive and living in China, I mean."

Angry color stained the East India Company Director's cheeks. "You leave my wife out of this. Do you hear?"

"Then tell me about the child."

Without a word, Forbes slammed open one of the building's ornate front doors and walked outside.

Sebastian kept pace with him as he turned down the narrow cobbled lane toward the river, the company's vast brick warehouses looming around them. "The sums are rather simple to do," said Sebastian, "even with the limited information available. Chantal de LaRivière was killed in April of 1796, six months after the late Earl of Seaforth flew into a rage over his youngest son's elopement and cut him off without a penny. That means the elopement took place around September or October of 1795. If, as now seems likely, an unborn child was the reason for that hasty bolt to the border, then the baby would have been born—when? April? May?"

Forbes pressed his lips together and kept walking.

"What happened to the little girl? It was a girl, was it not?" When the man remained silent, Sebastian said, "According to Nicholas Hayes, you killed her."

Forbes drew up again and cast a quick look at the surrounding warehouses before saying with low, careful insistence, "I did not kill it."

"Her. Not 'it.' *Her.* And if you didn't kill the child, then who did?"

"No one did. Brownbeck gave the baby to a woman to nurse, and it died. These things happen."

"How did Hayes find out about the child's death?"

"I haven't the slightest idea. But given that the convict ship didn't leave for Botany Bay until the end of the year, someone obviously told him."

"When did the baby die?"

Forbes looked vaguely stunned by the question. "You seriously think I remember?"

"No, of course not."

The angry color deepened in the man's face, but he simply turned and started walking again.

Sebastian said, "You realize what this means, don't you?"

"No, but I have no doubt you've every intention of telling me. So let's humor you, shall we? What does it mean?"

"It means Nicholas Hayes had a very good reason to want to kill you."

"I had nothing to do with the brat's death. Brownbeck is the one who gave it to that drunken woman, not me."

*That drunken woman. Jesus.*

"You think that matters?" said Sebastian, his voice rough with revulsion. "What counts is that Hayes considered you responsible, and you knew it. He'd already tried to kill you once in Macau because of it, and he might well have come back to England specifically to try again. In China, he was protected by a powerful Hong merchant, so you didn't dare move against him. But in London, you could easily hire someone to quietly take care of him. Someone like, say, Titus Poole."

"Don't be ridiculous. If I'd known Nicholas Hayes was in England, I'd have simply informed the authorities and let them kill him. Legally."

"Perhaps. Except that Bow Street can be a tad slow at times, which means there was a chance that Hayes might get to you before they caught him. And what if they did catch him? A man in prison and on trial can talk. In fact, the newspapers love to interview condemned men, hoping for a lurid confession. I suspect you wouldn't want all of London reading what he had to say."

At some point they had quit walking again. Forbes's light blue eyes were reduced to two narrow slits, and his jaw was clenched so tightly, he had to practically spit the words out. "For the last time, I tell you I did not know that man was in London. But let me warn you: If word of this gets out—any word at all—I swear to God, I'll kill you."

"You can try," said Sebastian, and left the man standing there in a narrow slice of sunlight that slanted down between the towering masses of the surrounding warehouses.

*Chapter 38*

$\mathcal{J}$i played the dizi in Leicester Square that morning. The day was clear and warm, the crowd large. But less than half an hour into the pitch, the child saw a blind, lame woman enter the square from Green Street, a worn old hurdy-gurdy tucked up under one arm as she leaned heavily on her cane.

Ji had seen the older woman several days before, on the Strand, and for some reason he only dimly understood, the sight of her filled him with an odd combination of compassion and dread. At the time the woman had been led by a girl, but today she was alone. At the entrance to the square, the woman paused, her sightless eyes turning toward the sound of Ji's music.

Ji stopped playing and lowered the flute.

A warm wind gusted up, carrying the scents of ale and roasting meat from a nearby tavern, along with the furtive whisperings of two dirty, ragged older boys who'd been eyeing Ji in a way the child didn't like.

Uncomfortably aware of the two boys watching, Ji picked up the tin cup and dumped the coins in a pocket. *Don't run*, Ji almost whispered aloud. *Don't let them know you're scared.*

Tucking the flute out of sight, Ji walked rapidly away toward Castle Street, then ducked into a narrow passage.

It was a mistake.

Ji heard running footsteps, coming fast. One of the boys pushed past with a snickered "'Scuse me" as he slammed both hands hard between Ji's shoulder blades.

Ji staggered and drew up, caught between the two boys. They looked to be perhaps fourteen or fifteen, their faces gaunt and grime smeared, their tattered and patched clothes held together with pieces of twine.

And they had Ji trapped between them.

"Ho there," said the first boy, his lips pulling back in a sneer. He was larger than his companion, his teeth so big and crooked, they didn't seem to fit in his mouth. "That's right. I'm talkin' to ye. Goin' someplace, are we, me fine lad?"

Ji was finding it hard to breathe. "What do you want?"

"What ye think we want, then? Eh, me bright little boy?"

"I don't rightly know."

"Hear that, Davey? He *don't rightly know.*" The one Ji was starting to think of as Big Teeth shared a laugh with the other boy, eyes alight with a hatred that Ji recognized even as its origins remained unfathomable. "Ye talk real flash, don't ye, boy?" His scornful gaze swept Ji's coat and trousers. After days on the street, Ji's clothes were dirty and rumpled. But compared to the rags of Big Teeth and his friend, they were very fine indeed. "Dress flash too. Don't ye?"

Ji remained silent.

"Right, then," said Big Teeth, reaching out one grubby hand in a mocking, beckoning gesture. "Let's 'ave yer blunt. And don't even think about holdin' any of it back."

Ji stared at him. "I beg your pardon?"

"Yer money, bright boy."

Swallowing an ocean of rage and fear, Ji dug out that morning's take and held out the coins.

Big Teeth scooped them up with a triumphant whoop. "Right. Now, give us the rest of it."

"But that's all I have!"

Big Teeth's lips pulled back in an ugly smile. "Why don't I believe ye?" His gaze shifted to his companion. "Take 'im down."

The second boy, the one called Davey, hooked an elbow around Ji's neck and jerked. Ji fell back, spine slamming hard against the ground. Winded, eyes watering, choking on blind terror, Ji felt hands groping pockets, tugging off shoes, pulling at socks. Ji kicked out desperately, uselessly.

"Ho!" called Big Teeth in triumph as the coins Ji had hidden in one sock hit the cobbles with a clatter. "Knew it." The hands moved up Ji's leg. "What else ye hidin', then?"

"Please let me go. I don't have anything else. I swear it."

"No?" Big Teeth yanked the bamboo flute from Ji's grasp and peered at it as if it were something strange and vaguely repulsive. With a shrug, he snapped the dizi against his knee and threw the broken pieces against the nearby brick wall.

"No!" screamed Ji.

Big Teeth laughed. Then an older woman's voice said, "Let him go, you vile pack of mindless gallows thatches."

Two dirty, unkempt heads turned. The ruffians were surprised enough that their grips loosened, and Ji scooted out of the way just as the hurdy-gurdy player's cane whistled through the air.

The first blow caught Davey above the ear with an ugly crack. He let out a howl and took off running up the passage.

"Ye stupid ole woman," snarled Big Teeth. "Ye think—"

She swung again, the cane catching him flat across the middle of his face and breaking his nose.

"That's right, you nasty vermin," the woman shouted as Big Teeth scrambled after his companion. "Go on, get! Get!" Then she said to Ji, "You all right there, lad?"

Ji crawled to where the dizi lay trampled in the muck of the passage.

"Lad?" said the woman again. "You all right?"

Ji swallowed hard and said in a small, shaky voice, "Yes. Thank you, ma'am. How . . . how could you know what they were planning to do? You're blind."

Too late, Ji recognized it as a horribly rude thing to say. But the woman just laughed. "I heard them whispering. When you've been blind since birth, your ears get real good. Your ears, and a few other senses people don't seem to have a name for."

"Thank you," said Ji again, and started to cry.

"Aw. There, there now, tyke," said the woman, lowering herself awkwardly beside Ji so that the two of them sat side by side with their backs to the dirty wall. "It'll be all right."

"No, it won't! I hate this place! I wish Hayes had never brought me here. We should have stayed in Canton. Oh, why did he have to go and die? I wish I were dead too. I can't live like this. I just can't. I thought I could. I thought I could take care of myself, but I can't!"

She reached out awkwardly to pat Ji's knee. "How old you reckon I am, lad?"

Ji blinked at her. "I don't know. Why?"

"I'm sixty-two. Because I was born blind, they taught me to be a musician. That's what they do with the blind, whether they're any good at it or not. And I'll be the first to admit I never was very good. But I've been playing my hurdy-gurdy on the streets for forty-six years now."

Ji stared at her. "How? How could you possibly survive?"

She gave a soft laugh. "I won't try to pretend it hasn't been hard sometimes, especially now that I'm getting older. But there've been some good times too. Lots of good times."

Ji was crying unashamedly now, great, gasping sobs that felt as if they'd never end. "But they broke my flute!"

"Did they? Oh, now, that was real mean, it was. You play like an angel, you do."

"How do you know?"

"Heard you when I first came into the square. I was planning to just rest and move on to find another pitch when you stopped and didn't start up again. You did that for me, didn't you?"

When Ji remained silent, the woman smiled. "You're a good lad. I used to have a girl to guide me, but she took up with a fellow and left me a couple of days ago. I find it sorely difficult to get around without her, and I'd be right grateful if you'd agree to take her place—at least for a little while. I don't usually earn more than ten or twelve pence a day, but if we're real frugal, maybe we can save up enough to buy you a new flute. What do you say?"

Ji sniffed and wiped a grimy sleeve across wet eyes. "I don't even know your name."

"It's Alice. Alice Jones."

*Chapter 39*

$\mathcal{T}$heo Brownbeck was seated at a large, cluttered desk in the library of his Bedford Square house, surrounded by untidy piles of manuscripts and books, when a footman showed Sebastian in.

"As you can see, I'm busy," announced Brownbeck, throwing down his quill with enough force to send ink splattering across his page. "This had better be important."

He didn't rise or step from behind his desk. Nor did he invite Sebastian to sit. So Sebastian wandered the room, taking in the tall bookshelves overflowing with well-thumbed religious volumes, the worn leather chairs beside the empty fireplace, the portrait of a pretty young woman in powdered hair and eighteenth-century dress he took to be the wellborn but long-dead former Miss Julie Osborne. "Working on a new article, are you?"

"I am. On the shocking number of young pickpockets that infest our sadly beleaguered city."

"Making up the 'statistics' as usual, I assume?"

Brownbeck's nostrils flared. "My statistics are based on careful reasoning and precise analysis. If you're here simply to insult me, you can go away."

Sebastian stopped before a strange, disturbing print of what looked like the Archangel Gabriel handing the world to a personification of Britannia. "Actually, I'm here about your granddaughter."

Brownbeck's eyes narrowed. "I have no grandchildren and you know it."

"Not anymore. But you did have, once. A baby girl born to your daughter, Katherine, and Nicholas Hayes in the spring of 1796. What happened to her?"

Brownbeck rose to his feet, his face dark crimson, his plump hands pressing down flat on the surface before him. "Get out. Get out of my house this instant."

Sebastian held the older man's furious gaze. "I'll go if you insist. But you have a choice: You can answer my questions here and now, or I can ask them elsewhere in a manner I can guarantee you'll find highly embarrassing."

Brownbeck swung away to where glasses and a carafe of brandy rested on a surprisingly plain tray. He poured himself a hefty measure without offering Sebastian any and threw down half of it before turning to say, "How did you know?"

"It doesn't matter. The point is, Nicholas Hayes knew about the child. He knew about her birth, and he knew of her death, and he blamed you for it. You and Sir Lindsey Forbes."

Brownbeck took another mouthful of brandy and rolled it on his tongue before swallowing. "The child died. Children die all the time without anyone being to blame."

"Unless they hand the babe over to a drunken wet nurse." When Brownbeck remained silent, his glare pugnacious and unapologetic, Sebastian said, "What did she do? Roll over on the child in a drunken stupor and accidently smother her?"

"I never asked for the particulars. And it wasn't a wet nurse, by the way. It was a foster mother."

"What was her name?"

"I don't recall."

"Of course not."

Brownbeck took another drink. "This is all ancient history. What purpose can possibly be served by digging up the past?"

Sebastian studied the rich, self-satisfied old man's broad, fleshy face, the coarse-grained skin and small, angry eyes. "Nicholas Hayes was dying of consumption and he knew it. That explains why he didn't worry about being hanged if he came back to England—he probably figured he'd die before anyone could put a noose around his neck. But it doesn't explain why he would want to return in the first place. I think he came here to revenge his baby's death by killing either you or Forbes. Or both."

A noticeable sheen of perspiration showed on the older man's face. "You're mad."

"Am I? Why do you think he came back?"

"I neither know nor care!"

"You should. Because if Hayes came back to London to kill you, it means you had a very good reason to kill him."

Brownbeck stared at him for a long moment, then raised his glass with a shaky hand and drained it in one long pull. "This is nonsense. I didn't even know the rogue was in London. And you're mistaken if you think he cared enough about that dead child that he'd risk the freedom of his last remaining days on earth to come back here and revenge its death."

"*Her* death," said Sebastian. "Not 'it.' Her."

Brownbeck waved a dismissive hand through the air. "You think Hayes cared about my daughter? Well, let me tell you, he didn't. All he cared about was getting his hands on her inheritance. And when that slipped through his grasping fingers and his father disowned him, he took up with some disreputable tavern wench." His lips twisted in an ugly, suggestive sneer. "Maybe that's why he came back to London—to see his lowborn paramour."

"What are you talking about?"

"The woman who ran the flash house where Hayes took refuge. Within months of abducting my daughter, he was carrying on with her in the most disgusting way imaginable. I know—"

"Nicholas Hayes didn't 'abduct' your daughter," Sebastian said quietly.

Brownbeck tightened his jaw and rolled determinedly on. "I know because I was worried he might try something else, so I had my people watching him."

A silence fell on the untidy library. It could have been a lie, of course. But it had a ring of the truth. Hadn't Sebastian himself suspected something similar?

Aloud, he said, "A troubled man can take comfort in the arms of an understanding woman and still nourish an abiding hatred for those he holds responsible for the death of his child."

"You didn't know Nicholas Hayes. I did."

"Did you? How well?"

"Well enough to know he was hot-tempered, unpredictable, and dangerous."

"In other words, well enough to be frightened of him if you discovered he'd somehow managed to return to England."

Brownbeck slammed down his empty glass. "You're right in that, at least. If I had known of Hayes's return to England, I probably would have been frightened. But I did not know." He walked over to give the bellpull a sharp tug. "This conversation is over."

A footman appeared in the doorway, and Brownbeck snapped, "His lordship is leaving."

Sebastian settled his hat on his head. "Where were you last Thursday evening, by the way?"

Rather than answer, Brownbeck went to sit heavily in his chair and reached for his quill. "Good day, my lord. And don't come back."

# Chapter 40

$\mathscr{Y}$ou're stuck, you bleedin' fool!"

Sebastian could hear Grace Calhoun's husky shout even before he turned into Chick Lane.

A wagon carrying a load of long wooden beams had tried to cut the corner too sharp and was now wedged between a chandler's and the butcher shop opposite. Grace Calhoun stood tall and imposing in front of a nearby greengrocer's, her hands on her hips, her eyes narrowed as she watched the wagoner uselessly whip his horses. "You can beat them poor beasts to death, but all that'll get you is a dead team. It won't do nothin' to move your bloody wagon. You're gonna need to back up and take that corner wide, the way you should've done in the first place."

Sebastian reined in, and for an instant Grace's gaze flicked to him. But she gave no other indication she either saw or recognized him. She stayed where she was until the cursing, grumbling driver began to back his team. Then she turned to Sebastian and said, "What are you doin' here again?"

Sebastian handed his reins to Tom and hopped down. "We need to talk about Nicholas Hayes."

She huffed a low laugh and started walking toward the Red Lion. The afternoon had turned sultry, with a solid covering of high white clouds that somehow brought no relief from the heat.

"Ain't got nothin' more to say about him."

Sebastian fell into step beside her. "Did you know he had a child by a rich man's daughter—an infant that died?"

"And if I did?"

"Is that why he came back to London? To punish those responsible for his child's death?"

She turned in through the ancient narrow arch that led to the Red Lion's dilapidated old stable yard. "I told you, I don't know why he came back."

"Were you his lover eighteen years ago?"

That stopped her. She drew up in the shadow of the arch, her lips twisting into a hard smile that nevertheless managed to carry more than a hint of sadness. "Lover? Nah."

"But you were more to him than just the owner of the inn where he found refuge."

When she remained silent, he said, his voice low and earnest, "I need you to help me understand him."

"Why?"

"Because . . ." What could he say? Because bringing this man's murderer to justice was more important to Sebastian than he could begin to explain, even to himself? Because he felt driven to prove that Nicholas Hayes had been wrongly convicted so long ago? Because while nothing could be done at this point to alleviate the tragedy of the dead man's life, it was somehow vitally important that the tragedy be both recognized and remembered by someone?

But Sebastian could say none of those things. And so he said, "Because I don't want whoever killed him to get away with it. To go on living his life while Nicholas is just . . . dead."

She stared directly into his face, and he wondered what she saw there—if she understood perhaps better than he did himself why he was doing this. Then she drew a deep breath that parted her lips, and her eyes became unfocused in a way that made him think she looked within. Just when he thought she would tell him to leave her, she said, "All right."

They sat on an aged stone bench in the shade cast by the inn's crumbling high walls and talked of long ago. The courtyard smelled of damp stone and the lichen staining the worn pavers near the largely unused stables, deep in the shadows, the exposed ancient bricks had taken on a pink glow.

She told him of a troubled, lonely young man bereft of the woman he loved and a child he would never see. Of a son cast off by an unforgiving father and adrift. At twenty, Nicholas Hayes had been wellborn, handsome, refined—everything a brilliant, beautiful, but lowborn and uneducated woman raised in the hardscrabble back alleys of London had never dreamt could be hers. But for a time they had come together, and in her mature, understanding arms, he had found a measure of solace and a temporary respite from the soul-crushing pain into which his once-privileged life had descended. Then came a brother's suicide and a young countess's death, and the young man's life turned into a living hell.

Sebastian said, "How did he learn of the death of the child?"

She glanced up at a couple of house martins darting around the eaves of the inn, then fixed her gaze on Sebastian. "There was this East India Company man—I can't remember his name."

"Forbes?"

"Yeah, that's it. Forbes. He taunted Nicholas with it."

Sebastian sucked in a breath that hissed between his teeth. "With the child's death?"

She nodded. "He went to see Nicholas in Newgate not long before he was due to be loaded on the transport ship. That man, he hated Nick real bad. Seems he'd offered for that rich man's daughter once, and the rich man, he was more'n happy to bless the marriage. Only because of Nick, she'd refused him the first time."

"And then turned around and married him?"

"Does that surprise you? Her a gentlewoman with a babe on the way?" Grace Calhoun gave Sebastian a look redolent with all of a woman's contempt for male ignorance. "That East India Company man, he told Nicholas the rich man's daughter was his now and the baby was dead. And then he laughed."

Sebastian found that his hands had curled into fists, and he had to force himself to open and press them flat on his thighs. He said, "Did you know Nicholas was dying of consumption?"

She was silent for a moment, her face pinched. "Not for sure. But he was coughing something fierce, and I know the signs. I asked about it, and he said he reckoned he wasn't gonna make old bones."

"You haven't seen the boy Ji since Nicholas was murdered?"

"No. Reckon something musta spooked the lad, made him think he ain't safe here."

"Like what?"

"I don't know. Maybe he seen somebody hanging around he didn't trust."

"If he were spooked, where would he go, do you think?"

"How would I know?"

Sebastian suspected she knew a great deal that she still wasn't telling him, but all he said was "Do you think it's possible Ji could be Nicholas's son?"

"I never figured him for anything else."

"But Nicholas never said anything?"

"No."

He watched her head jerk toward a distant *thump* somewhere in the depths of the inn, and he found himself wondering not for the first time about the life's journey that had brought her to the position she occupied in London's dangerous underworld. He said, "Do you have any idea what Nicholas did during the weeks he was in London? Where he went? With whom he met?"

"No. There was one time—a few days before he was killed—when I could tell he was upset about somethin' that'd happened. But he didn't want to talk about it. I think maybe he might've gone to see his sister, but I couldn't swear to it."

Sebastian stared at her. "Nicholas Hayes has a sister?" *Bloody hell*, he thought; no one had mentioned the existence of a sister.

She gave an incredulous laugh. "You didn't know? Anne is her name—Lady Anne."

"Were they close?"

"No. Nicholas said she took after his da too much for them to ever get along. But she's all he had left, so I reckon he could've seen his way to maybe contacting her."

"Would she betray him, do you think?"

Grace pushed to her feet, her attention all for shaking out and brushing off the skirt of her gown. "To Bow Street, you mean?"

"Or to his enemies." *Like maybe her cousin, Ethan.*

She looked over at him. "You think the likes of me knows anything about the likes of some earl's daughter? Why don't you ask her? She's Lady Bradbury now." Her gaze flicked away from him to a cat stalking a mouse in the shadows beyond the stable door, then came back. "So she ain't gonna be buryin' him?"

"No. I am. This evening, at St. Pancras. If you know where Ji is, you might let him know."

She shook her head. "I keep tellin' you, I don't know where the boy is." And such was the flare of worry and sorrow he glimpsed in her eyes that, for the first time, he found himself believing her.

*Chapter 41*

Lady Bradbury—born Lady Anne Hayes—was the wife of a dour, stout Yorkshire baron some fifteen years her senior. His lordship's town house on Stratton Street was not large, but it was extremely well-appointed and richly furnished, thanks to her ladyship having outlived all three of her brothers and thus unexpectedly inheriting a handsome sum from her late father, the Second Earl. Sebastian knew these things because before approaching her, he stopped by Park Lane to talk to his aunt Henrietta.

"You didn't ask about any sisters," said the Dowager Duchess in response to Sebastian's somewhat testy question. "I was under the impression you were interested in Seaforth's sons because of the succession." Which he had to admit was true.

"Are there other sisters?" asked Sebastian.

"She's the only one who lived to come of age. If I remember correctly, she was six or seven years Nicholas's senior, and was married and off in Yorkshire by the time he ran into trouble. Most of her children are grown, although I believe there may still be a girl in the schoolroom and a boy at Eton."

"What's she like?"

The Duchess pressed her lips together in an expression that told him more about her opinion of Lady Anne than words ever could. "To put it bluntly, she's a sanctimonious, moralizing prude. I've no doubt that if she'd been born into a bourgeois household she'd be one of the Chapham Sect. I swear, they're proliferating these days. If they have their way, we'll all have to give up dancing and playing cards, and start fainting at the mere mention of a piano's 'legs.'"

"She doesn't sound like the kind of person Nicholas would approach for help."

"Not if he knew his sister—and one assumes he did."

"Perhaps she was different when she was younger."

"Oh, no, she's always been like that. Most of the Hayes family are." She gave a disdainful huff. "A bunch of insufferable killjoys that range from the merely unimaginative to the profoundly hypocritical."

"What's Lord Bradbury like?"

"Much the same. But then, he's from Yorkshire, and the family never used to be very flush. Needless to say, the match was far from brilliant for an earl's daughter, even if Seaforth's title was of only recent origin and Irish to boot. And I see that smile on your face, Sebastian, and I know what you're thinking, but these things do matter. My point is, she didn't make a particularly good marriage because at the time all three of her brothers were alive and her dowry was rather small. But in the end she came into an unexpectedly large inheritance when her father died."

"Which means she was either lucky or unlucky, depending on how one looks at it."

"Oh, believe me, she imagines herself to be most unlucky. Those kind always do. I'll be surprised if she agrees to see you. Most people know by now that you're looking into Nicholas's murder, and Lady Anne likes to pretend he never existed." She glanced at the ormolu clock on the drawing-room mantel. "And now you must go away and leave me in peace so that I can dress for Lady Cartwright's dinner in honor of the Grand

Duchess of Oldenburg. The vast majority of the visiting Allied Sovereigns are dead bores, but I admit to finding the Tsar's sister entertaining—in the same way that one is amused by a fireworks display."

"I thought they were all up at Oxford for the next couple of days."

"Most of them are. But the Grand Duchess has elected to remain in London, hence tonight's dinner." The clock began to strike the hour, and she stood up and shooed her hands at him. "Now go away."

Sebastian's knock at Lady Bradbury's door was answered by a gaunt-faced butler who looked dubious when Sebastian presented his card, but bowed and went away to see if her ladyship was receiving visitors. He came back almost immediately with her ladyship's apologies. Lady Bradbury would shortly be preparing for an evening at Drury Lane and was thus unable to see him.

"Drury Lane? How fortuitous. Please tell her ladyship that since she can't see me now, I'll make it a point to find her at the theater later this evening. I have some important questions about her brother I'm looking forward to asking her, and will try not to inaccommodate her too much." The butler's eyes widened in alarm as Sebastian gave one of his nastier smiles. "You will give her ladyship my message, won't you?"

He turned away and walked slowly back to his curricle. He'd hopped up and was gathering his reins when her ladyship's front door flew open and a liveried footman came pelting down the steps.

"Lord Devlin! Lord Devlin, please do wait." The young footman skidded to a halt beside the curricle. "Her ladyship has reconsidered your request and decided that it will be convenient to see you now."

She received him in an elegant drawing room hung with pearl-colored silk delicately painted with a Chinese pastoral scene. A life-sized, full-length portrait of her ladyship, painted à la Diana by Lawrence when she was perhaps ten years younger, dominated a room finely furnished with more satinwood pieces than it could comfortably hold.

Like her brother, Lady Anne was of above-average height with dark hair threaded with gray. She also had her brother's long nose and fierce straight brows, although the effect was not as attractive on her. Sebastian wondered if that was owing to a difference in proportions or if the problem was simply that over the years Lady Anne's personality had stamped itself on her face. When he was a child, Sebastian's mother used to laughingly tell him whenever he pulled a face that his features would freeze that way. And while he knew she said it to tease him, he'd also come to realize there was an element of truth to that age-old warning. It didn't happen instantly, of course, the way children thought. But there was no doubt that over time most people's personalities showed on their faces for all to see. And Lady Anne's face told anyone who cared to look that she was a haughty, selfish, self-absorbed, and petty woman.

She stood beside the room's empty hearth, one hand resting on the expensive white marble mantel, her head tilted back at a belligerent angle and her face pink with indignation. But she refused to acknowledge that he had successfully maneuvered her into agreeing to see him. Instead, she bowed her head in a condescending way and said, "I'm told you have some questions you wish to ask."

She did not invite him to sit.

"Thank you for agreeing to see me," said Sebastian, wandering the room in a way she obviously did not like but was unable to stop since she refused to invite him to sit. "I'm wondering, did you know your brother Nicholas had returned to England?"

"Of course not."

Her haughty disdain reminded Sebastian of Sir Lindsey Forbes's response to the same question. Both tone and words were identical. He said, "Do you have any idea why he came back?"

"I do not. My brother and I were never close, and I have spent the last twenty years trying to forget he ever existed."

"Then I suppose you don't have any idea who might have killed him either?"

"Seriously, Lord Devlin? What difference does it make who killed him? The man was an escaped convict, long thought dead. The world is better off without him."

Sebastian searched this cold, smug woman's face, trying to understand how two siblings could come from the same set of parents and yet be so different. "What about the current Lord Seaforth? Is your cousin, Ethan, capable of such a thing, do you think?"

Her long nose quivered. "Good heavens, no. This is beyond outrageous." Reaching out, she gave the bellpull a sharp tug. "I must ask you to leave now."

"Can you think of anyone Nicholas might have contacted since returning to London?"

"I told you," she said icily, "my brother and I were never close." She glanced over at the young footman who had appeared at the entrance to the drawing room. "Lord Devlin is leaving." To Sebastian, she added, "And if you come back, I will not be at home."

He inclined his head in the polite bow that civility required and yet still managed to make her stiffen. "I think you've told me everything I need to know."

*Chapter 42*

They buried Nicholas Hayes that evening in a quiet corner of St. Pancras's churchyard. Shortly before dusk, the sky took on a peculiar color, like a washed-out cloth tinged with hints of old brass, and a hot wind gusted up that felt gritty and dirty against their faces yet carried no hint of coming rain.

It wasn't the "done thing" for ladies to attend funerals, but Hero was there, as were Jules Calhoun, Mahmoud Abbasi and his young son, Hamish McHenry—looking half-drunk and half-sick—and Mott Tintwhistle. Sebastian was wondering how the old cracksman-turned–dolly-shop owner had known. Then Grace Calhoun arrived, dressed in unexpectedly severe black and accompanied by her beefy barman. She stood silent and stony-faced through the short graveside service. And then she left.

Afterward, Sebastian and Hero stood alone beside the raw grave, with the gusting wind flattening the rank grass of the churchyard around them. "I wonder how he would feel about lying here," Hero said suddenly.

"He knew he was dying when he came back to England. I suspect he didn't much care where his body ended up."

She stared off across the jumble of moss-covered tombs and headstones, toward the wind-thrashed treetops of Pennington's Tea Gardens. "I wish Ji could have been here."

"I know." Sebastian was silent for a moment, the wind buffeting his face. Then the wind dropped and the air smelled of dust and lichen-covered stone and old, old death. He said, "I should have realized Kate Brownbeck was with child—that only a baby would have precipitated that disastrous, hasty elopement."

Hero drew a painful breath. "And then they took her baby away and she never had another. The poor woman."

The sun was sinking lower in the sky, bathing the world in that strange brassy light. He said, "I must admit I can sympathize with Nicholas Hayes for coming back here with murder in his heart. I think about the lot of them—Brownbeck, Forbes, Seaforth, and LaRivière—and it's hard not to be consumed with vicarious rage."

"Of the four, I'd say Forbes and LaRivière are by far the strongest and most dangerous characters—and the most likely to kill."

"Yes. But weak men can also kill, especially out of fear. And a sickle in the back strikes me as the act of a weak man."

"It does, doesn't it?" The church bell began to ring, tolling out the hour, and the mournful peal seemed to press down upon them. The air was heavy with the smell of freshly turned earth, the hard sky criss-crossed with birds coming in to settle for the night. Wordlessly, Hero reached out to take his hand. He laced his fingers with hers, and she said, "Is it wrong that I find myself wishing he'd succeeded in doing what he came here for?"

"I don't think so. Not at all."

She looked over at him and smiled.

*Chapter 43*

*Wednesday, 15 June*

The next morning, Hero and Calhoun shifted their search for Ji away from the areas around Pennington's Tea Gardens and the Red Lion.

Someone had told Calhoun about seeing a boy who might have been part Chinese playing a bamboo flute in Leicester Square. Calhoun had spent hours Tuesday evening combing the area without any luck, but it started him thinking. "Maybe the lad is deliberately staying away from places Hayes's killer might know about," said Calhoun. "Maybe that's why we can't find anyone who's seen him."

"You might be right," said Hero. And so with that possibility in mind, they decided to try Clerkenwell.

Lying to the north of London's old city walls, Clerkenwell had once been the site of four rich monastic institutions. After the Dissolution, Henry VIII doled out the land to his noble supporters, and for a time Clerkenwell was an area of fine houses and exclusive spas. But those glory days belonged to the past. The nobility had long since shifted west to Mayfair, leaving Clerkenwell to poor tradesmen, artisans, and prisons.

What was still called Clerkenwell Green no longer bore any resemblance to the idyllic village green it had once been. A narrow space shaped like a squished, elongated triangle, it had the intimidating bulk of the Sessions House taking up the entire wide end and Clerkenwell Churchyard at the point. What wasn't paved over was reduced to hard-packed earth, and the whole was hemmed in by two converging streets thick with drays, carts, and carriages. The dusty space in between was given over to stalls, pickpockets, stray dogs, and itinerant street performers. It was noisy and crowded and smelled of urine and dung.

While Calhoun walked up Clerkenwell Close to the church and then back down to St. John's Square, Hero interviewed the only musician on the green—a lame, blind woman who said her name was Alice Jones.

"Been blind all my life," said Alice, who looked to be somewhere in her seventies but said she was only sixty-two. Her clothes were ragged but clean, her soft gray hair neatly platted and wrapped around her head in two braids. Her eyes were an eerie milky white. "Played the hurdy-gurdy all my life too. That's what they taught me in the blind school, you see."

"When did you leave school?" asked Hero, tilting her parasol against the fierce sun.

"They kicked us out when we turned sixteen. My parents were both dead, so that's when I started playing on the street."

Hero looked up from scribbling notes. "You've done this ever since?"

"Oh, yes. Forty-six years." Alice Jones laughed at what she must have heard in Hero's voice. "Can't imagine it, can you?"

Hero ruefully shook her head, then remembered the woman couldn't see her. "How much do you make a day?"

"Ten or maybe twelve pence, if I'm lucky. More if the weather's good, less when it's not."

"Do you always play here in Clerkenwell?"

"Oh, no. You need to move around, you know. Some street musicians just go wherever the fancy takes them, but I'm not like that. Tuesdays for Leicester Square, Wednesdays for Clerkenwell, Thursdays are for Kensington, and so on. I've always been like that. Gives a certain sense of order and control to life, if you know what I mean?"

"Yes, I can see that."

The woman tilted her head as if she were studying Hero, even though her eyes were sightless. "Why'd you say you're writing this article?"

Hero didn't think she had said why, only that she was writing it for the *Morning Chronicle*. "I believe it's important for people to understand the life stories of those they see on the streets. Those who are less fortunate than they."

The skin beside the woman's empty eyes crinkled with her smile. "The wretchedly poor, you mean."

"Well, yes," said Hero, oddly uncomfortable to hear it spelled out so bluntly. The wind gusted up, and she had to tighten her grip on the parasol. It wasn't easy juggling a notebook, a parasol, and a reticule that was heavier than usual, thanks to the little brass-mounted muff pistol she'd started carrying after her unsettling experience in Snow Hill. "I'm particularly interested in interviewing street performers who were born elsewhere. I understand there's a Chinese boy on the streets, although I'm not sure if he performs. Do you know anything about him?"

The woman laughed. "All children look the same when you're blind."

"This child may play the flute."

"Oh? And he's Chinese, you say?"

"Perhaps only half-Chinese. A lad of eight or ten."

Alice shook her head. "Sorry. I don't believe I've heard of him."

A shout brought Hero's head around. A ragged boy was crossing the green, his clothes dirty and torn, his head bowed, his lips moving silently as if reciting a prayer. Then someone shouted, *"That's 'im! Grab 'im."*

The boy's head came up, his gaze jerking toward the shout as he broke into a run. After nearly a week on the streets, he was dirty and disheveled, his coat torn at the shoulder, his dark, straight hair limp. But Hero recognized him instantly.

"Ji," she cried as three men closed on him.

The boy was running toward Hero. He dodged a stall selling sweetmeats, a plump woman with a shopping basket, a juggler whose balls went tumbling in the boy's wake. He was young and nimble and frightened, but the men's legs were longer, and one of the men was particularly fast. Ji had almost reached Hero when the fastest man managed to reach out and catch the boy's arm. Ji wiggled away. The man swore and was starting after him again when Hero stepped forward to thrust her parasol between the man's legs.

He tripped and went sprawling. One of his friends swerved around him while the other leapt right over him. Hero was vaguely aware of the hurdy-gurdy woman whacking the first man on the head with her cane and pounding the second man across the shoulders. The downed man at Hero's feet lay as if stunned, then rolled onto his back just in time to see her draw the muff pistol from her reticule and point the muzzle at his face.

"Move and you're dead," she said calmly, thumbing back the hammer.

He froze.

"Wise," said Hero. "Now, tell me who hired you."

The man looked to be somewhere in his thirties, his face unshaven, his hair badly cut, his coat, waistcoat, and breeches worn and greasy. He stared at her, his jaw sagging. "I cain't tell ye that!"

"I see you need some persuasion." She shifted the muzzle slightly to the right and down. "I suppose you might not bleed to death when I shoot you in the arm—if you're lucky, that is. Of course, you'll probably lose the arm, but—"

"You wouldn't do that!"

"Oh, believe me," said Hero, enunciating each word carefully, "I would." She extended her right arm, her finger tightening.

"Wait! Don't do it! Oh, God, don't shoot me. I'll tell ye. I'll tell ye! It's Seaforth—the Earl of Seaforth. He hired us. I swear to God, that's the honest truth."

"Why should I believe you?"

Greasy Coat's eyes bulged. "Gorblimey, lady. I couldn't make something' like that up if'n I wanted to. Some lord, hirin' me t' find a half-Chinese lad? Ain't no way I could come up with a tale that batty."

"Did he hire you to kill Nicholas Hayes too?"

"What? I ain't never killed nobody!"

"If you—" Hero broke off as one of the man's confederates who must have circled back around slammed into her.

"We lost 'im, Jack!" shouted the man as Hero staggered. "Come on and let's get outta 'ere!"

He took off running again, but he had successfully distracted Hero long enough to give Greasy Coat a chance to scramble to his feet. He darted out into the street that ran along the north side of the green, oblivious to the team of shires bearing down on him.

"*Oy there!*" yelled the dray's driver as the near horse reared up in fright, its big, flailing hooves knocking the man down. The driver was reining in hard, but it was too late. The off leader plunged, then reared up to come down on the man as he tried to roll out of the way. The thudding hooves crushed the man's head with a sickening crunch.

"Dear God," said someone behind Hero.

From the far side of the green came a child's shout. "I hope you're reborn as a hungry ghost!"

But when Hero turned and looked, Ji was gone.

*Chapter 44*

*C*lad in natty yellow trousers and a coat with exaggerated shoulders, the Third Earl of Seaforth was in Bond Street shepherding three of his sons and a very pregnant wife through Dubourg's Celebrated Exhibition of Cork Models of Roman Antiquities when Sebastian walked up to him and said quietly, "We need to talk. Now. I've spoken to the owner and he has kindly offered to lend us a private room for a few minutes."

Seaforth gave a startled laugh. "Good God. Not now, man."

He would have turned away, but Sebastian caught him by the arm and hauled him back around. "You sorry son of a bitch," hissed Sebastian, still keeping his voice low. "It's only the presence of your family that has kept me from landing you a facer here and now. The men you hired just attacked my wife."

"I didn't hire anyone—"

"You did. You hired them to get rid of the boy Nicholas Hayes brought back from China. But that's the problem with hiring killers. They can be a wee bit hard to control."

"Papa," said the eldest of Seaforth's red-haired, freckle-faced boys, pointing to a projection on one of the buildings. "What's this supposed to be?"

Sebastian glanced at the child, who looked to be perhaps eight or nine. "I suggest we take advantage of that private room. You don't want your wife and children to hear what I have to say."

Seaforth yanked his arm from Sebastian's grasp and stalked toward where an anxious-looking Mr. Dubourg was waiting to usher them into a small, untidy office.

"You're wrong, you know," said Seaforth as soon as the door closed behind them. "I didn't hire those men to kill the boy. I simply told them to make him go away. I thought perhaps they could sell him to a chimney sweep or something."

"He's too big for a sweep's boy. Apart from which, nine out of ten children sold to chimney sweeps don't live to see their freedom, so it's basically a death sentence anyway. The truth is, you don't care what happens to that child as long as he disappears."

"Of course I don't care. Are you telling me you wouldn't do the same in my position?" Seaforth's voice had taken on the aggrieved tone of a man who always, always, sees himself as the undeserving victim of his own failings and deficiencies.

Sebastian gave a faint, disbelieving shake of his head. "Is he Nicholas Hayes's legitimate son?"

"I don't know! You think I could afford to take the time to inquire into the particulars?"

"Did you pay the same men to kill Nicholas?"

Seaforth's jaw went slack. "No! I swear it!"

"I don't believe you."

"Ask them! They'll tell you! I hired them the morning after Nicholas was found dead."

"Used someone else to kill Nicholas, did you?"

"No!"

"Why the bloody hell should I believe you? You obviously not only knew Nicholas had come back to England, but you even knew he'd brought a boy with him. A boy who might well be his son and thus heir to everything you thought was yours."

Seaforth's tongue darted out to wet his lips. "You can't know that. No one knows that. In all likelihood, he's nothing more than a half-Chinese by-blow. Even if he were by some miracle legitimate, I seriously doubt he could prove it."

"I suspect Ji knows. And he could have the papers to prove it."

Seaforth looked confused. "Who is Ji?"

"The child you've been trying to kill."

A spark of aggrieved fury flared in the Earl's pale gray eyes. "So what precisely are you suggesting I should do? Allow some dirty little foreigner to claim everything that is mine? *Become a peer of the realm?*"

Sebastian was having a hard time keeping his fists at his sides. "How did you know Hayes was in London? Did you see him?"

Seaforth shook his head. "No."

"So how did you know?"

Seaforth glanced toward the door. But Sebastian was between the Earl and the exit. He was trapped and he knew it.

"Answer me, damn you," said Sebastian.

"Brownbeck! Brownbeck told me."

*Bloody hell,* thought Sebastian. "How did Brownbeck know?"

"He saw them. I don't know where or how, but he told me because he thought I should know."

"You mean, he told you because he was hoping you might kill them."

Seaforth simply stared back at him, the freckles standing out stark against his pale flesh.

Sebastian said, "Did he tell anyone else?"

"He didn't say, but I know he also told Forbes—Forbes and LaRivière. I know because I thought it best under the circumstances to warn them, only both men said they already knew."

"Did you tell anyone else?"

"No. I swear to God."

"Right," said Sebastian with a hard smile.

"Who else would I tell?"

"I've no idea. Did Nicholas have any other enemies?"

"Not that I'm aware of."

"Was the boy with Hayes when you killed him in Pennington's Tea Gardens?"

Seaforth sucked in a startled breath. "I tell you, I didn't kill Hayes! I swear it. My wife wasn't feeling well that day, so I spent the afternoon at my club, had dinner, then went to the Regent's reception. I won't deny I wanted the man dead, but I've never killed anyone in my life."

"You hire other people to do your killing for you, do you?"

The other man's gaze slid away, telling Sebastian all he needed to know.

Sebastian said, "When did Brownbeck warn you about Hayes?"

"Last week sometime. Maybe Monday or Tuesday—I don't recall precisely."

"When did you speak to Forbes and LaRivière?"

"The same day. I think it may have been Monday, actually."

"And you'd have me believe you didn't hire the men to go after the child until Friday?"

"I swear it! Ask the men. They'll tell you."

"Unfortunately, the only one who was in custody is now dead."

Seaforth's eyes widened. "You killed him?"

"Not exactly."

Sebastian advanced on the other man, backing him up until Seaforth slammed his shoulders against the nearest wall with his hands splayed out at his sides. "When we walk out of here," said Sebastian, "you're going to collect your wife and children and take them home. And then you are going to contact those men you hired and you are going to call them off. Am I making myself perfectly clear? You are going to call them off *right now*. Because I want you to understand this, and I want you to understand it well: If anything happens to either my wife or that little boy, you won't live long enough to rue the day you were born. Is that clear?"

Seaforth's nostrils flared. "You can't just go around threatening people like this. I am a peer of the realm! I—"

"What you are, sir, is a fool. Your men threatened the daughter of the Regent's dear, dear cousin and most trusted advisor. If you think I might hurt you, what do you think Jarvis would do if he found out?"

Seaforth's face quivered as his nose began to run. "You haven't told him, have you? Oh, God. Have you?"

"Not yet. At the moment you're more useful to me alive than dead. I suggest you do your utmost to keep me in that frame of mind."

From the far side of the door came a child's voice. "Mama, where's Papa?"

At some point, Seaforth's hat had been knocked to the floor. Sebastian picked it up and handed it to him. "Now take your family and get out of here."

*Chapter 45*

Theodore Brownbeck came hurrying out of the Bank of England's massive portal with his head down, his thoughts obviously far away. He had a sheaf of papers tucked up under one arm and was worrying his lower lip with his front teeth. He'd crossed Threadneedle and was almost to Cornhill before he realized Sebastian had fallen into step beside him.

"What do you want?" demanded the banker, throwing Sebastian an angry sideways glance.

"The problem with lying in response to questions about a murder," said Sebastian pleasantly, "is that it tends to make you look guilty."

Brownbeck kept walking. "Am I supposed to somehow divine what you're talking about?"

"Sir Lindsey Forbes, the Count de Compans, and the Earl of Seaforth. It turns out that all three men knew by the beginning of last week that Hayes was in England, and they knew because you'd told them."

Brownbeck's face was a transparent study in his shifting thought processes as he first registered surprise at the discovery of his lie, then hovered over the possibility of denying everything before finally deciding to bluster forward in an attack. "I did not kill Nicholas Hayes, if that's what you're suggesting."

"I don't believe you did. Men like you don't usually do their own dirty work; they get others to do it for them. So you told Nicholas Hayes's enemies that he was back in the country, presumably in the hopes that one of them would quietly kill him."

Brownbeck made a scoffing sound deep in his throat. "Who thinks like that? I told them about Hayes because they needed to know."

"Why is that?"

"Because the man was a dangerous murderer, in case you've forgotten!"

"So why not inform the authorities and have him arrested?"

Brownbeck cast him a scornful glance. "And have the past dredged up again for everyone to titter about? Risk having my daughter's name dragged through the mud? It's been bad enough with him being found dead. Can you imagine the papers if he'd been taken alive?"

"True. But surely that possibility pales to insignificance if you genuinely believed Hayes had come back here to kill someone. Someone such as, say, you."

"Don't be ridiculous. Why would the man want to kill me?"

"Because you let his baby die."

Brownbeck drew up abruptly and cast a swift look about before saying in a low, icy voice, "I didn't 'let' the child die. How was I to know that woman was in the habit of dosing the infants in her care with opium?"

*Jesus*, thought Sebastian. He'd heard of venal foster mothers giving their helpless young charges opium to keep them quiet and dull their hunger. Most of them simply quit eating and died. No wonder Nicholas hated the East India Company's enthusiastic investment in the production of opium. Aloud, he said, "You'd have known if you'd bothered to check into the woman before handing the infant over to her. You obviously didn't care."

"Of course I didn't care! It was bad enough I had to pay to have someone take the thing. If you think I shed any tears over its demise, you're mistaken. The brat is better off dead."

For a moment, Sebastian could only stare at him. "That 'brat' was your daughter's only child. Your grandchild."

Brownbeck set his jaw. "I make no claims to it. Begotten in sin, fathered by a vicious murderer, born into infamy! What would I want with such a disgraceful legacy?"

The hot wind gusted up, whistling down the narrow street and buffeting them with the reek of horse droppings and urine and dust. Sebastian said, "How did you know Hayes had returned to England?"

"I saw them—him and that child he presumably brought back from China with him."

"Where?"

"Near Russell Square. They were walking down the street as I was exiting a friend's house. Hayes didn't see me."

"But you recognized him? After nearly twenty years?"

"I have an excellent memory for faces. He was older, obviously, but his appearance hadn't altered that much. And the ways in which he had changed simply meant he'd grown to look more like his father. I followed them a ways—discreetly, of course—just to make certain. But as soon as I heard his voice, there was no doubt in my mind."

"What was he doing when you saw him?"

"I told you, simply walking down the street with the boy."

"And then you told Forbes, Seaforth, and LaRivière?"

"Not right away. I thought about it a day, and then I told them. As I said, I thought they deserved to know so that they could be on their guard."

"Who else did you tell?"

Brownbeck looked puzzled. "Who else would I tell?"

"You weren't tempted to hire someone to take care of the problem for you?"

"No, I was not. And even if I were, do you seriously think I'd know how to go about finding someone like that?"

"Well, you do write extensively about London's criminal underworld."

"I *write* about the criminal class. I don't know any of its members."

"So you're saying you don't actually know what you're writing about?"

"One does not need to be intimately acquainted with vermin to know they must be exterminated." Brownbeck's voice grew aggrieved as he launched into one of his favorite themes. "What this country needs is a proper police force to patrol the streets, bring criminals to justice, and safeguard public morality. We need a police force, and we need a series of severe prisons along the lines of the Panopticon system advocated by my friend Jeremy Bentham."

"I suspect we'll eventually get both, God help us all." Sebastian watched a dog sniff at something in the gutter, then brought his gaze back to the plump, sweaty face of the man beside him. "So, which of the three men do you think killed Hayes? Forbes, Seaforth, or LaRivière?"

"Don't be absurd. It's more than obvious that Hayes was killed by some underworld acquaintance of his."

"Oh? Why do you say that?"

"Because anyone else would have had more sense than to leave the body on public display in the tea gardens, of course."

"Perhaps they hired someone who wasn't very good at his job," suggested Sebastian.

Brownbeck made a derisive sound with his tongue against his teeth. "The problem with you, Lord Devlin, is that you refuse to accept the obvious. The man was known to consort with thieves and low, lewd women. No doubt he quarreled with one of them and finally paid the ultimate price for his infamy."

"I suppose it's possible."

"Not simply possible, but probable."

Sebastian glanced up as the wind banged a loose shutter somewhere overhead. "Did you know Forbes had seen Hayes in China?"

Brownbeck hesitated a moment before answering, as if considering his response. "As it happens, I did, yes. Perhaps that's why I recognized Hayes so easily when I chanced to see him by Russell Square—I already knew he was alive. Why do you ask?"

"Just curious."

Brownbeck's lips tightened. "That's the trouble with young men to-day. They're bored, aimless, and restless, with nothing to do besides indulge in idle curiosity."

"Oh, it's not idle," said Sebastian with a smile that seemed only to irritate the banker even more. "Believe me, it's not idle at all." He politely tipped his hat. "You've been a great deal of help. Thank you."

And then he walked away, leaving Brownbeck scowling after him, the papers beneath his arm snapping in the hot, dry wind.

Sir Lindsey Forbes was down at the East India Company's docks, talking to a weathered, white-whiskered sea captain, when he became aware of Sebastian watching him. The growing wind whipped at the gray water and seagulls screeched overhead as the East India Company man continued his conversation. But he kept glancing in Sebastian's direction. After a moment, he nodded to the captain and turned to walk up to where Sebastian stood with one shoulder propped against the corner of a saltpeter shed, his arms crossed at his chest.

"What the devil are you doing here?" Forbes demanded.

Sebastian pushed away from the wall. "You lied to me."

Forbes stiffened. It was considered a grave insult to accuse a gentleman of lying. "I beg your pardon?"

"When you said you didn't know Nicholas Hayes had returned to England. Turns out, you learned of it from both Lord Seaforth and Theo Brownbeck."

Forbes heaved a heavy sigh, like a weary soul disappointed in the foibles of his fellow men. "Setting aside for a moment the extraordinary rudeness of one man prying into another's life, I fail to understand what makes you think I owe you an honest recital of the minute details of my existence."

"Not all of it—only those parts directly related to the murder of Nicholas Hayes."

"Has it occurred to you that your obsession with that wretch's demise verges on the unhealthy? Eighteen years ago, a wayward young man committed an atrocious murder and was sentenced to death for it. Unfortunately, the authorities in a paroxysm of unwarranted mercy commuted his sentence to transportation for the term of his natural life. He was then dispatched to the antipodes, where by rights he should have perished. Except that by some oversight on the part of providence, he managed to escape and eventually worked his way back to England, where he presumably was set to recommence his life of crime when his miserable existence was finally brought to an abrupt end."

"That's one way to look at it."

A loud clatter jerked Forbes's attention to where some men were loading a lighter. "There is no other way. The appeal of such a tawdry tale to the more unscrupulous elements of the press is obvious, but even they have finally moved on. Why you continue to involve yourself in matters that are really none of your affair is beyond me."

Sebastian kept his gaze on the East India Company man's smooth, lying face. "Did you tell anyone else that Nicholas Hayes had returned?"

"I did not. Whom would I tell?"

"I've no idea."

Forbes's deceptively soft blue eyes narrowed as if with thought. But Sebastian was beginning to understand just how much of everything this man said and did was for show. "I'll admit I did consider warning McHenry," said Forbes. "But in the end I realized it was unnecessary."

Whatever Sebastian had been expecting, it wasn't that. "You mean Hamish McHenry?" It came out more sharply than he'd intended.

"Yes. Why? Do you know him?"

"How do you know him?"

"As it happens, I met him in India, although I understand he's in England at the moment."

"What made you think he might need to be warned of Nicholas Hayes's reappearance?"

Forbes gave a negligent shrug. "I suppose because he was involved with Chantal de LaRivière himself at one time. That, and because he worked in the Foreign Office with Crispin Hayes."

"He did? Both of them?"

Forbes's lips curled into their habitual, smug little smile. "They did indeed. I understand it was shortly after Crispin's death that McHenry decided to buy a pair of colors. I always thought there was more to that tale than met the eye, but unlike you, I am not given to tilting at other people's windmills."

"So why didn't you warn McHenry?"

"I probably would have done so, except I haven't seen the man recently. And then Hayes was dead, so there was no point."

"And in the midst of all this ruminating, it never occurred to you to notify Bow Street?"

"It did, obviously. However, I decided against it. And to forestall your inevitable next question, I decided against it because I happen to value my family's privacy and had no desire to see the unpleasantness of the past paraded in public again for the amusement of the hoi polloi."

"Hayes tried to kill you on the waterfront in Macau. You weren't concerned that he might try again?"

"As it happens, he caught me unawares that day in Macau. After all, I thought the man dead and had no anticipation of encountering him in China, of all places. But forewarned is forearmed, as they say." The smug little smile was back. "I have every confidence in my ability to defend myself."

Sir Lindsey Forbes was a much smoother liar than Brownbeck. He'd obviously had years and years of practice at it. Sebastian said, "Did you tell your wife Nicholas Hayes was still alive?"

The smile faded from the man's features, leaving him looking considerably less pleasant. "You leave my wife out of this."

Sebastian gazed beyond him, to where a man with a barrel was selling ale to the dockworkers. "Odd, don't you think, that four men—you,

Brownbeck, Seaforth, and the Count de Compans—all knew that Nicholas Hayes was in England, and yet not one of you ostentatiously upright, law-abiding pillars of society felt moved to inform the appropriate authorities?"

"As I said, I am not the type to constantly be busying myself about other people's affairs."

"You might not be. But Brownbeck has made it his life's work—that and amassing a fortune, of course."

"Then I suggest you direct your questions toward that worthy," said Forbes with the faintest of bows. "And now you must excuse me."

Sebastian watched the East India Company man turn back toward the water, the breeze off the river lifting the tails of his finely tailored coat as he walked past the sweating, ragged dockworkers and seamen. The vague outlines of a possibility were beginning to occur to Sebastian, an idea so outlandish that he wanted to immediately discard it.

And yet he couldn't.

*Chapter 46*

$\mathcal{S}$ebastian had left Tom with the curricle beside the jumble of sheds, shops, hovels, and low taverns that trailed away from the docks toward East India Company Road. The docklands were busy this time of year, for June was the month for the return of the great East Indiamen with their deep draughts and precious cargoes of tea and spices, silks and salt-peter. The wind gusting off the big artificial basins was cool and damp, the air heavy with the scent of wine and cinnamon, and so absorbed was Sebastian in his contemplation of the various possibilities suggested by that day's revelations that he almost missed the men who fell into step behind him as he neared his curricle.

They did not strike him as being either seamen or lumpers.

His hand going to the double-barreled pistol he'd slipped into his pocket that morning, Sebastian met Tom's eye and then swung around. "Have something you wish to say to me, do you, gentlemen?"

There were four of them, their weathered faces sun-darkened and unshaven, their clothing the tattered remnants of the uniforms of men who'd fought for years against Napoléon. The clothes could have been stolen or bought secondhand, but Sebastian didn't think so. He knew ex-soldiers when he saw them—which meant the men now ranged against him were exponentially more dangerous than your typical dockland ruffians.

They drew up abruptly, their widening eyes and slack jaws betraying a shattered expectation of remaining undetected until they were ready to move in for the kill. But these men were not easily deterred. One of them—a tall, gangly fellow with a sergeant's chevrons on his stained, ragged red coat—exchanged a quick, significant look with his fellows and laughed. "Wot? Us?"

Sebastian drew the pistol from his pocket and pulled back the first hammer with an audible *click*. "Just out for a stroll, are you?"

"Ain't no law agin that, now, is there?" said the sergeant.

"Strolling? No."

Sebastian was aware of Tom nudging the horses forward to bring them closer. He didn't expect the situation to escalate. The men would have to be mad to continue an assault against a victim now armed and ready for them.

But the men were obviously desperate. They'd faced death often enough in the past for far less pay than they'd doubtless been promised by whoever had hired them to kill Sebastian. He saw the sergeant's sideways glance and quick jerk of the chin, and said, "Bloody hell," as they rushed him.

His first bullet took the sergeant high in the chest, spinning him around and sending him sprawling. Sebastian thumbed back the second hammer and shot another man in the throat. Then, dropping the flintlock, he yanked his knife from the sheath in his boot.

The two surviving assailants broke and ran.

Sebastian threw a quick glance at his tiger. "You all right?"

The boy was staring at him openmouthed. He swallowed and said, "Aye, gov'nor. Who are they?"

Sebastian went to check first one, then the next of the downed men, looking for weapons. They weren't dead yet, but they soon would be. In the coat of the second man, he found a bloodstained letter written in a woman's hand that began, *Dearest Richard, I can't begin to express to you the excitement with which I await your long-anticipated, safe return home.* . . .

"Damn," said Sebastian, swiping the back of one gloved hand across his sweaty forehead. *Damn, damn, damn.*

"Do you think Forbes set them after you?" asked Sir Henry Lovejoy as he and Sebastian walked along the terrace of Somerset House.

"Perhaps. Although the site of the attack could simply have been coincidental. The truth is, they could have been hired by any one of the four men who seem to be implicated in all of this."

Lovejoy stared out over the wind-whipped river. "Four men. I can't believe four men knew Hayes was in London and yet not one told the authorities."

"LaRivière still isn't back from Oxford, so I haven't had a chance to confirm it with him. But I can't see any reason for both Brownbeck and Seaforth to lie about that when they seem to be telling the truth about the rest. So yes, I'd say four: Brownbeck, Forbes, Seaforth, and La-Rivière."

Lovejoy shook his head as if still finding the information too difficult to absorb. "The involvement of Seaforth and LaRivière I understand. But Theo Brownbeck? Sir Lindsey Forbes? What have they to do with Nicholas Hayes?"

"It's . . . delicate," said Sebastian. "It involves the reputation of a lady, which makes it difficult for me to talk about. Let's just say both men had a very good reason to worry that Nicholas Hayes had returned to England specifically to kill them."

"And yet neither felt moved to make a report to Bow Street when they realized he had returned?" The magistrate's voice was rough with his disgust. "It's unbelievable."

"Yes. And suggestive."

Lovejoy looked over at him. "Meaning?"

Sebastian chose his words carefully. "Brownbeck came right out and admitted that he considered going to Bow Street but decided against it because he didn't want the embarrassment of having the past dredged up again. It's a sentiment shared by Seaforth and Forbes and, presumably, LaRivière as well." He'd decided against telling Lovejoy about Hamish McHenry. Forbes's casual mention of the major had been too pat not to be suspect, and Sebastian wanted to talk to Hamish himself, first. "I'm beginning to think the four men may have made a pact—either explicitly or implicitly—to simply have Hayes quietly killed."

"But he wasn't killed quietly," said Lovejoy.

"No, he wasn't, which makes it damnably confusing."

Lovejoy's face tightened into a pained expression. "The involvement of two prominent men such as Seaforth and LaRivière was bad enough. But now you're saying Forbes and Brownbeck are implicated as well? Merciful heavens. We're fortunate the palace is preoccupied at the moment with the visiting Allied Sovereigns. When are they due back from Oxford?"

"Tonight."

The Green Man was not a favorite with military men. Located in an ancient, tumbledown part of Westminster, the tavern was a place of dark, low ceiling beams, age-blackened wainscoting, and uneven flagstone floors. The medieval glass in the leaded windows was thick and wavy, the tables and benches were all scarred, and stray dogs regularly ran in and out looking for scraps.

Hamish McHenry sat alone in a darkened corner, a half-empty bottle of Scotch and a glass on the table before him. His head fell back and he blinked when Sebastian slid onto the bench opposite him. "How the blazes did you find me here?"

"Were you hiding from me?"

The major raised his glass to his lips and took a deep drink. "Not exactly."

Sebastian turned to order a brandy, then waited until it arrived before saying, "You didn't tell me you were in the Foreign Office with Crispin Hayes—before you bought yourself a pair of colors and went off to do your best to get yourself killed."

One corner of the man's lips quirked up into a shadow of a smile. "How did you know?"

"That you went to war hoping to die? I did something similar myself . . . although for a slightly different reason."

"Ah." He lifted his glass in a half salute. "Who told you I was with the Foreign Office?"

"That was Forbes."

"He's a nasty, sneaky son of a bitch."

"That he is. I assume he told me in an effort to deflect suspicion from himself onto you."

"And did it work?"

"Not exactly. Although I'll admit it helped me see a few things more clearly."

McHenry leaned back against the old-fashioned bench, his forearms lying limply on the table before him. "Then I suppose he achieved his purpose, didn't he?"

Sebastian said, "Tell me about Chantal de LaRivière."

McHenry brought up both hands to scrub them down over his haggard face. "She was so beautiful. She had the smile of an angel, a laugh like the gentle peal of the bells of heaven, and a body that could tempt a man to sell his soul to the devil."

"And did you? Sell your soul to the devil, I mean."

McHenry's bloodshot eyes met Sebastian's. "Metaphorically speaking, I suppose you could say I did."

"She seduced you?"

McHenry reached for his glass and drained it. "In every way."

"Let me guess. And then her suitably outraged husband caught you in flagrante delicto."

The major splashed more Scotch into his glass. "Not a very original scheme, I'll admit. But nevertheless highly effective. The Count played the outraged husband to perfection. At first he threatened me with a crim. con. case, of course. I was twenty-three years old and a frightened fool. I told him I had no money."

"And so he said he was willing to allow you to pay him with what you did have: access to information."

McHenry wrapped his hands around his glass, but did not drink. And for a moment he seemed to shrink in on himself, becoming less than what he had been a moment before.

Sebastian said, "How long did it go on?"

The major sucked in a deep breath and took a drink. "Not nearly as long as LaRivière hoped, as it turned out. I made a wretchedly unsatisfactory traitor, you see. Took to drinking. Considered killing myself. Showed up to work falling-down pissed and puking on myself. Grenville—he was the Foreign Secretary at the time—was an old friend of my father's, but even he couldn't put up with it for long and dismissed me. I suppose in some weak, twisted way it was what I was hoping would happen."

"And so LaRivière set his wife to seducing Crispin Hayes next?"

McHenry nodded, his jaw clenched. "I was so sunk in my own misery and a useless orgy of self-loathing that I didn't know what was happening until it was too late. It was simply by chance that I saw them together in the park one day and realized what she must have been doing. I tried to warn Crispin, but of course he wouldn't listen. He was hopelessly in love and utterly convinced Chantal was in love with him. Then I came along, trying to tell him she was a scheming little whore. He almost killed me for it."

"You told him she was trying to get him to spy for France?"

Dark color stained the major's cheeks and he shook his head. "Not exactly. I was too ashamed to be as explicit as I could have been. I only told him she was playing with him. Using him. Setting him up."

"How long between when you told him and the night he killed himself?"

"Less than a week. I don't know for certain exactly what happened, but I assume that somewhere in there Chantal and the Count sprang their trap and Crispin got caught. It's the only thing that makes sense of what happened next, isn't it? Crispin found out that he'd been fooled— that the woman he loved so desperately was using him. And then he ei- ther killed himself or he confronted LaRivière in a rage and LaRivière killed him."

"Which do you think is the most likely?"

"Honestly? I don't know."

A half-grown pup bumped its head against Sebastian's hand, and he reached down to pet it. "After Crispin was found dead, when Nicholas came to see you, did you tell him the truth? That LaRivière was using his wife to seduce young clerks in the Foreign Office, I mean."

McHenry scraped his hands down over his face again and nodded. "I thought I was being noble—finally doing the right thing, coming clean, making amends for being a weak, sniveling coward. Except that all I ended up doing was ruining Nicholas's life."

"Why didn't you come forward after he was arrested and tell the truth?"

McHenry let his hands fall. "You don't want to know."

Sebastian met his gaze. "Yes, I do."

"I tried. I had a long, extraordinarily difficult talk with Grenville. Then I went back to my rooms, expecting to be arrested. Instead, I re- ceived a visit from . . . someone. Someone important. He told me that a Frenchman like LaRivière could be useful. That rather than be exposed and ruined or killed, LaRivière had agreed to act as a double agent, sending false information back to Paris. I was warned that if I said anything more, I would simply disappear. It was suggested that I leave the country and that I might find the army a good new career."

"Why didn't Nicholas say anything?"

The major lifted both shoulders in a helpless shrug. "Maybe he was willing to be a martyr for king and country. Maybe he did it to preserve his brother's good name. Maybe he didn't believe they were really going to find him guilty of murder and ship him off to Botany Bay. Or maybe my visitor threatened someone he loved. I don't know."

Sebastian drew a deep breath, his chest so tight it hurt. "It was Jarvis, wasn't it? The man who came to see you and warned you to keep your mouth shut about LaRivière. It was Lord Jarvis."

McHenry started to take another drink, then changed his mind and pushed the glass aside. His gaze met Sebastian's, and after a moment he gave a slow, silent nod.

## Chapter 47

Charles, Lord Jarvis, was tired. In the past three days he'd traveled to and from Woolwich, then up to Oxford and back to London again. He'd attended more dinners, banquets, balls, levees, and various other ceremonies than he could count. As he climbed the steps of his Berkeley Square town house, he was thinking about a drink, a bath, dinner, and his bed.

"Good evening, my lord," said his butler, taking his hat and helping his lordship off with his dusting coat.

"It's good to be home," said Jarvis.

Grisham paused with Jarvis's coat over one arm, his expression one of wary resignation.

"Well, what is it?" snapped Jarvis, watching him.

"Mrs. Hart-Davis is dining with friends this evening," said the butler, referring to the cousin of Jarvis's late wife. "But Lord Devlin is here to see you, my lord. In the drawing room, my lord."

"What the devil?"

"He's been here for some time, my lord. Quite insistent he was in waiting for your lordship."

Jarvis was already heading for the stairs. "Oh, he was, was he?"

He found his son-in-law sprawled in a high-backed chair by the cold hearth. "What the devil is the meaning of this?" demanded Jarvis, closing the door behind him with a snap.

Devlin had been reading a book—one of Jarvis's own books, he realized, recognizing the distinctive burgundy leather binding that characterized the volumes of his extensive private library. But at Jarvis's entrance, the Viscount set the book aside and rose to his feet.

"You didn't tell me LaRivière was passing false information to revolutionary Paris for you. I assume he continued to do so well into the Napoleonic era?"

Jarvis walked to the table that held a selection of carafes and poured himself a glass of brandy. "I'd offer you some," he said without looking up, "but I know you well enough to assume you'd have helped yourself if you'd been thirsty."

"I'm not thirsty. Thank you."

Jarvis carefully replaced the carafe's stopper and turned, glass in hand. "It's a peculiar fantasy you nourish, this idea that I should impart all sorts of privileged information to you simply because you have taken it upon yourself to right all the perceived wrongs of the world."

"Not all of them. Mainly murders."

Jarvis gave a noncommittal grunt and took a sip of his brandy.

Devlin said, "Was the information he was feeding to Paris false before or only after the death of his wife?"

"Only afterward. Before the lovely Chantal's demise, the information he was sending was quite genuine—although not, fortunately, of a particularly sensitive nature."

"So you didn't know of his activities until after Hamish McHenry had his little conversation with Lord Grenville? How . . . remiss of you."

Jarvis's eyes narrowed. He took another drink.

Devlin said, "Did LaRivière kill Crispin Hayes?"

"I honestly don't know."

"Nor do you care?"

"Of course not. Why would I? The man was a fool."

"I'm surprised you allowed Hamish McHenry to live."

"He can thank Lord Grenville and the Foreign Secretary's friendship with his father for that. I assumed the wretch would die soon enough in India, but he seems to have the devil's own luck." Jarvis sipped his brandy. "So, are you here for a reason or simply to blow off steam over what you imagine to be my reticence?"

The younger man's nostrils flared. "Did you have Nicholas Hayes killed?"

"Why would I?"

"To keep him from killing you. And to keep LaRivière's secret, obviously."

Jarvis huffed a soft laugh. "Do you realize how long ago that was? Virtually every Frenchman of title or property has switched sides and danced a duet with either the revolutionary government or Napoléon at some point in the last twenty years. The Bourbons understand these things."

"And yet you warned me away from inquiring too closely into La-Rivière's affairs just a few days ago. Why was that? I wonder."

"Surely it's not such a puzzle that I have no desire to see the French King's representative accused of murder in the midst of the Regent's grand fete."

"So you have reason to think LaRivière did kill Nicholas Hayes?"

"I see it as a vague possibility—presumably for the same reasons as you."

"Because he feared Hayes's revenge? Or because LaRivière has reason to fear the Bourbons might not be so understanding after all?"

"He may fear it. That's not to say such fears are reasonable. But then, fears often are not."

Devlin's jaw hardened. "Eighteen years ago, you allowed an innocent young man to be convicted and transported to hell for a murder you knew he didn't commit."

"I don't know what happened to Chantal de LaRivière eighteen years ago, any more than you do. Nicholas Hayes went to Dover Street that night with murder in his heart. But whether or not he actually killed that woman pales to insignificance when seen in the larger context of affairs of state. In case you've forgotten, we were at war—in the first years of what would be a long, brutal, bloody war we were by no means guaranteed to win. The benefits to be derived from turning someone like LaRivière to our purposes far outweighed the paltry considerations of whatever injustice some hotheaded young man may have suffered."

"Paltry considerations."

"That's right."

Something blazed in his son-in-law's eyes, something so hot and dangerous that Jarvis instinctively took a step back.

"You and your ilk sicken me," said Devlin.

Then he turned and left.

For a moment Jarvis stayed where he was. Thoughtfully, he drained his glass and, setting it aside, walked over to lift the book Devlin had been reading and left open on the table beside the chair.

It was a selection of Montaigne's essays, and Jarvis found his gaze caught by a familiar line. *A straight oar looks bent in the water. What matters is not merely that we see things but how we see them.*

## Chapter 48

$\mathscr{G}$ilbert-Christophe de LaRivière was drinking a glass of port in solitary splendor at his own table when Sebastian walked into the Frenchman's dining room, trailed by the Count's French butler frantically sputtering, *"Mais, monsieur le vicomte! Vous n—"*

LaRivière's languid gaze met Sebastian's. Then he glanced at the butler now wringing his hands and said, "Leave us." Leaning back in his chair, the French Count took a slow sip of his port. "Bit high-handed even for you, isn't it, Devlin?"

Sebastian shut the door in the butler's face. "We need to talk. Now."

LaRivière waved one slim white hand in the general direction of the two long rows of empty chairs. "By all means, do have a seat."

"Thank you, but I'll stand."

A faint suggestion of a smile hovered about the Frenchman's thin lips. "As you wish."

"You know why I'm here?"

"I presume it has something to do with the events that gave rise to the rather hysterical message I recently received from Lord Seaforth."

"Something. But not all."

"Oh? Do tell."

Sebastian wandered the room, taking in the gleaming walnut wainscoting, the exquisite Venetian chandelier, the heavy Sheffield plate. The life-sized painting of one of the most beautiful women Sebastian had ever seen.

"Your wife?" said Sebastian, pausing before the portrait.

"My late wife."

She was breathtakingly exquisite. She'd been painted with her glorious fair hair loose and unpowdered and her gown slipping off her shoulders in a style that was reminiscent of the Restoration era. Her face was heart-shaped, her enormous eyes a brilliant violet, her mouth full and pouting and seemingly made for kisses and everything sinful. It was a beguiling combination of innocence and seduction, vulnerability and power that had beckoned more than one man to his doom.

"She was lovely," said Sebastian.

"That she was," agreed the Frenchman, still lounging at his ease.

"Was she a willing participant in your little seduction schemes? I wonder. Or did you force her compliance?"

"Oh, Chantal enjoyed seducing men, believe me." Again, that faintly derisive aristocratic smile. "You've been talking to someone, have you?"

"Several people."

The Count gave a very Gallic shrug. "It was inevitable, I suppose."

"Is that why you tried to have me killed?"

The amusement deepened. "Did someone try to kill you? How . . . distressing."

"That they tried? Or that they failed?"

"What do you think?"

Sebastian continued his perambulation of the room. "Eighteen years ago you set your lovely wife to seduce a green young man with a promising career at the Foreign Office. He tumbled desperately in love with her and in due course also tumbled into bed with her. At which time you—playing the part of the outraged husband, no doubt to perfection—charged in and caught them in flagrante. It's an old, rather tired game, but it still works, doesn't it? The husband threatens a crim. con. case that would both disgrace and bankrupt the victim, and the victim begs to settle out of court. Only, in this instance the victim had no money. He did, however, have access to information—information that could be passed on to Paris. Not for ideological reasons, mind you, but for vulgar monetary gain."

LaRivière sipped his port. He was no longer smiling. "I see you judge us harshly—an easy thing to do, no doubt, when one has never seen their country ripped apart and destroyed by revolution. We did what we had to do to survive. Vulgar and otherwise."

"You were living in this house at the time. It's not as if you'd been forced to take refuge in a chicken coop." Sebastian had seen French countesses and duchesses reduced to living in old barns.

"Believe me," said LaRivière, "it was not nearly so well-appointed twenty years ago."

"Your two masters have paid you well, have they?"

"Well enough. I also made some extraordinarily wise investments."

"Based on tips passed to you by your two masters?"

"Perhaps."

Sebastian resumed walking. "Unfortunately for you, the same sensibilities that made the first of the young men in question susceptible to Chantal's seductive wiles also meant that playing the role of traitor to his own country preyed upon him to a disastrous extent. He quickly fell apart and was dismissed from the Foreign Office."

"I presume you're going someplace with this?"

"I am; bear with me. Your first victim having thus lost his usefulness, you then set your sights on Crispin Hayes. Except this time you chose poorly. Oh, he was every bit as susceptible as his friend to Chantal's seductions—she must have been an extraordinarily talented woman. But when you came barging in and played your practiced role as the outraged husband, Crispin didn't react quite the same way as his friend— perhaps because his friend had tried to warn him about Chantal."

LaRivière gave a regretful sigh. "I should have killed McHenry as soon as he was dismissed from the Foreign Office."

"I'm surprised you didn't."

"A miscalculation on my part. I feared his death might arouse unpleasant suspicions."

"And yet that apprehension didn't stop you from killing Crispin."

LaRivière took a slow sip of his wine. "I didn't, you know—kill him, I mean. I'm not saying I didn't consider it. But he beat me to it by killing himself. The dupe was utterly besotted with Chantal, convinced that she loved him with a fervor to equal his own and was looking to him to save her from her evil husband—me. Then he discovered he'd been played for a rank fool and he couldn't bear it. Some men find that sort of shame impossible to live with, I'm afraid. It was his own frailty and damaged sense of amour propre—combined I suppose with the pain of unrequited love—that drove him off that bridge."

"I don't believe you."

Again, the shrug. "Believe as you wish. It makes no difference."

"Was that why Nicholas came here that night? Because he thought you'd killed his brother? Or was the argument all about Chantal?"

"I really don't recall."

"Oh, you recall, all right. You argued, one of you pulled a pistol—I'm assuming that was you—and in the ensuing struggle the pistol went off and Chantal was killed."

"That's one theory."

Sebastian came to rest his hands flat on the tabletop and leaned into them. "You're lucky Nicholas Hayes didn't shout the truth about your treason to anyone and everyone who would listen."

"Ah, but by then your estimable father-in-law had already made his move. Jarvis convinced the noble young man to keep quiet for the sake of both his brother and king and country—and, presumably, for the sake of his own skin. I wonder when he realized his mistake. As they were loading him on the transport to Botany Bay? What a fool he was."

"You're suggesting, I take it, that Nicholas had reason to want to kill Jarvis as well?"

"I would, if I'd been treated so shabbily. Wouldn't you?"

Sebastian pushed away from the table. "Perhaps. Except that I sincerely doubt Jarvis knew Nicholas Hayes had returned to England. But you knew."

"I did. However, so did a number of other people."

"Oh? Whom did you tell?"

"No one. But as you are doubtless already aware, neither the Earl of Seaforth nor Theodore Brownbeck was anywhere near so reticent."

"So why didn't you try to kill Nicholas?"

LaRivière gave what sounded like a genuinely startled laugh. "Perhaps I've mellowed in my old age."

"No, you haven't."

"Oh, believe me, I have. Eighteen years ago I was desperate. You may consider yourself a moral, ethical, and honest man—loyal and true and all that rot, as you English like to say. But you have no idea how you would behave in adversity. No idea at all."

"I spent six years at war. You think I haven't faced adversity?"

LaRivière's eyebrows arched. "Perhaps you have. And would you have me believe that you have done nothing of which you are ashamed? I've heard whispers of things that happened in Portugal . . . when was it? Four years ago?"

Four years before, Sebastian had beaten a French captain to death with his bare hands. The raw, surging bloodlust of that night—and the unspeakable events that had led up to it—still haunted Sebastian's dreams. But all he said was "Did you kill Nicholas Hayes?"

"And if I said I did not, would you take me at my word?"

"No."

"I thought not. But the truth is, I didn't kill him. On the evening in question, I dined with the Regent before attending his Carlton House reception for the Allied Sovereigns."

"You could have hired someone to do your killing for you."

"I could have. But I did not."

"Again, I don't believe you."

LaRivière made a soft *tssking* sound and shook his head. "Such an untrusting person you are. Tell me, my lord, do you fence?"

"Yes."

"We must have a match sometime."

"I think not."

"No? A pity, but as you wish." LaRivière drained his glass, then held the stem between two fingers and twisted it back and forth so that the fine-cut crystal caught the candlelight and danced it across his cold, dark eyes. "Why do you do it, anyway? Devote yourself with such indefatigable passion to this quest to catch the killer of someone you never even met." He glanced over at Sebastian. "That's an honest question, by the way. I genuinely would like to know."

"For the same reason I would step in to stop a man from whipping a tired horse, or a cruel child from tormenting a stray dog. Because it's the right thing to do." *And because I believe we are all connected, every living thing one to the other, so that I owe to each what I would owe to myself.* But he didn't say that.

LaRivière shook his head as Sebastian turned toward the door, obviously finding the concept too alien to comprehend. "What a waste of a life."

But Sebastian only laughed.

That night, Sebastian lay awake long after the last gentleman's carriage had rattled up the street, long after the creatures of the dark settled down into silence with a final furtive rustling and the wind died in the hours before dawn.

"You can't stop thinking about it all, can you?" said Hero, rolling over to rest her hand on his chest.

He slipped his arm beneath her to gather her close. "No." He had told her some but not all of what he had learned that day. Jarvis's role in the events of eighteen years ago he had kept to himself.

She said, "I think Seaforth did it. I think he killed Nicholas but missed Ji, so the next morning he hired someone to find the boy and eliminate him."

"Seaforth spent the afternoon at White's. Lovejoy's men confirmed it."

"You don't think he could somehow have left and come back without anyone noticing?"

"Possibly." Sebastian buried his face in the heavy fall of her warm, soft hair. "I wish we could find that child."

"We came so close today," said Hero. "Thank God I was there, even if he did then slip away. Do you believe Seaforth has indeed called off those men?"

"Surely he knew I wasn't making an idle threat. Although I plan to pay him another visit in the morning, just to impress the point."

But by morning, the Third Earl of Seaforth was dead.

*Chapter 49*

<br />

Thursday, 16 June

"*W*ho found him?" said Sebastian, staring down at what was left of the late Earl of Seaforth. His lordship sat slumped against a grimy brick wall just inside the arch to Leen Mews, less than half a block from his North Audley Street house. The early-morning air was cool, the light pale and diffuse, thanks to a cover of high white clouds. Around them, the exclusive streets of Mayfair were only just beginning to come awake.

"A dustman," said Sir Henry Lovejoy. "Right before dawn. At first glance, he thought his lordship must have imbibed too freely last night and fallen asleep. Then he took a closer look."

"That must have been a shock."

"I daresay it was."

Seaforth sat with his thin legs in their natty yellow nankeen trousers splayed out before him, his arms hanging limply at his sides, his bare head bowed. It wasn't until Sebastian hunkered down beside the dead man that he could see the Earl's wide, staring eyes. A trickle of blood had dried beside his lordship's slack mouth; a larger, dark red rivulet stained the cobbles near the wall.

Lovejoy said, "According to Lady Seaforth, her husband went for a walk late last night and didn't come back. She says he's been troubled by something lately and hasn't been sleeping well."

"'Something' being the reappearance and murder of his cousin Nicholas?" suggested Sebastian, studying the blood pooled on the cobbles.

"Presumably."

Sebastian rose to his feet. "From the looks of things, I suspect that when we move him, we'll find he's been stabbed in the back."

"Lovely." Lovejoy pushed out a long, pained breath. "The palace isn't going to like this. They aren't going to like it at all. The talk about Nicholas Hayes was finally beginning to die down. Now it's all going to start up again, only it will be even worse. First an earl's son, now an earl."

Sebastian glanced around at a clatter of horses' hooves. A groom was leading a pair of smart chestnuts out of the stables at the far end of the mews. For a moment the two men's gazes met; then the groom looked away. "Perhaps we'll be lucky and find someone who saw something."

Lovejoy nodded. "I'll have the lads talk to everyone in the area." Yet even as he said it, both men knew it was unlikely to turn up anything. Nicholas Hayes's death might have been messy, but the two killings since then were something else entirely.

Seaforth's top hat lay upside down where it had fallen on the cobbles beside him, and Sebastian found himself staring down at the dead nobleman's thinning, vaguely untidy hair. The Earl had been both selfish and scheming, an ugly combination of weak and vicious. And yet . . .

"Why Seaforth?" he said, thinking aloud.

Lovejoy looked over at him. "What do you mean?"

"I can see any one of four men—Forbes, LaRivière, Brownbeck, or even Seaforth himself—murdering Nicholas Hayes out of fear he'd come back to England to kill them. And I can see the same frightened killer then deciding to eliminate Pennington when he realized the gardens' owner would be able identify him. But why the bloody hell kill Seaforth?"

Lovejoy's lips pressed together in a frown. "Well, he is the one who told you they all knew Hayes was in London."

"Revenge, you mean? For having too loose a tongue? I suppose it's possible."

"But you don't think so?"

"I think it more likely that Seaforth knew who murdered Hayes and was panicking enough to begin talking about it, and that's why he was killed." *Or perhaps because he was behind the attack on our carriage and Jarvis found out about it,* thought Sebastian. But he decided not to say it.

"Perhaps someone is acting on a violent grudge they hold against the Hayes family," suggested Lovejoy.

"Now, that's a possibility I hadn't considered."

"Who's the new Earl?"

Sebastian thought about the three eager, redheaded little boys he'd seen with their father and mother on Bond Street. And about another child, this one dark-haired and exotic, who might or might not have a claim to his murdered father's titles and lands. "It's one of two children, both about eight or nine."

Lovejoy's face had taken on a pinched look. "Let us hope I am wrong."

Hero spent the first part of the morning in a chair by the drawing room windows, going over the notes from her various interviews. Yesterday's near miss with Ji had been encouraging, frustrating, and frightening. They now knew Ji was still alive. But if Hero hadn't been there . . .

"Was that the lad you was looking for?" Alice had said, coming up to Hero afterward as the crowds gathered round the ruffian's broken body.

"Yes," said Hero. "Why? Do you know him?"

"No," said the old woman. "Sorry. I only play Clerkenwell on Wednesdays, you know. What was it you said you wanted him for?"

"Just to interview him."

"Ah. Well, I'm right sorry you missed him, then."

Hero was planning to move their search to Westminster next. But she had this niggling feeling she was missing something—something that would be obvious if she only knew where to look. Yet after several hours of reading and rereading the same scribbled notations from her talks with a dozen or more street performers, she was beginning to suspect that the vague, fanciful notion was nothing more than wishful thinking.

"'Orses," said Simon, who'd been playing with a small wagon at her feet but now looked up at the sound of a carriage dashing down the street. Simon had trouble with his h's—amongst other sounds—with the result that he had a disconcerting tendency to sound like a Cockney street urchin.

"'Orses," he said again, scrambling up into the chair beside her to lean against the caned back and peer out the windows overlooking the street.

The clatter of hooves and the rattle of trace chains drew Hero's attention to a smart barouche and team drawing up before their steps. As Hero watched, a gentlewoman in an elegant sapphire blue walking dress and broad-brimmed hat appeared in the carriage's doorway, then paused to thank the footman who'd let down the steps. Even from this distance, she projected an aura of rare grace and self-possession. A pigeon taking flight with a whirl of wings from the pediment of a nearby house caused her to look up, the brim of her hat lifting so that the morning light fell full on her face.

"Come, Simon," said Hero, setting aside her notebook to lift the child from the chair. "Let's go find Claire, shall we?" And then she went to ring the bell and send word to Morey that she was at home to Lady Forbes.

# Chapter 50

"Thank you for agreeing to receive me at such an unfashionably early hour," said Lady Forbes.

"We keep very unfashionable hours around here," said Hero with a smile. "Please, have a seat."

Lady Forbes did not sit. Instead, she stood just inside the entrance to the drawing room, her face abnormally pale, her breathing noticeably agitated. Once, this woman had loved Nicholas Hayes enough to run away and seek to marry him. But after almost nineteen years, people changed, thought Hero—particularly when their circumstances altered so radically. Looking at her now, Hero found herself wondering how much of the passionate, willful nineteen-year-old girl Kate had once been still lingered within this poised, awe-inspiringly composed woman. Or had that vulnerable girl been squashed and left behind long ago?

The woman who was now the wife of Sir Lindsey Forbes jerked at the ribbons of her hat as if suddenly finding them too tight. "I've just heard that Lord Seaforth was found dead this morning. Is it true?"

"Yes," said Hero baldly.

"Dear God." Katherine Forbes turned away, one hand coming up to press against her lips as if she was momentarily overwhelmed by what she'd just heard. And it came to Hero, watching her, that this was a woman who'd long ago learned to hide every wayward emotion and betraying thought. That what Hero had at first taken as calm self-possession was actually a painstakingly constructed facade.

And that facade was cracking.

She watched as Katherine Forbes carefully set about tucking away everything she didn't want seen. When she turned to face Hero again, head held high, only her unnatural pallor betrayed her. "I ask that you and Lord Devlin keep what I have to tell you in the strictest confidence . . . if at all possible."

"You have my word."

"Thank you."

She sat then, tensely, on the very front edge of the sofa facing the windows, her reticule gripped with both hands on her knees as if it could somehow protect her from the consequences of what she was about to say. "I'm here because Lord Seaforth's death has led me to fear that my previous lack of honesty may in some way I don't understand have contributed to the Earl's death."

She paused, as if unable to go on, and Hero said quietly, "You saw Nicholas, didn't you?"

Kate sucked in a quick breath, then nodded. "We were just returning to St. James's Square—Sir Lindsey and I. We'd been visiting acquaintances, and it was early evening, that time of day when the setting sun lends such a glorious golden light to everything. I looked across at the square, thinking how pretty it all was, and . . . I saw Nicholas standing there, by the fence around the water basin."

"You recognized him?"

She nodded again. "Immediately. He was older than the young man I remembered and dressed like a tradesman, but the instant I saw him, I couldn't look away. It was as if all the noise and color of the square faded and there were only the two of us." She paused as if vaguely embarrassed by what she had just said. "I realize how fanciful that sounds."

"No, please—" Hero's throat suddenly felt so tight, she had to work to push out the words. "Go on."

Kate's voice was hushed, her chest jerking with each strained intake of air. "For a moment, I couldn't look away. Then I remembered Sir Lindsey was beside me and I was terrified lest he turn and see Nicholas too."

"Did he?"

"No." She paused as if reconsidering this. "At least, I don't think he did. Nicholas told me afterward that he hadn't intended to approach me, that he was simply hoping to catch a glimpse of me from a distance. He hadn't meant for me to see him."

"But he did approach you?"

"Yes. Four days later. I was with my maid Molly at Hatchards, in Piccadilly. We spoke for only a few moments, but arranged to meet again. Someplace private."

"Where?" said Hero, sharper than she'd intended. "Where were you to meet?"

Kate swallowed. "In Pennington's Tea Gardens, on Thursday evening."

"Dear Lord," whispered Hero. "That's why he went there."

Kate pressed her lips together and nodded. "I knew Sir Lindsey would be busy with all the events surrounding the Allied Sovereigns' visit. When the day came, I told him I wasn't well and had decided to stay home. He was furious, of course—he likes having a wife with him at such events." She said it as if any wife would have sufficed as long as she was attractive and presentable enough for Sir Lindsey to consider her an asset, and Hero suspected that was true enough. "But for once I didn't give in to him. He grumbled, but in the end he went alone."

*For once I didn't give in to him*, thought Hero. What a miserable marriage. Aloud, she said, "You were with Nicholas in the gardens that night?"

"No. Just as I was about to leave the house, one of the kitchen maids scalded her arm quite badly. I had to deal with it, and it took so long that by the time I reached Pennington's Gardens, they were closing." Her face had acquired a pinched, haunted look. "All I could do was sit in the hackney and watch the stream of happy, laughing people leaving the gardens. I kept hoping I'd see Nicholas, but he never came." She swallowed convulsively and bowed her head. "I was devastated. I was certain he must be thinking that I'd changed my mind, that I'd decided I didn't want to see him after all. But by then he was already dead, wasn't he?"

"Did you see anyone you recognized in the crowd?"

Her head came up, and it was obvious from the consternation in her face that it had never occurred to her that she might unknowingly have seen Nicholas's killer. "No. No, I didn't."

"And then you went home?"

"Yes. I had the hackney stop by the apothecary's so I could pick up a headache powder on the way. That was the excuse I'd given for going out, you see—and my explanation for having the footman call a hackney rather than go through all the bother of having the horses put to and the carriage brought 'round. Of course, I was gone a ridiculously long time for such a simple errand, and I could have sent one of the servants for it in the first place. But I didn't expect anyone to inquire too closely. I mean, why would they?"

*Why indeed?* thought Hero. Servants were accustomed to accepting their employers' little prevarications and obvious outright lies without a blink. "Did Nicholas have a child with him when you saw him—a little boy of perhaps eight or nine?"

"Not when I spoke with him in Piccadilly—or at any rate, I didn't see the boy then. But I remember there was a child who seemed to be with him in the square. A pretty boy, with very dark hair." She paused. "Why? Who is he?"

"His name is Ji. We don't know for certain what his relationship is to Nicholas Hayes, but the two came together from China."

"Is that where Nicholas has been? In *China?*"

"Yes. He didn't tell you?"

"No. But we spoke so briefly. I was afraid someone might see us. Where is the child now?"

"We don't know. He disappeared after Nicholas was killed. I saw him yesterday morning, but some men tried to grab him, and he ran off again."

"Good heavens. Who would want to hurt a child?"

"Lord Seaforth, actually. He was afraid the boy might be Nicholas's legitimate heir, and thus able to challenge the succession."

Kate stared at her. "And is he? Nicholas's child, I mean."

"I think he probably is."

Kate was silent, and Hero had the impression that all of her focus, all of her thoughts, had been drawn into herself. Eighteen years before, this woman had given birth to Nicholas Hayes's child—her only child, a child who had died. Hero wondered how such a woman would react to the discovery that the man she'd once loved so desperately had fathered a child by another. But with Kate, such things were almost impossible to discern.

Hero said, "Nicholas didn't say anything to you about the boy?"

"No."

"Did he say anything—anything at all that might help explain his murder?"

"No. As I said, we spoke for only a moment or two."

"Can you tell me what he said? It might help."

Kate nodded, the skin of her face tight, the struggle to maintain her composure so obvious as to hardly be worth the effort. "When he first walked up to me in Hatchards, I said something like, 'Dear Lord, it really is you.' I think by then I had somehow managed to convince myself that I must have imagined seeing him. I said, 'What are you doing in England? If they find you, they'll kill you.'" She paused.

"And?" prodded Hero.

"And he said, 'I know. It doesn't matter.' I remember I was suddenly furious with him. I said, 'What do you mean, it doesn't matter? It matters to me.' And then he smiled this strange, crooked smile and said, 'You still care? Even if it's just a little?'" She paused again, her gaze dropping to where her fingers were playing aimlessly with the strings of her reticule.

It was a long moment before she could go on. "He said . . . he said, 'You still care?' and I told him I'd loved him with every breath I've taken for more than nineteen years." She looked suddenly fierce, a challenge in her eyes when she glanced up as if daring Hero to judge her.

When Hero remained silent, Kate said, "I told him it was madness for us to be talking like that where anyone might see us. And then I suggested we meet at the tea gardens, because no one fashionable goes there anymore. I remembered there used to be a small clearing in the shrubbery, with a bench, near the access gate in the western wall. . . ."

Her voice trailed away, and in the silent, wounded depths of her gentle blue eyes, Hero could see hints of a pain and a heartache that would never go away.

Hero said, "Was anyone close enough that they might have heard you?"

Kate looked at her blankly. "I don't believe so, but . . . Dear heaven, do you think it's possible?"

"Perhaps," said Hero as gently as she could. But there was no way to soften this woman's realization that their planned meeting might somehow have inadvertently contributed to the death of the man she'd loved for so long. "Did he say anything else? Anything at all?"

Kate gazed out the open windows. The flat morning light was soaking the upper stories of the row of houses across the street and turning the small visible slice of sky an almost brilliant white. Then suddenly everything darkened, as if a heavier cloud had passed over the sun. "I don't think so. Except . . ."

"Yes?"

She frowned with the effort of memory. "I don't recall his exact words, but he said there was something he wanted to ask me. I said, 'Ask. Ask me anything,' and he smiled in a way that made him look so much like the boy he once was that it . . . it hurt. He said, 'You don't even know what it is yet,' and I told him I didn't care. Then the smile went out of his eyes and he said, 'I thought I could count on Anne, but she let me down.'"

Hero sat forward. *"Anne?* Do you think he meant his sister, Lady Bradbury?"

"I assumed so. Why do you say it like that?"

"Because Lady Bradbury told Devlin she had no idea her brother was in England. She said she hadn't seen him since their father banished him nineteen years ago."

*Chapter 51*

Thursday's schedule of events for the entertainment of the visiting Allied Sovereigns included a dinner to be hosted by Lord Castlereagh, a visit to Drury Lane Theatre, and a ball at the home of the Marchioness of Hertford. But for those dignitaries unfazed by their recent lightning trip to Oxford and looking for a diversion earlier in the day, the palace had arranged for them to view the annual charity children's procession and service at St. Paul's Cathedral.

Sebastian arrived at St. Paul's to find the sky above white with thin, high clouds and the air warm and humid. Somewhere a band was playing, although the musicians struggled to compete with the wind's noisy snapping of the banners carried by each of the various charitable institutions.

Lady Bradbury was standing near the cathedral steps in a section reserved for people of quality. She wore a green sarcenet walking dress with bunches of yellow ribbons on the tucked sleeves and an enormously wide-brimmed bonnet of the type popularized by the Tsar's sister the Duchess of Oldenburg. When Sebastian walked up to her, she was clapping politely, a vaguely bored smile plastered on her face as she watched the end-less parade of carefully scrubbed and neatened-up pauper children.

She cast him a quick glance, then said in a smug, self-congratulatory tone, "It's an uplifting sight, is it not? A grand tradition that honors our rich heritage of British benevolence."

"That's one way to look at it."

She gave a polite titter. "Is there any other?"

Rather than answer, he said, "I know about your meeting with Nicholas."

Her hands froze midclap, her eyeballs swiveling sideways. She recovered almost immediately, that fixed air of amused condescension never slipping. "I don't have the slightest idea what you're talking about."

"Yes, you do."

A pretty child in a sashed dress stepped forward to recite a short, breathy speech no one could hear before presenting three posies to the Lord Mayor, the Tsar of Russia, and the Prussian King.

Lady Anne clapped again. "This is hardly the place for such a discussion."

"Then walk apart with me. I doubt anyone will either notice or complain."

"Don't be ridiculous."

"If you are counting on me to either be quiet or go away, I fear you are doomed to disappointment."

She hesitated, her lips flattening into a thin, unattractive line. Then she turned and stalked off toward Ludgate Street, her head held high.

Sebastian fell into step beside her. He thought she might continue to deny having seen her brother, but she obviously thought he knew more about the meeting than he did. She said, "Do I take it you think I should have informed the authorities?"

"Not at all. Although I must admit I'm surprised you didn't."

She looked beyond him, her attention seemingly all for the next troop of charity children filling the narrow street, banner waving. "And deliberately provoke the kind of wretched scandal I've been forced to endure for the past week? Why would I?"

"Ah. So that's why," said Sebastian in a way that caused her ladyship's eyebrows first to lift, then to draw together in a frown. "Is that the same reason you refused to honor your brother's request?"

She huffed a scornful sound that was not a laugh. "As if I would take his grubby little foreign-born by-blow into my home."

Sebastian stared at her, at the tilt of her chin and the still faintly curling line of her lips. "Nicholas asked you to take care of his child?"

"Yes. Can you believe it?"

"So the child is illegitimate? Are you certain?"

"I assumed it must be, although I don't believe he actually said. He wanted to introduce me to her, but naturally I refused."

"*Her?*" For a moment, it was as if the off-tune band, the jostling children, the cheering crowd all faded into a haze. "Are you telling me the child is a girl?"

"That's what he said. Obviously I don't know for certain, but why would he lie? Di is her name, or Gi, or some such outlandish thing. I believe he said she was twelve, but needless to say I wasn't paying a great deal of attention."

"Twelve?" Sebastian found everything he thought he'd known about the missing child spin around and realign itself to create a different picture. He thought about the child he'd glimpsed so briefly standing beside that lamppost in Brook Street, and realized that instead of a nine- or ten-year-old boy, he'd actually been looking at a small, fine-boned twelve-year-old girl with cropped hair. "What else did he say about her?"

Lady Bradbury gave a high, ringing laugh. "He was at pains to impress upon me that she's intelligent, well educated, and well mannered, and that her English is perfect. As if that would make any difference."

Sebastian looked at this woman's hot, flushed face and saw the petty, all-consuming nature of her self-regard, the self-absorption that defined everything and everyone by its impact on her. He said, "Did Nicholas tell you he was dying of consumption?"

"He did, yes. He said that was why he'd come back to England, because he was dying and he was hoping I would agree to take care of the girl after he was gone. Can you believe it?"

Sebastian found he had to look away from her, to the street filled with endless thousands of orphaned pauper children. "What do you find so unbelievable? That he would risk giving up the few remaining months of his life to try to provide for his child? Or that he had such misplaced faith in his only sister's goodness?"

Two splotches of color appeared high on her ladyship's cheeks. "Nicholas forfeited any claims he might have had on his family nineteen years ago."

"And what about his child? What about your niece's claims?"

Lady Anne gazed at him with righteous, scandalized horror. "She's *Chinese.*"

"And therefore means nothing to you?"

Her ladyship drew up abruptly and turned to stare back at the Cathedral. "This is a preposterous conversation."

"One more thing: Did Nicholas say anything else—anything at all—that might shed some light on his murder?"

"I don't think so. I was frankly appalled to see him and stunned by his request. I cut off our interview as quickly as possible and left."

"Where did you see him?"

"He accosted me last Sunday as I was leaving church, of all places. I was beyond mortified. What if someone had seen us talking and recognized him?"

"Perish the thought. *Did* anyone see him?"

"No, thankfully."

"You're certain?"

"Reasonably so, yes. Obviously, I was concerned."

"Did you tell anyone you'd seen him?"

"Seriously? As if I would."

"No, of course not." Sebastian touched his hand to his hat with only the vaguest of polite bows. "Thank you for your time, Lady Bradbury."

He was turning away when she reached out unexpectedly with one elegantly gloved hand to touch his arm. "You won't—you won't tell anyone I spoke to him, will you?"

He studied her thin, crimped mouth. "What worries you more? The possibility that someone might find you lacking in common decency and humanity? Or the fear that people might mistakenly believe you actually loved your own brother?"

"Don't be a fool," she said. Then she turned to walk back toward the Cathedral, the yellow silk ribbons on her pin-tucked sleeves fluttering in the wind.

"So that's why Nicholas came back," said Hero later that afternoon. They were seated on the terrace overlooking the house's rear gardens with Simon and the big, arrogant black cat named Mr. Darcy at their feet. It was still hot, but the clouds overhead were becoming thicker and darker, the light more diffuse. "He didn't come back to kill Seaforth or LaRivière or even Forbes, but because he was dying and he hoped his sister would agree to take care of his daughter after he was gone."

Devlin stared out over the gardens, at the neatly edged parterres banked by more natural shrubbery bending now with the growing wind. They could hear a horse neighing in a nearby stable and a hawker out on the street shouting his wares. "Mahmoud Abbasi told me that Nicholas was no longer the hot-tempered man he'd been when young—that he'd studied the teachings of Buddhism and was one of the most calm and controlled men Abbasi had ever met. But I didn't pay enough attention . . . or perhaps I didn't believe it enough to think everything through the way I should have. A man like that wouldn't dedicate the last remaining months of his life to exacting revenge on those who'd harmed him in the past. His thoughts would all be for his child. His *daughter*." Abbasi had also told Sebastian about a girl child, he realized. A girl who would now be about twelve. But they'd both simply assumed the child must have died.

A lizard paused at the edge of the flagstone paving, head up and alert as it attracted the attention of both the cat and the baby. Hero said, "Why put Ji in breeches? Why cut her hair and make everyone think she's a boy?"

"Presumably for her safety during all those endless months on the ship. That, and because Hayes was familiar with the rough area around the Red Lion where he hoped to be able to hide here in London. How ironic that by dressing her as a boy to keep her safe, he almost got her killed because Seaforth thought she might be the rightful heir to the earldom."

Hero was silent for a moment. "I can't believe Lady Bradbury turned her brother down. Because his child is half-Chinese? My God."

"That, and a by-blow—or so her ladyship assumes."

"What a despicable woman."

They watched the cat start to stalk toward the lizard. But the lizard took fright and ran away, so Mr. Darcy sat down and began cleaning himself as if that had been his plan all along.

Devlin said, "One of my favorite parts of her tale is her indignation at the fact that Nicholas approached her as she was leaving Sunday services. He's begging her to take care of his orphaned daughter— practically on the steps of her church—and all she can think about is that someone might see them."

Hero tipped back her head, her gaze on the clouds above. The sky had taken on a darker color, and the trees were alive with a chorus of birds coming in to roost ahead of the approaching rain. "It's why he decided to contact Calhoun, isn't it? Because his sister had just turned him down and he was desperate to find someone who would be there for his little girl when he died."

Devlin nodded. "I suspect it's also why he approached Lady Forbes and arranged to meet her in Pennington's Tea Gardens."

Hero watched Simon push up from the flagstones and toddle over to place his hands on his father's knees. She said, "I'd always assumed that if we found the person he'd gone to meet that night, we'd know who killed him. So I suppose the question now becomes, Who besides Lady Forbes knew he was going to be in the gardens? Sir Lindsey?"

Devlin reached to lift the little boy up onto his lap. He was silent for a moment, then said, "Given that Lady Forbes was at Hatchards with her abigail, it's possible her woman overheard them making the assignation and told Sir Lindsey. It's also possible that Titus Poole simply followed Nicholas to the gardens that night and killed him, although the sickle in the back has an amateurish, unplanned feeling to it that argues against that. So I'm beginning to think it more likely that Poole overheard the conversation and reported it to whoever was employing him, and that person went to the gardens to confront Hayes."

"Katherine Forbes said Sir Lindsey was gone by the time she meant to call a hackney for the gardens. She assumed he went straight to the dinner, but what if he didn't? What if he went to the gardens and met Hayes in the clearing? If he didn't get any blood on his clothes, Sir Lindsey could conceivably have killed Hayes and then gone on to Carlton House."

"I'd say so, yes. I think I need to pay another visit to Mr. Titus Poole."

## Chapter 52

The rain started just before Sebastian turned his horses into New-gate Street. There was a clap of thunder, a hush, then a sudden down-pour that roared in their ears. The temperature felt as if it had plummeted twenty degrees.

"Never thought I'd be glad t' see the rain," said Tom, grinning as the water ran off his hat and nose.

Sebastian drew up near the arched entrance to the Bell's yard. "There's no doubt the city can use a good cleaning." He handed the reins to the boy and hopped down. "In more ways than one."

It was raining harder now, the clouds bunching up thick and dark overhead, the wind gusting enough to try to grab the door to the tap-room when Sebastian pushed it open and walked into an atmosphere redolent with the smell of wet wool and beer. The room was crowded, for the rain had driven a score or more of men inside, their coats and hats sodden, the men laughing as they wiped shining, wet faces and called for ale or wine. A comely girl of about sixteen was behind the bar, her hair as fair as that of the towheaded child Sebastian had once seen playing with a ball in the inn's yard.

"Is Titus Poole around?" he asked, pushing his way through the crowd to the bar.

The girl glanced up from filling a clutch of tankards. She did not smile, and something about the way she stiffened told Sebastian she was not overly fond of her stepfather. "He was here a bit ago. I think he said something about going out to the stables."

"Thank you," said Sebastian. But she was already turning away.

The Bell's stables were ranged along the far side of a yard running deep with water, with more falling every second from the angry sky. Sebastian suspected Tom was regretting his enthusiastic welcoming of the rain.

He found the stable doors standing open wide. Inside, a lantern had been lit against the gloom, casting a pool of golden light in which the inn's master stood in conversation with an ostler. The roar of the rain masked Sebastian's footsteps so that he'd reached the doorway before Poole turned away from the ostler and saw him. For an instant, the disgraced Runner checked. Then he came on, his bull-like head thrust forward with the arrogant belligerence of a man who's spent his life using his size to intimidate his fellows.

"What ye doin' back here?" he growled, drawing up some five feet away, his big hands dangling at his sides alternately opening and closing into fists.

Sebastian had paused just inside the doorway, the rain dripping from his hat and running in a cascade of rivulets from the caped shoulders of his driving coat. "I thought you might like to know that I've come to the conclusion you probably didn't kill Nicholas Hayes."

Poole's eyes narrowed, as if to better hide any betraying emotions that might lurk there. "Oh, ye have, have ye? And ye thought this might be of interest to me why?"

Sebastian let his gaze drift around the warm, golden-lit stables, taking in the row of stalls filled with horses now munching on oats, the pitchforks and other tools arrayed along a nearby wall, the ostler watching silently from the shadows. The lad was young, probably no more than eighteen, with the same pale blond hair as the girl in the taproom. Sebastian wondered if he shared his sister's opinion of their stepfather.

"Don't get me wrong," said Sebastian. "I still think you were hired to at least follow him. But one assumes that if you were hired to kill him, you were meant to do so quietly, whereas Hayes's death was . . . not quiet. A sickle in the back suggests a killer who's not in the habit of carrying his own weapon, and somehow I suspect that description doesn't apply to you."

Poole's gaze flicked for one telltale instant to the listening youth. "I don't know what yer talking about."

"Shall I spell it out more clearly? You admitted you were following Hayes—for days. That suggests you were in a position to overhear when Hayes arranged to meet a friend in Pennington's Tea Gardens. You could have gone there yourself and killed him, but you didn't. For some reason, you told your employer about the assignation, and your employer killed him, which means you're protecting a murderer." Sebastian paused. "And in case you've forgotten, the authorities tend to frown on such activities."

The threat was not subtle. Sebastian watched the fury leap into the man's eyes—fury driven by fear and accompanied by the quick calculation that the easiest way to shut Sebastian up was to kill him.

Now.

With an angry roar, Poole seized one of the pitchforks from the nearby array of tools, leveled it at Sebastian's chest, and charged.

Titus Poole was big and strong, but in the manner of so many big, strong men, he was not overly light and agile on his feet. Sebastian avoided the pitchfork's ugly iron tines by the simple expedient of sidestepping at the last moment.

Poole's charge carried him through the open doors and out into the storm. Drawing up, he swung around, the rain coursing over his balding head, his cheeks darkened by a tide of anger augmented by a suspicion of just how ridiculous he looked. "Ye bloody bastard," he howled, and charged again.

Sebastian glanced toward the towheaded ostler, but the boy stayed where he was, the features of his young face tight and watchful and indicative of someone who was not at all inclined to interfere. "Don't be a fool," Sebastian told Poole, pivoting away from the new assault. "A taproom full of men heard me walk in here and ask for you. You stick me with a pitchfork and you'll hang. Just tell me the name of the man who hired you."

Poole tightened his hold on his weapon. "Oh, I'll stick ye, all right. I'm gonna spit ye like a rabbit ready for roasting. I'm gonna gut ye like a fish on its way to market."

Leaping away from the next wild thrust, Sebastian grabbed a hay rake and brought it up before him. He was worried that if he pulled his knife, the confrontation would only end with Poole dead, and Sebastian really, really needed the man to talk. "Just stop."

Poole looked at Sebastian and laughed, for the tines of the pitchfork were forged of iron, while the hay rake was a simple implement of wood. "Ye think that's gonna stop me? It's only in here 'cause it's got a crack in the handle that wants fixing." Shifting his hold on the pitchfork, Poole swung it like a cricket bat so that the heavy iron head crashed against the end of the wooden rake and shattered it.

Sebastian was left holding a four-foot handle that ended in nothing.

"Aw," sneered Poole, his dark little eyes alive with contempt and lethal purposefulness. "What ye gonna do now, my pretty little lordling?"

With a laugh, he closed in for what he thought would be the kill.

He was still laughing when Sebastian ducked for the fourth and last time, then spun around to drive the jagged broken shaft into the big man's heart.

"You're fortunate the man's ostler wasn't too fond of his employer," said Sir Henry Lovejoy, the rain pounding loudly on the stable's roof as he bent to peer down at the bloody corpse at their feet.

"Stepfather," said Sebastian.

"Ah."

The disgraced Bow Street Runner lay flat on his back, legs splayed, arms flung wide in the straw. His eyes were open and staring, his mouth sagging as if in faint surprise. The broken end of the hay rake was still buried in his chest.

"I was trying not to kill him," said Sebastian, his shoulders propped against a nearby support beam, his arms crossed, the mist blowing in through the open doors wet against his face. "I wanted to talk to him."

"Yes. It's a pity," agreed Lovejoy, straightening with one hand at the small of his back. "No one is going to be getting any answers out of him now." He glanced over at Sebastian. "You've still no idea who hired him to follow Hayes?"

"No. There are four obvious possibilities—namely Forbes, Brown-beck, LaRivière, and Seaforth."

Lovejoy looked over at him in surprise. "You suspect Seaforth, even though he's dead?"

"For all we know, Poole got nervous and killed him. The problem is, while I have some suspicions, I've nothing specific that ties any of the four to Poole. They all knew Hayes was in England, and each had good reason to believe he was here to kill them. But that doesn't mean one of them decided to kill him first."

Lovejoy gave a sad shake of his head. "And you say that all the while, Hayes was here simply trying to find someone to take care of his child after his death. What a tragedy it all is. You've seen no sign of this little girl?"

"Not since Lady Devlin stopped Seaforth's men from grabbing her in Clerkenwell."

Lovejoy shook his head again. "At least we know she was still alive as of yesterday."

"Yes," said Sebastian.

But he knew from the pain in Lovejoy's eyes that the magistrate found no more comfort in the thought than did Sebastian himself.

Later, after the men from the deadhouse had carried away Titus Poole's body and the officials from Bow Street left, Sebastian sat with the newly widowed Mrs. Poole beside the Bell's big, old-fashioned kitchen fireplace.

She was a plump woman probably somewhere in her forties, with a massive bosom and a plain, sad face. The extraordinarily fair hair she had passed on to her children was now mingled with white. She huddled close to the fire, for with the rain had come a cold that felt biting after so many unseasonably hot days. She was shivering with reaction, her shoulders rounded as she held a handkerchief to her eyes with one hand.

Sebastian said, "You need to tell me who hired your husband to follow Nicholas Hayes." He'd almost said *to kill Nicholas Hayes,* but he reasoned he'd be more likely to get an answer out of her if he didn't force her to admit she'd known her husband was in the habit of killing people for money.

She gave a faint shudder and sucked in an audible breath, but otherwise she remained silent.

Sebastian said, "Poole is dead. He just tried to kill me in front of your own son. Telling me whom he was working for won't stain his memory any blacker than he's already done himself."

She brought her hand down to twist the handkerchief between her fingers in her lap. Her face was pale and distorted with shock, but he was surprised to see that her eyes were dry. "I don't know," she whispered, keeping her head bowed. "Truly I don't. He didn't tell me those sorts of things."

"Do you know when he was hired?"

She pressed her lips together and nodded. "He came home maybe two weeks ago, flush with money and bragging about how he had a new job. But he didn't say who for."

"Do you know if he'd worked for this particular man in the past?" Sir Lindsey Forbes had admitted to knowing Poole.

"No. He didn't say."

"How much did you know about the work he did?"

She shifted her gaze to the fire, the orange glow from the flames touching her ashen face with hellish color. "He'd talk to me sometimes about how clever he was, working deals with both thieves and their victims. There wasn't nothing he liked better than talking about himself, unless maybe it was hearing other people talk about how grand he was. Sometimes I'd hear him bragging in the taproom about how he'd threatened someone and they'd knuckled under, or how he'd cheated some flat."

"Did you know he killed people?"

She was silent for a moment, her heavy breasts lifting with her strained breathing. "When he was courting me, he was ever so nice. I'd never known anyone so gentlemanlike. I thought I was the luckiest woman alive, that he'd chosen me. But we hadn't been married a week when he hit me—slapped me on the side of my face with the palm of his big, hard hand. Knocked me clear across the room, he did. Said he was sorry afterward, of course—although he also said it was my own fault for talking back to him." She brought up the handkerchief to press against her lips. "Sometimes he'd hit me for just looking at him wrong. Hit Jonathan and Mary too—even little Rose. So you see, I ain't sorry he's dead. And if I knew who'd hired him, I'd tell you."

It was an old story, of a man pretending to be something he wasn't to lure a woman into marriage or into his bed. But Sebastian's sympathy for this woman was tempered by the fact that she'd surely known the sordid history of Poole's activities as a Runner. She might have been a widow with three children, but she was also the owner of a tidy inn; she hadn't married Poole out of any pressing financial need, but because his attentions had flattered her. She hadn't been bothered by the fact he'd once sent innocent, impoverished men, women, and children to their deaths. She simply hadn't expected him to hurt *her*.

Aloud, Sebastian said, "Can you remember anything—anything at all—that he might have said about the man who hired him?"

She was silent for a moment as if with the effort of thought. "Well, I know he was a nob, because that's what Titus called him—'that stupid nob.' Titus was right proud of himself because after Hayes was found dead over in Somer's Town, Titus went to the nob what'd hired him and claimed to have killed Hayes himself. That nob, he wasn't exactly happy—you see, Titus was supposed to kill the fellow quiet-like and then dump the body someplace it'd never be found. That way no one would ever know the fellow had even been here."

She paused, obviously feeling compelled to explain how she'd come to know so much. "Titus didn't usually tell me about his work in any detail. But he was bragging about this, you see. Said that nob weren't happy with the way everyone was talking about Hayes being murdered—said it made folks remember all that'd happened in the past. So he only gave Titus half of what he was to pay him if the job was done right. Normally Titus would've been more than a bit miffed about something like that, but he thought it was a great joke because he hadn't really killed the fellow himself. He didn't know who'd actually done it, only that he'd been smart enough to get himself paid for it."

## Chapter 53

Late that night, a new wave of storms swept in from the North Sea, bringing with it an even fiercer wind and great pulses of lightning that split the sky.

Sebastian lay awake, watching the quick electric flashes light up the room and listening to the rumble of the thunder and the patter of raindrops hitting the window glass. He kept going over what he knew about the day Nicholas Hayes died and trying to tease out how what they'd learned from Kate Forbes and Mrs. Poole should alter their perception of the critical hours surrounding the murder. Then he became aware of a subtle change in the room's energy and looked over to find Hero lying awake beside him, watching him. "Maybe if you got some sleep," she said, "it would all make more sense."

He gave a smothered laugh and drew her close. "You're always saying that."

"Because it's true . . . even if it is impossible."

She fell silent, her head on his chest, one hand resting on his stomach, and he knew that she too was running through the day's revelations and what they meant. She said, "It's somehow the height of irony that whoever hired Poole to murder Nicholas Hayes now thinks that Poole actually did kill him, when he didn't. Someone else did."

Sebastian ran his hand up and down her bare arm. "I suppose it's possible 'the nob' killed Hayes himself and simply paid Poole to make the ex-Runner go away and shut up. But I doubt it."

"So of the four men who had reason to worry that Hayes came back to London to kill them, one tried to have him murdered and another actually did kill him. Nicholas Hayes had a collection of ugly enemies."

"That he did. It's also rather ironic that whoever hired Poole is the one person we can be fairly certain didn't actually kill Hayes. He only thinks he's responsible."

"Is it possible that Seaforth hired Poole, and then Poole killed him?"

"It's possible, although I can't imagine why Poole would have killed him."

"Perhaps because Seaforth only paid half of what he'd promised," suggested Hero.

"According to Mrs. Poole, Titus was laughing about how he'd suckered 'the stupid nob' into paying him. So while Poole only received half of what he'd been promised, he knew he hadn't actually done anything to earn it." Sebastian paused as the wind gusted up, throwing the rain against the house in hard sheets. "Although that's not to say that Poole didn't kill Seaforth—only that I don't think the money was the reason."

She propped herself up on one elbow so she could see him better. "Now that you know Titus Poole didn't kill Hayes, the alibis of your suspects become more important, don't they? Didn't Seaforth say he spent the afternoon at his club before going to the Regent's reception for the Allied Sovereigns?"

"He did. And Lovejoy confirmed it. Which means that unless the Earl somehow managed to leave and come back without anyone at White's noticing, it's unlikely that he was responsible for the sickle in Nicholas Hayes's back. As for LaRivière, he wasn't only at the reception.

He even dined with the Regent—as did Sir Lindsey, according to his wife. But given the timing of the murder, it's not beyond the realm of possibility that either man could have worked in a quick trip to the tea gardens before going to Carlton House."

"Gibson did say it's unlikely the killer had much blood on him."

"He did."

"What about Brownbeck?"

"Brownbeck refused to give any account of his movements that day, and it's hard to ask Lovejoy to look into the man without giving away Lady Forbes's secrets."

"So he could have done it."

"He could have."

"Lady Forbes had her abigail with her in Hatchards when she spoke to Hayes. It's possible the woman overheard them making the assignation and told Forbes. But she also could have told her mistress's father. I wouldn't be surprised if Katherine Forbes has had the same abigail since she was Miss Kate Brownbeck."

"Now that's something I hadn't considered," said Sebastian, thrusting his splayed fingers through the heavy fall of Hero's dark hair to draw it away from her face. "I think I might take another trip up to Somer's Town tomorrow."

Her gray eyes shimmered in a sudden pulse of lightning. "Why?"

"I want to talk to that gardener whose sickle somehow or other ended up in Nicholas Hayes's back."

"Surely you don't think he's responsible?"

"No. But I've been thinking about that testimony he gave at the inquest—how he said he'd been cutting grass in the clearing and didn't realize he'd left his sickle until he found it missing the next morning."

"You don't believe him?"

"Not exactly. I suspect that by the time Nicholas's body was discovered near the west boundary wall, that gardener knew damn well he'd forgotten his sickle. Only for some reason he didn't want to admit it. And I want to know why."

Friday, 17 June

The next morning dawned overcast and chilly, with a flat white light that made the day feel dreary and vaguely depressing.

"I know it ain't really cold," said Tom as they drove through gloomy, rain-drenched streets. "But it *feels* cold."

"It's cold," said Sebastian as a fine, miserable mist hit them in the face.

Bernie Aikens was up on a ladder, tying in the arching new-growth canes of the roses on an arbor near the tea gardens' central ornamental pond. The rows of climbing roses were covered with fresh green leaves and thick with swelling buds only just beginning here and there to burst into blooms of soft pink and a white so pearlescent as to almost glow in the gloom of the cloudy day. The smell of wet vegetation and damp earth and the sweet perfume of the roses hung heavy in the air, and Aikens was whistling as he worked, the tune a vaguely familiar sea ditty Sebastian couldn't quite place.

The gardener cast a quick glance toward Sebastian as he paused beside the nearest arch, then ignored him. But when Sebastian continued to quietly watch him, the gardener grew visibly self-conscious and finally said, "Can I help ye there, yer honor?"

"You're Bernie Aikens, aren't you?"

A wary look settled over the man's weathered features. He had a long, bony face so lean that the structure of his prominent cheekbones and jaw was clearly visible beneath his sun-darkened skin. "Aye."

"I'm Devlin."

The man's hands stilled at his work. He might not have remembered Sebastian's face from the inquest, but the name had obviously stuck with him. He stood motionless on the ladder, his hands now gripping its sides, his gaze fixed on nothing in particular in the distance.

"I mean you no harm," said Sebastian quietly, watching him.

Aikens sniffed. "Yer here 'cause of that dead man, are ye?"

"Yes."

"I said everything I got t' say at that inquest. Don't know nothin' else."

Sebastian tipped his hat back on his head. "I've been wondering if your ability to recall that day might have been hampered by the stress of testifying at an inquest. It's a shocking thing, murder. It can make it difficult for a man to remember the exact sequence of events." Sebastian paused. "Wouldn't you say?"

"Aye," said the gardener, the big bones of his jaw flexing beneath the skin.

"I'm told you're a good, reliable gardener, a responsible man." It wasn't true, of course; Sebastian knew nothing about Aikens beyond his own observations. "That kind of man tends to check his tools and make certain they're clean and in good order before he puts them away for the day. So I'm wondering if perhaps you actually realized you'd left your sickle in that clearing earlier than you thought when you were trying to remember things at the inquest. Now, some men might simply shrug and put off retrieving a tool until the next morning. But a responsible man like yourself wouldn't do that, would he, Mr. Aikens? That kind of man would go back right away."

Aikens stared out across the rose garden to where a couple of crows were pecking at a section of recently turned earth. When the silence stretched out, Sebastian said, "About what time was it when you reached the clearing?"

For a moment, Sebastian thought his gambit had failed. But Bernie Aikens was obviously a man with a conscience, and the lie he'd told at the inquest must have been weighing heavily upon his soul. He leaned his body into the ladder and brought up both hands to swipe them down over his face and cover his mouth. "I don't know what time it was, exactly," he said, his voice half-muffled by his hands. "We start picking up and puttin' stuff away an hour before closing time, so it was about then."

"And Nicholas Hayes was already dead by the time you arrived at the clearing?"

Aikens nodded and swallowed hard.

"What did you do?"

He squeezed his eyes shut, as if he could somehow block out the bloody vision that he must be seeing over and over again in his mind. "I didn't know what to do. At first, all I could think about was just grabbing me sickle and gettin' out of there. But I realized quick enough that'd be a mistake. I mean, what if somebody'd seen me with that bloody sickle and thought I was the one who'd killed the fellow?"

*You'd have been hanged,* thought Sebastian. But all he said was "So what did you do?"

Aikens swallowed. "Nothin'. I jist turned around and walked away. I was shakin' so bad, I was afraid me legs was gonna give out beneath me."

"Did you see anyone else in that part of the gardens?"

"No. No one. I was walkin' fast, trying to get as far away as I could, and it was late enough that the gardens was already startin' to empty— folks know we close early on Thursdays. The only person I seen in that part of the shrubbery at all was Mrs. Bowers."

"Who's she?"

"A milliner. Comes here often, she does, which is how I happen to know her."

Sebastian took a breath, and for a moment he was seeing not dripping trees and a heavy gray sky but an aging widow with a bruised neck lying dead on a stone slab. "A milliner?"

"Aye. Heard she was found murdered herself just the other day. I'm tellin' ye, the streets has gotten right dangerous, they have. I mean, who'd want to kill some old widow woman who never done anybody any harm?" Bernie Aikens turned his head to look directly at Sebastian as if earnestly seeking an answer to his question. "Who'd do that?"

*Chapter 54*

$\mathcal{M}$rs. Bowers?" said Paul Gibson, staring at Sebastian. The surgeon was in his favorite pub, sitting on one of the high-backed benches and eating a plate of roast beef when Sebastian tracked him down. "Why do you want to know about her?"

Sebastian slid onto the bench opposite him. The day was so dark and cloudy that the pub had its oil lamps lit against the gloom. "Because I think the same man who killed Nicholas Hayes also murdered her."

Gibson's jaw sagged and he stopped chewing, his eyes widening. Then he swallowed, hard. "Seriously?"

"Seriously."

"But . . . why would he?"

"For the same reason he killed Irvine Pennington: because she saw him that evening."

"But . . . how would he even know who she was? Dozens of people must have seen him at the gardens that night. What's he going to do? Kill them all?"

Sebastian turned to order a pint, then laid his forearms on the scarred old tabletop and leaned into them. "According to the gardener whose sickle ended up in Hayes's back, Mrs. Bowers was wandering around the western shrubbery that evening. Seems she was one of the gardens' regulars, which is how the gardener happened to know who she was."

Gibson frowned with the effort of memory. "At the inquest, the gardener said he left that area around midday."

"That's what he said. But the truth is, he realized just before closing time that he must have left his sickle in the clearing and went back for it. That's when he saw Mrs. Bowers."

"And the killer? Did the gardener see him?"

Sebastian shook his head. "He says the only person he saw was Mrs. Bowers—and Hayes, of course, with the sickle in his back."

"If he lied at the inquest, he could be lying to you."

"He could be, but I doubt it." Sebastian leaned back to let the young barmaid set his ale on the table before him. "Mrs. Bowers was killed on Saturday?"

"Friday night."

"Our killer moved fast, didn't he? He took care of Pennington in the morning and then Mrs. Bowers that night. I'm glad no one else saw him."

"No one that you know about," said Gibson. "It's not like there was anything obvious linking Mrs. Bowers to Hayes."

"True." Sebastian paused to take a long, deep drink. "If I remember correctly, she was strangled with a strap, wasn't she?"

"She was. From behind. She was a small woman and arthritic, so it wouldn't have been too difficult a thing for someone to manage." He paused. "The inquest concluded she was murdered by footpads. Her earrings and wedding ring were missing, remember?"

"A thief could have come along and robbed her body. Or the killer could have taken them himself to make it look like a robbery."

Gibson took another bite of his roast beef, chewed, and swallowed. "If that's true, then your murderer used three different weapons in his little killing spree: a sickle, a knife, and a strap. A knife was used twice—once on Pennington and then again on Seaforth—although I'm not convinced it was the same knife. And while Pennington was stabbed multiple times, your killer got the Earl on the first try."

"Are you suggesting we could be looking for two different murderers?"

"It's possible, although it's also possible your killer simply aimed better the second time he used a knife. One assumes it's easier to be more exact with that sort of thing when you do your killing on a deserted street at night."

"You've finished Seaforth's autopsy?"

"I have. The cool, damp weather has calmed everyone's tempers enough that I've finally been able to get a few things done. Not that there was much to see with him. He was stabbed in the back with a dagger and then presumably dragged into the mews." Gibson cut another slice of beef. "So what does all this tell you?"

"It tells me that Nicholas Hayes's killing was, in all likelihood, impulsive. The killer either flew into a rage and grabbed the sickle because it just happened to be lying there, or he'd been wanting to kill Hayes, saw an opportunity, and decided to take it. Hayes might have been sick, but he was a tall man and still in the prime of his life. A man like that wouldn't be easy to strangle, and the killer probably didn't have a dagger on him. It's not something most people carry. "

"Unless they're carrying a sword stick."

"True."

Gibson was silent for a moment, his roast beef forgotten. "Your killer must have gone home that night, thought about anyone and everyone who could possibly link him to Hayes's murder, and then set about deliberately eliminating them—this time making certain he had a more appropriate implement with him. What a charming fellow."

"He was desperate. His killing of Hayes was messy, dangerous, and probably unpleasant. But this killer isn't a stupid man. He recognized that what he'd done was a rash act that left him vulnerable. So he decided to fix it by killing the two people he knew could tie him to the tea gardens that night. And then he killed Seaforth too, perhaps because he was afraid the Earl could also somehow identify him." Sebastian paused. "Except that he was wrong when he thought his little killing spree would fix his vulnerability, because by killing Mrs. Bowers he's given us a way—maybe—to find him. What do you know about her?"

"Not a great deal. Adele is her name—Mrs. Adele Bowers. I'm told she was a milliner up until maybe ten years ago, when her eyesight started to go and the arthritis in her hands got so bad, she couldn't keep making hats. She was living with her daughter at the time she was killed. That's who we released the body to—the daughter. Or, rather, to the daughter's neighbor."

"Do you recall the daughter's name?"

"Aye, thanks to the fact that she was named after her mother and has never married: Miss Adele Bowers, of Charles Street."

Like her mother, the younger Adele Bowers was also a milliner, and kept a small shop just off Oxford Street. It was a respectable area, and the hats in her shop were well made and fashionable even if they weren't particularly inspired—the work of a milliner who was able to follow a pattern but lacked the creativity to give her work an innovative flair.

A woman somewhere in her thirties or forties, the younger Adele Bowers was built short like her mother but plump, with a round face and small dark eyes and unremarkable features. Her hair was a lifeless shade somewhere between dark blond and brown, and she wore it tucked up under a neatly starched cap. The cap, like her gown, was of unrelieved black as befitted a woman in deep mourning.

Sebastian's presence in her shop obviously flustered the milliner greatly. She kept dropping curtsies and calling him "your lordship" or "my lord." At no point did it seem to occur to her that she didn't have to answer his questions; nor did she appear to give any thought to why he was there expressing interest in the death of a retired milliner. Her mother's recent murder was currently consuming Adele's life, so it didn't strike her as odd that someone else should find it interesting.

"Sorry about the smell, your lordship," she said, her hands fisting in the skirt of her black mourning gown. "The thing is, you see, we—or, rather, I suppose I should say 'I' since it's just me now—live upstairs. And we—that is, my brother, Henry, and I—haven't been able to bury Mama yet. So she's still up there in our—or my—rooms. We're hoping to have the funeral tomorrow night, God willing. But they're ever so expensive these days, aren't they? Funerals, I mean. And my brother, Henry, he says we can't bury Mama without having two mutes at her funeral—two mutes, six bearers, and all those expensive ostrich plumes on the horses' heads! So it's taking more time than we expected to get everything together. Thank goodness for this cold snap we're finally having."

Delays of seven to ten days between a death and a funeral were not uncommon, mainly because of the need to organize—and pay for—an increasingly elaborate funeral. Many people also delayed funerals out of fear of burying an unconscious loved one alive, but in this case, that obviously wasn't an issue.

Sebastian said, "Your mother was killed last Friday?"

Miss Bowers nodded vigorously and dropped another curtsy. "Last Friday night it was, my lord. She'd gone out the way she did every evening at about that time to take a short constitutional around Soho Square. Only, she never came back. After a while, I got to worrying. She was ever so regular in her habits, you see, and she was never gone long. So I sent Robert—that's the neighbor's boy, Robert Owens. He's a good lad, Robert. Runs errands for us all the time, he does, and is ever so reliable."

She paused for a moment, the confused look on her face suggesting she'd lost herself in her own parenthesis.

Sebastian said, "You sent Robert to look for her?"

"Oh, yes, your lordship. I sent Robert, and in just a few minutes, he was back again. White as a sheet, he was, and his eyes staring out of his head with fright."

"He'd found her?"

Miss Bowers nodded. "Somebody'd dragged her back into the alley just off the square. It was Mr. Owens—Robert's father—who called the constables. He told me not to go look at her, so I didn't."

"That was probably wise," said Sebastian. "Did your mother go to Pennington's Tea Gardens much?"

"She did, yes, my lord. In fact, she went there the day before she died. She loved walking in those gardens. She had ever so much trouble with the arthritis crippling her hands, you see, so she couldn't make hats anymore. Sometimes her hip bothered her too, but she said the walking helped ease the stiffness. So she'd walk up to those gardens nearly every afternoon. She'd sit on one of the benches for a time and then walk back. Sometimes I worried about her going up there all alone like that. But she'd just laugh at me and say the earth and green growing things and the birds soothed her soul and gave her energy."

Miss Bowers paused, as if vaguely embarrassed by what she'd said. "Mama was a bit peculiar in that way."

"I can understand it."

"Can you?" Miss Bowers looked at him as if he must be a bit peculiar too, even if he was a real viscount. "I never could. But then, Mama was different from me. I've always been good with my needle, but Mama was the one with what she called 'vision.' She said she could *see* her hats in her head before she started making them."

"You don't?"

"No."

"So where do you get your ideas?"

She nodded to a nearby stack of well-thumbed editions of *Ackermann's Repository* and *The Ladies' Monthly.* "From fashion plates, of course."

"Of course," said Sebastian. "Do you by any chance know if your mother was acquainted with either the Count de Compans or the Earl of Seaforth?"

Miss Bowers stared at him blankly. "I don't think so, my lord."

"How about a Major Hamish McHenry?"

"No, your lordship."

"Sir Lindsey Forbes?"

Miss Bowers shook her head. "Mama used to make hats for her lady-ship when she was Miss Katherine Brownbeck and living in Bloomsbury. But I don't think she ever met Sir Lindsey, no."

Sebastian knew a quickening in his blood. "So she knew Theodore Brownbeck?"

"Oh, yes, my lord. In fact, she was telling me just the other day that she'd seen him up in the tea gardens. Ran into him in the shrubbery, she said. She mentioned it because he was all red in the face and acting peculiar, and she thought the heat must have got to him."

"What day was this?" asked Sebastian, his voice sharp enough that Miss Bowers looked momentarily taken aback.

"Must have been Thursday of last week, my lord—the day before she died. I remember because it was so hot that afternoon—the day she was killed, I mean—that she decided not to walk up to the tea gardens and said she'd only go for her evening constitutional after the sun was down. That's when she told me about having seen Mr. Brownbeck the day before and thinking the heat must have got to him because he was acting so queer."

# Chapter 55

Sebastian reined in near the corner of St. James's Square, his gaze on the impressive home of Sir Lindsey and Lady Forbes.

He found himself remembering the angry visit from Theo Brownbeck that had followed so hard on the heels of Hero's first call on Lady Forbes. At the time they had simply assumed Sir Lindsey must have sent word to his father-in-law of Sebastian's involvement in the investigation of Hayes's death. But it now appeared more likely that the warning to Brownbeck had come not from Forbes but from her ladyship's abigail—the same abigail who had accompanied her mistress to Hatchards in Piccadilly and doubtless overheard her arrange to meet Nicholas Hayes in Pennington's Tea Gardens.

Had the abigail always spied on her mistress for her former employer? Sebastian wondered. Or had Brownbeck's chance sighting of Hayes that afternoon in Russell Street prompted him to task the abigail with watching his daughter's every move? However it had come about, that was obviously how Brownbeck had learned of the planned meeting between Hayes and the former Kate Brownbeck. And so he had gone to the gardens that night to— What? Break up the assignation? Warn Hayes to stay away from his daughter?

Kill him?

The latter seemed unlikely, Sebastian decided, given the choice of murder weapon. Far more likely that Brownbeck had gone to the gardens that night planning to confront Hayes. No doubt the two men had exchanged heated words. And then what? What would a man steeped in the teachings of Buddhism do when confronted with the angry father of the woman he still loved?

Walk away, of course.

And so Nicholas had turned his back on Theo Brownbeck. Whereupon that esteemed pillar of society, that pious writer of endless tirades against the lowborn "criminal" classes of society, had grabbed the sickle left by a forgetful gardener and buried the blade deep between Hayes's shoulder blades. Then he had run away, red in the face and shaking with reaction, and unfortunately encountered an arthritic old widow who'd once made his daughter's hats.

The killing of Nicholas Hayes had been impulsive, a product of rage and seething impotence. But the murders of Adele Bowers and Irvine Pennington were deliberate and planned. After a night's agitated reflection, Brownbeck must have cold-bloodedly decided on the need to quickly silence the two people he knew could tie him to the gardens that night. And then he'd set about doing it.

And Seaforth? Why kill Seaforth? Had the Earl threatened Brownbeck in some way?

Still pondering that question, Sebastian handed the reins to his tiger. "Walk them, will you? I've no idea how long I'll be."

"Aye, gov'nor," said Tom, scrambling forward to the seat.

Sebastian hopped down and was turning toward the Forbeses' town house when he noticed Lady Forbes herself standing alone at the railing surrounding the square's central basin. The day was cool and overcast, with a blustery wind that ruffled the gray surface of the water and tugged at the green ribbons of her ladyship's fashionable straw hat. She was watching him, and Sebastian changed direction to walk toward her.

"Sir Lindsey isn't here," she said as he drew nearer. She was wearing a stylish muslin walking dress with an elegant hunter green spencer, and looked every inch like what she was—the daughter of one very rich man and the wife of another. And between them, those two rich, supremely selfish men had made her life miserable.

"Actually," said Sebastian, pausing beside her, "I've come to see you."

She turned her face away to stare off across the vast expanse of ornamental water. "You've figured it out, have you?"

Sebastian studied her beautiful, pale, carefully composed features. "Have you?"

She gave a faint laugh that held no real amusement. "I'll admit I've been frightfully thick about a few things. But a bit of calm reflection made it all rather clear."

"You know your abigail was informing on you to your father?"

"I didn't. But I know now. She burst into tears when I confronted her with it. Swore she'd done it for my own good, and then cried even harder when I dismissed her without a character reference." She paused, her features hardening. "Given everything that's flowed from what she did, she's lucky I didn't murder her. I honestly think I could have, in that moment." She swung her head to look at Sebastian, and he saw the raw fury and everlasting grief in her eyes. "Does that shock you?"

"No." He stared across the water to where a pigeon was preening itself atop the head of the equestrian statue of William III in the center of the basin. "Have you seen your father?"

She shook her head. "I went there—to Bloomsbury—meaning to confront him about it all. But it seems he's missing. The servants say he went out last night and never came back. I'd be inclined to believe he's simply given them orders to put me off, except that they were obviously quite frightened and unsure as to what to do next."

WHO SPEAKS FOR THE DAMNED

"Have you told Sir Lindsey?"

"That Father is missing?" She gave another of those strange, ragged laughs. "That would be rather difficult, given that Sir Lindsey also seems to have disappeared."

"You're serious?"

"Very. He went out last night as well, and hasn't been seen since. According to Simmons—that's our butler—he sent one of the footmen for a hackney, which is most unusual. You must know that hackney carriages are quite beneath the touch of Sir Lindsey Forbes."

"And you've no idea at all where he's gone?"

"None."

"Have the authorities been informed?"

"Not to my knowledge. You know what servants are like. We train them to ignore all our eccentricities and reprehensible behavior, don't we? So how could they dare go to the authorities when their master might walk in at any moment and be furious with them for causing such a stir?"

Sebastian was thinking, *What about you?* when she said, "He can be rather nasty when he's put out, you know—Sir Lindsey, I mean."

And he understood.

She looked away again, blinking rapidly enough now that Sebastian realized just how great was this woman's struggle to hold back her tears. "Was Forbes a part of it, do you think? Killing Nicholas, I mean. And Seaforth as well?"

"I honestly don't know."

She was silent for a moment. Then she said, her voice quieter, "Have you found the little boy yet? Nicholas's child?"

"No. Although we have seen him—or I should say we've seen *her,* because we've discovered the child is a girl. She's the reason Nicholas came back to London—because he was dying of consumption, and he was hoping his sister would take care of the little girl after he died."

Katherine Forbes stared at him. "And Lady Anne turned him down? How could she?" She brought up one hand to cup her mouth, then let it fall. "That's what Nicholas was going to ask me, isn't it? He wanted to ask me to take care of his child after he died." Her voice broke. "Dear God. And my father killed him."

"I suspect so." Sebastian hesitated, then said, "Do you have any idea—any idea at all—where your father might have gone?"

"No. He's never gone off like this before." The wind tugged at the brim of her elegant, expensive hat, and she put up a hand to catch it. "How did you know? How did you know it was Father?"

"He was seen in the gardens that night."

"Then perhaps he's run away. France is open these days, isn't it?" She glanced back at her grand house on the eastern side of the square. "And Forbes?"

"He knew Hayes had returned to London. But I don't believe he played a part in his death."

"Then where has he gone?"

Sebastian met her gaze and saw there a flare of hope that he understood only too well. "I don't know."

"They're *both* missing?" said Hero when Devlin told her of the disappearance of Brownbeck and Forbes. "Are you certain?"

"It looks like it. I swung by Brownbeck's house in Bloomsbury on my way to Bow Street. The servants tried to cover up their master's strange behavior, but it didn't take me long to get the truth out of them. Seems he went out shortly after dark—in a hackney, same as Forbes—and never came back."

"That sounds ominous."

"It does, doesn't it?" Devlin went to pour himself a brandy from the carafe that stood on the table near the drawing room fireplace. It was dark now, the room lit by golden candlelight and a small fire laid on the hearth to drive away the evening's chill. "Lovejoy is doing what he can to look into it, but it's rather delicate, given the prominence of the two men involved."

Hero was silent for a moment, her gaze on the leaping flame of the candle at her side. "I'll confess I've always despised Theo Brownbeck. He's sanctimonious, hypocritical, and—given the hateful 'statistics' he invents—basically dishonest. But I never would have pegged him as a murderer."

"He's a weak and supremely selfish man. I suspect he struck out at Hayes in a moment of rage. And then, rather than own up to what he'd done, he went on a killing spree to eliminate anyone who might be a threat to him."

"Including Seaforth?"

"One presumes so."

"Do you think he has now killed Forbes?"

"I had the distinct impression that Lady Forbes is hoping her husband is her father's latest victim."

"I can't say I blame her."

"No."

Hero watched him take a long, slow swallow of his drink. "Do you think LaRivière is now in danger?"

"I don't know. I keep coming back to the fact that while Brownbeck obviously killed Nicholas Hayes, one of the other three men—either Seaforth, Forbes, or LaRivière—hired Titus Poole and thus mistakenly believes that he himself is responsible for what happened up in Somer's Town." He paused. "Although I suppose in the case of Seaforth, I should say *believed*."

The distant sound of a door opening echoed up from below, followed by a crash and running footsteps on the stairs. They heard Morey's warning hiss, then Tom's excited voice shouting, "But 'e's gonna want t' know."

An instant later, the tiger burst into the drawing room, bringing with him the smell of horses and warm boy and London air. "They're dead, gov'nor! Both o' 'em! Forbes and Brownbeck. Some ex-soldier found 'em in the ruins o' the old Savoy Palace o'er by that new bridge they're buildin'. Brownbeck 'as been shot, and Forbes 'as got a knife stickin' out of 'im!"

## Chapter 56

Sebastian arrived at the ruins of the old Savoy Palace to find the site illuminated by the hellish glow of flaring torches and a scattering of bobbing horn lanterns. A sizable crowd was beginning to gather despite the softly falling rain, with a couple of constables fighting to hold people back.

"Sir 'Enry's waiting for ye," called one of the constables when he recognized Sebastian.

Leaving the curricle with Tom, Sebastian worked his way down the wet slope, past scattered piles of stone and rough timbers. Lying between the Strand and the Thames, Savoy Palace had once been the grandest nobleman's house in all of medieval London, home to the uncles and sons of kings. Now it was mostly gone, marked only here and there by a half-demolished tower or the fragment of a wall, with most of the rest swept away for the construction of the grand new bridge slowly inching toward completion. Only the small fifteenth-century chapel of Henry VII was to be spared, and it was there that the bodies of Theo Brownbeck and Sir Lindsey Forbes lay.

"How long have they been here?" asked Sebastian, walking up to where Lovejoy stood huddled beneath an umbrella.

The magistrate looked pale in the torches' light. "A while, I suspect— most likely since last night. They were only discovered by chance when an ex-soldier went searching for someplace to get out of the rain. From the looks of things, it appears that Brownbeck knifed Forbes, and then, as he was dying, Forbes shot Brownbeck."

"Lovely."

The two men were near the southern end of the old Tudor chapel, their bodies hidden from both stray passersby and the bridge's workmen by the crumbling remnants of the stone walls that had once connected the chapel to the rest of the complex. Forbes had fallen on his left side, his head thrown back as if in agony, his right arm extended. The knife that had killed him was still buried in his chest; a flintlock pistol lay in the rubble-strewn weeds near his outflung hand. Brownbeck was flat on his back some eight to ten feet away, one knee bent awkwardly, the chest of his old-fashioned waistcoat dark with his blood.

Sebastian went first to hunker down beside the dead banker. Forbes's shot had caught Brownbeck square in the chest and probably killed him almost instantly. His jaw was slack, his eyes open and sunken, his body stiff with rigor mortis and wet from the rain.

"I think you're right about the timing," said Sebastian, pushing up to go take a better look at Forbes. The knife had been thrust into the East India Company man's chest at such an angle that it had slid in under the ribs, right into the heart. And that struck Sebastian as odd.

"What in the bloody hell were they doing here last night?" said Sebastian, rising to his feet.

"It's peculiar, isn't it?" A wind gusted up, and Lovejoy hunched his shoulders against the driving rain. "A couple of the lads were interviewing Mr. Brownbeck's servants when word came that the bodies had been found. According to his valet, Brownbeck went out late in the afternoon of Nicholas Hayes's murder and came back several hours later with blood on his cuffs."

"The valet is certain of the day?"

"He is. He's been with Brownbeck for more than twenty years, and when he read about Hayes's murder in the papers the next morning, he naturally found himself thinking about that blood. So he spoke to Brownbeck's coachman and discovered that Brownbeck had driven up to Somer's Town that evening."

*And yet neither man said a thing,* thought Sebastian. But then, good positions were hard to find.

"We sent word to the palace as soon as we knew what had occurred here," Lovejoy was saying. "The papers are to be told that footpads were seen in the area, and a couple of ruffians will no doubt pay the ultimate price—quickly, of course, to calm the inevitable public nervousness."

"Of course," said Sebastian.

Lovejoy blew out a long, troubled breath. "At least it's over and the murderer is dead, even if his infamy will never be known."

It was raining harder now, and Sebastian stared off across the darkened ruins toward the looming shadow of the unfinished bridge. "I think there's little doubt that Brownbeck killed Nicholas Hayes, Irvine Pennington, and Adele Bowers. But I'm not convinced that all is as it seems here."

Lovejoy stared at him "You're not?"

Sebastian found himself studying the ungainly sprawl of the banker's body. "What are the odds that Theo Brownbeck—whom I suspect never killed anyone in his life up until just over a week ago—would manage to hit Sir Lindsey's heart with his first dagger thrust?"

Lovejoy frowned. "It's unusual, I'll admit."

"And then Sir Lindsey—who admittedly began his career in the military but was already dying with a knife in his chest—likewise managed to shoot Brownbeck right in the heart?"

Lovejoy blinked against the wind-driven rain. "Oh dear."

Sebastian said, "You've sent to the deadhouse for a couple of shells?"

"Yes. They should be here soon."

"Good. I'd like to hear what Paul Gibson has to say about this."

*Saturday, 18 June*

Gibson must have started work on the autopsies early the next morning, because by the time Sebastian arrived shortly after breakfast, he was already gory up to his elbows and had his hands deep in Sir Lindsey's chest.

"Bow Street told you how the men were found?" asked Sebastian, trying not to look too closely at what Gibson was doing.

The surgeon lifted Forbes's dripping heart from his chest and set it aside in a shallow basin. "They did. Not sure I believe it, though."

Sebastian transferred his gaze to the ceiling. "Oh? Why not?"

Gibson grinned. "Part of it's the angle of the shot. They're saying Forbes was knifed first, then fell and somehow managed to shoot Brownbeck. But if that were true, then the bullet should have been traveling up from below when it hit his body, and it wasn't. It was obviously fired by someone who was standing."

Sebastian shifted his gaze to where the banker's naked, eviscerated body lay on one of the wide shelves running along the back of the room. "It's possible Forbes could have shot Brownbeck before he fell. I've seen men stabbed in the heart run a couple of hundred feet before collapsing."

Gibson reached for a rag and wiped his hands. "I suppose. But that's only the first thing." He turned to pick up the knife that lay on the shelf beside the bloody basin. "This is what's really telling. Look at the knife your East India Company man had in him." It was a small, common knife with a simple horn handle and a wide blade some six inches long.

"Now, look at this." Setting the knife aside, Gibson grabbed the dead man's shoulder and rolled the body onto its side.

Sebastian found himself staring at a small purple slit high up between the man's shoulder blades. "Bloody hell. The blade went all the way through him."

"It did. And if you'll notice, it was a narrow blade. A very narrow blade."

"What are you saying?"

Gibson eased the body back down. "I'm saying I think your man was killed with either a dagger or, more likely, a sword stick. And then, after he was dead, the killer thrust that knife into him and left it there to make it look like that's what was used."

"Huh." Sebastian went to stand at the open door, his gaze on the clouds that were beginning to blow away and reveal patches of blue sky.

Gibson watched him. "That's all you have to say? *Huh?*"

Sebastian turned, his hands dangling loose at his sides, a feeling of helpless frustration welling within him. "I know exactly who did this. But I'll be damned if I can figure out how to prove it."

*Chapter 57*

After leaving Tower Hill, Sebastian drove first to the Bell in Warwick Lane. Having moved on to Mayfair, he had a brief but useful conversation with LaRivière's servants. Then he headed back toward the Tower again, this time to the ancient, picturesque church of St. Dunstan-in-the-East.

Drawing up outside the old lych-gate, he handed the reins to Tom and said, "If he kills me, you know what to tell Sir Henry."

Tom scrambled forward to the high seat. "Ye don't think ye meybe oughta let Sir 'Enry know what yer doin' *before* ye talk to that Frog?"

Sebastian smiled as he hopped down into the narrow lane. "Somehow I doubt Sir Henry would approve of what I'm about to do."

Lying between Great Tower Street and the Thames, St. Dunstan's was one of the few medieval London churches to have survived the Great Fire of 1666. The afternoon was glorious, with high, puffy white clouds scattered across a brilliant blue sky and a light breeze that took the sting out of the sun's heat. Gilbert-Christophe de LaRivière, the Count de Compans, sat on a stool in the midst of the vast old churchyard, a sketchbook propped on one knee and a small folding table at his side to hold an elegant but well-used case containing various drawing implements. A sword stick leaned conspicuously against the table, for this was a rough section of London and the churchyard was deserted. He had his eyes narrowed against the glare of the sun, a faint smile curling his lips as he rendered the old church with quick, sure strokes.

"Nice day for it," said Sebastian, walking up to him.

"It is," agreed the Count, his attention all for his sketch. "I assume you've gone to the bother of tracking me here for a reason?"

Sebastian let his gaze drift around the quiet, leafy cemetery's mass of gray, lichen-covered tombs and crowded headstones. "You've heard about the deaths of Brownbeck and Forbes?"

LaRivière studied the Gothic-style tower and steeple added to the old church by Wren after the fire. "I have, yes. Such a pity, isn't it? Official word is that it's the work of footpads, although I'm hearing whispers that they actually killed each other—or else one killed the other and then committed suicide."

"Oh? I hadn't heard any rumors of suicide. Who started that?"

LaRivière gave a very Gallic shrug. "I've no idea. You know how people are."

Sebastian leaned his hips against a nearby tomb and crossed his arms at his chest. "Titus Poole didn't kill Nicholas Hayes, you know."

"I'm sorry; who?"

"Titus Poole, the man you hired to quietly murder Hayes and then hide the body someplace it would never be found. That's why the killing was so messy—because Poole had nothing to do with it. When he came to see you the day after the murder and took credit for it, he was lying. It's the only reason he was willing to accept half what you'd promised him in payment—because Poole hadn't actually killed Hayes. Brownbeck did."

LaRivière paused with his pencil hovering over the sketch for a moment before lowering it to his paper again. "I haven't the slightest idea what you're talking about."

"Yes, you do. The only part you didn't know is that Poole played you for a fool. After he talked to you, he went back to the Bell and laughed with all his mates about how he'd convinced 'that stupid nob' to pay him for a murder he didn't even commit."

The Frenchman's lips tightened into a thin line, but he said nothing.

"At first I didn't think Poole could have been working for you," Sebastian continued, "because he told me once that he didn't like foreigners, especially the French because they'd killed his brother. Except I just checked with the newly widowed Mrs. Poole, and it turns out Poole didn't even have a brother. The man was quite the accomplished liar."

LaRivière squinted thoughtfully at the delicate tracery of the old medieval windows, then went back to his sketch.

Sebastian said, "Did you know Brownbeck was paying his daughter's abigail to spy on her? That's how he discovered Lady Forbes had arranged to meet Hayes in the tea gardens. Brownbeck actually drove up there that evening in his own carriage. That's a mistake you never would have made, but then he obviously lacked your expertise in arranging these things. Then again, I don't think he intended to kill Hayes." Sebastian paused. "It's ironic, isn't it? While Brownbeck was quietly eliminating everyone he feared could tie him to Hayes's murder, you set about doing the same thing. I wonder why you started with Seaforth. Was it because he was so weak and nervous? Did you tell him of your plan to hire Titus Poole? Were you afraid he would betray you?"

"Have you considered a career writing for the stage? You appear to have a definite flair for dramatic invention."

"You should have stopped there, with Seaforth," Sebastian continued. "I assume you kept your little killing spree going because you feared Seaforth's death would panic the others. But eliminating Brownbeck and Forbes was definitely excessive. Of the four men who originally knew of Nicholas Hayes's return to London, you're now the only one left alive . . . which is more than suggestive."

LaRivière dropped his pencil into its case and calmly snapped the lid. "An interesting theory, I'll admit. But that's all it is. Just a theory with no proof."

"Well, we do have the bodies of the men who attacked me at the docks," said Sebastian, pushing away from the tomb. "Are you so certain those men can't be traced to you?"

The Count laughed out loud as he closed his sketch pad and set it atop the drawing case. "Do you imagine that was me? It wasn't, you know. If you do ever discover who hired them, I believe you'll find they lead you to a dead man. Forbes was quite put out by your interference in something that's really none of your affair."

Sebastian kept an eye on the Frenchman's sword stick and said softly, "You're forgetting the man who attacked my carriage last Monday night."

LaRivière was still smiling, but his eyes were cold and hard. "Was your carriage attacked last Monday night? I had no idea. How . . . unfortunate."

"More unfortunate than you know, given that the man has been identified as someone who worked with Poole. He says the attack was made on your orders."

It was a lie, of course. Bow Street had never found the man responsible for the attack and probably never would. But LaRivière didn't know that.

The Frenchman laughed again as he stretched to his feet. "And do you seriously think anyone would take the word of some lowborn, common scum against that of a count? Or that your Regent would ever allow the official representative of the French King to be accused of such a thing, let alone stand trial?"

"Probably not," said Sebastian. "But you made one serious miscalculation. My wife was in the carriage with me that night. The bullet fired by your 'lowborn, common scum' came within a handsbreadth of killing her. You have met my wife, have you not? The former Miss Hero Jarvis, daughter of the Regent's dear cousin Lord Jarvis? So you see, you don't need to worry about anyone trying to arrest you. Once he learns what happened, Jarvis will take care of you himself. Quietly and efficiently."

Lunging sideways, LaRivière snatched up his sword stick and, with a quick twist of his wrist, freed the blade to bring it hissing through the air. "I think not," he said, settling into *en garde*. "I did offer to fence with you, did I not? Only you seem to have forgotten to bring your sword, *monsieur*."

Sebastian leapt sideways as the Frenchman lunged forward in a straight attack, the steel of his blade flashing in the sunlight. Circling around him, Sebastian grabbed the wooden campstool and brought it up before him.

"Interesting shield," said LaRivière, his blade tracing a mocking figure eight in the air.

Sebastian smiled. "Not much of a saber."

"Yet it can be amazingly lethal," said the Count, launching another attack.

Sebastian ducked behind a tombstone. "I saw what it did to Forbes. That knife was a decidedly clumsy attempt at misdirection, by the way."

"But obviously effective." LaRivière moved in with a lightning flicker of steel.

Sebastian dodged behind a table tomb so badly broken that its inhabitant's scattered bones were clearly visible amidst the rotten remnants of his coffin and shroud.

"Hiding behind the dead now, are we?" said LaRivière with a smile.

The Frenchman was light on his feet, his shoulders straight, his wrists strong and agile. Darting out of reach of another quick strike, Sebastian pitched the campstool at the Frenchman's head and then reached down to yank the dagger from his boot when the man ducked.

LaRivière straightened with a laugh. "Oh dear, *monsieur le vicomte*, I fear your blade is a tad too short."

Sebastian shifted his hold on the knife. "It's long enough," said Sebastian, raising his arm to send the dagger spinning through the air.

The blade sank into LaRivière's chest with a dull *thwunk*. The Frenchman looked down, the confident, contemptuous smile sliding off his face to be replaced by an expression of bemused horror.

Sebastian watched the sword stick slip from the Count's fingers, watched the man's knees buckle and his eyes roll back in his head. "That's for what you did to Nicholas Hayes, you lousy son of a bitch."

## Chapter 58

*I*n a sense they all killed Nicholas, didn't they?" said Calhoun. He was standing beside the empty hearth in Sebastian's dressing room and staring unseeingly at the cold grate. "Brownbeck might have been the one to swing the sickle, but they all contributed to bringing Nick to that moment."

Sebastian looked up from washing his hands and face at the basin. "I think you can say that, yes."

Calhoun turned to hand him the towel. "I'm glad they're all dead."

"So am I."

The valet started to say something, then hesitated.

"What?" prodded Sebastian.

Calhoun drew a steadying breath. "I wasn't strictly honest with you, my lord. When I told you how Nick came to escape Botany Bay, I mean. I said the soldier caught in that flood with him was already dead when Nick found him. But Nick told me he killed the man. Said he was desperate to get away and the man was one of the guards who'd tormented him something fierce. But the killing still bothered Nick, even after all these years."

"Why did you feel the need to change the story?"

"I don't know. I suppose I was afraid you'd think less of Nick if you knew the truth. See him as the rogue everyone claimed he was rather than the admirable man I knew him to be."

"He was admirable," said Sebastian, taking the clean shirt Calhoun held out to him. "Loyal, brave, and strong. I wish I could have known him."

His lips pressed into a tight line, Calhoun met Sebastian's gaze and nodded.

"The papers will be told LaRivière died of an apoplexy," said Jarvis later that evening, his face dark with anger as he stood in the center of Sebastian's library.

"Not footpads this time?" Sebastian poured himself a brandy, then raised the carafe toward his father-in-law. "Are you certain you won't have a drink?"

"No, thank you," said Jarvis. "Fortunately, the French have agreed to keep the truth quiet."

"The truth? Do they know the truth?"

"As much as was considered necessary."

"Oh? For their sake, or yours?"

Jarvis's jaw tightened. "A French count, a British earl, a Director of the East India Company, and the man expected to become the next Lord Mayor of London are all dead because of you, and you consider this a time for levity?"

"Ah, yes, if only I had minded my own business and allowed four powerful, loathsome, murderous men to continue to walk unmolested amongst us, we would be so much better off."

Jarvis's eyes were now two narrow slits. "You find it amusing that you've just killed a close friend of the newly restored King of France?"

Sebastian took a sip of his brandy and shook his head. "Louis never liked him. He was only close to Louis's brother Charles, and you know it."

"Charles will be king soon enough."

"Undoubtedly. But he won't rest easy on the Bourbons' newly recovered throne. I wouldn't be surprised if the French have another revolution in ten or fifteen years."

"You're mad."

"You think so? Ideas can be repressed for a time, but they can't be buried forever."

"By which I take it you mean this ridiculous notion of democracy?" Jarvis sneered the word. "If we lose the legitimate rulers given us by God, we'll simply have more tyrants like Napoléon thrown up by the mob—except they'll be worse."

"Worse than the crowned tyrants? It's possible, I suppose. But what the people raise up, they can also pull down."

"Is that the kind of world you want to live in?"

"I'm not convinced we're going to have a choice."

"Of course we have a choice. But you just imperiled it."

Sebastian laughed out loud, then drank long and deep. "I think you give me too much credit."

*Monday, 20 June*

Kate Forbes sat on a gilded, satin-covered chair in the midst of her spacious, beautifully appointed drawing room. She wore the deep mourning that society expected of a woman who'd just lost both husband and father, but Hero thought her attitude was more that of someone who'd just been set free.

"I'm glad they're dead," she told Hero, her face set hard. "Does that sound horrible? The only reason I agreed to marry Forbes was because my father told me he'd take away my baby if I didn't. Forbes promised that if the child was a girl, he'd raise her as his own." She paused to draw a shaky breath. "You know the survival rates for infants left to the parish or given to foster mothers; they almost all die. I realized there was no way I could save a son. But if by marrying Forbes I could save a daughter, I decided it was worth it." She twisted her hands together, her head bowed. "Of course, it was all a lie."

"I'm sorry," said Hero, her heart breaking for the desperate young girl this elegant woman had once been.

Kate's head came up, her eyes fierce. "I've hated Forbes for eighteen years. Hated them both. I feel like a hypocrite, wearing black for them." Pushing up, she went to stand at the window. Outside, the day was sunny and warm, with just the hint of a breeze. From the distance came the laughter and shouts of children playing around the square's water basin. "No one's found any trace of Nicholas's child?"

"I caught a glimpse of her this past week, when I was interviewing a blind musician in Clerkenwell Green. And in thinking it over, I've realized I may know how to find her."

*Tuesdays for Leicester Square,* Alice had said. *Wednesdays for Clerkenwell.* It could simply have been a coincidence that Ji had reportedly been seen in Leicester Square on the same day Alice always played there. But the more Hero thought about that morning on the green, the more she'd become convinced that Alice had been lying, that the blind woman and Ji had been there together. So far Calhoun's attempts to track down the hurdy-gurdy player had been unsuccessful. But tomorrow was Tuesday. . . .

Kate turned, and Hero saw the leap of hope in her eyes. "You do? Even before Forbes died, I was determined to find a way to care for her. But now I can do whatever I want and I want that child more than anything in the world. Can you take me to her right away?"

"Not right away," said Hero. "But I have an idea. . . ."

*Tuesday, 21 June*

Early that morning, Ji helped Alice set up in her favorite spot in Leicester Square, then moved a ways apart—close enough to protect Alice's cup from thieves but not so close as to attract attention. Sitting cross-legged on the ground, Ji began silently reciting sutras. She prayed, first for the man she had so shamefully wished would be reborn as a hungry ghost. Then she prayed for Hayes.

It was the twelfth day after his death. If Ji were in Canton, she would be burning incense and giving cloth to the monks on Hayes's behalf. But she wasn't in Canton. Never again would she smell its sweet plum blossoms or see its gentle waterways, and that hurt. But it didn't hurt anywhere near as much as the knowledge that she would never again see Hayes.

When Ji was a little girl in Canton, she used to stare at the faces of random women in the street, looking for the faintest suggestion of a resemblance—the arch of a brow, the curve of a lip. And she'd wonder, *Are you my mother? Are you the one who conceived me after lying with a man your family considered a 'barbarian' so that when I was born, they took me from your arms? Were you horrified when you looked down at my face and saw the truth of your shame written there for all to see? Were you relieved when they carried me away to leave me on the banks of the Pearl River to die? Or did you cry out and grieve for your loss? Do you miss me still, the way I miss you? Do you search the faces of the little girls you see in the street, hoping against hope to find me?*

"Oh, Ji," Hayes would say, holding her close, "I'm so sorry."

He could have lied. He could have told her that she was his child, that she'd been born in love to that woman who'd died in childbirth just hours before Hayes—devastated and wishing for his own death—had stumbled upon an abandoned, wailing infant on the banks of the river. But instead he had told her the truth: that his child had died along with her mother. That was his way.

"Even a well-meaning lie can sometimes cause incalculable harm," he was always telling Ji. She had seen the look on the face of Hayes's friend Jules Calhoun when Hayes told the story of his escape from Botany Bay. About how he'd killed the ex-soldier caught up in the floodwaters with him, and then bashed in the man's face so that everyone would think it was Hayes who had died. Another man might have lied and said the soldier was already dead. But not Hayes. Years later, he was still reciting mantras for the benefit of the man he had killed.

Ji let her head fall back, her gaze blurry with unshed tears as she stared up at the gray English sky. "I miss you," she whispered.

Swallowing hard, she lowered her gaze to scan the crowd in the square, looking for potential trouble. That was when she saw him—Hayes's friend Jules, standing at the corner of Cranburn Street. And there, nearby, was the awe-inspiring woman from the Red Lion, Grace Calhoun.

The more she looked, the more familiar faces Ji saw. The man from the Turkish baths whom Hayes had pointed out to her as an old friend. The extraordinarily tall gentlewoman who'd been interviewing Alice the day those men tried to grab Ji in Clerkenwell Green. And that other lady, dressed now in the severe black that Hayes had explained English-women wore when in mourning. Ji recognized her as the woman they'd watched from a distance in St. James's Square—the one Hayes told Ji he'd once loved.

That he still loved.

The woman in black came closer. She stood for a time listening to Alice play her hurdy-gurdy before stooping to drop some coins in the tin cup. Then she turned and walked right up to Ji.

Ji rose shakily to her feet, ready to run.

"Do you know who I am?" said the woman.

Ji studied her pale face and yearning eyes. "Yes."

"Once, long ago, I loved your father. I—" The woman's voice cracked, and she had to start over. "I love him still. I'm told he came back to England, hoping to find someone to care for his daughter when he died, and I would be honored if you would allow me to do that. For his sake, and for yours."

Ji felt a breeze kick up cool against her face. Heard a child laugh and a dog bark somewhere nearby. It would be so easy to let this woman go on believing a lie. So easy. But even a well-meaning lie could sometimes cause incalculable harm.

It was the hardest thing Ji had ever done, but somehow she forced herself to say, "I'm not his daughter. Not really. He adopted me after he found me abandoned by the river the day his real daughter and her mother died. People think he named me Ji because it means 'good fortune' and I was lucky he found me. But he always said I was *his* good fortune because I gave him a reason to keep living."

Ji saw the woman's chest jerk with a quickly indrawn breath and knew just how much her words had hurt the woman—that she'd been holding on to the comforting thought that a part of Hayes still lived, and Ji had just taken that away from her. Then the woman gave a strange smile and shook her head. "If he adopted you, then he loved you and you are his daughter. That's all that matters. Will you let me do this, for him?"

Blinking hard against the threat of tears, Ji glanced over at Alice, who was no longer playing her hurdy-gurdy and was instead simply holding it and listening to them. "What about Alice? We've been taking care of each other."

"Ach, child," said Alice quickly, "don't you be worrying about me. I'll be fine."

"If Alice has been taking care of you, then I think it's only fair that we continue to take care of her." The woman held out her finely gloved hand. "Will you let me? Please?"

For one suspended moment, Ji hesitated. Then she reached out and felt the woman's hand close protectively around hers.

# Historical Note

The Allied Sovereigns' visit to London in June of 1814 was, if anything, even more of a whirlwind of activities than depicted here. I have tried to stay as close to the actual schedule as possible, although I shifted a few events. The reception at Carlton House was not held on the evening of 9 June, and the barge expedition down the Thames started earlier in the morning.

The barges on the Thames were the stretch limos of their day. For a good six hundred years, virtually every guild, official organization, and wealthy family had its own elegant barge, complete with a liveried crew. On the Thames side of Somerset House, you can still see the arched entrances to the building's old barge house, and several surviving examples of the carved, gilded barges are preserved at the National Maritime Museum in Greenwich.

The British East India Company was basically an example of capitalism run amok. A joint-stock company with its origins in a Royal Charter from Queen Elizabeth I, it eventually turned into an empire-building enterprise with the right to acquire and rule territory, raise an army and navy, make war, and mint money. By Sebastian's time the company controlled most of the Indian subcontinent and had an army of more than a quarter of a million men (twice the size of the British Army). It was when the Directors of the company ran into financial difficulties in the eighteenth century that they convinced Parliament to pass the Tea Act of 1773, which of course helped spark the American Revolution. The Indian Rebellion of 1857 led to the end of company rule in India, with the Crown taking direct control of what then became the British Raj.

The Canton System and the East India Company's trade with China were essentially as described here. One of the most helpful books I read on the subject was Paul A. Van Dyke's *The Canton Trade: Life and Enterprise on the China Coast, 1700–1845.*

Both the process for producing tea and the plants themselves were once closely guarded Chinese secrets. The East India Company did eventually manage to send in spies to discover the secret to tea production and steal some of the plants. They then began to grow their own tea in India and what was at the time called Ceylon.

The story of Britain's role in the production and spread of opium use is sordid. By forcing Indian farmers to produce opium rather than wheat, the East India Company did cause massive famines. The worst was in 1777, but smaller famines continued to occur throughout the eighteenth and nineteenth centuries. Rather than carry the opium in their own ships, the company sublet the operation to what were called "country traders"—private ships used to smuggle the opium from India to China. The silver thus earned was then used by the company to buy the Chinese luxury goods they shipped back to Britain. By the beginning of the nineteenth century, addiction levels in China had soared and were becoming a huge problem. When the Qing dynasty finally moved decisively to put a stop to the smuggling, Britain declared war on China—twice. As a result of what became known as the Opium Wars, the Chinese government was forced to legalize the opium trade. The Opium Wars also helped to spur a wave of Chinese immigrants to the West Coast of the United States. And yes, they brought opium with them.

Hero's interviews with street musicians are based on the reports of Henry Mayhew. Most street musicians of the time were either blind or of foreign birth.

The character Mahmoud Abbasi is loosely based on a man named Sake Dean Mahomed, a former captain in the East India Company who ran what is believed to have been the first Indian restaurant in London. The Hindoostane Coffee House opened in George Street in 1810 but was forced to close the following year, after which Mahomed went into the "shampooing" business. Turkish-style baths became increasingly common in the late Regency (one opened near Jamie Knox's old tavern at Bishopsgate churchyard in 1817), although it was under the reign of Victoria that they really exploded when they were widely recommended for "medicinal purposes."

British use of Lascars continued well into the twentieth century. There were more than fifty thousand Lascars working on British ships at the outbreak of World War II, and when I took a P&O ship from Australia in the 1970s, the ship's crew was still almost entirely Indian or Goan. Many of the eighteenth- and nineteenth-century Indians who ended up in Britain took local wives, with their children being absorbed into London's population. There were no legal restrictions on mixed-race marriages in nineteenth-century England, and in 1817 a magistrate of the Tower Hamlets wrote with "disgust" about the number of local white women marrying Indian seamen. For an interesting firsthand look at the life of a half-Indian, half-British man growing up in nineteenth-century London, see Albert Mahomet's *From Street Arab to Pastor.*

There was a ship called the *Earl of Abergavanney* that struck the Shambles off the Isle of Portland in a dense fog, but that was in 1805 and it sank. Its captain, John Wordsworth, was a brother of the poet, and he went down with his ship.

The medieval church of St. Dunstan-in-the-East managed to survive the damage of the Great Fire of 1666, but some of the repairs were done badly. By the early nineteenth century, the weight of the roof had forced the walls seven inches out of perpendicular. In 1817, it was completely rebuilt in a similar style, only to be heavily damaged by bombing in World War II. Rather than tear it down or rebuild again, the ruins and the churchyard were turned into a lovely park that can still be found today near the Tower of London.

Read on for an excerpt from the next Sebastian St. Cyr mystery,

# WHAT THE DEVIL KNOWS

*Available soon from Berkley*

# Chapter 1

Saturday, 8 October 1814

Molly Maguire hated the fog. Hated the way it reeked of coal smoke and tore at her throat. Hated the way the damp, suffocating blanket could turn even the most familiar lane into something ghostly and strange.

It was always worse at night, when the temperature plummeted and folks lit their fires. That's when the mist would drift up from the docks, swallowing the dark hulls and tall masts of the big ships at anchor out on the river and creeping along the mean streets and foul alleyways of the part of East London known as Wapping. Sometimes Molly would dream of a different life, the life she'd once known, when cold, wet nights were spent safe and dry in a warm, gently lit cottage. But that life belonged to the past. In this life Molly walked the streets at night.

She'd been on her own since before she turned thirteen, and she told herself she should be used to it by now. Yet after three years, she still shrank from servicing men with foul breath and rough hands and urgent, rutting manparts. It didn't hurt anymore like it had at first, at least not usually. But Molly still hated it even more than she hated the fog.

The bell in the clock tower of St. George's-in-the-East struck midnight, the dull clangs sounding oddly loud in the dense fog. If business had been good, Molly would have given up and gone back to the small, wretched room she shared with five other girls. But she was desperate for money. It might be Saturday night, but the fog had driven most potential customers off the streets. She'd had a couple of drunken seamen who took turns on her, one right after the other, then demanded a discount. But even they weren't as bad as the fat old magistrate who'd pinned her against one of the looming towers of St. George's.

A man like him, he could've bought himself a fine piece of Haymarket ware and tumbled her in the back room of a Covent Garden coffeehouse. Instead he'd picked up a cheap little Wapping doxy and taken her up against the soot-stained old stones of the church, his big hands tearing at her bodice and painfully squeezing her breasts as he thrust into her hard enough to make her wince. She could still smell the stink of his spilled snuff and fine brandy clinging to her. And when it was all over and she'd asked for her money, he'd laughed at her.

"I don't pay whores," he said, buttoning his flap over his ponderous gut.

"Wha-aat?" she'd wailed. "What you think? That I did this because I—"

He backhanded her across the mouth, splitting her lip against her teeth. "Consider yourself fortunate that I've decided not to have you committed."

"Fat old wagtail," Molly muttered now to herself. It felt good saying it out loud, so she said it again. "Fat old wagtail. Should've lifted his bloody watch, that's what I should've done. He owed me, he—"

She broke off as a dark, bulky shadow emerged from the fog swirling up near the corner. Probably old Ben Carter, she thought. She'd already tangled with the watchman once tonight and was in no mood to deal with him again. The black mouth of a noisome alley yawned beside her, and she ducked into it, gagging as the stench of rotting fish heads, rancid cabbage leaves, and what smelled like raw entrails enveloped her. She had her head turned, looking anxiously over her shoulder for the watchman, when her foot caught on something and she pitched forward.

"Mother Mary and all the saints," she swore softly as she came down on what felt like a big overstuffed sack. Her outflung hands slid over warm, smooth cloth and something else. Something wet and sticky.

Rearing back with a gasp, she stared down at the man before her, at the familiar greatcoat with silver buttons, at the hideous yawning wound in that fat neck, at the fine once-white cravat now soaked dark with blood. More blood matted his bushy gray hair and swooping side-whiskers. She sucked in a quick breath and smelled him, smelled the brandy and the snuff and the blood.

A scream rose in her throat, but she choked it back. In her mind she was screaming, screaming over and over again, her heart pounding in her chest. She heard the sound of heavy approaching footsteps and threw a panicked glance back at the mouth of the alley in time to see Watchman Ben pass with his lantern.

"Twelve o'clock on a foggy night and all is well," he called.

She pushed to her feet, ready to run as soon as the watchman was safely gone. Then her gaze fell on the body before her, on the gold watch and chain spilling from that blood-splattered silk waistcoat, and she hesitated.

Molly might be a whore, but she'd never been a thief. Still, the man did owe her, didn't he?

She told herself he owed her.

# Chapter 2

The Frenchman was nervous.

Small, lithe, and dark-haired, with a hawklike nose and hooded, nervous eyes, he stood beside the fire crackling on the hearth of Sebastian's library, hands stretched out to the blaze. The morning had dawned cold and gloomy, the sky leaden, the city wrapped in mist. "They're watching me," said the man, his French low and quick. "Even here in London, I've been followed."

Sebastian St. Cyr, Viscount Devlin, heir to the powerful Earl of Hendon, stood with his hips resting against the edge of his heavy, dark oak desk, his arms crossed at his chest and his gaze on the man who'd been on his payroll for the last five months. "Do you know why?"

"Who can say? When the Bourbons drove into Paris, they claimed the past would be forgotten. They spoke of healing wounds and uniting all Frenchmen together again." The man's lips pulled away from his teeth into a rictus of a smile. "They lied. Louis himself might mean well, but his brother and niece are vicious snakes. They're beginning to move against anyone they consider their enemies, bringing back the Jesuits, strengthening the power of the church. . . . There have already been deaths. There will be more. I'm not going back."

"Where will you go?"

"Louisiana, perhaps. I hear they speak French there." The man, whose name was Labourne, rolled his shoulders in a Gallic shrug. "I'm sorry I do not have more to report."

Sebastian nodded, swallowing his disappointment and frustration. It had been more than twenty years since the sun-spangled summer morning when his mother, Sophia, the beautiful, gay, scandalous Countess of Hendon, had sailed away from Brighton, never to be seen again; three years since he'd discovered she hadn't drowned that day, as he'd always been told. At first, war with France made tracing her difficult. But with the abdication of Napoléon, Sebastian had assumed the task would become easier.

He'd been wrong.

"Can you recommend someone who could take up where you left off?"

Labourne frowned thoughtfully at the nearby wall of leather-bound books. "There are one or two who might be willing. When I have spoken to them, I will send you their names."

Sebastian pushed away from the desk. "Thank you."

He was standing at the library window and watching the Frenchman stride swiftly down the wet street when Hero came to rest her hand on the small of his back.

"I'm sorry," she said softly.

He turned to take her in his arms, holding her close, breathing in the sweet familiar scent of her. She was a tall woman, nearly as tall as he, dark-haired and Junoesque in build, brilliant and strong, and he loved her and their son with a ferocity that filled his life with joy and, sometimes, terror.

After a moment, he drew a deep breath and said, "Do you think I'm wrong to keep trying to find her?"

Hero lifted her head from his shoulder to meet his gaze. "No."

"She obviously doesn't want to be found."

"Perhaps not. But she owes you answers."

"Does she?"

"I think so, yes." She paused, and he expected her to say, *I just hope you're ready for whatever answers she might have to give.* But all she said was, "The man has no idea where she might be?"

"He says she was in Paris, then traveled to Vienna. It was when he followed her to Vienna that he realized he was being followed himself."

"By agents working for the Bourbons?"

"He thought so, and I'm inclined to believe him."

"But . . . why? Because of what he used to do in the past, or because of what he was doing for you now?"

"I'm not sure." Sebastian glanced down the street again. The Frenchman was gone, swallowed up by the mist. "Her presence in Vienna is . . . puzzling." In the wake of Napoléon's defeat, the representatives of Europe's leading states were gathering in the Austrian capital, intent on hammering out a long-term peace plan and rebuilding the world's power structure. The city was crowded with an influx of powerful Englishmen and their hangers-on; it struck him as the last place to appeal to the errant wife of the Earl of Hendon.

"I assume she no longer calls herself Lady Hendon?"

"No. *Dama* Cappello."

"Cappello? Why?"

"Labourne didn't know."

A hackney coach drawn by a big, rawboned bay appeared out of the fog, and they watched together as the ancient vehicle drew up before their steps with a rattle of trace chains.

"Who's that?" asked Hero as a beefy, bushy-browed man in a brown corduroy coat swung open the carriage door and hopped down.

Sebastian felt a sense of foreboding settle upon him. "One of Sir Henry's constables. Something must have happened."

## Chapter 3

*Y*ou'd think an East End magistrate'd have more sense than t' go wandering around someplace like Wapping in a stinkin' fog."

This piece of worldly wisdom came from Tom, the small, sharp-faced young tiger who perched at the rear of Sebastian's curricle as he drove east through the city. Once, Tom had been a pickpocket. But after serving as Sebastian's groom for more than three years, the lad had ambitions of someday becoming a Bow Street Runner.

Sebastian guided his chestnuts around a plodding brewer's wagon, then said, "It is rather curious, I'll admit."

"It's bleedin' harebrained, that's what it is."

Sebastian ducked his head and smiled.

They drove up the rain-drenched expanse of the Strand at a spanking pace, then passed through Temple Bar, that ancient division between Westminster and the City of London itself. By now the fog had mostly cleared, with only stray wisps still hovering over the river and clinging to the city's countless belching chimneys. The farther east they traveled, the older, narrower, and more decrepit the houses became, the more ragged the men, women, and wretched children on the streets, the more foul the air. By the time they reached Wapping, they were in an area dominated by the ships rocking at anchor in the Pool of London, by vast docks and looming brick warehouses. This was a district of sailors' victuallers and boat and mast makers, of endless taverns, rowdy seamen, thieves, and whores.

Turning into Nightingale Lane, Sebastian drew up near a shuttered apothecary shop. He could hear the cry of seagulls and the flapping of furled sails from the ships tied up in the nearby basin; smell the reek of tar and resin and dead fish that hung heavy in the air. "That wind has a cold bite to it," he told the boy. "Best walk 'em."

Tom scrambled forward to take the reins. "Aye, gov'nor."

"And keep your ears open. You might hear something useful."

Tom grinned. "I kin do that, too, yer lordship."

Hopping down to the wet, worn cobblestones, Sebastian turned toward a group of somber men huddled in conversation at the mouth of a nearby alley. At his approach, one of the men stepped away from the others and said, "Lord Devlin. My apologies for bringing you out on such a miserable morning."

His name was Sir Henry Lovejoy, and he was one of Bow Street Public Office's three stipendiary magistrates. Small and slightly built, he had a balding head, pinched, unsmiling features, and a serious demeanor. Once, Lovejoy had been a moderately successful merchant. But the tragic death of his wife and daughter some years before had shifted the trajectory of his life, leading him to adopt a severe religious belief and devote himself to public service.

Sebastian had known the dour little magistrate since those dark days when the Viscount had been on the run from a false accusation of murder, and Lovejoy assigned the task of bringing him to justice. Since that time, the two men had cooperated in solving a number of murders, for Sebastian's access to and knowledge of the rarefied world of the Haut Ton made him an invaluable ally when it came to cases involving either the nobility or the royal family. This death was decidedly different, although Sebastian suspected he understood only too well why Lovejoy had reached out to him.

"It's certainly bracing," said Sebastian, walking up to him. Then his gaze went beyond the Bow Street magistrate to the bloody ruin of a man lying farther into the alley, and he whispered, "Good God."

Stout and gray whiskered, the man was sprawled on his back, his heavy arms flung wide at his sides, his legs splayed. What had once been a white cravat was now soaked dark with the blood that had gushed from the gaping slash across his throat and the shattered, sickening pulp that had been the side of his head. The grimy brick walls of the narrow alley were splattered with gore and what Sebastian realized with a twist of his gut must be brain matter. He'd spent six years at war as a cavalry officer, but the sight of violent death still bothered Sebastian, and he suspected it always would.

"Ghastly, isn't it?" said Lovejoy.

Sebastian studied the dead man's full-cheeked, gape-mouthed face; the vacant, staring eyes; the open, buttonless greatcoat; the striped waistcoat; the old-fashioned breeches. Below that, the man's feet were completely bare.

"Someone's helped themselves to his shoes and stockings, I see."

"And his hat, buttons, purse, and watch," said Lovejoy. "I can easily imagine footpads bashing in his head. But why would they bother slitting his throat, as well?"

"It does seem rather excessive."

Lovejoy squinted up at the seagulls wheeling noisily overhead. "I'm told that ten days ago, a seaman by the name of Hugo Reeves was killed not far from here in Five Pipes Fields in Shadwell. His head was smashed in just like this, his throat cut so viciously his head was half off. No one thought much of it at the time. The streets near the docks are always dangerous, although the brutality of the attack was seen as unusual even for around here. But after this . . ."

His voice trailed away, his nostrils flaring as he sucked in a deep breath. "You can imagine what people are now saying."

Sebastian met his troubled gaze. "They're saying it's like the Ratcliffe Highway murders."

Lovejoy pressed his lips together and nodded.

Less than three years before, in December 1811, the East End of London had been terrorized by two horrific sets of murders. First, on 7 December, four members of a family—a twenty-four-year-old linen draper, his young wife, their three-month-old baby, and a fourteen-year-old apprentice—were found with their heads bashed in and their throats slashed. No explanation for the carnage was ever found. Then, just twelve days later, while the city was still reeling from the first attack, the killer struck again at the King's Arms on nearby New Gravel Lane, butchering the fifty-six-year-old publican, his wife, and their maidservant.

Within days of the second murders, a suspect was arrested. But before he could be brought to trial, the man was found hanging in his cell in Coldbath Fields Prison. The authorities immediately declared the case closed. There were whispers, of course: suggestions that the magistrates were too eager to blame the killings on a conveniently dead man. But the ugly, senseless murders ceased. And so with the passage of time, the panic and whispers died down.

"Do you think it's possible?" said Sebastian, his gaze on the stiffening dead man before them. "That this could be the work of the same killer, I mean."

Lovejoy hunched his shoulders against a cold gust of wind. "It always seemed to me that there were certain . . . anomalies in the official version of events. When the murders ceased, I assumed I must be wrong. But now . . ."

Sebastian hunkered down beside the blood-drenched corpse. Despite the cold, the coppery-sweet smell of spilled blood and raw flesh was strong—the stench of death. He had to stop himself from cupping his hand over his nose and mouth. "You say he's a magistrate?"

Lovejoy nodded. "Sir Edwin Pym, of the public office in Shadwell High Street."

Yanking off his glove, Sebastian touched the back of his hand to the dead man's cheek. "He's stone cold. But then, the night was cold. Any idea when he was last seen?"

"According to his housekeeper, he went out last night around ten. She was expecting him back before midnight, but obviously he never returned."

"Does she know where he was going?"

"She claims she does not."

Sebastian glanced over at him. "You say that as if you don't believe her."

A quiver of revulsion passed over Lovejoy's features. "I'm told Pym had a habit of trolling for harlots at night—the younger the better."

"Lovely." Sebastian pushed to his feet, his gaze taking in a nearby pile of smashed hogsheads, a row of overflowing dustbins, the slick gleam of a mound of rotting fish heads. "The alley's been searched?"

"In a preliminary fashion. I'll have the lads tear it completely apart once we've moved the body, but I'll be surprised if they find anything."

Sebastian brought his gaze back to the bloody, shattered ruin of the dead magistrate's head. "What would do that, do you think?"

"An iron bar? A large hammer? I've sent for a shell to have him carried to Gibson. Perhaps he can tell us."

"If anyone can," said Sebastian. A former army surgeon who now made his home in Tower Hill, Paul Gibson could read the secrets a dead body had to tell better than anyone Sebastian had ever known. "The Ratcliffe Highway murderer used a maul, didn't he?"

"For the first set of killings, yes. A seaman's maul. Although I believe there was some confusion as to what he used to cut his victims' throats."

Sebastian studied the gaping wound in the dead man's neck. "This looks like it was done with a sharp razor, but I could be wrong."

Lovejoy started to say something, then paused.

"What?" prompted Sebastian.

Lovejoy cleared his throat. "It may mean nothing, but Sir Edwin Pym was one of the leading magistrates involved in the investigation of the Ratcliffe Highway murders."

Sebastian looked over at him. "And the other victim you mentioned— Reeves? Was he involved in any way?"

"Not that I'm aware. But then, I was at Queen Square Public Office at the time, so my knowledge of the inquiries is limited to what I read in the papers like everyone else."

Sebastian glanced toward the group of men still standing near the mouth of the alley, silently watching them. He recognized the constable who'd been sent to fetch him and a couple of Lovejoy's other lads, but the rest were undoubtedly local. "There are plenty of magistrates in the East End. Why were you brought into this?"

Lovejoy looked vaguely uncomfortable. "Lord Sidmouth has asked me to take over the investigation of the murders." As Home Secretary, Henry Addington, Viscount Sidmouth, was officially in charge of all the stipendiary magistrates of the metropolis's nine public offices. "I'm to report back to him as soon as I leave here."

"An unenviable interview."

Lovejoy pushed out a harsh breath. "Indeed. I'm told the Home Office is most anxious to prevent a resurgence of the panic that gripped the entire city in December of 1811."

"Bit hard to do, once word of this spreads beyond Wapping—as you know it will, soon enough." Sebastian found his gaze drifting back to the dead man's bare feet, now a bluish white. "What do you think? Did the killer strip him of his boots and valuables? Or did someone else come along later and help himself to the easy pickings?"

"The latter scenario, surely? We'll be watching all the pawnshops, of course—although even if some of the stolen items turn up, I doubt it'll tell us much about the murder itself."

Sebastian nodded. "You mentioned Pym's housekeeper. What about his family?"

"He lived alone. His wife died some years ago, and his only daughter is married and lives in Stepney. I'm told there's a son, as well, but he's a sea captain with the East India Company."

"You said the man killed last week was a seaman?"

"A ship's carpenter, yes."

"The man blamed for the Ratcliffe Highway murders was also a seaman, was he not?"

"He was, yes. But then, most people around here are connected in some way to the maritime trade."

"Given the three-year gap between these new murders and what happened in 1811, it's possible we're dealing with a seafaring man—a killer who sailed away three years ago and is now back."

"How perfectly ghastly to think about. But why would such a man go after an unknown sailor and a Shadwell magistrate?"

"You assume this murderer has a logical reason for what he does." Sebastian let his gaze drift over the gore-splattered wall beside them and felt a new ripple of disquiet sluice through him. "If I had to guess, I'd say it's more likely that whoever did this simply enjoys killing."

*Photograph by Samantha Brown*

**C. S. Harris** is the *USA Today* bestselling author of more than two dozen novels, including the Sebastian St. Cyr Mysteries; as C. S. Graham, a thriller series coauthored with former intelligence officer Steven Harris; and seven award-winning historical romances written under the name Candice Proctor. A respected scholar with a PhD in nineteenth-century European history, she is also the author of a nonfiction historical study of the French Revolution. She lives with her husband in New Orleans and has two grown daughters.

CONNECT ONLINE

CSHarris.net
◼ CSHarrisAuthor